CRY HAVOC

J K Mayo has, in Harry Seddall, created a new archetype of the undercover agent: a man seeming at one moment cynical, at the next showing glimpses of integrity, but always ambiguous, self-mocking, ironic, and scornful of the accepted hypocrisies of society. After featuring in *The Hunting Season*, Harry Seddall went on to take the lead role in *Wolf's Head*, a thriller described by Martin Cruz Smith as "an absolutely terrific book. The most fun I've had since my first James Bond" and by John Coleman in The *Sunday Times* as "an adventure thriller done with intent savagery and brilliant, teasing verbal sophistication". The fourth Seddall thriller, *A Shred of Honour*, has just been published by Harvill.

J K MAYO

Cry Havoc

Fontana
An Imprint of HarperCollins*Publishers*

First published in 1990 by Collins Harvill

This edition first issued in 1993 by Fontana
an imprint of HarperCollins*Publishers*
77/85 Fulham Palace Road,
Hammersmith, London W6 8JB

1 3 5 7 9 8 6 4 2

ISBN 0 00 617932 0

Set in Bembo

Printed and bound in Great Britain by
HarperCollinsManufacturing Glasgow

To Christopher MacLehose

1

The man who had been struck by the nine iron in the pit of his stomach lay on the floor of Calder's house with his mouth open as if the blow had paralysed his respiratory system, and his eyes shut tight as if he did not want to look at a world that had hurt him so much. Calder thought about hitting him on the head as well, but decided there was no need.

He took the length of black electric cable he had cut from the television set and which hung ready on the back of the swivel chair, and turned his victim face down. The victim's fists were still pressed into his abdomen, and as Calder pulled the man's arms behind his back a sad little sound came from the gaping mouth. When the wrists were securely tied with many turns of the black cable, Calder took from the back of the swivel chair the length of brown cable he had cut from the desk lamp, and lashed the man's ankles as thoroughly as he had the wrists.

Then he picked up the pistol which the assassin had let fall and satisfied himself – Calder had no experience of pistols – that its extravagant length was due to a silencer being attached to the barrel. This meant that he could allow himself an extra minute, since the assassin's accomplice sitting at the wheel of the car parked outside the house would not be waiting for the sound of a shot; even two shots, if the assassin was in the habit of firing a coup de grace.

He looked through the window and the fly-screen – all the windows were closed and screened, he had made sure of that – and saw the driver was displaying no sign of doubt or impatience. The man was making a good show of being perfectly relaxed, with his arm along the back of the seat and an elbow resting on the door. Passers-by would think he was waiting for a friend to come out of the house; which was what he was doing, more or less.

"So far so good," Calder allowed himself the thought, because so far he had followed a pre-arranged plan and the plan had worked. Now, however, he must improvise.

Soon after he had learned, from something said during the lunchtime bridge session in the Master's office, that an imminent attempt to murder him was likely, Calder had decided that only a methodically prepared plan could preserve his life. He was not a logician of any sort, indeed his subject was English Literature, but he had noticed it of himself that as he moved towards old age (he was sixty-seven) he became, by degrees, more methodical in his behaviour. How best, he asked himself when he had time to put his mind to it, to act in such a crisis? The answer was, in a way that suited his own nature. Accordingly, earlier in the afternoon, he had made a plan to deal with the assassin.

He could not put his mind to it at once, however, because he was so startled to hear that his assassin had arrived on campus that on a hand which he hoped to play at four diamonds he bid himself into trouble.

"Five diamonds," Calder said. "What did you say, George? A student looking for me? One of *my* students?"

"Why are you so goddam surprised?" George asked. George was the university physician. He drank quite a lot and used a good deal of profanity, which Calder found pleasantly old-fashioned in a country much given to the four-letter obscenities. "Yeah, one of your students."

"I'll double your five diamonds," said Bill Livingstone, the master of the college. "The reason he's surprised, George, is that he has no students. James is an honorary fellow, you know that."

"Hell, I didn't know he had no students though. You *do* have students, you've talked about them."

6

"Not this semester," Calder said. "Did I bid five diamonds?"

"You did, partner." This in the dry whisky voice of the master's secretary Dinah. "No bid. Are we in five diamonds and doubled, George?"

"What? Yeah, I guess you are. No bid."

Bill led his card, after a no bid from Calder, and Dinah began to lay down dummy.

A peculiar thing was happening to Calder. His mind was becoming aware that he had known, as soon as George mentioned the mythical student, that a man had been sent to kill him; it was being slow to admit what the rest of him knew by instinct, that was all; it had gone into spasm, as his lumbar muscles did when he put his back out. Hence the five diamonds instead of four, and doubled of course. If he took the ruff and the finesse he might do it.

His mind, he was pleased to discover, appeared to be recovering from shock faster than afflicted lumbar muscles ever did. He thought he would make his five diamonds, and he began to think he would contrive a way to deal with the assassin as well.

When that was done, he would have to start running: whether he was killed or survived, his disappearance would be sudden. His mind, now recovering wonderfully (he let them have their two tricks and began to play his hand like a demon) decided to prepare the ground for his early departure from New York State.

"I've no students this semester or next, George, because I'm set to finish my book this year. No, doctor, my trick." George withdrew his fingers reluctantly, wearing an expression he often wore at the bridge table, which said effectively: "Foiled again!"

"In fact," Calder said, while George went into a brown study over his discard on the next trick, "I'm flying to England tomorrow to put in a spell at the British Library."

"I thought London was two weeks away," Livingstone said, his round face as bland as it always was, but in his voice the reflexive amount of petulance proper to the master of a college who, even at so informal a university as Wade, is not being kept

7

informed. Livingstone was in the third year of his three-year tenure of the mastership, because although Wade University had been modelled on the Oxford system of separate colleges, the founders had boggled at the idea of autocratic college masters in place for life, and the master of each college was appointed every three years from among the full professors. Calder himself had been master here rather a long time ago; he knew that a token gesture towards an explanation for his sudden departure would be enough.

"It turns out I have to be in London Friday," he said, gathering in the trick which had successfully transferred the lead to dummy, "so I'm off tomorrow."

"Well, Jim Calder," said Dinah, who was watching his play like a hawk, "just who do you think is going to make a fourth at bridge in the lunch break?"

Even while the words of her question came out, Calder was simultaneously asking himself: how does this assassin propose to kill me? He felt suddenly in tremendous form, keyed-up, scared stiff, but alert and intelligent.

The tricks came obediently to his hand, he was conducting himself in such a way that none of the others suspected that this was not simply a day like any other, and already – in this very moment past – he had resolved to give himself after this bridge game no more than one hour in his office to work out how to oppose the assassin before going home, instead of leaving, as he usually did, between five and six. For this reason, that it would greatly reduce the chance of the assassin installing himself in the house before he himself returned.

"Tony Skolnikoff's a good player," he said, collecting his last trick and trying to remember which windows he had left open, which shut; whether he had closed the screen door when he came away this morning.

"Tony Skolnikoff," George said, "would never have made that five diamonds. Mind you, neither would I."

"Tony's all right," Livingstone said.

"Five diamonds, doubled," Dinah said. "Tony's all right, but he is not you, Jim."

She meant more than Calder the bridge player, and though by his own way of it he was an unemotional man, Calder experienced within himself a moment of loss, then a doubt, and at last a deeper fear than he could regard as being scared stiff. For a man alone at sixty-seven friendships were, apparently, better than death. And what happened after today, supposing that he did manage to defeat the assassin? Such things must not be thought on after these ways, he told himself, doing great violence to the sense of the original.

"Hey, George," he said, while Livingstone shuffled the cards, "this so-called student of mine, what did he want, did he say what he wanted?"

"Nope. I only spoke to him because he was hanging about in the doorway of your office, to tell him you weren't going to be back till after lunch. I think maybe he was English. He had that kind of accent. He said something about an essay."

"It's always something about an essay," Livingstone said. "Got the wrong office, that's all."

"Freshman?" Calder asked.

"How do I know? Not one of the younger ones, anyway."

"Are you guys going to play bridge?" Dinah asked, caustic to the last.

Not one of the younger ones for a student, maybe, but young for an assassin. Yet how long did assassins live? Calder had now completed the first part of the improvisation on the original plan. He had stuffed as much of one tea towel as he could into the assassin's mouth and tied another round his head to hold the gag in place. He turned the fellow over, on the basis that the young man was quite likely to choke to death and that if he ever opened his eyes before he did so, there was something rotten about expiring with your face flat on the carpet.

He became aware that the eyes were open now, staring at him with a great amount of feeling in them, some of it, certainly, looked to be panic. "If you'd come alone, you idiot, I wouldn't have had to gag you, not so soon, anyway," Calder said. "How was I to know there would be two of you?"

He looked out of the window and saw that the other man was not making nearly such a good show of looking relaxed. His arm was no longer lying on the back of the seat and he was staring at the house as if he, too, was getting ready to improvise.

Calder opened the bottom drawer of his desk and took out a small box, grabbed from off the top of the bookcase (exclaiming "Tsk-tsk!" at the dust) the canvas rifle case with the Remington in it, put the sling over his shoulder, and went quietly out of the house and down the porch steps. He loped gently, as became his age, across the thirty yards or so of grass to the scrappy woodland of birch, aspen and maple which he called the wilderness, went in among the trees a little way and sat down.

He watched the house, letting his breathing settle, an essential prerequisite to a steady aim, and slid the rifle out of its case. From the box at his knee, labelled Remington .222 Long Cartridge, he loaded the weapon. He stood up and found a comfortable stance in the stand of birch. He knew he was imperfectly concealed, but the sun was bright behind him, and it was safe to assume that when the driver finally left the car and came to see what was keeping the assassin, his attention would be concentrated on the house.

The house had been built with its back to the road, and facing south-west, in order to catch as much of the day's sunlight as possible, and up to now this had given him a number of advantages. When it came to shooting the assassin's partner, however, the position of the house confronted Calder with a problem. The bullet fired from the Remington long cartridge treble two had extremely high velocity, and while it would wreak an effective amount of havoc on the Second Murderer (Calder was bound to have thought of him in this way sooner or later) if it hit bone, were it to pass through his flesh or miss him altogether, it would cause this havoc to anyone passing along the road or to anyone a good way beyond the road who happened to get in its way.

Calder did not in the least expect to miss his target altogether, but he had been brought up to behave conscientiously with guns, in the knowledge that accidents happen even to the best of us. He would have to wait, therefore, until the Second Murderer had the house behind him, so that if the fellow failed to stop the bullet, the house would, with any decent amount of luck, do so instead.

"Let him come creeping and careful," Calder said to himself. "Let him not come swift and darting. I am too old of eye for snap-shooting."

Creeping and careful he came. First the head, peering warily round the corner of the house and looking not at all into the wilderness where Calder lurked.

Calder spoke silently again, "I'll have to kill you, my dear chap. It's the only safe way for me," he said, making up his mind to it even as he thought the words.

The dear chap, observing that his head was beside the railing of the porch that ran along the front of the house, set himself to climb over it. The sun was brilliant on the house, and as the man spread himself against the wall to look in through the window – why did he spread himself like that, was it because people did it in the movies? – Calder aimed at the centre of his torso and fired twice.

The man bounced off the house and fell over the porch rail, where he hung with his arms dangling and jerking while his mouth emitted a gush of blood. At the moment when he bounced off the house there had been a lot of perceptible motion of some sort in the air about him, and Calder felt briefly unwell, because he knew that this was composed by droplets of blood forced out by the intense pressure created by the impact of the bullet.

The bad feeling, however, soon passed, and Calder was pleased to find himself so callous, for there was still much to do.

By the time he reached the house the man had died, which was all to the good. However callous Calder was proving to be, he would have found it difficult to treat a badly injured man simply as an incubus to be disposed of. Still carrying the Remington, he went quickly into the house, where he saw that the assassin on the floor was still securely bound and gagged, and now breathing as well. This last fact, he noticed, gave him a fleeting sense of irritation, and he wondered if he was going to find himself, at a convenient time, killing the wretched fellow in cold blood.

He went to the front of the house, and found that the assassins' car had been left with the engine running. He drove it round the house, a Buick coupé with a large trunk, and backed it over the grass to the body lying draped on the porch rail. He took a good look at the blood on the porch and went inside and took his clothes off, filled a bucket with warm water and detergent, threw a cloth in it, and went out again onto the porch. He laid the bucket down clear of the spattered blood, got the keys from the car and opened the trunk and went up onto the porch, trying to tread in as little blood as possible.

"Now, my boy," he said, whether to himself or the corpse he was not sure, "all treats have to be paid for," and took the dead man's ankles and heaved him off the rail into the trunk of the Buick.

It took him seven buckets of water and detergent, and liberal use of the yard hose, to clean the porch, the rail, the wall and the window. Each time he went into the house for warm water, he first hosed blood off his skin. By the time it was done he was extremely tired, so he went inside and made himself some coffee, put some Scotch in a glass and sat down to rest.

He watched the man on the floor watching him for a long time, and gradually an idea came to him, a thing to say to the defeated assassin. He did not expect it to bear fruit, since the man would probably die of thirst before he was found, or of some constriction of the blood or throat for all Calder knew. And for all Calder knew, he might yet decide to shoot the

12

fellow. Life and death play strange tricks, he told himself sententiously, under the influence of fear, adrenalin, euphoria, fatigue and whisky.

What he had thought of saying sounded in his mind faintly comic, something straight off the screen, but that after all was presumably where these people lived, in some unreal movie of their own. And if the man swallowed it, and if he survived, who could say what effect it might not have.

So he watched the man's eyes watching him, and swirled the drink in his glass. "You're going travelling with your buddy, in the trunk of the Buick," he said. Then he spoke the line: "What did you think you were playing at, sonny? Didn't they tell you who I used to be? They set you up my boy. They set you up, didn't they?"

Calder thought he had tried too hard, over-done it, but then it hardly mattered. There was a lot going on in the man's eyes, but that could mean anything.

Long after dark that night he parked the Buick at a beauty spot beside a lake in the foothills of the Adirondacks, and hiked the fifteen miles home. Walking was Calder's exercise, so he took pleasure in the journey over moonlit meadows and through the darkness of the woods taken at a good measured pace, taking his time but covering ground; waiting, when he saw the white flare of a skunk ahead of him lit by the moon, until the preoccupied creature shuffled off into the forest.

"Carry your latent stink off with you," Calder said aloud, to his own surprise. Standing there, hearing the words last on into the silence, he felt his face draw in and pain strike between his shoulder blades. After that the walk was different, no longer part of the clear run of thought and action that had persisted since he had made that little slam in diamonds and had begun to create the events that had brought him here to stand, a lone still figure, among the still figures of the trees.

When he went on again he knew the exalted confidence that

13

had brought him through the day had seeped away like the tide, and that the aftermath – whatever that might be – was flowing in. He walked on, clenching his will against the onset of this new state, but knowing that a grim spirit now went with him through the woods.

The moon vanished, her behaviour as appropriate in life as in literature, he thought to himself with a flash of gloomy wit, and the same dour humour stayed with him as he stumbled through a tangle of old beaver workings in a dried-out swamp. When he had crossed it, going sometimes on all fours like an animal, arriving on the other side scratched, scraped, and splintered by the godforsaken mess of twined and broken timber, he was exhausted but still, as it seemed to him, resilient in spite of all.

He sat with his back to a solid vertical fir to break out the sandwiches and the flask of coffee from his hiker's pack. "Resilient in spite of all," he told the tree, and reached behind him to pat its unresponsive trunk.

"There's life in the old dog yet," he said to himself, with coffee warming his belly and bread and cheese in his mouth. He was becoming aware of the aftermath, and this was the time to find the courage to look at it. He knew guilt was rising in him, but he had a sense which he found hard to accept, that the guilt was not for what he had done to the two men who had come, after all, to kill him; on the contrary, he felt guilt because he was not blaming himself for what he had done. Despite the doubtful state that was in him now, he was still tolerably chirpy about what he had done. He thought it was quite funny too; it amused him to be as old as he was, and to have turned the tables on two professional assassins.

All the same, he could not help noticing that he liked the complete and in its way quaint – yes, quaint was the word for it – ruthlessness with which he had dealt with them. He found it worth observing that he had not had time to meet them. If they had been men with strong and belligerent personalities, which they very likely were in their business, and he had been forced to face either or both of them across a room and start from there, he would have been defeated. He thought this because he did not see himself as being a strong personality. Adequately assertive was as far as he would go, not one of your competitive men, not one of your aggressive human beings.

Human beings – he had hardly seen them as that at all. As to the danger of it, in a way he had hidden from that as well. In his fear and excitement he had seen things to do, and he had done them. He had enjoyed doing them. He had been full of glee.

He did not like that at all. An old, or nearly old, man, full of glee and killing people. What did that sound like? It sounded like a demented nearly old man; the absence of guilt, or of the expected kind of guilt, sounded demented as well.

Look what he had done with them, after. He had put the still living one in the trunk of the Buick, bound and gagged, along with the bloody corpse of the other. There was a good chance the living one would die before anyone burst open the trunk of the Buick, attracted by the fact of it standing there for so many days, after a while; or by, after a while, the smell of decomposing flesh.

He knew that rotting meat, after not too many days, produces white maggots, and he had thought of that too when he was putting the living man in with the dead; but it had not deterred him, he had thought of it only as a piece of bad news for the living one, if he lived in there long enough for the maggots to begin their existence.

He had thought it all through, and remembered it all, and yet he had no remorse. What else could he have done, that would have left him time to get away? As for his sanity, he thought that in all truth it was as sound as a bell. He had no genuine feeling that he was a closet psychopath who had been triggered into madness by an attempt on his life.

He poured the last of the coffee and lit a cigarette, breaking the match in his fingers before he threw it away, because of the risk of fire. He perceived the irony, but did not smile at it. Staring into the blackness of the woods past the glowing coal on the end of his cigarette, the nature of the fear that was

15

chewing at him reached him with terrible speed. It was an ancient fear, and here in the forest, alone among the sounds and silences of the night, was the place to feel it. It was the fear of vengeance. The two men who had come for him during that day had come only to kill him, but the men who would be sent after them would be crying vengeance at his heels.

Calder dropped the cigarette end into the dregs of the coffee and threw the waste on the ground. Six or seven miles to go. Terror did not follow him through the trees, but he knew it was growing behind him, in the car he had left up there beside the lake.

2

He was wearing the navy blue blazer and grey flannel trousers, the white shirt and dark crimson tie, of those peripatetic American businessmen who check in at Sheraton Hotel reception desks and shed boarding cards as they pull out their ID. He told the doorman he was expected and gave his name. He told the security man who sat at a table between the door and the elevators his name, and both the man sitting and the other one standing beside him stared objectively at the visitor's face to see whatever they could see there, as if it was a code they might crack and find a sinister message hidden in it.

They saw a thick-necked blocky individual with cropped fair hair and a head that looked made of tough bone, like a British rugby forward. He had deep brown eyes with an intelligent and watchful spark in them, as if they had seen too many jokes turn sour. The sitting man made a phone call and passed him to the elevator.

On the twenty-first floor the security set-up was the same, and here the guard standing at the desk relieved him of a Walther automatic. The one behind the desk asked him his business.

"My name is Carmichael," Carmichael said, "and I am expected."

"Yes?"

"Yes," Carmichael said.

"I meant, yes, and . . . ?" the man said.

"I know what you meant," Carmichael said.

"So?" the other said. He was a man over forty with hostile blue eyes and dead black hair, probably over six feet when he

17

stood up, a man with the look of early retirement from some government agency, making a second career: another hard case.

"I bet you eat your Wheaties dry," Carmichael said, and lay down on the good deep carpet and put his hands behind his head and closed his eyes. He had not liked it in the trunk of the car with his dead colleague, and his sleep had not been good since. He was tired.

The man said, "Get up," and some other things, but Carmichael tuned out and felt his spine begin to relax and the bad humour leave his mouth, and let his head rest in the crook of his arm.

After a while Mendham's voice said: "Hallo, Alexander."

Carmichael opened his eyes and saw cloth in two minimally contrasting shades of blue falling onto a black shoe. "That's a very nice cloth," he said. "These guys are full of shit."

"Of course they're full of shit," Mendham said, "That's why I hire them. In the security business you have scared clients, so you hire people who will scare them more, and that helps them to feel that your people will scare the other people."

"You heard that at some business school?"

"I just thought of it," Mendham said, "a thing to say. Do you want to rest there a bit, or will you come in now?"

As Carmichael followed Mendham to his office the man at the desk said: "You're a limey."

"Ah," Carmichael said, in the rueful but accepting voice of a pool player who has driven the cue ball off three cushions and watches it strike the colour to the lip of the pocket instead of into it. He took out a pack of Marlboros and a lighter, and watched the hostile blue eyes while he lit up.

"What is it you want of me?" he said. "Is it this?" and he made a step forward and mashed the cigarette out on the man's face.

The man yelled and half got up, but Carmichael went on pushing the disintegrating cigarette into his face and he went over backwards carrying the chair with him. He scrambled up from the floor and one hand went to his face and the other to his belt, but his sidekick who had taken Carmichael's revolver

18

moved in and warned him: "No, you don't want to do that."

The blue-eyed man said to Carmichael: "I'll kill you for this."

"Well," Carmichael said, "before you set about it, think of the years you've had and the years you want to have."

He went on into Mendham's office.

It was a big corner room windowed on two sides. Carmichael thought that even for an office it was one of the most artificial rooms he had seen. The sense of artificiality was so strong that it made the dome of the Capitol, distant but clear against its blue sky, look like a backdrop. The furniture might have been chosen for a film set, the super-top-executive desk, the leather couches and chairs, the conference table with seats for ten.

He couldn't quite make out what was wrong. Everything in the room was appropriate but the result was a caricature. It was Mendham's room, so if it was making a statement then the statement was Mendham's.

Mendham was not making statements just now. Mendham was asking questions. "So how did it happen?" Mendham asked.

Carmichael laid himself along one of the mammoth couches. "So that's what's wrong," he said. "Everything's too big."

Mendham, the exile, made himself very English. He squatted on his toes, with his hands clasped and his elbows resting on his thighs, and bounced a little to show that he was comfortable. His face was leaned towards Carmichael.

It was a pale sharp-boned face, with pale brown hair and eyebrows, and would have made a modest impression except for the eyes. They were dark blue eyes, so dark that they should have been deep and warm enough to redeem the blandness of the face, the kind of eyes women liked to have near their own eyes. But something had died in them once, and been replaced by something else, and even Carmichael felt bad when they looked down at him.

"What happened," he said, "was that you didn't tell me Calder was an old pro. He shot Jerman full of holes and he nearly gutted me."

"Calder is not an old pro," Mendham said. "Calder is an old professor of English Lit."

"Even if that was all he was," Carmichael said, "we'd have a problem, because his syntax is thicker than my loins. But Calder is an old pro. He told me himself."

Mendham bounced twice and made an agile move that brought him easily to his feet.

Carmichael felt relief at once. He relaxed with a long stretching of the spine, and had a sudden image of himself as one of those big circus cats, all deadly teeth and claws, that submits to the mastering eye of the lion-tamer. It made him surly.

"I could have got killed. You could have got me killed," he said. "Your briefing was full of holes."

"Have a drink," Mendham said. "Better still, let's go and have lunch."

"It's tea-time," Carmichael said.

Mendham looked down. "It's a damned dismal carpet this," he said. "I went too far with the carpet."

Carmichael looked at the carpet. It was half an acre of undertoned black, a depressive colour that made him think of the Sargasso Sea. "Went too far?" he asked, hoping for an insight into Mendham's system of decoration.

"There's something odd about this," Mendham said. "What did Calder say to you, about his being an old pro?"

Carmichael despaired of being offered a drink and got up and off the couch to look for it himself. "It's on the tip of my tongue," he said. "It's been engraved there since he said it. The words are these: 'Didn't they tell you who I used to be? They set you up, my boy. They set you up, didn't they?'"

Along one wall, on a steel bench, was an array of electronic equipment that could have been anything from a missile control system to a sound mixing lab. It was so incongruous that it reassured Carmichael. It was the only part of the room that did not seem phoney, and it drew him to the metal cupboards underneath the bench, hopeful that if there were such a genuine article as good whisky around that was where it would be.

Mendham sat behind his desk. "They're locked," he said, as Carmichael tugged at one of the cupboards. Mendham touched a switch, and the door next the unreal view of the Capitol admitted a Daughter of the American Revolution.

Mendham said formally: "Alexander Carmichael, Mrs Jane Winder."

"How do you do?" she said, and Carmichael straightened from his aborted search for Scotch, and said the same.

"Alexander is looking for the whisky," Mendham said.

"You're such a bad host, John," Mrs Winder said, and went out again.

"Calder is not a pro," Mendham said, "but we're supposed to be, so let's stop playing around with this. Debrief yourself; tell me the tale; whatever."

Mrs Winder came in with a tray and put it on a table at one of the massive couches. She distributed glasses and sat on the couch beside Carmichael. His surprise showed. "Don't worry," she said, "I can keep secrets better than John does."

When Carmichael reached the point in his story where Calder had locked him in the trunk of the car with Jerman's corpse, he grew agitated and went over to look down into the street, speaking with his back to them. A bluejay came out of nowhere and lunged at the window. It fell to the ledge where it sat and stared at him.

"Piss off," he said to it, and slapped the glass with his hand, but the bird went on sitting and staring. Nausea came up in his throat and he turned away.

"Come and sit down," Mrs Winder said, and when he did she took his hand and held it on her thigh.

He looked at her and she looked back calmly: a woman of middle age in a white cashmere sweater and trousers, a woman with black hair and grey eyes and a pleasant face with plenty of peace in it.

"I kill people," he said. "You don't need to be nice to me."

"I do," she said. "I have a need to be nice to you. It's not for you, it's selfish."

21

"Sweet Jesus!" Mendham said.

"Shut up, John," Mrs Winder said, and went on allowing Carmichael to learn her face.

She saw the question he was not going to ask; and what was behind it. "I'll be fifty next birthday," she said, "and I think I may be old enough to be your mother, but today that may be a good thing, so you'll come home with me."

Mendham could not stand this. He came out from behind his desk. "You two are on my time now," he said, "and this elaborate foreplay is not what my time is for."

He poured himself a drink, and shoved the tray along and sat beside it on the table, and made himself a tensed spring leaning towards them. "So if Alexander will kindly tell us how he got out of the trunk of the car," he said, "we can put our fine Italian minds together and plan the next move."

"I was lucky," Carmichael said. "This old coot with about ten cameras in his car came by looking for scenery to photograph and pulled in. So I made a lot of noise and finally got him to open the trunk and let me out."

Mrs Winder squeezed his hand and gave it back to him. She took a cigarette from a pack on the tray. "I don't have to smoke," she said to Carmichael. "If you don't like the taste I shan't smoke any more today."

"No, no," Carmichael said. "Go ahead. I smoke myself."

Mendham swung his hand gently and made a whirlpool of his whisky. He peered into this as if he had fathomed some secret of nature.

"Tell me," he said. "How did the old coot let you out?"

"That's the odd thing," Carmichael said. "Calder had left the keys in the ignition."

Mendham lifted his head. Carmichael met his gaze, and felt like a man falling overboard just before he goes into the winter sea off Labrador. Mendham said: "Calder left the keys in the ignition." He went back to the maelstrom in his glass. After a while he said to it, "Some professional," and then drank it down in a gulp, Old Father Neptune hitting the bottle.

Carmichael said: "Everything else he did was professional. Even professionals make mistakes."

"I know they do." Mendham became coarse. "You're the living proof."

Mrs Winder said: "That's unfair. Jerman was a good man, extremely good, in fact, and Calder was good enough to zotz Jerman."

"Zotz?" Mendham said with amazement. "Where do you get words like zotz? I've never heard zotz."

"I have this *nostalgie de la boue*. I like to go to New York and meet the underworld," Mrs Winder said. "They don't kill guys any more, they zotz the little fuckers." When Carmichael heard her well-bred voice saying these words he experienced a number of beneficent sensations.

"All right," Mendham said to her. "You know as much as I know about Calder. Do you think he's a pro?"

Mrs Winder dropped a light and deprecating touch on the back of Carmichael's hand. "I'm sorry, Alexander. No John, I don't think so. I think he's a man who turns out to be resourceful, and is fortunate enough to be ruthless as well. He has the ruthlessness of the old, of old age."

Mendham was deeply interested in this idea. "The ruthlessness of old age. Why do you say that? How would you know? You've been ruthless and amoral all your life."

"Not all of it, but yes, long enough. Now, even at fifty, it feels healthier," Mrs Winder said, "a natural thing, part of the selfishness of growing old. I think it will be a great standby in old age. I think it has been a standby for Professor Calder. I'm rather drawn to the idea of Professor Calder. I suppose it is essential to zotz him?"

"You made the contract, for pity's sake." Mendham was cross. "You know what it's worth and you know who it's with. It would do us a lot of harm to back out now. Do you want to tell Alexander, or shall I?" He had laid the faintest sneer of distaste through the question, against her offering her bed to Carmichael.

Her head moved, first to Carmichael and then back again, and the calm grey eyes thought about Mendham for a little while. That was all that happened, but it was as if a shark had come into the room.

Carmichael began to doubt. Then he saw that this might be foolish, and then, he felt an excitement he had not felt before. It was a rather grisly excitement.

"I'll tell Alexander," she said. "We think it is ninety per cent certain Calder will go to England," she told Carmichael, "so that's where you go."

Carmichael may have felt himself between the shark and the deep blue sea, but he knew when the time came to look out for himself. "I'm not sure," he said, "that I feel happy about going back to England."

"Yes, I know about that," she said, "but I really think it will be perfectly safe for you. No one is looking for you now, you're forgotten. You'll be going under a new name, and you'll know at once if you're spotted and if you are spotted we can think again."

"That sounds nice," Carmichael said, "but I don't think it makes me happy enough."

"Try this." There was a note like kindness in Mendham's voice. "We think you'll find yourself up against Harry Seddall. Does that make you happy enough?"

Carmichael felt skinless, his emotions exposed to the world, and a wish to burst into tears nearly overcame him. He remembered how *well* he hated Harry Seddall. "Yes," he said, "that makes me happy enough."

"Good man," Mendham said, an atavistic echo from some old British film or other.

Mrs Winder, more sensibly, said, "You can always zotz the little fucker."

"Yes," Carmichael said, "I can always do that."

She gave Mendham the calm grey look again, a warning. "Now, Alexander, you and I will have dinner," she said, "and then we'll go home."

3

James Calder lay on his bed in the Hotel Rosita and wondered how long the depression would last. It had come on him this first night in the hotel. The early signs of it, in the dining room, had taken him by surprise and their significance had not at once been clear to him. It had been five or six years since he had suffered depression, and he had thought during most of those years that he had reached a place where he was in reconciliation with all his life.

On the ship from Baja California Mexico he had been full of himself, walking with elation about the decks, the fugitive who had escaped his enemies, and traversed the length and breadth of the United States. To himself, if to no one else on board, he was a figure of mystery. As the ship came into the bay he looked down at the solemn weight of a pelican drifting through the air just below him, and spoke to it silently.

"I am an ageing English scholar who has fought for his life against evil men," he said, "and killed one of them – would you believe that? – and perhaps left the other to die; or rather, left the other perhaps to die."

The pelican, indifferent to his pedantries as to his presence, coasted on, following its shadow over the sparkling sea. Its grave attendance upon this silent monologue drew further confidences from the man at the ship's rail.

"Perhaps I make too much of this," he said. "Certainly it has its hold on me. Do you think I am trying too hard to reassure myself that having escaped thus far I am away, scot-free? I have come far and deviously," he explained, "and by unlikely roads."

It came to him that the pelican, who knew of predators on shore and in the sea, would be unimpressed by this argument, and at this moment it turned from the ship in a clumsy curve and went its way.

Calder saw that the ship was up to the berth and turned his eyes to the land, and felt no more than the faintest semblance inside him of a shadow like that on which the pelican rode.

He liked the simplicity of the Hotel Rosita, in its white town rising to the green hills; a real family hotel for Mexicans. He felt himself to be engaged in, a part of, the human society of the hotel, and when he came downstairs for dinner, he detected (this may have been purely subjective, to fulfil a need of his own) a benevolence among the people in the dining room, in which he shared and to which he contributed.

It was only when the champagne he had ordered to celebrate his arrival was foaming in the glass that the sudden fatigue came on him. He went through the bottle fast enough, but had to force himself to eat. At last, when he had moved into the bar area – an internal courtyard with its seaward end open to the night – he asked for coffee and brandy and prepared to relax.

So early in the year the hotel was not even half full, and since most of the diners were still at their meal he was almost alone. Among tables that would have seated perhaps a hundred people there were only himself, two young couples with five children between them sitting together on the far side of the room, and three elderly people: two women and a sombre man of military bearing, they sat at a remove of one table from him.

The stiffness of respectability that can afflict an almost deserted public room had fallen upon the two families, and the unfortunate children were being restrained from every impulse of high spirits. The elderly trio were equally reticent, but Calder had the sense that this was their custom.

Out of this unspeaking emptiness isolation came to him. It was not the simple feeling of being one man by himself where others, both here and in the dining room he had just left, were in company. The thing that simultaneously descended upon him and rose within him was his old enemy, the long-forgotten despair and the fear it brought with it, of feeling himself a meaningless and incapable creature, born to sorrow as the sparks fly upwards.

He rose, ready to escape to his room and himself, at the same moment that the waiter returned. Calder had come to his feet and set off so abruptly that he knocked into the man and nearly sent flying the tray balanced on his hand, but he had nothing left to cope with this, and kept on his way.

"Señor!" the man said. "The brandy, the coffee!"

"No matter," Calder said, a phrase which could mean nothing to a man with little English. By now he had stopped and turned round, but could find no more words, although the waiter, in his bewilderment at the violence of Calder's movements and the violence of feeling he was receiving from him, went on saying things, seeking perhaps no more than the decency of response which Calder was unable to give him.

Calder felt all the eyes on him of both the decorous families, and saw people arrive now from the dining room and look over at the little scene he and the waiter made. He could neither speak nor move, but some instinct drew his eyes to the table nearby, to the two women and the soldierly looking man.

The man dropped his head, as if in acceptance or resignation, and then raised it and spoke quietly a few words. To Calder it was as if by magic – the waiter became calm, set down the contents of the tray, and went away.

The soldierly man then stood up, excused himself to his companions, and came over to Calder. When he spoke it was in beautiful English, with only the faintest foreign turn to the pronunciation.

"Would you care to sit with us?" he said.

Calder found his tongue. "Thank you," he said. "I think I must go to my room."

"I shall go with you," the man said. "It is when it would be

27

insupportable to meet idiots upon one's way that one meets idiots, and for you just now it would be insupportable."

He pulled a card from his waistcoat pocket and presented it. Calder was able to discover his spectacles, and learned that his benefactor was German: the Freiherr Geyr von Harma.

Calder took him to be fifteen years his senior, a man of about eighty whose face went in upon its bones like the mask of a fox, tall and still straight in the back, but with the old man's fall of the shoulders and an exhausted look to him as if life, by continuing so far, had asked too much of him. The eyes were a faded blue, one of them with a broken blood vessel, and their expression was bleak.

The stereotype of a Prussian aristocrat, Calder thought, not the man you would expect to find cast as your benefactor. He felt an ironic smile in him, and saw it appear, as if by osmosis, on the face opposite him.

"I come from Brandenberg," von Harma said.

"You are *geboren*," Calder said, surprised to find he could amuse himself, and to be so sure that the other would not be offended.

"It is what we used to call ourselves," von Harma said. "Nowadays I should have thought it vulgar of you to say it, had you not been mocking me. Come, let us take you upstairs."

"Your English is quite perfect," Calder said, as they left the room. "You have lived in England."

"Long ago. I was in our military attaché's office in London," von Harma said.

Calder was aware that he was being humoured, and knew he was babbling partly as a reaction to this, doubtless temporary, easing of his depression and in relief at being rescued from his dilemma. He noticed too that von Harma guided him, by example, towards the stairs, and realized that without this he might well have stopped where he was and babbled on.

"You knew how to help me," he said. "How was that?"

"Up the stairs, now," von Harma commanded him, and they reached Calder's room in silence.

28

Calder sat on the edge of his bed and von Harma, very upright, on a wooden chair. "I have been extremely rude," Calder said. "My name is James Calder. I am an academic, English Literature."

Von Harma bowed where he sat. "Will you sleep?" he asked. "I do not sleep easily, and can give you some pills that will ensure you four or five hours, at any rate."

"Why should I not sleep?" Calder said, and after a little. "How did you know what was wrong with me?"

"We have the same difficulty, you and I. I also suffer from depression," von Harma said. He stood up. "My room is two doors away, across the corridor. I shall fetch the pills for you, in case you want them. Later, when I come to bed, I shall knock lightly on your door, and if you are awake and want to talk, you shall say so."

"I feel myself fortunate," Calder said. "I could not have been more fortunate. You are extremely kind."

"There is no kindness in it," von Harma said, and left him.

Calder took the well-worn letter from his hip pocket and stretched out on the bed. He did not read it at once, but laid it on his stomach and lay with his hands behind his head. Through the open window came the sound of the Pacific breakers throwing themselves on the beach, and of a rising wind sweeping over the trees on the hills above the town. They were welcome sounds. He knew that a night of utter silence would have been hard on him.

He thought von Harma was an odd fish. In appearance and manner he was as cold as steel, but what he had said and done had brought Calder some ease. He had another thought about von Harma, which was that if he had been a junior officer in the immediate pre-war years, the difference in age between them might not be so great as he had thought. He supposed von Harma had suffered some debilitating illness.

Calder adjusted the angle of the bed lamp and turned to Marion's letter for the hundredth time.

My dear Jim,

There is no way to start but to say that this will be a posthumous letter, and that what we feared for a while long ago, but did not any longer seriously expect, has happened. It is hard to believe, so long after the event, but to someone somewhere what we know has become a threat, and therefore we have become a threat.

It seems to me that we were hardly more than children at Bletchley Park during the war, when we found that punt on the lily pond; but that was not quite the case, or we should not have made what was, for us then, the happy use of it we did.

But that is no more than an old photograph in the memory for us, and I write to you now with no feeling but that of fear. That fear, and the certainty that it is justified, have brought me to a place with myself where I am almost wholly winnowed from life, and writing this to you it is as if I write from one human soul to another, not as from a person to a person; so expect no emotion, and experience none, except that of fear on your own account.

I send you this warning only because it is my fault that you are in peril, since had I not been half in love with X (no names, even now) as well as half in love with you, I would not have told him that from our punt we had overheard his meeting with the traitors that night, and urged him to turn them down; for although we simply knew of them as Communists in those days, and did not yet know to think of them as traitors, I knew there was a wrong in them that he should not be part of. I have ended that sentence with a preposition. You always jumped on that – not quite so winnowed from life as I thought then, am I Jim? I wish to God I were. I am deadly frightened.

A dose of whisky later, and with some clenching of the will, I am back to you. Where was I?

Well, all those years ago, he married, and the wife being who she was I phoned you from a hotel when I was in France and you were staying in Magdalen for that conference. I felt smug about that – from a hotel where I was not staying to an Oxford college where you did not belong seemed particularly safe. Such precautions even then, so many years after the event!

We decided then that we had best let sleeping dogs lie, partly since we knew nothing to tell us that he had become a traitor like Philby and the others, and partly because of the risk to ourselves. Or did you persuade me to let it be, Jim? I rather think you did. If that's how it was well, now of course I rather wish we'd made up our minds to do something about it then – one way or another it would have been settled long ago. But that's me crying over spilt milk, and what use is that?

After that, Jim, we went back again to the yearly Christmas cards. I wonder why we sent them, and only them?

That this last sentence had been expressed as a question came again to Calder, as it had at every reading of the letter, as an instant of appalling pain. It came not from the recollected tenderness of having loved her those many years ago, nor from their not having grown into any kind of friendship except to the degree that there was (this had long been a belief of his, which he applied equally to scholarship and to other aspects of life) something of everything in everything else. The pain sprang from her vivid wish, which he felt so clearly expressed in those nine words and that question mark, to be in dialogue with him – since that would mean this letter of hers would not be posthumous. It was the most bitter paradox he had ever encountered, and it hurt him that he should perceive it in this way, as no more than a figure of speech – but how could he fail to? – which reduced the words of Marion's sorrow for her death to being filed in his mind under a label already inscribed, a label from his own safe life in the university world: what had been his own safe world until a month ago.

Now, he had for himself the same sense of doom that had overwhelmed, before she died, the woman who had written this letter to him. To that life of literary scholarship – his real life – he had already said goodbye. To this life that was left he anticipated only some violent, and he must hope sudden, ending. Meanwhile, unlike her, at least he could run, for she had given him somewhere to run to. (Poor Marion. He had given up grammatical obsessions, such as that with eschewing the final preposition, decades ago.)

He picked up the letter, which he had let fall to the bed cover, and read it through to the end.

All right, Jim, after another dose of whisky: this is a lonely house, which is why I chose it, since I like my solitude, and these last forty-eight hours there have been men, three men, fishing the hill lochs and the burns, and they know damn all about fishing. There is always one of them watching the house from somewhere roundabout. I have walked close to them and they have that clumsy look MI5 used to have, the vulgar hat and belted trenchcoats look, and though they are wearing brand new Barbour jackets and rustic breeks I know that's what they are underneath.

The phone has stopped working. Two days ago the car refused to start. Last night, Jim, one of them was IN THE HOUSE, creeping about like a hippopotamus. All that is bad enough, but the worst thing is, that my cats have sloped off, and to me that is the final portent. I know my fear has made them nervous, but I am certain also that they know these men mean death.

So I am writing you this letter, and am going to walk innocently to the road end with a bundle of mail, as if I had been catching up on my correspondence, and post this among it, c/o my lawyer: one of those letters lawyers get, to be forwarded in the event of . . . Well, in the event of. Then I shall try to walk out, but it is five miles to the village and I fear, and oh yes, it is such dreadful fear, that they will stop me. With luck they'll be overconfident and think they have gone undetected and so you will get this letter.

What you will do is up to you. If you felt the fear I am in, you would simply up and run. I can give you only one name that a friend of mine, my only friend in high places and whom I shall *not* name, once recommended to me some years ago when I had the vaguest and at that time quite illogical feeling that harm might one day come to me. The name is Seddall, and he is in some form of military intelligence. That is all I can give you to find him, except that I know he has a house in the West Country. This Whitehall friend of mine warned me that if I ever met Seddall – which I did not – I might not like him at first meeting but would find him a good man to have on my side if I had trouble, especially if the trouble should come from the Establishment.

At that time I was not more seriously concerned than one is about fire when one insures one's house, which is to say looking to an improbable event in the future; all the same, for some melodramatic reason – what did I have in mind? "Avenge me if . . .!"? – I made the highly placed friend and (without asking or telling him) the unfortunate Mr Seddall joint executors of my will.

I can't write more. I am losing my nerve fast now, and shall have one more tot of whisky which on top of nothing but coffee for breakfast will make me a little drunk, and then I shall set out to meet my fate.

Good luck, Jim,
Marion

Then, as if the tot of whisky had been half a glass or more, came a last scrawled line.

PS. Well, I name her: Julia Heron.

It had come to seem to Calder that he read and re-read this letter as if doing so were a penance; but a penance for what, he did not know. It was not his fault that Marion had been killed. He had not failed to grieve for her. Indeed the grief he felt, each time he took out the letter and heard her speaking to him, was beyond the natural amount of grief for a woman with whom he had been in love for a summer forty years ago. By this time he knew the grief was fuelled by guilt, and that this had brought him the idea of penance, but he could make no sense of it.

The thinking stopped, and listening to the waves on the shore and the wind in the trees, and with the light still on, he slid into the half-waking state which brings much the same warmth that follows the first seconds after an injection of morphine, and went off to sleep.

When von Harma tapped lightly on the door, Calder came awake at once.

"I have disturbed your sleep," the German said.

"No," Calder said. "It is not a disturbance."

"Then I shall sit down for no more than five minutes," von Harma said, and settled on the wooden chair. Calder swung his legs over the edge of the bed and, rested by his sleep, smiled at the visitor.

". . . I fell asleep without taking your pills," he said. "A good sign."

"Yes," von Harma said, "a good sign." He bent stiffly and took from the floor a page of the letter Calder had been reading, and handed it to him.

Calder had been thrown on his own resources for too long to quench the impulse that rose in him. It was more than an impulse, it was a longing.

He took the page and put it with the others and offered them to von Harma. "Will you read it?" he said.

Von Harma looked at him. "You are certain you want me to read it? Then I shall." He took a pair of spectacles out of their case, and began to read.

After the first few lines his eyes lifted to Calder. They rested on him with no change in the bleakness of their expression, and returned to the letter. Calder stood up and went to the window and leaned out, and waited. The town slept, and the sky was bright with stars.

He waited a long time, longer than it could have taken to read the letter, before von Harma said: "So, you have run. You escaped before they came for you."

"No," Calder said as he turned back to the room. "They came for me."

Now it was von Harma who waited. "I killed one of them," Calder said, "perhaps both. Then I ran."

"Tell me," von Harma said.

Calder told him everything.

When he had finished von Harma looked at the letter, not at the words but at the letter itself, as if it were a small marvel. "Dear God," he said. "Is each of us then a piece of history?"

He leaned forward and put the letter on the bed, and then sat back and looked at his hands, the backs of them and the palms, as if to bring himself away from history into the present again.

"You have done incredibly well, but you are out of your ground."

An alteration that Calder did not like took place on von Harma's ancient face. It was as if one of the skull-faces on a medieval painting of the Dance of Death had been portrayed as enjoying a ghastly joke.

"If you will accept an unlikely ally," von Harma said, "I shall help you to England."

"Good heavens," Calder said. "I can't ask that."

"You have not asked," von Harma said. "It is I who ask this of you. Do you think I should not enjoy it?"

Calder stared at him, and found himself unable to answer.

"I am no older than you," von Harma said. "You are fitter than I, but this," and he tapped on the side of his head, "is more apt for such a campaign as you are embarked on. Also, I think it likely I have resources you cannot call on."

He bent on Calder a look it was difficult to receive, and said:

"There is, however, one thing that you may find an obstacle to accepting an alliance with me."

The look became even worse, and it was all Calder could do not to turn away from it. "Tell me," he said at last.

"The reason I look so much older than you," von Harma said, "is that I was many years a prisoner in Russia. I was sentenced for war crimes." He had a moment of difficulty in speaking. "I was guilty of them," he said.

Von Harma came to his feet. "You must have time to decide," he said. "Give me your decision in the morning."

His face might have been carved from ice.

Long after the door had closed behind him Calder sat and stared at it, while the wind, which had risen to something like a gale, rattled the shutters at the window and howled at the night.

In the morning Calder was up early and went out to walk on the beach. The sky was clear and brilliant and the air hyperoxygenated after the night's winds, but the pelicans sat unmoving as if it was too soon for them to wake.

He went into the hotel feeling that he had an appetite. Von Harma and the two women were already in the dining room. Calder went over to their table.

"Would it be an impertinence," he said, "to ask if I might join you?"

The women inclined their heads, and seemed not displeased.

Von Harma looked at Calder, and Calder at von Harma, then Calder pulled out the fourth chair and sat down.

For the first time since he had killed and run, he began to have a real hope that he might reach the man Seddall, whom Marion had designated for his saviour.

36

4

"What *is* this?" Harry Seddall demanded, his eyes large with surmise.

"It's two Arbroath smokies taken aff the bone wi' a bit sauce," Mrs Lyon said, and clouted the large spaniel which was salivating, not with desire for its master's breakfast, but with the frustration of not being able sufficiently to express its love for this bony old Scotswoman.

"I'll murder ye the day," she told the dog Bayard, and bent down to give his face and scalp a furious friction rub and deliver a few wallops to his haunches, which would have distressed the inspectorate of the Royal Society for the Prevention of Cruelty to Animals, but sent the spaniel out of the room crooning from an open throat to digest these joys solitary in its basket.

The terms of her original contract called for Mrs Lyon to clean house three days a week, but she had long since modulated this arrangement to suit her own ideas, one of which was that a man would not be allowed to leave for the day's work without a good breakfast inside him, so long as she was there to cook it.

Harry took in another forkful of the strongly smoked fish wrapped in the bland white sauce. "It is by-God delicious," he said.

"There's no need for blasphemy all the same," Mrs Lyon said, and to the black cat Sacha who sat, pooled in sunlight on the breakfast table a yard from the exhilarating haddock, and venomous with proudly concealed greed, she exclaimed with her head on one side: "Oh, but ye're a bonnie wee bugger."

37

"Don't swear at the cat," Harry said triumphantly, reckoning the score at fifteen-all.

"Bugger's no swearing," Mrs Lyon said, a fast passing shot that returned him to *The Times* crossword as she left the room.

"Eighteen across," he read aloud to the cat. " 'Criterion followed by a cavalry regiment.' Eight letters, beginning with 'S'. We should be able to get that one, Sacha, we belong to a cavalry regiment."

Mrs Lyon's grizzled head showed itself round the door. "Standard," she said smartly, Navratilova to the last, and disappeared again.

"I want the bloody stairs polished from top to bottom," Harry yelled after her.

"Aye, that'll be right!" she yelled back. "I'll no get near the stairs the day, I'm turnin' out your drawing-room."

"Mind you," Harry said to Sacha, "this is the best damn breakfast in London."

As he polished off the fish and reached for the marmalade, the black cat's eyes gleamed, daggers of nephrite.

Harry Seddall walked at a smart three and a half miles an hour through Kensington Gardens and on into the Park, digesting like anything and basking in the ebullience of the spring day. The lusty daffodil and the slight narcissus flourished in the grass, some trees budded and others leafed, and across a sky as blue as the Virgin's robe in a Sienese painting the white clouds passed steadily from the south-west and shone in the sun.

Despite the beauty of the day, they were clouds that threatened rain, or even snow, for that freshness was in the air. Seddall, however, warmly coated and well hatted, handled his umbrella cheerily and recked nothing of the weather. He noticed, instead, that in the two years since Monique had left he had not felt so beforehand with life.

Seddall mounted the steps to what, in his obsolete fashion, he alone still called the Office. He displayed the usual credentials, accepted the usual salutations, and went so far as to eschew the lift and to essay briskly the wide staircase in what became, however, the diminishing progression of canter, trot, walk. He should take more exercise, get a bicycle, go beagling, travel through the Carpathians with a mule.

Maggie Donovan, making her mail round, fell into step beside him as he strode with recovering breath along the corridor to his room.

"The general would like it if you can make time to see him at eleven," she said.

"Reassure the general," Seddall said. "I can do this."

"My, we're frisky this morning," she said.

"Ho, yes," he said. "Come the three corners of the world in arms, and we shall shock 'em."

He unlocked the door and waved her in, followed, threw his coat and hat on a chair, and went to the coffee maker.

"I'll do that," she said, "and you shouldn't hold doors for me. You're four ranks higher than I am."

"Senior officers are always being polite like that," he said. "It means nothing, as you must have noticed." He opened the window wide and sat on the sill. "Or are you, by any chance, a feminist?"

"Certainly, I'm a feminist," Maggie Donovan said, measuring coffee with a spoon into the filter.

"Then why are you making the coffee?"

"Because it is my will," she said.

Seddall lit a cigarette, and listened again to what she had said. It sounded as if she meant it.

She switched the filter machine on and joined him at the window. She bent over the miniature narcissi in his window box. "They do you credit," she said.

"You said I'm four ranks higher than you," he said. "No one says it that way. Why do you?"

She looked down into the courtyard where the stonework was lit and shadowed by the sun. "Have you ever sat in the courtyard at Burlington House, and really looked at it?" she asked.

"Yes, I have. Why do you say four ranks higher?"

With neat and callous fingers she took a petal from one of the bright young flowers. She held it out and let it go, and watched it swirl uncertainly in the air. "It puts it in perspective. Four ranks: if I can make the next step, colonel's not so far off."

"I've heard of this," Harry said in a drawling voice, "it's called ambition."

That drawl had sounded like contempt. She came in from leaning out of the window and stood opposite him where he sat with one leg on the sill and the other idly swinging. The clear daylight on his face did not make him blink, but either from its brightness or some other influence, the green in his eyes faded until they were almost entirely yellow.

The smell of coffee had now joined itself to the influences in the room: the freshness of the breeze that stirred the flowers; the sunshine in which the blue smoke of the French cigarette basked, coiling and stretching, before it curled up round the sash of the raised window with a sudden rush as if to give itself to the spring day – the sunshine which, not yet coming directly into the room, lit it with the early promise a day will make (a promise sometimes false, sometimes true; but still, while it lasts, a promise) of beneficence to come; the room itself, high and well-proportioned and friendly to the evocation of well-being offered by such simple harmonies of the morning; and lastly the man on the windowsill, for whom it seemed the most apt and natural thing in the world to sit among these satisfactions, and listen to the pigeons cooing out of sight on the pediment above his head.

For Maggie Donovan, however, the eyes that watched her from the man who seemed so pleasurably at his ease, flung a sudden doubt on the innocent nature of the scene. It was as if, looking at a picture of the lush imagined Africa painted by the Douanier Rousseau, she had seen one of his nice safe jungle animals bring its stare to life, and open fanged jaws at her.

"What's up, Donovan?" the unlikely tiger in the window said. "We were talking about your race for promotion."

"It's not a race," she said, "and I don't know that it's ambition either. It's planning a career-path, that's all."

"My," he said. "Is that where I've been all these years, walking along a career-path?"

"I'll pour some coffee," Maggie said.

"Do that," he said, and dropped his cigarette end out of the window, and watched it roll down a few slates into the gutter, and went on watching where down on the ground official cars came in and were parked just so, and were at once inspected by Ministry of Defence police for bombs, pocket sub-machine guns, matchbox cameras, and anything else undesirable and alien. She was a good-looking, red-haired woman, he thought, and on the way to being quite a warrior. He wondered what else he would think, if he knew her better.

She had to switch the coffee-maker off, since it had not finished its run, and fiddle with the cups and the filter, which was still dripping through; and doing this she glanced at him now and then, thinking that she did not recognize, altogether, the man who had been described to her; the character that had been sketched for her.

There was more to him than she had thought at first, despite the sloppy appearance he made of himself, sitting there inside what had obviously been a perfectly good suit on the hanger this morning, but wearing it with such a comfortable air of being a man at home and in his pyjamas – how did he do this, in Whitehall, of all places? – that the cloth, obedient to its owner, was already crumpling about him as if he had slept in it; while his tie, a breezy herbaceous number, had begun to walk round his neck and bend the collar of his shirt.

In her few months in the Ministry, exchanging only perfunctory greetings with him in the mornings, and in the evenings sometimes catching sight of him – a drifting figure whose appearance, by that time of day, had become close to slovenly – she had supposed him to be, by contrast with the variously pin-striped and uniformed staff who habitually displayed enterprise and initiative by the cut of the jib and the vigour of the stride, a man of little moment waiting for the retirement axe to fall.

Well, she thought, they had told her and she had not believed, but she knew different now. That motionless stare he had laid on her while his eyes flickered against the slant of the sun; that minutely watching stare from the yellowish brown eyes, as cold and objective as the real hunting beast looking out from its real jungle: that had taught her different.

She thought it again: You were told Maggie, but you didn't take it on board. Well, sweetie, now you've been *warned*. She knew that the glowing image of Rousseau's tigers was mocking her, but pouring coffee into the cups she said to herself: What's the old cliché about being confronted by one of the fiercer animals? Don't let it sense your fear? This was just a man, fucking hell, darling, just another of *those*.

So she took the coffee over to him, and thinking to defend herself against his questions by posing one of her own, she asked as she gave him the cup: "Why three corners of the world? You'd think it would be four."

To avoid, however, the excessively scrutinizing eyes, she took his hat and coat from the chair where he had flung them and hung them on the coat-stand.

"Three corners? I dunno." He drank coffee. "Perhaps he felt he was standing on one corner already. Sometimes one does."

She stood at his elbow now, sipping her coffee. "There's your letters," she said ungrammatically, still shunning the direct exchange with him. "That's a funny one on top."

"Don't read my mail," he said. "It's private, secret, confidential and classified."

"*That* one isn't," she said. "It's from some kind of nut."

"All the same. It's a bad habit in a place like this. People could misconstrue it."

He eased himself off the windowsill and settled behind the desk. "Give me some more coffee, there's a good . . . person.

Saved by the bell!" he said, smiling, pleased with himself, but with a lot of irony there, at least half of which seemed to be not for her, but for him.

She got the coffee, and as she put it on the desk he said: "What's all this about, Donovan? Making the coffee, hanging up the coat? Pissing around in here when you should be toting that mail about? We've hardly exchanged two words together before."

"Well, you seemed a bit more jolly and approachable this morning," she said. "At least you did at first. I mean, I do work here too, you know. If I've got enough clearance to tote the mail about, as you put it, I've got enough damn clearance to talk to you. Sir."

"Ouch," he said.

He looked at the letter on top of the mail in front of him. It was headed in large cheap-looking type: 'British Association for Strategic Harmonisation'. The address was in West Hartlepool. She was right, it looked as if it came from some kind of nut.

"I've been rude," he said. "I'm sorry. What about dinner tonight, or do I mean tomorrow night?"

"You have a great way with women, don't you?" she said. "Which night do you mean?"

"Help me, Heaven!" he said, and stood up making a despairing gesture with his hands. "It's just that there's something in the back of my head that tells me I'm doing something on one of these nights. And no, if there's one thing I don't have, it's a great way with women. At least, not lately."

"I don't know," Maggie Donovan said. "I don't know about that. There are things for and things against, so far. I really came in, it's a bit impertinent of me, to tell you . . ."

He smiled a very young but sardonic smile, that seemed to have survived long into the grown man's face, and had some relic of kindness in it. "Tell me," he said.

"I shouldn't," she said, "but anyway, I think there's something grim about your meeting with the general at eleven, and Lord Findo's coming in too."

"Uhuh," he said, not at all disconcerted. "Findo? Yes, yes. He's the one tipped to chair the new security committee, if they can get themselves sorted out about who's to be on it. Well, I don't see anything in that. He's just a politician. One of the Great Unwashed."

"You're a pretty esoteric kind of snob."

"That I am," he said. "Listen, you were wrong to say anything to me about how the general seems to feel about this meeting, so thanks, but just don't do it again. Now scoot, we have things to do, do we not? Oh, may I call you about dinner, or did I lose that one?"

"I don't know yet myself," she said. "If you call, we'll find out."

She looked fine, she looked a good cool sort of woman in that uniform, with her hair bobbed round her neck, a pretty old-fashioned way of doing it surely. She looked like what's-his-name's driver in *The Life and Death of Colonel Blimp*, Roger Livesey's driver, who was it, Moira Shearer or Deborah Kerr? She looks like a ruddy fantasy for a man like me, he thought. That *means* something, Seddall, you take care.

"All right, then," she said, and gathered up the rest of the mail.

"Sure," he said, "so long."

5

"Harry, you're looking good," said the general, who knew that he himself was looking absolutely best. He knew this because he always did look absolutely best. Major-General Aubrey Kenyon, in his shining coat of health, appeared to Harry as a horse in prime condition.

He had too much bulk for a racehorse but he was full of bounce and go, and might have made an admirable hunter except for something crafty in his eye. He was large, fit and full of energy. There were days when the vigour of his personality brought up a smile in Seddall, and other days when it made him feel he had woken up tired.

This was a different sort of day altogether. Kenyon looked as glossy as ever, the big face glowed, the brown eyes were bright, the blue suit could not have hung from a more erect frame, but the ebullition was not flowing.

"Sit down and give me one of your filthy cigarettes," the general said, and then wandered away down the room and revolved the large globe that stood in a corner, with the British Empire showing red all over it circa 1939.

Harry took out a cigarette for himself and tossed the pack onto the teak slab the general had shipped home after the campaign in Malaya, and which was now the top of his desk. Rugs from India and Persia, wall hangings and pictures from Africa, the chunks of onyx from the Far East that had been carved into ashtrays, were a record of Kenyon's life in the Army. They made the office as if it were part of his home. There was nothing warlike or military to be seen, not even a regimental photograph.

Kenyon came back and helped himself to a cigarette, which he did not light. He held it and examined it. He gnawed at his moustache with long white teeth. He put back his head and gave Seddall an uninterpretable look.

"We're in some kind of soup, Harry," he said. "I don't know what kind, whether its your genuine Brown Windsor or the real bortsch or just something thin that we can swim out of." He leaned forward and Harry leaned forward and lit the cigarette for him.

"You and I are in this bortsch, Aubrey?" Harry said. "Or I'm in it and you're being a good old soul and pretending it's both of us?"

The general looked a bit more crafty, like an evil horse gauging how amusing it might be to drop Harry into the next ditch, but Harry did not think he would do that. He thought he trusted Kenyon, though he had worked for him less than a year. He thought the general would not drop him into any ditches unless the going got really rough, and that even then he might not.

He was inclined to trust Kenyon because he had been shunted into Harry's section in the Old War Office building for a reason. Kenyon was an officer with a good career in armour behind him, but once in Whitehall he had depressed the Government with his intellectual superiority in opposing its tank policy, and was in danger of being chopped by fair means or foul.

It therefore became important to his friends to place General Kenyon where he had nothing more to say about tanks, and here he was, smoking diffidently a Gauloise and talking about bortsch and Brown Windsor.

The phone rang and the general looked at it warily before he picked it up.

"Yes?" he said.

Then he said: "Can't talk to him just now."

He said: "Lord Findo will have to wait. I am occupied."

He put down the phone and tapped it gently with the palm of his hand. "That," he said, "is the cause of the trouble. Tell me what you know about him."

"Findo?" Harry said. "Don't know much. Long-time politician, made a corner in Defence when he was an MP, chairman of the party Defence committee, had a Ministry, forget which but not Defence, inherited the title five, six, seven years ago. Even for a politician rather not one to like, at least not for me to like, though I don't like any of 'em. But he and the Prime Minister like each other, and," Harry said with great earnestness, "they do deserve each other, so two years ago he gets to be chairman of this committee of Privy Counsellors that's been looking at the intelligence and security services. Title's a Lloyd George creation."

"Lloyd George creation?" the general said. "What's that to say to anything?"

"It tells us," Seddall said in a drawling voice, "that his great uncle paid in thousands for that title."

"So what?" Kenyon said, with the air of a man trying to converse in a language he is not sure of. He made a messy job of putting out his cigarette and said without looking up from it: "For someone who doesn't know much about Findo, you seem to know an awful lot about him, if you see what I mean."

Seddall brushed ash unsuccessfully off his waistcoat. "You could say so. I thought at first his committee was just looking at Five and Six," he said, "and then I heard he'd got them looking at all of us, so I boned up on him." He waited till Kenyon lifted his head and he could talk to his face. "Findo's a dangerous little bugger, Aubrey. So what's up? He's after me about something?"

Kenyon pulled back his cuff to see his watch, as if he would have liked to plead another engagement, then he met Seddall face to face. "Yes, he's after you about something, and he's more dangerous than you think. That committee of his has made preliminary recommendations, suggesting that Five and Six should be merged —"

"Merged," Seddall said in a flat voice and with an uncompleted smile. "Arkley is going to love this." Sir John Arkley was the head of MI6.

"Merged," Kenyon went on, "and much we care. I mean anything would be an improvement. Why Arkley? What about Considine, and the Curzon Street mob?" Considine's MI5 was headquartered in Curzon Street. It was Kenyon's habit to refer to them as if they were a bunch of American gangsters.

"I can talk to Arkley," Seddall said. "I mean I don't like Arkley, but I can talk to him. I can't talk to Considine."

"Quite so," Kenyon said vaguely. He was coming to the difficult bit. "The thing is this, Harry. The Lord Findo is making a move on us."

"Oh, yes," Seddall said carefully, "but we of the Armed Forces have our Secretary of State to deal with mountebanks like Findo."

"There's no need to be so bloody sarcastic about it," Kenyon said. "You know damn well the PM doesn't like our man, and you know what that means with this Government."

Seddall said: "Sure. It means lots of leeway for Findo in case he comes up with something good." He remembered the bortsch. "So how is he making his move on us?"

This made General Kenyon unhappy. He combed his moustache with those long white teeth. "He's picked on you, as a way of getting at me, at us," he said.

"Well, for God's sake spit it out," Harry said, "or I'll start thinking it's worse than it is."

"It's an insult, really, more than anything. He wants your security classification downgraded until further notice. What he wants is that you should be, in his own words, kept amused with matters of no importance until the question is cleared up satisfactorily."

For a moment Seddall knew a sense of anticlimax; then he frowned. "Question? What question are you talking about, Aubrey? You haven't mentioned a question, or did I miss something?"

Kenyon reached across the desk and took Seddall's lighter and cigarettes and lit one. His glance skated across Seddall's and he stood up. As he moved round the desk he came out of his jacket, which he put on the coat stand by the door. He went off down the room again but did not get as far as the British Empire, being waylaid by the corner of a Kashan rug which was trapped under a chair leg.

He tilted up the chair and smoothed down the rug with his toe, releasing as he did so an unfortunate smile, which although it pretended merely to deprecate the housewifeliness of the act, lingered too long, so that it betrayed a larger sense of apology than could have been inspired by idle fiddling with rugs.

At all this displacement activity, Seddall felt a sixth sense come to life. It whispered to him so strong a warning of menace that, though he remained slouched in his chair, he was as wary as a fox that has heard the cry of hounds in the next valley.

"According to Findo," the general said, "there is a question about you."

Seddall heard himself speak in a strange and formal voice. "Are you able to be specific about the nature of this question?"

The general stayed where he was, even though it meant the lengthening ash of his cigarette falling onto the Kashan. He preferred to keep the distance between them.

"I can quote Findo easily enough," he said, "because that's all he came up with: 'There is a question about Seddall'. He wouldn't add to it. I told him he couldn't leave it at that, and he said, oh yes, he could, as I would find out if I failed – failed was his word – to do what he wanted."

"And what does he want?" Seddall asked with a brutal smile. "Because you'e going to give him what he wants, aren't you, sir?"

Outright antagonism the general could handle, and he came back to his desk and sat down and stuffed out the cigarette. "Don't call me 'sir' in that tone, Harry. I've never sold a man of mine down the river yet. I don't plan to start with you."

"Oh, come on, Aubrey. You're not in the Army now, you're in intelligence. There have been more men grubbily manoeuvred out of intelligence than were ever sold down the Mississippi," Harry said, and sat himself up. It took him, to his surprise, some kind of effort. "I have to suppose that 'a question about me' means about my security, about my loyalty, as the good old Un-American Activities Committee used to put it. If the Lord Findo is feeling his oats and has decided to say I'm unsecure, there's not going to be much you can do about it."

The general found all this irritating. "Don't go chickenshit on me, Harry. I may be tolerably new to this business but I'm not going to jack it in and go and cultivate my garden just because an opportunist like Findo declares war."

Seddall let this rhetoric go by him. "What does he want?" he insisted. "Apart from such minor matters as having my security rating lifted?"

The general rubbed his face vigorously as if this might clear his mind. "No," he said. "He doesn't want either of those things. Pretty odd, isn't it? He said he didn't want you to be on anything big, give Seddall some unimportant odds and ends to do, he said. Until he had more to go on."

The two men looked at each other.

Kenyon said: "That's right: he can't really do this, unless we let him. A vague accusation for which I have his word alone, and no more than a personal word from him saying you should do nothing but odd jobs until God knows when."

"But Findo is Findo," Harry said, "and is in big at No.10."

"Yes," Kenyon said.

"So he's playing poker with you," Harry said, "and you don't know if he has cards."

The general waited. His right hand stroked the dark teak and he watched his fingers as they moved.

"Findo has no executive authority, so far as we know," Seddall said, "but he is stirring a big pot, and Downing Street thinks he may be the man to drag MI5 and MI6 screaming towards the twenty-first century."

After that the two of them sat there, each of them in a brown study, until the general said: "So we should be a bit careful."

He stood up. "I'm taking Jean to lunch," he said, and removed his jacket from the hanger. "One thing occurs to me,

Harry: is there anything you've done in the past that Findo could get you for?"

Seddall grinned, surprising them both. "I've done plenty he could get me for," he said. "I've cut a lot of corners and annoyed a few people about here," and he waved a hand out towards the windows over Whitehall, "but that's not what he's talking about, as you well know. He's talking about me being a security *risk*."

"Yes," the general said, and stood there, a man waiting in his office before lunching with his wife, silently asking Seddall if he was – what? a security risk? a traitor?

"No," Harry said in a grim voice. "Nothing like that." He got up and moved to the door. "As for the rest," he said, "the work I'm doing is routine, even that talking-shop with the French you've landed me with. The most exciting thing on my horizon is going to the opera tonight."

The general had collected his hat and umbrella but left his coat in order to put a hand on the door handle and forestall Seddall's imminent and indignant exit.

"Harry," he said, "I had to hear you say it, you know that, damn it."

Seddall's wary eyes let humour come up in them and he came out with one of those mordant half-smiles of his. "Sure, I know that," he said.

"We'll go along carefully," the general said, "until we know more. I need to know, Harry, are you going to trust me?"

"Uh-huh," Seddall said, "and I'll go along carefully all right, which means I'll watch my back. This," he made little waves with his fingers in the air between them, "light touch Findo is using. I don't like it, I think it's as sinister as all hell."

"So do I," Kenyon said. "So do I."

As they went down in the lift the general said, "Enjoy your night at the opera. What is it?"

"*La Bohème*," Harry said.

"Well, by God, nothing to worry Findo about that," the general said.

51

6

"An executor!" Harry Seddall said crossly. "An executor? Why me, of all people?"

In the pit the oboe sang again, and strings and tympani continued to screw themselves to fine pitch like mechanics preparing Concorde to race Apollo across the sky.

"Why not you? You've got a head on your shoulders," Mrs Heron said. She bent a critical scrutiny on the audience, which apparently passed muster. "A nice old-fashioned evening," she said, as one delivering the imprimatur. "I value the Bergs and Brittens and Birtwistles, but this need not mean we must do without Puccini and Verdi, far less . . ." She flirted a hand to see off the unfinished sentence.

"Well, go on," Seddall said. "Far less what?"

"I was," said Mrs Heron, "going to add far less Mozart and Wagner, but when I find myself expatiating in measured periods I try to stop myself. It is the result of sitting at too many conference tables, and writing too many memoranda."

"Memoranda," he said, "I like it. No one's said memoranda since Bismarck."

"Oh, surely," she said. "I'm not that antiquated."

"I liked the word," he said. "I never suggested you were antiquated. Don't play games with me."

She smiled rapidly. He remembered that smile of hers. It came and went as fast as a whip looped and straightened. "Am I playing games with you?"

"What do you mean, are you playing games with me?" He leaned towards her. "I am delighted to see you again," he said, "but we've only met twice. You call me to say you've got a box for *La Bohème* and as soon as we've sat down you shove this letter from a Scotch lawyer into my hand saying that you and I are co-executors of this woman I've never heard of. That, Mrs Heron, is playing games. Damnation," he said, "if I'm going to be cross with you I can't call you Mrs Heron. What do your friends call you?"

"They call me Julia." She patted his knee. "I know I am going to be able to count on you," she said.

Seddall thought of telling her that this confidence was premature, but felt badly placed for argument. The stalls beneath them were filling and the orchestra was warming up. The piccolo trilled, brass brayed and whiffled, strings hung on a long note, and drums rolled.

"This woman," he said. "Who was she?"

"A friend," Julia Heron said.

"More," he said irritably. "The curtain will be up in a minute. I want something to chew on."

She looked down at her hands on her lap and her shoulders lifted and fell in what might have been a sigh. "Marion thought she might be killed, by which she meant murdered. She lived on the Isle of Islay, in Scotland, very remote. Her house was burned down last week, and she was found dead there."

The resentment that rose in him ran across to her and she turned to face him. The distinguished and still beautiful face of the woman not yet antiquated, and the rather round, not quite prepossessing face of the man fifteen years her junior, had hardly begun this confrontation when applause told them the conductor had made his entrance.

Seddall said: "Who did Marion think was going to kill her?"

Mrs Heron enunciated with great distinctness into the sudden silence of the darkening theatre, but such was her discretion that she did not sound the words. Seddall, nevertheless, had read them without trouble, and felt a chill on the back of his neck as if the axe was about to fall.

What she had said was: "MI5."

*

53

In the first interval, Mrs Heron said to him: "I have quite spoilt this for you, haven't I? I really am sorry. I meant to intrigue you with the letter and tell you the rest after."

Seddall glissaded past this with an easy absence of courtesy. "Whose box is this? Is it a Home Office box?"

"No," she said. "It belongs to a friend of mine. This is not Home Office business."

"How can it not . . ." he began, but there was a knock on the door and the sandwiches came in.

Seddall waved the attendant out again and opened the champagne. As he gave her the glass he said: "How can it not be Home Office business if it's" – and here he mimed the words as she had done, a heavy touch of sarcasm – "MI5?"

"We can't talk properly here," Mrs Heron said. "Where are you taking me to supper?"

"An Italian place round the corner," he said. "I don't know if I'll want to talk about it there either. We'll see when we get there. I don't get it, Julia, you're a Home Office person."

"Have a sandwich," she said. "I'm a private person too. Marion was my friend. She asked for my advice, in case anything should happen to her, because there was a man she wanted to warn who would be in the same danger as she."

"Dear God, Julia Heron," he said. "You're doing this on your own kick? You *are* doing this on your own kick! I feel the most appalling sense of doom. I wonder where they get their smoked salmon, it's good."

"We can find out easily enough," she said vaguely.

"You're not thinking straight," he said. "Time enough to find out after this business is over, because by the time it is over we may never need to know where our food's coming from again."

He remembered her, from the one conference table they had both sat at, as an intelligent but also rather abstracted woman. Abstracted or no, her focus on him was exact. She said: "I take it you give some credence to Marion's fears that you-know-who were a threat to her."

"No," he said. "I don't. I didn't know Marion. You can take it I believe you-know-who capable of anything, but killing friends of senior Home Office officials is more than I'd have included in that anything."

"Rubbish," she said. "You're hooked, aren't you?"

"I'm not landed yet, anyway," he said dourly. "What was Marion, that they should kill her? What did she know that they might have thought she shouldn't?"

"Until she retired two years ago, Marion was an academic. She taught European history at Edinburgh."

"Well," Seddall said. "It's true that a sense of history is not popular with our politicos, these days, but I wouldn't have thought things had gone that far."

Mrs Heron's grey eyes looked into his. "Try not to joke," she said. "The loss is recent, and I still feel it."

He bowed his head in acknowledgement, and faced her again. "Why was she afraid of them?"

"She would not say, in case it put me in danger too."

He felt the surprise on his face. "Even you," he said. "I'm not out to flatter you, but that would be reaching high."

"Tolerably high," she said, "and I think I've detected that you don't flatter people."

He grinned at her, and though there was a rueful quality in this which did not entirely lift the ironic twist from his mouth, she found it likeable. She knew him a little, and she had read him up, she understood that he did not excel himself to be liked. It was true there was a repelling aspect in his manner, but that was perhaps his own business, and certainly not relevant to the moment.

"I think," she said, "that it may go back to the war, when Marion was at the code-cracking centre at Bletchley Park; Enigma, and all that."

"The war?" he said. "Who cares now about the war? They don't even know there was a war."

"Some of them do," she said, and the house lights went down.

*

At the second interval, he said: "I'm not in the mood to see this out. Will you mind terribly if I meet you in the foyer afterwards?"

Mrs Heron said: "I'll come with you now."

On the stairs she said: "Unfair to you, and unfair to Puccini. I apologize to you both."

He stopped in the act of putting on his coat and stood against the wall. With the coat collar trapped in against his shoulders, as a result of the struggle to get it on, which had brought his scarf hanging to the knee on one side and hardly showing at the other, and had knocked his hat to the side of his head, he might have been an over-roistered man about town who had been trying his luck in the Quartier Latin, instead of merely watching it on stage.

A dowager on the arm of her escort in the foyer noticed him with a raised brow, inclined her profile and said, "Julia," to Mrs Heron as they went by.

"Listen," he said, knowing nothing of the picture he made but with the sense that some flicker of expression had lightened the gravity which beset Mrs Heron, "I don't want you to apologize for anything. I've been grumpy but I'm coming out of it. I'm just sorry that I've made you leave the bloody opera."

"Stand up properly," Julia Heron said to him, levelled off his scarf, gave him the hat to hold and tugged and fidgeted his coat collar into place. "There," she said, "now give your shoulders a heave. That's right, now you're more or less presentable."

"You must have been a good mother," Seddall said as they set off again.

"I was," she said, "and now I'm a good grandmother."

"Who was that woman? Have I disgraced your reputation?"

Outside they found the night air brisk and the sky clear. Seddall put on his hat, not too far off the straight.

"Lady MacSomething," Mrs Heron said. "Whoever she is, my reputation is hardly in her keeping. In any case, I'm quite pleased to be seen out with a raffish man."

"I'm not raffish, damn it. For that you can walk to your dinner."

She said: "I'd like to walk."

He thought this woman had everything going for her. He had noticed the shoes, and ascribed them to Charles Jourdain. Black and elegant enough for the grey silk dress, but with a heel low and fat enough for walking.

They had come along the north side of the Opera House down into Covent Garden, and as she looked up at the Tuscan portico of St Paul's Church she caught his glance on her.

"Yes," she said, "it's a pity," and tucked her hand inside his arm.

"What is?"

"That if our ages had been reversed, we could have made something of it."

"People do," he said, struggling for a frankness to match hers, but knowing he was not up to it.

"Only if they start younger," she said, "unless in exceptional cases, of which this is not one."

"Dear Jesus, Julia," he said. "I've never met anyone like you."

"You probably have," she said, "but you wouldn't recognize it until they were my age."

St Martin's Lane was busy and the restaurant full. They were taken right down the room where they sat side by side with their backs against the wall. He asked for dry sherry, asked in fact for a double helping, and she for a very dry martini, Gordon's gin, ten-to-one.

"Now listen," he said. "If we get into this business of your friend Marion and those whom at this table, at least, we shall simply refer to as They, you and I must not meet until it is over. If I do it then *I* shall do it, and you will keep well clear of it, and clear of me."

"If you do look into it, you may need me."

57

"If I do get into it," he said, "there will be no point in my dragging you in until I'm six lengths ahead going down the straight. And believe me, Julia Heron, when it comes to the chances of that happening, a darker horse never spoke before the off."

"I don't like this," she said.

He gulped down more than he meant to of his sherry, which had that instant arrived.

"You are ready to order?" the waiter asked.

"No," Seddall said. "Not now. Later, please. On second thoughts, I'll have another of these. Julia?"

She shook her head with one of those disappearing smiles at the waiter, and he went away.

"Of course you don't like it," he said. "Marion – Marion what was her name again?"

"Marion Oliphant."

"Right. She was your friend, and you got me into this, if I am in, and you know damn well that these people, They, are dangerous and that in any case some of them would love to see me go down the plughole. They're dangerous because too many of them are stupid, and you know that too, I mean they're run by the Home Office. You sit on committees that deal with these people. And the Home Secretary may not be fool enough to think the sun rises and sets on Them but they're by God his people, part of his empire on which he has to think the sun rises and sets, and they're full of power, and dangerous with it. So for my sake as well as yours, Julia, you'll have to steer clear. They're not all stupid; some of them are very sharp. They're very dangerous cookies indeed, and if I get into the same oven as them the chances of my coming out looking like a fresh . . . a fresh whatever instead of a small heap of cinders are slim indeed. I don't think that metaphor quite worked."

"No," Mrs Heron said, "but it was sufficiently expressive."

She thought he was expressive to watch, as well. Even by so mildly intimate a talk as theirs had been on the walk through Covent Garden he had been thrown off his stride; indeed he had behaved like a nervous horse caught in heavy traffic without blinkers.

Now he was transformed into a different man altogether, a man who knew he was committing himself to a bad battle, which would be fought on ground he would not have chosen and with the odds against him.

What he had just finished telling her with such vehemence was that the prospect of it put the fear of God into him, and she knew he meant it, but for all that he did not look like a man in fear. He looked full of energy, his eyes set on her one moment and then everywhere the next, as if hoping they would fall on some excuse for instant action. His head thrust out at her, and the chin as well, as if the musculature of the lower jaw had been designed to rip at his enemies. Perhaps it had: Mrs Heron knew little of the ways of neanderthal man.

"What would you like?" neanderthal man said.

"Parma ham," she said, "and melon." She took the card from the waiter. "And I think some veal, what is this, yes, *scaloppina arciduca*. Thank you."

"I'll have the same," Harry said. "What wine, Julia?"

"None, perhaps. None. Pellegrino."

Seddall waved a hand, and the waiter, a tall lank pale-faced black-haired thin-moustached fellow, was offended by this discourtesy. He went inside himself and stared at some length, thinking dark Calabrian thoughts behind black unspeaking eyes.

"I do beg your pardon," Harry said. "I am not quite myself."

The waiter stirred, the merest acknowledgement, and went away.

Seddall sat leaning on the table with his arms folded, rubbing his chin against the knuckle of his thumb: a man brooding.

"Are you worried," Mrs Heron said, "about being rude to the waiter?"

"What? No, no," Seddall said. "He's a human being. He'll understand."

"Then what is it?" she asked. "I feel a little *plantée la*, as they used to say."

He sat up. "I do apologize. It's true – I am *not* quite myself."

One hand touched her arm, but the fist of the other was clenched on the table cloth.

"I can see that," she said impatiently. "But what is it that's upsetting you?"

He looked down the restaurant and then back at her. "I feel watched," he said. "Is it possible you're being followed? Is your interest in Marion Oliphant known?"

The ham from the caves of Parma arrived. The assassin poured the water of San Pellegrino. Seddall looked at him and nodded, and won an inclination of the head in return.

"You're forgiven," Mrs Heron noticed.

"Of course," Harry said. "Italians have moods too. They understand other people having them. They especially like Englishmen having them, it makes us seem human."

"You think they don't find the English human?"

"*I* don't find the English human, for God's sake. Not many of them. Tell me about this Marion business," he said. "For a start, who knows you knew her? No one or everyone?"

"No, not everyone. It was an early friendship. We spent a few holidays together before I married, but time and distance matured it into a meeting for lunch when Marion was in London. All the same," she said, "I suppose an intelligence profile of Marion might show me on it."

"Oh, yes," Seddall said. "Oh, yes," and he spoke as if some light had gone out of the day. "Then we should not be here. We should not have met like this."

"I hardly think . . . ," Mrs Heron began, but he interrupted her.

"Julia," he said, "you rely too much on your high position, on your years in the Establishment. You think no one would dare lay a hand on you. Sure, you've got powerful friends, but believe me in this kind of business they're nothing. It's like being a member of the LTA and knowing you have a seat for the finals at Wimbledon, and finding when you get there that the place has been taken over by men with Kalashnikovs. There's no

60

point *then* in showing your credentials or waving your ticket. When that sort of thing happens, Julia, when *this* sort of thing happens, anarchy's in. We're in the shit already, and we haven't even started."

Mrs Heron was offended. "I don't like being told I'm a fool," she said, "and I don't like foul language." It was true. She thought she had moved well into modern life, but the semi-respectability of swearing which had come in had left her behind. She knew, all the same, that the remark was feeble.

It put Seddall in a rage. "Will you for God's sake come out of the bloody drawing room," he said. "Do you think the people who murdered your friend Marion are going around wringing their hands and saying: 'Oh, dear, we've murdered poor Marion Oliphant'? Damn it, Julia, guys like these take themselves to dinner at the Caprice on the strength of things like that, and they give themselves champagne to celebrate burning the bloody house down and wiping all the evidence into ashes along with Marion. Do you know what you've done, meeting me openly like this?" he said, as the tears came to her eyes at the force of this brutality.

"Do you realize that if I do this thing, and oh yes, I expect I am going to do it, because it is exactly the sort of thing I do, isn't it? *Do* you see what you've done? You've started me off in the middle of a bloody minefield. And can I ask you to please not offer me a bloody compass to help me out of it. Do you think you can manage that? Do you get the message at last, Julia? Do you get it?"

The best affirmative she could come up with was some jerky motions of the head, which, nevertheless, she turned to meet his eyes, despite the moisture which was still welling in her own.

"You're a thug," she said, "a cruel and beastly man."

"Yes, well," he said, and produced a large pristine handkerchief from an inside pocket and wiped her eyes with surprising delicacy of touch, and then gave it into her hand. "Here's a go," he said. "First of all you tuck me up all snug in my coat and

61

scarf, and now here I am drying your tears. What are we, playing at parents?"

"Playing at mummies and daddies," she said. "There are books about it. Start with Freud."

"Oh, I will," he said earnestly. "If I come out of this with a whole neck I'll start reading Freud first thing."

She gave her eyes what she hoped was a final ministration, and then regarded the linen in her hand. "Do you always carry a spare handkerchief for a woman? I find that rather touching."

"Damn you," he said.

They discovered that the waiter had come on them unawares and was all eyes and ears; it was clear that he viewed this table, of all the tables in all the restaurants in London's West End, as the best show in town.

When the veal and the salad and everything they could possibly desire were in front of them, Harry said. "Now, I propose that we avoid talking shop, if that's the word for it, until we've eaten this, and then I'll ask you to tell me about Marion."

"I shall welcome the respite," Mrs Heron said, and he looked at her suspiciously.

So they discussed pleasant nothings, such as which arciduca the scaloppina could possibly be named after – surely not the Austrian invader, said Harry; perhaps that Francis of Lorraine who succeeded the last of the Medici, suggested Julia – until they had finished eating.

Mrs Heron took her first sip of coffee, gazing down the room. "Have you actually seen anyone watching us?" she asked.

"No," he said. "From now until the blood has stopped running in the gutters, I shall simply assume that there are people who want to know what I'm doing every minute of the day. Now tell me about Marion."

She told him about Marion.

"You told me you had to collect a Bugatti," Harry said, and being surrounded by the babble of foreign tongues, he expanded his voice to something like a shout. "Where is it?"

"It's here," Sorrel said, and hoisted a bag onto the table. "It's for my godson. Do you want to see it?"

"A toy?" Harry said. "I am much chagrined. I thought I was going to drive off in style with the most desired woman in Soho."

"I'm not sure how to take that," Sorrel said, "but coming from you I suppose you're being evil."

"If the cap fits," Harry said, "wear it. Let's see this Bugatti."

Sorrel took a box out of the bag, and a blue racing car out of the box. Harry held the car with reverence and then ran it back and forward on the café table.

"God, I would like one of these," he said.

"I'll get you one tomorrow," Sorrel said, "if you're a good boy."

"I mean a real car, you twit, as for grown-ups," Harry said. He set the toy on his forearm and squinted at her across the bonnet.

"You do *look* like a schoolboy," Sorrel said.

"And you do look . . . ," he said, but lost his nerve. Anyway she did not look like anyone he would want to malign, even in his most rotten mood of mischief; and being with Sorrel made him feel good. Sorrel was a reassurance about some of the better things.

It was not just the way she looked, although her hair flourished in a golden tumble about her head and her eyes were the blue of the best skies; Sorrel was straight, tough, and independent in ways of her own that Harry knew nothing about, but they shared common ground where it counted, and where it counted was in the business that Seddall was in. Sorrel was the right stuff; she would do to ride the river with; all that sort of thing.

So he did not insult her. Instead, talking under that babble which made the Patisserie Valerie more secure than a bench in the middle of Hyde Park, he told her first about his meeting with General Kenyon, and then about his evening with Julia Heron.

63

The coffee and the mineral water came and were renewed, and came and were renewed again. The smoke from Harry's Gauloise hung in the air between them and sometimes Sorrel brushed it with her hand, and he said, "Sorry," and she shook her head, Don't bother about that, and always the strong blue eyes were close on him and what he was telling her.

When he had done, Sorrel said: "This is a heavy scene, this of Marion Oliphant. Do you believe she was done in by our friends at Five?"

"Of them I can believe anything," Harry said, "and I seem inclined to believe they killed her, even perhaps by mistake, and burned down the house to cover up. Or that they were using a freelance team who fouled it up for them. Whatever *it* is, or was."

Harry ran a loving finger over the blue body of the Bugatti, a caress that he might have made on the skin of a woman. Sorrel thought he had good fingers. She thought it was perhaps a good thing they'd never had an affair, or even more. If it had been more he would never have let her go on working with him. His view of women would have forbade it, since the work put her in danger. She had worked with him since she was, what, twenty-two? Yes, twenty-two, and five years on they had a friendship that had grown from the work they did together, and she liked the work, because it tested her, it gave her risk.

So, perhaps it was good that they'd never had an affair, or even something more. But she said again, to herself, and said it without thinking, aloud: "Perhaps."

"Perhaps what?" Harry asked her.

"I was having a private muse," Sorrel said. "Quite off the point."

"So was I," Harry said. "I was thinking what an innocent object it is, this toy Bugatti."

"Harry," she said. "You are absolutely not interested in innocence. What you mean is, that your life has got complicated all of a sudden, and not at all for the first time, do I have to point out? And you're trying to pretend to yourself that you don't like

64

it, and that you'd rather go home and put your feet up on the couch and have nothing to do but think about dinner. Which is a load of old codswallop. You *live* for it, having your life complicated like this."

"Not this time, I don't," he said. "This time I don't like it at all."

Sorrel said: "Then it's not Mrs Heron's tale that's eating you, is it? It's what Kenyon told you about this Lord Findo person."

He held down the flap of the cardboard box and steered the car into it as if it were a garage, and closed the box."

"So much for innocence," he said. "Innocence is not what we are in among, but there's no harm in remembering that it exists."

"Here and there," she said. "In spots."

"In sometimes surprising spots," he said. "Bits of it in surprising people. Yes," he said, "it's Findo first and foremost that's worrying me, and that and the Marion Oliphant saga coming together, at the same time, that worries me too. I'd like to be handling one or the other."

"Ah, well then," Sorrel said. "That's good. I'd hoped that's what you wanted. You want me to make some moves on the Marion Oliphant question."

"Discreet moves," he said. "Only the most tentative moves. I don't want you to engage the enemy, if there is an enemy. It's true that I'm thinking it may well be down to Five, but it may not be. Marion may have been paranoid, Julia may be, *I* may be, God knows I've cause. Perceive yourself as a reconnaissance patrol, no more. Your job is to get the feel of the ground, see if there is an enemy on it, and on no account to be noticed yourself. Let's take this one easy and slow. None of this rushing in headlong."

"Do I rush in headlong?" Sorrel said.

"People who buy Bugattis rush in headlong," Harry said.

"It's a toy," Sorrel said, "for my godson."

"It is well known that half the time when grown-ups buy toys for kids, they're into wish-fulfilment." He looked at her. "Hell," he said. "Sorrel, if you can't be good, be careful."

7

Calder stood outside his hotel in the Pink Zone of Mexico City and watched the ancient lorry come slowly down the street. On the back of it stood about thirty students, some of them holding up placards and strips of canvas with slogans on them. The slogans recommended liberty and an end to poverty, and education for all.

Those on the lorry and those coming behind them on foot, two or three hundred of them in an unkempt, unmarshalled, but homogeneous procession, shouted out the slogans. They did not seem to Calder to be enthusiasts or revolutionaries. Their bearing was resigned but resolute, as if they knew they must do what they were doing, but did not expect much result from it.

At the end of the street other lorries and a dozen or so police cars waited for the students to arrive, and there were police all over the place, seriously obstructing the progress of people going about their business, apparently indifferent to the imminent clash of social forces.

At a respectable and unmenacing distance from the police blockade the student lorry stopped, so that the tail of the procession was level with Calder. The students went on waving their banners and shouting their slogans. Pedestrians edged past between them and him, showing neither respect for their cause or irritation with the marchers, who were crowding up now round the lorry so that Calder had to move back against the wall or become one of them. Calder was not that kind of academic. He moved back against the wall.

The police, most of them extraordinarily small men, ran up in untidy separate groups, isolated the lorry from its supporters, and pulled and pushed the boys and girls with their banners down onto the road. The shouting diminished, less because of the waved pistols than because of the difficulty of shouting while being forced into involuntary physical movement. They were hustled along to the police blockade and climbed into the police lorries.

The marchers waited until the police had made a selection from them; rounding up the usual suspects, Calder thought, pace Claude Raines in *Casablanca*; and then variously stood about and drifted off.

As he slanted across the road to the restaurant the victorious police team was slamming the doors of its many vehicles and driving away, its klaxons wailing that two-note phrase which reminded Calder of a *mouvement perpetuel* by Poulenc.

Von Harma was waiting for him in the restaurant, the grey and etiolated figure in a grey suit. He had been watching the street and when he saw Calder raised a hand from the table, not very far, as much as a pianist might when about to play the Poulenc.

After the scene outside, von Harma occurred to Calder as a member of the occupying forces. Not expecting to say it, he said: "It takes you back, I dare say. The round-up in the street."

He was at once shaken by what he had said. Von Harma, on the other hand, was not. "Takes me back?" von Harma said. "Hardly at all."

Calder was sure the German had put no control on himself, in the face of this blatant aggression, this reminder of who he was, of who he had been: he was sure that von Harma was genuinely undisturbed.

"It must," Calder said, blundering wilfully on.

"It does not take me back," von Harma said, and his eyes were so many fathoms deep in himself that Calder thought he would need a decompression chamber to surface again. "Not back," von Harma said. "Time past is present in time future, is that what Eliot wrote? I am always what I have been. I am always where I have been. I do not need to be taken back. I am there. What will you drink? The local brew, a margarita?"

"Is that a pink gin?" Calder asked, looking at the glass in front of von Harma. "I'll have one too."

"What survivals we are," von Harma said. "Pink gin."

He lifted the hand again – no more than to caress a sound from the keyboard – and a waiter arrived as if he had skated there, a rapidity Calder had discovered to be rare in Mexico.

Von Harma dropped his eyes briefly to the glass. "Two of those," he said. "*Dos.*"

The drinks came in no time.

"You are still willing for this enterprise?" von Harma said.

"Yes," Calder said. "I'm at my wits' end. You are Heaven-sent."

"I doubt that, my dear Calder. Let us drink to our success. To your success."

They drank. A small girl, a child of about eight or nine, gave Calder a flower. "That's extremely kind," he said fatuously, and held it in his hand.

The child stood there and waited.

"She is selling it to you," von Harma said. "She is a beggar." He looked at his Patek watch.

Calder found some small notes and gave them to the girl. She went on her way.

"She did not offer to sell one to you," Calder said.

"No," von Harma said. "They never do."

On the summit of Popocateptl, which was covered with snow, the setting sun made miracles of changing colour as Calder, in the Boeing 747, drew level with it and passed it. Some of the passengers exclaimed spontaneously at the sight.

Calder, finding himself in danger of sympathizing with Wordsworth's childlike sense of a mystic presence in nature, quoted Nashe instead.

"Brightness falls from the air," he said.

"Ah! Metaphysics," von Harma said. "Do you know that there are two other mountains outside Mexico City? They are mountains of garbage, and on each of them lives a tribe, each with its own king. They make their living off these festering piles of human waste. The authorities leave them to themselves, and the two kings hold judgment over all, and exercise the death penalty, or whatever other penalties they please. There they are, those few hundreds of people, living like dung flies on human excrement. It is, in some ways of regarding it, a paradigm of the human condition. Could you write a metaphysical poem on that, do you think?"

"No," Calder said. "I could not. Thomas Mann might have written a novel on it, or Camus. They had the same rubbish dumps outside Paris until the fourteenth century, but no one wrote metaphysical poems on them that I'm aware of."

Von Harma gave a little diagonal nod of appreciation. "I don't recall that the Paris dumps were colonized in quite that way," he said, "but at least Philip the Fourth had them done away with. As to your novelists, Camus perhaps, but Mann would never have done it. Mann could only write about chaos as an opponent of civilization, not as a separate and self-fulfilling creature."

Calder had not thought it was this notion that made Thomas Mann objectionable to the Nazis, or they to him, but he had no wish to share von Harma's tolerance of time, and discuss the Nazi regime's view of the arts as if it were still relevant, or had been in operation only last week.

There was an empty seat between them, and von Harma inclined his head a little into that space. "You feel a revulsion," he said, "from me."

Calder met those eyes, as bleak and lifeless as the heart of a flintstone. "No," he said honestly. "I would have expected to, but I don't."

"That is because it is so great," von Harma said. "It is too hard for you to look at. You will acknowledge it sooner or later."

Calder knew he should have felt revulsion from being in von Harma's company, even more from being in his care. The German had made it plain that for whatever war crimes he had been sentenced, he himself knew they included atrocities that would have appalled Calder. All Calder could deal with now was the fact that he had been offered a protector against his pursuers, an escape line, and a route to the man Seddall named in Marion's letter.

An escape too, perhaps, from the police. He had seen nothing in the English language newspapers in Mexico to suggest that there was an international police hunt for Professor James Calder, wanted for the murder of two men found in the trunk of a car in New York State; but for all he knew about such things the police might make no announcement to the press, might say nothing until they caught up with him.

He had no way of knowing if they were looking for him. He had made a thorough job of cleaning up after him at the house. Unless the assassins' car had been noticed for the brief time it stood outside the house, unless he had been noticed driving away in it, then he might be in the clear, unconnected with the two bodies – if there were two, if the survivor had not been released from the trunk of the car: in which case the survivor would hardly name Calder to the police, or would he?

Assuming that the police were not looking for him, the assassins certainly were. He had travelled down and across America by bus and train: how long would they take to pick up his trail? He had used no credit cards, cashed no cheques. His only stop at Wade that last morning had been to take $7,000 from his bank, and everywhere he went he had paid cash. He knew they would find him though. He had a superstitious awe of what modern organizations could do in the way of finding people, and this was intensified in him by the fear that had grown in him as he made his way through the forest after depositing the car up on that lonely road, with one dead man and one living cramped together in its trunk. The fear that had come to him in the night, in the stillness of the trees, in the silence and sounds of the forest, the fear of vengeance, had settled into him.

He had been all fear until he met von Harma. If this was a Faustian bargain he had made with von Harma, he did not feel it yet; he did not feel he had sold his soul to the Devil. If he had, his instincts and his mind were refusing to look at it just now.

What he was saying to himself just now was nothing more nor less banal than: "Any port in a storm."

He came awake later, not knowing how long he had slept. It might have been for minutes or hours. The plane had reached its impious height, was in the blue of the empyrean above the endless plain of white cloud. He felt von Harma's eyes on him and turned to meet the passionless and impervious gaze.

"You were thinking," von Harma said, "before you fell asleep."

"No doubt," Calder said.

"Quite so. I was thinking too. I wondered how you had thought to reach Europe from Mexico."

"I had thought," Calder said, "to see if I could find passage on a cargo boat with passenger berths, if there were any left. That was as far as my thinking had gone. Failing that, there was a vague notion of trying to bribe my way, as a private deal. Probably absurd. I had even thought there might be an ocean-going yacht making its way back to the Mediterranean, even to England, something like that."

"Why not?" von Harma said. "These yachts cross back and forth to the Caribbean. It would not be so absurd."

"Why are you doing this?" Calder said abruptly. "Why are you doing this for me?"

"For what advantage to myself?" von Harma said. "*Cui bono?*"

"Perhaps," Calder said.

"You have considered that it might be an attempt at reparation," von Harma said. "How can it be that? If I had sought to make my life a penance, to seek to make reparation by doing good to humanity, I should not have waited until now."

The plane lurched gently on some whim of the atmosphere outside, as if to assure them it was alert to its place in the scheme of things, that it knew it had no divine right to be up here; any more than its occupants had.

"I think," von Harma said, "I am doing it partly because I can, and partly because I had a curiosity about you. The curiosity was because you killed one man and stuffed the other, still alive, in beside him, and this was lying on your conscience. Yet both of these men had come to kill you. I do not presume, I do not presume to suggest even to myself, that I made any sort of identification with this conscience of yours. It was part of the first impulse I felt towards you, when I saw that you were incapacitated by depression in that hotel, though I did not know then the cause of that depression. The other cause, one of the other causes, I should say, since depression is not so simply explained, after all, was the fear in you. It may be that this drew me to your predicament more than anything."

Von Harma ran the tip of a forefinger along the crease of his grey silk trouser leg. "That would be corrupt, of course, the impulse towards fear, it would be an echo of earlier life, for me. Certainly I feel no wish to alleviate your fear, not consciously, not from any virtuous or humane motive. Perhaps I simply want to observe what happens to you if the fear is alleviated, though that is not a desire of which I am conscious either, I speak of motivations within, to which my mind, so to speak, is not party."

"I don't," Calder said, "want to hear more of this."

"How could you?" von Harma said. "I don't want to hear more of it myself, if it comes to that. I am doing it partly because I can do it, as I have said. I have reached that position of prosperity where my wealth is unfailing. There is hardly anything I can do that would cause it to stop increasing, far less disappear. My financial – and industrial – interests are not publicised, little known. I am a very private figure. They are more than considerable, these interests, they are more than merely extensive. Anything your opponents can do, I can do, and probably more. I can

72

produce ten gunmen to their one, for example. My sources of information are as good as theirs. We of the multinational world, you must be aware, have powers greater than those of nations."

Calder sought for a moral standpoint, and knew what banalities he could utter if he found it. He uttered none of them, but said what was foremost in him to say: "And these powers are on my side," he said.

"Yes," von Harma said. "They make better odds than you started out with."

In any other man the words would have a jovial ring to them. From von Harma they came inflexionless, as if they had come from a statue.

"They're certainly that," Calder said.

The two men became silent. The plane went on its smooth way, with one of those gentle lurches now and then.

For Calder, however, the flight was not so smooth as it had been. He settled as well as he could into the cradle of security that von Harma had provided for him, but far within him, though he felt it no more than the plane felt those slight shudders as it passed across the sky, a turbulence had begun to move.

Their arrival at Schipol Airport was the first real test of von Harma's 'resources', as that conspirator had referred to them. It was one thing to leave a country on a false passport, but another to seek entry.

The Canadian passport in the name of Edward Gage was scrutinized and snapped shut in the same way as all the others in the line, and Calder and von Harma were met, as soon as they were clear of the emerging crowd, by a man dressed as a chauffeur.

"Take us to the car, Peter," von Harma said, "and then you can come back for our luggage. Professor Calder will describe his to you."

8

Mendham decided to have sugar with his coffee this morning; and ginger snaps; and after that a cigarette with a bit of taste to it instead of the low tar efforts he smoked all the time. For Mendham decisions like these, on a morning when he was feeling lousy, were a form of conscious therapy, looking after himself, giving himself a treat.

There was a knock on the door. Mendham gave himself two spoonfuls – or was it spoonsful? He thought he would use spoonfuls when talking to himself, and spoonsful when talking to Americans – of sugar. "Come in," he said.

The Weasel came in. Mendham didn't think the sugar and the ginger snaps and the Marlborough were going to do it for him. He disliked the Weasel. It was just that the little twerp was an absolute ace at hacking into other people's computers.

The Weasel was a sharp-faced five foot six with a doubtless furry tongue that spoke, however, six languages, dark red-brown hair and eyes of the same colour and the most lack of interest in other people Mendham had ever seen in anybody. He was wearing a pink cashmere V-neck sweater with no shirt beneath it, and the words LOVE ME – I DO embroidered on it in scarlet (presumably by some infatuated lover of God knew what sex, probably a new one invented in the laboratories) and jeans torn off at mid-calf to let you see he had no socks on his feet, only those scruffy jogging shoes the state of whose interior Mendham shuddered to contemplate. He had sharp little pointed teeth. Mendham imagined him using them to get that good shreddy trim to the end of his jeans.

"What do you want?" he said, in a bitter voice.

"Hi!" the Weasel said, exactly as he would have said it if he had come into the room and found that Mendham had fallen off a ladder and broken many bones. "This Professor James Calder, I've found him."

Mendham, who was dipping a ginger snap in his coffee, held it there too long, so that when he lifted it half remained in the cup. Great day in the morning!

"Jane!" he yelled.

Jane Winder came in, astoundingly elegant in a pink silk brocaded suit.

"What's up?" she said to Mendham, and to the Weasel: "Good morning, foxy."

"Hey!" the Weasel said, pleased, and "Great threads," he noticed. "We match."

"Whose office is this?" Mendham demanded. "Jane, darling, look what I've done to my coffee. Can I please have another cup?"

"Poor lamb," Jane Winder said. "Of course you can."

"You've found Calder?" Mendham said to the Weasel. "How did you do that?"

The Weasel made the irritated face of the adolescent who finds trying to communicate across the generation gap a terrible pain.

"Howdya think I did it?" he said. "I programmed the computer with your profile of this Calder and told it to find a match."

"Just like that," Mendham said.

Jane came back with a fresh coffee cup for him.

"Sure, just like that," the Weasel said. "Lookit me and Jane," he said, and plucked at his pink sweater so that for a dismal moment Mendham saw his (certainly unclean) navel. "Pink, right? Same as Jane's suit. We match, right? I want the computer to look for Jane, I don't just put pink in the programme or the computer's gonna find me as well as Jane. Crazy." How the Weasel cackled at this simple jest. "So I put in that Jane's a

75

woman," he said, "and that she's this high and has those big bedroom eyes and those kiss-me lips and has those great tits . . ."

"Zwimmer!" Mendham said, for such was the Weasel's name. "Shut up! You're not telling me anything except that you've got a dirty mind. I know what a comparison is, you twit."

The Weasel was affronted. "I *like* Jane," he said.

"Thank you," Jane Winder said, leaving the room again. "I think those were very sweet things you said."

"See," the Weasel said.

"Yes, yes," Mendham said. "What I need to know is, where did Calder show up and how sure are you that this is Calder you've found, or the computer has found?"

This time he did not dip his ginger snap in the coffee, but cracked it on his elbow for luck. It broke into three pieces, which made him feel better.

"Okay," the Weasel said. "Come over here," and he went over to the hi-tech complex and switched things on. Two screens came to life, and the Weasel played tunes on two keyboards.

"There," he said. "Read those."

Mendham had eaten only two pieces of the ginger snap. He swallowed some coffee, said: "Damn!" He'd forgotten to put sugar in. He lit a Marlborough and went over to join the Weasel, and looked at one of the screens. He read his own description, or rather his own wording of the description of Calder.

Professor James Calder. Age 67. Height 6 feet. Weight approx 180 pounds. Face long; no facial hair; ruddy complexion. Eyes brown. Eyebrows brown, bushy. Hair mostly grey, traces of brown still; hair also bushy. Note well: distinguishing mark, scar of deep incision, vertical, three-quarters of an inch, descending from hairline, on back of neck just to right of centre line.

Other habits and characteristics: has habit of plucking at eyebrow when tense or pensive; has a stoop of the shoulders, no doubt from years of study at desk, so that his head is always held forward and tilted up, giving an aggressive impression; is a fast and energetic walker.

Mendham moved to the other screen and began to read it.

Following copied from U.S. Embassy Mexico City consular section message to Attorney-General's Department, Washington.

Message is sent with reference to possible prosecution of Ukrainian war criminals resident in U.S. and with reference to movements of possible witness Geyr von Harma.

Message:

Geyr von Harma left Mexico City Airport KLM Flight KL259 ticketed to Schipol, Holland, 08:30 hours this date.

He was in company of Edward Gage, Canadian passport, description: Elderly, say 65; grey hair; brown eyes; 6 ft; 175–185lbs; stoops forward at shoulders; vertical scar 2–3 cms back right portion neck.

"Dear God!" Mendham said. "That's him. That's Calder all right. What's the date of this?"

"This message," the Weasel said, "is dated tooodaaay!"

"You mean they're in the air now?" Mendham said.

"Where they are," the Weasel said. "Up there. On their way to Europe right this minute."

"Weasel," Mendham said, "I mean, Zwimmer, you're a genius."

"What's with this Weasel?" the Weasel said.

"Slip of the tongue," Mendham said. "Forget it."

"No," the Weasel said. "Wait just a minute. You call me Weasel? Is that what you call me?"

Mendham went behind his desk and put sugar in his cup and topped it up from the coffee pot. "It's a private joke," he said. "Nothing to get excited about."

"Listen," the Weasel said. "'Weasel'? I like it. It's cool."

"That message," Mendham said, "who copied it? Where did you lift it from?"

"Would you believe the Mossad?" the Weasel said, and danced a little.

"No, I would not," Mendham said. "Indeed, I'd rather not."

"Believe it," the Weasel said.

"Can they tell we've been into their computer?" Mendham said. He lit another Marlborough. He took in smoke too fast and coughed. He felt slightly nervous. The Mossad scared Mendham. They had those dreadfully logical minds. If they wanted to stop people hacking into their secrets, they'd do something very thorough about stopping them.

"*We* have not been into their computer," the Weasel said. "It was me got into it, and if you think I left my signature in there, man!" He shook his head, and picked at the straggly hairs showing in the V of his sweater. Hunting fleas, doubtless, Mendham thought.

"You really have done awfully well," Mendham said, "Weasel," he tried.

"'Weasel'," the Weasel said. "I like it."

"The Weasel, actually," Mendham said.

"I get the special?" the Weasel said.

"You get the special bonus, all right," Mendham said. "Now scoot."

"Pop goes the Weasel!" the Weasel said. "Hey!"

He leapt in the air, a mini flashdance, and went out of the room to his own, very distant, drum.

Mendham flicked a switch. "Jane," he said. "The Weasel's found our Professor James Calder. He took a KLM flight out of Mexico City ticketed for Schipol Airport in Holland. Can you find out where it touches down and when it gets to Schipol? And get a fix on Carmichael, will you? We must talk to him quite urgently, don't you think?"

9

Seddall's progress through the chateau continued down stairways so composed of elegance and poise as hardly to be made of any fabric at all, taking him through luxurious salons whose walls were paintings by Masters of the eighteenth century, and on whose variously polished and Aubussoned floors rested Louis Seize chairs and sofas on some of which that unhappy monarch had undoubtedly rested his ill-fated bones, and buhl cabinets at which his Marie Antoinette had reckoned up her losses at cards.

From their ceilings hung proliferous facetings of chandeliers which, had they at a later time in the development of France fallen on the head of Bonaparte, would have prevented Tolstoy from writing *War and Peace*, and deprived Talleyrand of the occasion for some insulting epigrams. From their windows flowed terraces and gardens and cascades to which (even later) the Empress Eugenie had added the lustre of her beauty until she too was whisked away by history, whereupon France entered finally upon the era of the republics, and a chateau such as this became the domaine of bureaucrats and politicians.

Seddall's reflections on these evocative and Arcadian chambers soon lost their fluency under the hard eyes of the sentinels who lined his route. His passage was defined for him by continuous loops of red rope hung from brass posts. Behind the rope on either side the paratroopers stood at intervals, and behind them in the recesses of the rooms less disciplined men in suits variously sat, stood, moved about, conversed in quiet voices, and watched Seddall carefully when he passed by, as if he might go mad at any moment and require to be shot.

He came at length to the hall at the side entrance in the south wing of the chateau; a mere vestibule of thirty feet by sixty. The last arrivals were working their way through the check-in by the door opposite him.

"What efficient watchdogs our Gallic friends make," a voice said in his ear. "I had the gravest doubts as to whether I should be allowed in."

"Hallo, Arkley," Harry said.

"What are you grinning at?" Arkley demanded, coming round Seddall's shoulder into full view.

"Doubtless at the picture of them trying to turn you away," Harry said. "You're the doyen of the British contingent, after all."

"Doyen," said Arkley, rubbing a forefinger across the bristles of his black and white moustache and staring down at Seddall. "I don't think I like that word, it sounds elderly."

"Who could possibly be thought elderly in that suit, Arkley?"

The suit, of lightweight tweed in a small black and white check, and which might have been devised to match the pied hair and moustache of its proprietor, stood in a sartorial no-man's-land between a flash bookie's selection for Cheltenham and a stage designer's idea for the lead in a Feydeau farce.

Arkley fixed his face at Seddall.

"It does not do," he said, "to appear too English to the French, when we are trying to conciliate them."

"Is that what we're doing?"

A gleam of secret knowledge showed in Arkley's eye, and was gone. "You have not been briefed?" he asked.

"No," Harry said, "I have not." Nor had he. He had been sent here, on the face of it as Kenyon's deputy, but in fact to be out of Lord Findo's way.

Arkley either reviewed this information (if it was new to him) or appeared to do so, if it was not. "You must surely deprecate that," he said. "It is a surprise to you, it must be a surprise to you, to be sent here without being briefed. It is not how you are used to being treated." Arkley, acting, could be a character in Trollope, Dumas, or anyone that came into his head, and he was acting now, Harry decided, acting sympathetic disquietude.

"It seems," this actor said, "that you and I have a little agenda set out for us. Come and have a drink."

So Harry Seddall, in a suit that had known him for ten years, so that they were on good enough terms with each other to feel perfectly at home together wherever they went, accompanied Sir John Arkley, Director General of the Secret Intelligence Service, in his brand new puppy-tooth check and his head streaked like a magpie's plumage, down the hall towards the interior of the chateau.

Arkley put an arm round Seddall's back and held him lightly by the far shoulder, which allowed him to stoop slightly in a show of courtesy, and at the same time to celebrate his own advantage in height. "I am so glad we are able to do this," he said, with such a wanton intrusion of sincerity in his voice that Seddall became at once uneasy.

They approached a cordon of the plainclothes security men, and Arkley lifted the arm from Seddall's shoulder and held it out in a protective curve, a gesture which would have served equally well if Arkley had been escorting an arch-criminal to the gallows, or the heir of a royal house to his throne. This performance expressed a good deal about Arkley. It was political, since the security men were not in the way, and all Arkley was doing was to assume control of nothing in particular simply to keep himself in training; and it was a piece of play-acting, undertaken on the spur of the moment because Arkley found the idea of it amusing.

It had also the effect of adding to Seddall's uneasiness, but you could ask yourself whether this had been part of Arkley's intention until the cows came home. If it had been, it was finely judged, for even as Seddall decided it might be rather a bad idea to have this drink with Arkley, he found himself entering a room that had been made over into an outsized cocktail bar.

There were about twenty people there, but Arkley, as if he

had sighted someone he had arranged to meet, said, "Ah, here we are," and made off across the room. Seddall, seeing who he was aiming for, had his darkest expectations fulfilled; but he also saw Nick Churchyard, over by the windows, talking to a black man.

"With you in a moment, Arkley," he said.

He watched Arkley, with that delicate lope of his, as of a wolf testing the ice at every step, cross the room to sit himself by Considine: the head of MI6 going to meet the head of MI5; intelligence consorting with security. Does the wolf lie down with the fox? Seddall asked, and wondered.

"If that's whisky," Seddall said taking Churchyard's glass from him, "my need is greater than yours." He drank it off. "Thanks Nick. Do you want to get us some more?"

"My boss," Churchyard explained to his companion. "Colonel Seddall; Mr Doffene. Mr Doffene is with the Pentagon." Churchyard went away, taking Doffene's glass with him as well.

"Excuse this, Mr Doffene," Harry said as they shook hands. "I'm in the middle of being inveigled into meeting a character I'd normally cross the street to avoid."

"Charlie Doffene," the man from the Pentagon said, "and you're Harry Seddall, but I had been told you played them close to the vest." He nodded across the room. "I take it Arkley's the inveigler, since he brought you in, and Considine's the undesirable character"

Harry thought this was too quick on the uptake to be true. "I'm delighted to meet you," he said, "Charlie," he added, deferring to the American enthusiasm for first names. "But how did you get in here? This is an Anglo-French conference."

Doffene's face was strong, impassive and handsome. He let humour come up in it and go to sleep again. "I worked it, somehow. I'm francophone, a second-generation American of a Senegal family. The French do *relate* to francophones, you know," he said earnestly.

Harry could see that Doffene had some private comedy going here but he was too preoccupied to try and fathom it.

"Oh, absolutely," he said.

At this very English response Doffene was amused again. "I'm a bridge across a number of cultures. I'm here as an observer. I eat the food and I drink the wine, and I say nothing."

Doffene looked out of the window. He watched two of the light armoured vehicles of the in-lying patrol skim past each other, one going south and the other north. "The security here's a little crazy," he said, and turned back to Seddall. "The fact is, I hear you have a problem with Five."

"Well, by God!" Harry said. "What kind of poker is this, where all the cards are showing – except to me?"

"That's not your question, is it?" Doffene said. "Your question is, what's in the pot?"

The two studied each other as if they were two gamblers at the poles of that isolating axis that runs between the last men still in the game, when the stakes are at the night's high. From Doffene's tall, smooth-skinned face, its dark and careful eyes, Seddall had no sense of hostility.

He was, nevertheless, baffled by this meeting, which it was as possible Doffene had engineered as it was certain Arkley had engineered his impending meeting with Considine. Doffene's awareness of what he had called Seddall's 'problem with Five' had been dropped in with proper negligence, but it was impossible to believe that it was disinterested. Harry felt beset by meetings with interested parties, and it was not the time or place to seek enlightenment about this one.

"I like the tie," he said. Doffene's tie had small weathercocks on it.

"The Weathervane Golf Club, New Jersey," Doffene said, "but it's not a club of mine. I thought it was kind of pretty."

Churchyard came back. "Arkley caught my eye," he said, "took me a few minutes to get away. He inquires for you," he said to Harry.

"We should have dinner in London, perhaps," Harry said to Doffene.

"Yes, we should have dinner," Doffene said, in deliberate imitation of the phrase, "but perhaps *not* in London."

"My word," Harry said, "this is all very mysterious." To Churchyard he said: "Rescue me in five minutes," and to Doffene, by way of apology: "I'll need him."

"I think you just might," Doffene said, and took the glass Churchyard had brought him.

There were more people in the room now, but the level of sound had hardly risen since Seddall entered it. He supposed that when the Intelligence fraternity met together in these numbers – something between fifty and a hundred – it was a comment on their professional habit that they spoke in quiet voices.

There were few women, and from this and the low decibel count it occurred to him that it was as if he were moving through a convocation of clerics, enjoying what the British element would doubtless describe as their pre-prandial sherry. As he began to work his way through them, casting Arkley as a cardinal, and providing grudgingly a bishopric for the imminent Considine, he tripped over some object on the floor and was projected into a group of three, one of whom, a man of – under the recent dispensation – archidiaconal distinction, prevented his fall.

Seddall apologized and thanked the man.

"*De rien, monsieur,*" said this archdeacon, or archspy, "I am a specialist in crisis intervention. Besides, it is the fault of Barnavon and his absurd attaché case."

It was indeed an attaché case that had precipitated the incident, and its owner said he was desolated by what it had done, but pointed out that half of those in the room had so punctiliously interpreted the instructions received at the security check-in point, where the attaché cases had been given to each arrival, as to carry them about with them like so many diligent retrievers.

It was true. Near or between every other pair of feet, beside every other chair, stood one of the cases.

"It is ridiculous, all these attaché cases," the archdeacon said.

"Typical security overkill."

"*Absolument pas*," Barnavon replied with all the spirit of a small tubby young man defending his own service against criticism from the tall and elegant senior of another. "For this conference we have created a comprehensive security concept, of which the attaché cases are but a part."

"A concept," said the archdeacon, rejoicing ironically in this word, "is this the advertising world? Surely not."

"A concept that was approved at Highest Level three months ago," Barnavon repeated, ignoring the jibe. "Each attaché case is computer-linked, so that its whereabouts, and also whether it is being opened outside the conference hall contrary to the instructions, can be known at all times.

"Precisely," the third man intervened, "then why carry them about?"

Barnavon shrugged. "It is not essential. As you know the cases contain the conference agenda, and the first session is immediately after lunch. For my part I have mine with me simply for my own convenience."

"And it is part of the concept that each case with its contents will be returned and incinerated after the conference?" the archdeacon asked.

"Yes," Barnavon said. "You see a flaw in this?"

"I don't know," the archdeacon said. "I don't suppose I do. If anything it seems to me to be overdoing it, but I see no actual flaw."

Barnavon allowed himself to be a little supercilious to the older generation. "Our approach to security increases in sophistication at a remarkable pace," he said.

The archdeacon gracefully quit the field without giving any sense that he was failing to ride the *nouvelle vague*. "These things have always been a trifle arcane to me," he said.

Into the silence that followed this conclusion to their debate, Seddall said, without yet knowing why: "*Vous m'avez dit que c'est voici trois mois que ce concept pour la securité du conference est approuvé?*"

85

"*Mais oui, trois mois*," Barnavon said politely, but with some perceptible restraint at this further questioning. "*Pourquois, monsieur?*"

"It is impressive," Seddall said, "this thoroughness of your preparations," but as he left them he could see that Barnavon was not quite persuaded of the force of this compliment, and that the archdeacon was chewing his lip in thought.

10

Seddall worked his way among the humans and the attaché cases and came to where Considine and Arkley sat. He knew they disliked each other. He knew too that Arkley had a way of expressing this by regarding, or affecting to regard, Considine's people as vulgar, and would pass this idea across the space between the two men by no more perceptible process than simply holding it in his mind.

"Seddall," Arkley said now, "at last you have been able to join us. I see you have been meeting our new friend from America."

"Hallo, Considine," Harry said, and sank into a comfortable chair which let him stretch his legs out, as if about to fall asleep for the afternoon. "Doffene new, is he, Arkley?"

Considine nodded, no more, though there was something more than silence on his face. It was a face with a kind of simple-minded sculpture to it which suggested he was a clean-living man, though without offering any further proof. It was remarkably inexpressive, of whatever lived within it. The nose and mouth of this lifeless image were edged, the cheeks flat planes, the chin strong but dimpled, the ears large, and the head a mild yellow of wishful curls cut and lotioned into control.

"Doffene?" Arkley said, having fired a few glances back and forth between Seddall and Considine as if earnest to assure himself that they would enjoy one another's company. "Doffene floated into London from Washington on Tuesday. He is with what the United States Army is pleased to call its Intelligence Division. For how long he is to be in London, I do not know.

Considine is your man for that, surely? Considine deals with the home patch."

Considine's blank eyes looked at Seddall; it was like being regarded by a dugong. "Doffene has based himself in the military attaché's office in Grosvenor Square, but he is not accredited, not on Embassy staff even as temporary, though the Embassy has booked him into one of its flats near the Saville Club."

"Thank you, Considine," Harry said.

Considine began a nod in acknowledgement, but did not complete it, so that his eyes stayed down, sharing as it were a soothing absence of interchange with the carpet.

This led to a spell of silence, which though it suited two of them did not suit Arkley. "I must say," he said, "I should have thought you two had some pressing matters to discuss."

"You were going to fill me in on the real purpose of this conference, Arkley," Harry said.

"Oh, so I was!" said Arkley, hamming away like anything, the good host trying to keep the party going. "As you know, on the face of it this is a meeting to explore and share the wisdoms of our two countries on ways to combat terrorism, but the truth of it is . . . But tell me, Considine, is it safe to be frank? Your people have cooperated with the French, as I understand it, to provide the security arrangements for us all. But you will know: are the rooms bugged, is my chair listening to me even now, is that lampshade recording what I say?"

"Of course the rooms are not bugged, Arkley," Considine said. "What would be the point of that? This is not a meeting with the Soviets. We meet as allies."

"I don't know that we do," Arkley said, "not since France came out of full NATO membership, but I am always willing to be guided on security matters. If I am being lip-read I shall speak behind my handkerchief."

"You know, sometimes you remind me of the Knight Whose Armour Didn't Squeak," Harry said to him.

Sir John Arkley, who had no objection to being called to

order, and who was always pleased to be reminded of his knighthood, was delighted. "You are telling me I am overplaying the buffoon, Seddall. No doubt, no doubt. Very well. The truth of it is that we proposed this conference to the French because we have been giving them so much stick about the deals they do tend to strike with terrorists, that we – by we I mean Government, which is to say the politicians and their Permanent Secretaries – thought it would be statesmanlike to conciliate, *pour assoser l'entante*. The French are not inconsiderable politicians themselves, and unlike us they regard statesmanship not as an ideal attribute but a professional quality, which as a result they practise quite successfully at a useful level instead of aspiring to it on occasion as if it were an Olympic prize."

Here he stopped, though whether he had outrun his syntax, or his breath, or his thought, it was impossible to say.

Even Considine looked up, and Harry said: "I feel left in the middle of something, Arkley. Do you think you could round it off?"

"Preferably before luncheon," Considine said, and returned to his friendship with the carpet.

"No, no," Arkley said. "I've finished."

Seddall threw down a gauntlet. "You a friend of Findo's, Considine?" he asked.

The dugong looked up as if from his own sea-bound world, and said nothing.

"Of course he is," Arkley said. Arkley was tickled pink at Seddall's going for a confrontation, and showed it by giving off emanations of hyperactivity and falling into the argot of the Edwardians. "Considine and Findo are thick as thieves," he said. "Ain't you, Considine?"

Considine gazed at the carpet, or the ocean floor, or perhaps into his own mind. It was impossible to guess what was going on in him.

Arkley writhed his upper lip, flourishing his moustache; gleamed his eyes at Seddall before fixing them on the crown of Considine's bent head, and went at it again.

"What would you say, Seddall, to luncheons in a private room of the Compleat Angler at Marlow? To tête-a-têtes," Arkley said, "over supper in a rather unsavoury private club? They've been so terribly thick, lately, Findo and MI5, you might be forgiven for thinking they were having an affair."

Harry began to feel good. Arkley had always had it in for Considine, but it now seemed he had it in for Findo as well, and this might mean he would be an ally: an untrustworthy ally, but still an ally.

All the same, he wondered what Arkley thought he was doing, proclaiming his outright hostility to the Findo-Considine axis, if this axis in fact existed. Harry thought it probably did exist, and he thought it would be a tough combination to beat.

He perused Arkley, who sat forward with his hands on his knees, bright and brisk in his rotten new suit and a shining example to the wicked and wily. He thought Arkley was in his element, and probably knew what he was doing.

He could leave this stuff to Arkley, and meanwhile he had a question sitting in his mind.

"Considine," Seddall said, "the security here – your people have no part in it?"

"As a matter of fact," Considine said, as his head came slowly up, "it was part of the protocol that all the security would be handled by the French: *amour propre*, you know. We have taken no part."

"What do you think of these identical, numbered, computer-linked attaché cases?" Seddall asked him. He felt slightly foolish, asking this, because something about these attaché cases was eating him, and he did not know what it was.

"That's interesting." Considine's voice actually did sound as if he was interested, and there were faint signals of approval in the way he regarded Seddall, like some king in a fairytale who has been dying of ennui and comes across a man who might know how to amuse him.

It came to Seddall with some surprise that Considine's heart, or whatever he used for a heart, was in his job. It had not occurred to him that the man who ran his country's security service might find the security provision for a two-day conference worth his attention. For an absurd moment the notion flickered in his mind that this might be a redeeming aspect of Considine's character – flickered and was gone, for he had known the man too long.

Considine had reached an opinion. "These attaché cases of yours? I think they belong in the higher reaches of corporate finance where corporate heads have deals on hand and become paranoid."

Now he actually offered to Seddall an amiable smile. "You know, Seddall," he said, "the fact is that when you believe you have built in hi-tech apparatus to cover every chink that you can conceive of in your security armour, then you have surrendered yourself to the illusion that your security cannot be circumvented."

Considine gave a small crowing laugh. "After all," he said, "a man in armour can be cooked to death in boiling oil."

The laugh came again. It sounded dreadfully to Seddall as if Considine had seen this done; and it seemed to him that the arrival of so macabre a thought had shouldered away another thought he would have valued more.

Arkley had been up-staged, and was discontented, and let a sour note fall. "You will hardly, Considine, be relying on the French to protect the Minister," he said.

"Hardly," Considine said, and gave Arkley, and Seddall too, a shadow of his recent smiles before resuming the contemplation of what lay below him.

Another question, unexplained, occurred to Seddall.

"When does the Minister get here?" he asked Arkley.

"He addresses us after luncheon," Arkley said. The good humour he had been enjoying returned to him, and he allowed himself to be ridiculous. "Be there or be square," he said.

"For Christ's sake, Arkley," Harry said. "What are you, a child of the Sixties?"

Considine surprised them all. "Arkley was middle-aged in the Sixties, but you can just bet he was a child of them any time he felt like it. A regular chameleon, our Arkley." He rose to his feet. "There's a move towards the dining room, I do believe," he said, and left them.

"Beautiful manners, that Considine," Arkley said. "Coming, Seddall? I find I'm rather hungry."

"You carry on," Harry said. "I'll follow you."

He was hungry too, but not for food. He was hungry for the elusive thought that three minutes ago had been about to settle on the tip of his mind, when Considine's ghoulish laugh nudged it off the edge into the *ewigkeit*.

He sat there while the bar emptied, a rumpled, cross, inverted, inexplicably alarmed, scowling human object, trying against all the odds to let his mind be open and peaceful, so that the lost butterfly of a thought might flutter back to him of its own whim.

11

"I'm a Jewish princess," the girl with the long black hair said.

"What does that mean?" Nick Churchyard asked her.

"You don't know?" the girl with the long black hair that curled excellently around her shoulders said.

"No, I don't know," Churchyard said.

"It means I've been terribly spoiled by my Jewish Daddy," said the girl with long black hair that curled excellently round her shoulders, and enfolded her beautiful face when she bent down over the asparagus soup.

The phrase 'Jewish princess' was new to Churchyard, but he had seen movies and heard songs, and he knew that in most songs for a girl to say her heart belonged to Daddy did not mean it belonged to her papa, except in some of the senses of psychological role confusion. So he wondered.

"My name's Nick Churchyard," he said. "How do you do?"

"My name's Jennifer," the girl with the long black hair, kissable lips, but sophisticated eyes, said.

"Tell me, Jennifer," he said. "How do you keep your hair out of the soup?"

The sophisticated eyes gave him a long look, and towards the end of it he thought he saw some melt in there, of one kind or another. "Well, Nick, what I do," she said, "is lean over it until I feel comfortable and bring it to my lips and put it in my mouth, and I almost never get hair in it."

It was the way she said it that did it to him. He knew he was blushing, but he came from a good regiment and stood fire while he received more look, and was positive he saw some more of that melt in there.

"You're blushing," she said. "That's nice." It was nice. She thought he was the most man she had met since, well, maybe ever, and the blush was part of it.

"You're not blushing," he said. "I rather think that's nice too."

Churchyard was an honest man though, and felt he had moved too far out of his own character. "All the same," he said, "it's not as if we were halfway through dinner for two, we're only halfway through the soup, for God's sake, and we're at a public luncheon."

"There are rules?" she said, and tilted her head a little down and sideways so that she looked at him on the slant.

The table was not that broad, and her left hand was on it. He reached out and took her fingers onto his palm. "It's a good question," he said.

The people on either side of himself and Jennifer stopped their own conversations and looked at them. Jennifer gave him the best smile she had given him yet, so Churchyard kept his head poised where it was and waited in silence, and with rigid patience, until the four kibbitzers conceded that he had made his point and decided they had no points to make of their own.

It was at this moment that Nick Churchyard understood there was something to this woman that he really liked. Round about them sixty or so people were behaving the way sixty people lunching at a residential conference do behave – as if there were an established etiquette. Jennifer was behaving like Jennifer. Indeed, even now she had crooked her fingers and was running her nails down his palm.

"No," he said to her. "There are no rules."

"You said something about dinner," she said. " Was that an invitation?"

"First day we get out of here," he said. "Is it a deal?"

"Deal," she said.

They glowed at each other.

A male French voice came unwelcome into his ear. "Monsieur Churchyard," it said.

He looked round. A thin-moustached thinly built security man gave a thin stare at the joined hands on the table and offered him a sealed envelope, and went away.

"Excuse me," Churchyard said to Jennifer, and gave her back her hand. He opened the envelope and took out the note.

It read: "My room, instanter. H.S."

"Hell and damnation!" Churchyard said. "I've got to go."

God! What a good size he was, standing there, and how good he looked. He said all the right things, too. "I'm not going anywhere," she said.

A sensation of unbelievable quality passed back and forth between their eyes and went into their bodies. Each of them was overwhelmed, so wild for the other that unconsciousness seemed possible.

He began to turn away and when their locked gaze broke apart she remained staring where his eyes had been, and he stopped after only one step to collect himself.

Somehow he went back to her, close. "Your last name," he said. "In case I need to find you."

"In case you do," she said, "it's Fraenkel." She spelled it. "We never Americanized it," she said.

"The right thing," he said, meaning it greatly, and gave her a bad smile and went off and away, out of the dining room, out of sight.

"Do you have a fountain pen? What colour of ink?" Seddall asked. He was sitting at a Directoire desk at which, he fondly imagined, Fouche might have sat and got up to the kind of skullduggery he was getting up to himself right now.

"The most perfect blue, actually," Nick Churchyard said. Listening to his answer he realized the question had evoked from him thoughts of Jennifer's dress. Which matched her eyes. He must pull himself together.

Seddall was so preoccupied with what he was doing that he had noticed nothing. "Let's see it," he said.

He scrawled words on the sheet of paper in front of him. Other sheets, already scrawled on, made a clutter over the desk. "Yes," he said, "that's more like it, that's much more like it." He went on writing with Nick's pen, studied it as if he was an expert at Sotheby's and said: "What d'you think?"

Churchyard looked over his shoulder and read what he had written.

> To the Rt Hon. Christopher Walpole PC, MP,
> Secretary of State for Defence
>
> Sir,
>   It is most urgent that I see you BEFORE you go into the dining room to address the conference.
>   I would go so far as to say it is imperative.
>   Captain Churchyard, the bearer of this, will guide you to my room.
>
> Aubrey Kenyon
> (Major General)

"What do I think? I don't understand it. It's a joke?" Churchyard said.

"Of course it's not a joke," Seddall said. "Do you suppose I've been sitting here struggling to come up with a passable forgery of Kenyon's writing just to amuse you? The writing, man, the writing. Look, here's a note I had from Kenyon. Compare them. Tell me what you think."

"I think you're mad," Churchyard said. "You're going to ask me to take this to the Minister?"

"No, I'm going to order you to take it to the Minister," Seddall said, "and if you've forgotten what an order is I'll remind you at the appropriate moment, which is not yet. What I want you to do now is tell me if you think he'll accept that as if it had been written by Kenyon. He knows Kenyon. He's had dealings with Kenyon. He'll have seen his handwriting. Stop flapping and compare the two, and think, then answer me."

"Yes, it would fool me," Churchyard said. "I think it will fool the Minister, and I take it," he said in a disagreeable voice, "you want to fool the Minister."

Seddall folded the missive in three and put it in an envelope which he did not seal, but tucked in the flap. He got up from the desk. "Here," he said. "Put this in your inside breast pocket and don't take it out again until you're face to face with Brer Walpole."

Churchyard looked at the envelope Seddall was holding out, and then at Seddall. It was as if he were refusing a handshake from someone unworthy. When, at last, he took the envelope, he kept it in his hand.

"Damn it," he said, "I don't think I can do this. Kenyon's my regiment, Harry. I'm working for you because he brought me in."

Faced with this large, honest, reluctant young man Seddall knew an exasperating mixture of respect for his integrity, and a sense – for which he did not much like himself – of contempt for his innocence.

"Nick," he said, "put the bloody thing in your pocket."

Churchyard did this.

"Good," Harry said.

For the first time since he had begun to work for him, Churchyard thought he saw a shadow of anxiety pass over Seddall's face. "What's the problem?" he said.

"The problem is all these damned attaché cases they've issued to us," Seddall said. He took out his cigarettes and offered them, but Churchyard shook his head. "Because," Seddall said, in a cloud of French-smelling smoke, "it's like this: 'Where do you hide a leaf?' Answer: 'In the forest.' Do you recall that?"

"Vaguely," Churchyard said. "It's about hiding a letter by putting it on the mantelpiece. Sherlock Holmes, is that right?"

Seddall was pleased with that. "Or Edgar Allan Poe. I can't remember." He drew on his cigarette and watched Churchyard, hoping to be pleased again. "So where do you hide a bomb?"

Churchyard said: "Well, by that yardstick, you hide a bomb in an ordnance depot."

"Bloody hell, no!" Seddall was not pleased. "Where do you hide an attaché case bomb?"

"I get you," Churchyard said. "In among a crowd of attaché cases." Churchyard thought and worried. "Are we expecting a bomb? Has there been, well, intelligence to that effect?"

Seddall saw that he was failing to take the laddie with him, and in that instant he decided, with that comfortable old feeling of bullish cynicism, to lie to the Good Soldier Churchyard.

"You're entitled to an answer, and I'm not entitled to give you one," he said, and regarded Churchyard with, he hoped, no more candour than Churchyard would find credible. "I may not tell you we have intelligence to that effect, but I can let slip that there has been what I'll call a – " he pretended to hunt for the blameless word, though it had sprung up in his fertile head as naturally as a blade of wheat reaching for the sun " – what I'll call a susurration."

Churchyard said: "The French are running security for this. The French must have a word for susurration. Why are we making like Colonel Seddall's Private Army and sticking our necks out?"

Seddall produced a rather old-looking Smith & Wesson revolver and checked the cylinder and peered down the barrel and shut the weapon up again. "I'm getting tired of this, Nick," he said. "The French got their own susurration and decided to give it no credit. Their French logic tells them that security here is inviolable, so that even if they'd had it bellowed in their ear they wouldn't go to the bother of deciding whether they believed it or not. Logic will always drive the French into the Maginot Line mentality."

Churchyard only just glanced at him and went over to the window. He stood gazing out over the park, at a couple of scout cars that passed each other circling the chateau in opposite directions. The security seemed good to him. Somebody had certainly tried, and there were people and machines, never mind attaché cases, all over the place. It all looked to be highly organized and efficient and sophisticated.

"So what happens when I've lured the Minister up here?"

"We lock the door and keep him here," Seddall said in an expressionless voice. "By force, if necessary."

"You and me?"

"It will take two of us. His armed policeman may insist on coming. Are you carrying?"

"Yes, I'm carrying," Churchyard said.

All this time he had kept his back to Seddall, and now, in a lengthened silence, he showed no sign of moving.

"It's absurd for me to do this," he said at last. "You know that."

"Yes, I know that," Seddall said.

"It's all right for you. This is the sort of thing they talk about, when they talk about you. You've done crazy things like this before. They don't always work out, do they?"

"No."

"That's what they say. Sometimes they do, though," Churchyard said. "It must take more nerve than I've got."

"I doubt it," Seddall said. "You'll have to get down there, you know. You'll want to be at the front door in good time."

Churchyard to his surprise, suddenly thought of Jennifer – another maverick. Just my luck, he thought, or maybe it's something to do with me, with the sort of person I am. He turned back into the room. "Yes, I'll want to be in good time."

Seddall smiled his crooked smile. "I'll give you written orders, if you want."

"Don't spoil it," Churchyard said. He didn't say anything more. He touched the place where the forged letter lay, and tightened his mouth, and went out of the room.

The Minister came in playing his physical height and his matinée idol's charisma for more than they were worth, so that he appeared to be an actor in the part of himself.

This made sense to Seddall. A Cabinet Minister always knows the story-line of the day ahead, and Christopher Walpole had been dislocated from his script by the forged message from General Kenyon, so politician's instinct drew this energy field round him like a cloak to hide in, winning time for him to work out his own lines.

He saw Seddall, and no one else. "Where's General Kenyon?" he demanded, and shot his sleeve to look at his watch.

Churchyard, who came behind him, turned the shining brass key in the door, withdrew it, and put it in his pocket. At least, Seddall thought, when he decides to do it, he does do it.

Churchyard went to the window where he had stood before, as if that was the best place for dissociation.

Seddall said to Walpole: "I had you brought up here on false pretences, Minister. I think there's a threat to your safety and I have found that overriding. I wrote that note to you myself."

Walpole was a hard man behind the extravagant handsomeness, and under the polished black hair was a brain fast enough to drive his tongue, now that he had a glimpse of the scenario. "A threat to my safety here? That's rubbish, surely. I'll leave you now, Seddall." He discovered the time on his wrist again. He spoke low and close into Seddall's face so that Churchyard would not hear. "And just between you and me, Colonel, I'll have your fucking guts for garters as soon as we're back in London."

Churchyard, earnest to remain oblivious to the encounter between Seddall and Walpole, remembered thoroughly the girl downstairs and watched the world outside. He felt himself smile at the chestnut trees in their full flower, and was much struck to notice that although in his mind's eye he saw the fair Jennifer as clear as anything, he could see the trees with unobscured vision at the same time.

A scout car ran past below the window and from far off across the park he saw another coming over the grass towards him. At a cracking pace, too, he told himself, straight as an arrow for the house; and he saw Jennifer's dark, dark hair falling long, long, about her shoulders.

As the vehicle coming in from the perimeter cleared an avenue of beech trees he saw that it was different from the others, no mere scout car but a turreted armoured car with a pretty big gun, a seventy-five or ninety millimetre. Churchyard was an armoured car man himself, a dragoon, but it took him more seconds to recognize this one as a Panhard, which he could have sworn went out of service with the French Army ten years ago. He thought they had all been sold off to the Third World.

"You insolent bloody man!" shouted Walpole in a tearing voice behind him. Reluctantly Churchyard turned, to see Seddall with his back to the door and Walpole in his rage passionate to get at him, but held at bay by the pistol in Seddall's hand.

Churchyard – all vision of Jennifer gone – in a private moment of absolute anger at knowing he would have to intervene, cast his eyes in despair at the scene they had just left and saw the Panhard still making its straight reach at the house almost as if . . .

As if it was running in on its target.

The sudden gut reaction of an officer who had spent eight years in an armoured regiment overwhelmed all his reason, and told him the car was running in on its target, running in seriously on its target.

"That car's going to shoot," he yelled, "down, down, down," and hurled himself across the room to knock Walpole to the floor, and as he was going down on top of him shouted or tried to shout: "Hit the deck, Harry, hit the deck."

There was an enormous silence and then the gun cracked the air and the building shuddered, and again, three times more, and then another enormous silence, and then the high ripping clatter of machine-gun fire, and the gun again, and more automatic fire, sporadic and receding, until other closer sounds dominated the ear.

They were sounds that Seddall and the Minister had heard before, but Churchyard had not.

They were the sounds of masonry falling, and of the wounded and dying.

The three men lifted themselves from the floor and looked at each other in their own silence.

"What on earth was that?" Walpole said.

"I think Colonel Seddall may just have saved your life," Churchyard said. "That was an armoured car. I think it's shelled your conference for you," and remembered Jennifer, and tore the key from his pocket and leapt for the door.

12

The air was foul with dust from the still settling rubble, with the stench of high explosive, and with smoke from blazing timbers. The floor above had fallen in and oak beams that had been drying for over three hundred years were burning furiously.

At the smell of broiling meat from Arkley's leg Seddall recoiled a moment and then stooped over him again, and saw that the part of the leg trapped and sizzling under the flaming baulk of wood was detached from the rest.

He whipped off his tie and knotted it round Arkley's thigh and Arkley, whose face was as white as paper and who looked to be unconscious, shrieked. He lay there with his eyes closed, and went on shrieking.

The beam shifted and the flames feeding on it multiplied their violence. Seddall felt scorching on his head and face and knew it was now or never for Arkley. He put an arm under the shoulders and the other under the stump and the remaining knee, and began to carry the shrieking man to where the outside wall had been.

He was irritated by this shrieking. His mind focused angrily on the idea that men in shock, men who had just been savagely wounded, did not at once feel the pain.

With this bitter refrain starting in his head he stepped over the headless corpse of whoever had been next to Arkley, and set off on his journey through the carnage, through the burning, still collapsing, wreckage of the once beautiful salon.

He tripped on bodies dead or alive and stumbled off them again, trod on stucco cherubs fallen to earth when their heavenly ceiling flew apart and hurled them from their centuries of bliss, felt with revulsion his feet mire slippily in flesh and blood not recognizable for what it had been, met with his eyes the eyes of men, and of one woman, some of them silent and some moaning or crying out in their several agonies, some being tended by rescuers and others waiting, wondering if they would die there, if the fire that blazed about them would flare up and consume them in a last – how long? – passion of unbearable pain.

About him soldiers and security men, who had that morning so ineffectually laid their inhuman stare on all that passed, moved at their rescue work as clumsily as he. Like him they crept and crouched among the fallen ruins of the room above, and made their way among the burning timber and over patches of burning floor, as they worked to separate human debris from the debris of the chateau.

From all round him, as he lumbered on with Arkley's body in his arms, came the orchestration to Arkley's now monotonous, more widely spaced, but regularly repeated screams. It was the sound of other screams, of moans and whimpers, of calls for help and shouts of command; the sound of stones falling as new and changing stresses moved the remains of the deconstructed building; of creaks in the surviving structure as more of it moved towards collapse; of the busy crackling of fire; the straining and then the rushing sound of another segment of floor from the room that had been above, or of the ceiling above that, loosing its hold on the stronger elements that had secured it till now and falling upon corpses and survivors and rescuers alike.

Through a fog of powdered cement and plaster dust and smoke, through these sights and sounds that were to stay with him and become his own vision of armageddon, Seddall came at last to the place where the broken wall gave onto the stone terrace.

It was a certainty in him, however, that stone would not do. He could not lay poor Arkley down on stone. He knew he was beyond exhaustion, but he straightened himself up and crossed the old flagstones, and went down a little flight of steps, and laid Arkley on the grass of the park.

Arkley stopped screaming and opened his eyes.

Seddall fell to his knees beside him.

"Tourniquets, Seddall," the ghost of Arkley's voice said. "I thought tourniquets were old hat."

A man with a red cross brassard ran down the steps and went to Arkley's other side, one hand already feeling in his pouch.

"Maybe they are, Arkley," Seddall said. "It seemed like a good idea at the time."

As the drug went into the blood the vestige of an Arkley smile turned on the pale mouth in the pale face. There was a slight movement of the piebald moustache, but if Arkley had been trying to speak, neither of them ever knew what he had wanted to say.

"Will he live?" Seddall asked the paramedic.

The man moved a hand in a short arc from side to side. "*Peut-être*," he said, and rose and waved an arm, and an ambulance came over the grass and took Arkley away.

Seddall walked wearily round to the front of the chateau, passing the monstrous destruction of the wing from which he had just emerged, giving a wide berth to vehicles, hoses, men and women hastening here and there, shutting his ears to the klaxons of all kinds of emergency vehicles.

In the courtyard stood and sat groups and isolated figures of those entirely, or more or less, in one piece. One group of three moved towards him.

"Are you all right, sir?" Churchyard. Sir, from Churchyard?

"I'm fine, why?" Seddall said.

He could not see them clearly and struggled pitifully to get his handkerchief out. One of the three said, "Here," in a rich voice, and he felt linen put into his hand, and wiped his eyes with it.

His vision cleared and he saw Churchyard and Doffene and a dark-haired woman, and then he had to wipe his eyes again. "I'm most awfully sorry," he said. "Your handkerchief will be quite destroyed."

The rich voice belonged to Doffene. "They won't let us back inside," he said. "Let's go to my car."

The woman took Seddall's hand, the hand without the hand-kerchief, and led him along, while he wiped his eyes now and then and smiled with a strange happiness.

Doffene opened a black Cadillac and sat Seddall in the back with the girl beside him, and he and Churchyard got in the front. Seddall found a silver-plated cup put in his hand and immediately drank it down, whatever it was. It was cognac.

"I think I'm jolly nearly hysterical," he said.

"Pretty near," the girl said. "Drink this one too, though, and I think that will have been about the right amount."

Seddall took a look at her. "You're a grand girl," he said, "and I feel better, but is brandy the right thing for shock, or whatever this is?"

"No," she said, "but it's what we've got."

"That's a good answer," he said. "In fact it's just about what I said to Arkley. He said he thought tourniquets are old hat."

From the front of the car Churchyard said: "Arkley. Arkley's all right? You found him? They wouldn't let us in."

"I don't think they let me in either, now you mention it," Seddall said. "I just went. I felt bad about Arkley. I'd rather have tried to save his skin than Walpole's, but it was only a hunch, really, and I'd never have tricked Arkley out of there. The wrong hunch too, as it turned out." He swallowed cognac. "Who *did* it? Tell me that."

Doffene said: "*Anybody* could have done it. From Black September to the Red Brigades, except that it's not their style. An armoured car attack? Whose style is that? It's crazy!"

"Walpole," Churchyard said, "thinks you're Man of the Hour. So do I, rather, but Walpole can't wait to be all over you."

Seddall realized that he had a great wish to be out of there. "God," he said, "I wish I had a car. I'd be on my way like a shot."

"You can have mine," the girl said. "My name's Jennifer."

"Thanks," Harry said, "I'll take it." He smiled at her. It was the first time Churchyard had seen him smile a complete smile, with no trace of those other things, irony or scepticism or self-mockery, that usually came when he smiled. With the smile he said: "Where do I return the car?"

"It's Hertz," Jennifer said. "Drop it anywhere."

"Anywhere," Harry said.

"Will you be all right to drive?" Doffene asked. "You look bushed, you know."

"Best thing for me," Harry said. "I'll take it easy." To Churchyard he said: "Find where they've taken Arkley. Stick around for a few days, will you? He's lost some of a leg. I'll tell you what," he said to Jennifer, "if you were to visit him too, it would do him a world of good. He doesn't have friends, really, Arkley doesn't. I mean if you can spare a few days. I mean if Arkley makes it, actually."

"I can do that," Jennifer said. "Can't I, Charlie?"

"Naturally," Doffene said. "I hope he does make it. A lot of people won't. We were by-God lucky, Jen, you and I."

"Yes," Harry said. "How come? Were you in there? I mean, if you were, you must have been through the laundry afterwards."

"I had a call from Washington," Doffene said, "and this one . . ." He shook his head.

"This one," said Jennifer, speaking up for herself, "just couldn't face sitting there with all these stupid people after Nick Churchyard up and left."

Nick Churchyard lost, altogether, his countenance, but kept his head high and blushed gallantly at the maker of this declaration.

Seddall became kind. "I think I could smoke," he said, since it was all he could think of to say, and besides, it was true, "but I seem to have left my cigarettes upstairs."

Doffene leaned across Churchyard and took a pack of Marlborough from the cubbyhole. As he offered them to Seddall he said: "Have you heard of The Outfit?"

"The Outfit?" Seddall said. "Thanks." Doffene lit the cigarette for him. "No, I haven't heard of The Outfit. What is it?"

"Yeah," Doffene said. "Well, on the face of it, The Outfit is a private security consultancy in Washington. It's run by a man called Mendham."

An extraordinary number of things happened in Seddall's face. "Mendham," he said. "I know Mendham. I used to know Mendham. I knew he'd set up in that sort of business. I thought it had some ordinary sort of name. I didn't know it was called The Outfit."

Doffene said: "It has an ordinary sort of name, Mendham Consultants, Inc, but it also gave itself this unofficial name, The Outfit. It's a second identity, and goes well with that division of the operation. Kinda catchy, you know, and cool, for what they do. It helps to get the word to where it matters."

"What do they do?" Seddall asked, although from the cynical amusement in Doffene's voice he thought he had a fair idea.

Jennifer said: "They kill. They hire out to kill."

"They don't kill just anyone," Doffene said. "They mostly take a far right-wing stance when it comes to who they'll contract for. They're kind of respectable."

"Respectable!" Churchyard was outraged, and for the slightest moment this put the slightest frown on Jennifer's limpid brow.

"He means," Harry said, "though he won't say so, that a branch or branches of the US Government, or offices reporting to or financed by branches of the US Government, have used The Outfit."

"I certainly won't say so," Doffene said, "but I will say, other governments."

"Oho," Seddall said.

"Yes indeed," Jennifer said. "Oho."

"A man called Carmichael has just left Kennedy to fly British Airways to Heathrow," Doffene said. "That's what my call was about. Carmichael may have saved my life, I guess, but he's not flying to England to save anyone else's. You can bet on it."

Seddall looked at this. "Why tell me?" he said.

"Yes," Doffene said. "Mendham doesn't like you, does he?

You're the guy dropped him in the shit."

"He dropped himself in the shit," Harry said. "It just happened to be me that knew where to find the shovel."

Doffene showed his good white teeth. "I have no problem with that," he said. "That's for one thing. The other thing, well, the other thing's more vague. We think The Outfit has a deal going with someone in the British security and intelligence sector."

"For God's sake," Harry said, remembering Mrs Heron and getting suddenly shirty at the things people landed in his lap. "You're not going to leave me with that kind of garbage, Doffene. If you know that much you know more."

"No, he doesn't," Jennifer said. "You don't know how it is in Washington. It all comes down in drops like coffee from a filter, and every drop is the essence of grave deliberation by committees with proud security ratings. The coffee beans they hoard like misers with gold. It's not just power, it's fear too, fear of making mistakes, and getting caught at it."

"Proud security ratings," Harry said. "I like proud." He looked out of the car and saw the state of the afternoon sky. "I think I want to be on the road." He smiled at Jennifer again, but it was no longer that complete unqualified smile.

Churchyard took this to be a good sign. Seddall was feeling better than when he had just emerged from the shattered wing of the chateau, from what must have been a charnel house.

"You take care," Doffene said. "When you get to London, call us. Don't call the Embassy."

Jennifer scribbled on a notepad, and Harry took the number from her. "Don't worry about Arkley," she said. "We can't do what you did for him, but we'll do what we can."

Seddall was profoundly embarrassed, and did not know what to do with himself next.

"Let's go," Jennifer said. "I'll show you the car."

The car ran through the forest under a ribbon of darkening sky as if it was on the road to a dream. Seddall drove without lights, not wanting to let the night come before its time and mar his passage among the quiet ghosts of the trees.

He did not want the night to come at all, since he wanted only to drive on and on for hours within this calm and misting dusk. He would acknowledge that it was night when he saw his first star, and in this tunnel under the heavens that would be long after other stars were out.

He sped on in this secret world from which all but the last of the light had fallen, in which for miles he had been the only, the solitary traveller, and which wrapped him about like an endlessly comforting cocoon.

He watched the darkness gather between the woods, and kept an eye lofted for that first star, and fell asleep.

13

"To drive with no lights," the woman's voice said in English and French, "*c'est idiot, ça!*"

"No, no," Harry said, before he had returned all the way to consciousness. Returning a bit more, he said: "It wasn't that, I mean it wasn't only that." Returned altogether, "I fell asleep," he explained himself.

All of a sudden his head hurt like blazes, and he told her about that too and opened his eyes.

The first thing about the face was its seriousness and the remarkable amount of intelligent life in the eyes, which gleamed brown in the roof light of the car. The second was the beauty of it, a classic nordic beauty of face, open and smooth, and the straight cream-fair hair that lifted so well from the brown and had been allowed to blossom into fullness where it lay on her shoulders.

He was still in the driving seat of the car but resting more against the door than the seat itself. "How am I?" he said.

She smiled. "You tell me," she said.

"A bump on the head is all I can feel," he said. He sat himself up straight. "Apart from that I feel fine."

"Your car is not so fine," she said. "Climb out this side. You are in the ditch down there."

She withdrew and he clambered up and out over the passenger seat. She had a torch and threw its beam on the front of the car to let him see the damage.

"Yes indeed," he said. "I'm a lucky man."

The front end had come to grief against a culvert and was

more or less destroyed. The bonnet had sprung open and been pushed up against the windscreen which was starred, though it had not fallen in. The smell of ethyl rose from the burst radiator and mixed with the stink of petrol, and stirred the pain in his head, so that he stepped away from the wreck.

He looked about him. A three-quarter moon stood in the sky over the road he had followed, and when he turned from it to face the way he had been going he saw, rather late in the day, that first star which he had been searching for as he drove along. He sniffed the air like a dog, and breathed it in.

"It is better standing here," he said, "than just driving through it."

"Yes," she said, laying the alert eyes on him. "That's right."

"Listen," he said belatedly. "I'm being infernally rude. Thanks for stopping to help."

"I didn't exactly stop," she said. "I was in the woods walking, and was going to cross the road when I heard the car, which I could not see of course because you were driving along in the dark with no lights on at all, and then suddenly you were here cutting the grass – you call it cutting the grass? – and throwing the earth all over the place, driving yourself into the ditch." He caught a glimpse of her smile again in the backthrow of light from the torch. "You are an imbecile," she said. "I think you can walk to the house now, it is not far at all."

Her English was flawless, graced by French cadence and only just coloured by accent. Within the same instant he felt that he had fallen into a fortunate dream; and remembered carrying Arkley out of the carnage in the chateau.

"Can you walk?" she asked, and he understood that he was watching her too closely, as if there was a need in him.

"I'm sure I can walk," he said. "Where do we go?"

She turned her back to him and shone the torch across the road, showing him that a track opened into the forest. He heard the racket of a disturbed pheasant changing its roost up in the trees, and then another, before the beam dropped again.

"God," he said. "I do like this," and followed her across the road and into the forest.

He woke from a night of evil dreams but with a sense of having been comforted, and to the perfume she had been wearing the night before lingering in the air. He woke also to the sound of purring, and opened his eyes to see the face of a brindled cat inches from his own.

"Good morning to you," he said, and the cat, clearly an actor, pulled back its head to stare at him and then whipped off the bed and ran up the curtains to which it clung, despairing and amazed at discovering the force of gravity, before it half-fell half-jumped to the floor and shot out of the room.

When it was gone, daylight came peacefully through the curtains, linen-coloured and hanging to the ground. From somewhere below him Seddall heard the voices of two Frenchwomen raised in the morning babble of a household. He felt at home, though almost everything in the room told him he was in France. The exception was the dressing gown lying over a chair, whose tartan had a true Highland look to it, no flavour of the Paris imitation.

Naked in the bed, and seeing none of his clothes, he got up and wrapped himself in the tartan to find it came almost to his ankles. He looked once at the bed, and went out of the room.

A white stone staircase took him down to a flagged hall which ran the depth of the house. The front door was closed but the far end of the hall was open to the garden. He stood for a while taking the feel of the house. The stone, cold to his bare feet, the height and proportions of the hall, the long sunniness of the salon to whose entrance he was drawn, the thought of the high-entropy cat and the women's voices he had heard, all joined to bring him to a pleasant state with himself.

He went to the back of the house and out onto a terrace, where she was sitting at a table with the cat on her lap, smoking a cigarette and looking at her garden.

The thought was spoken as soon as it came to him. "You're very beautiful," he said.

"I don't set much store by it," she said. She turned her head to call into the house, and swung the rich fairness of her hair off her face. "Stephanie! Stephanie will bring coffee," she said. "Please, sit down. How do you feel?"

"Refreshed," he said, "rested. Also, I feel that I have been cared for, in the night."

"You were," she said, "so both of us were." The chestnut eyes were solemn on his, and the quick and candid smile came and went.

"You're a good woman," he said, "a fine woman."

He stroked the fair hair slowly and let his hand lie on her shoulder. She tilted her head so that her cheek touched the hand.

He held her head in both hands and kissed the crown of her hair, and she lifted her face for him to kiss her mouth. Their lips were dry at first and then their tongues moved slowly on each other, until it became a small exquisite pain for them to part.

He met the solemn look and knew what it meant. "There will be time enough," he said, answering it.

After a moment more the quick smile came, and she took one of his hands in hers and studied it, studied his face again, smiled again, and said: "Yes, there will. Sit down. Have a cigarette."

Stephanie came out of the house and put a tray on the table. She set thick white Apilco crockery with a pale blue line on it in front of each of them, and laid a cafetiere, a jug of warm milk and a basket with brioches in it at the centre of the table.

She was a lanky, gaunt-faced woman in her sixties with a grim expression, and spoke in French either too rustic or too rapid for him to follow. "*Non, non,*" he said. "*Vous parlez trop vite pour moi. Je ne comprends pas.*"

His hostess, this woman he had just kissed and who had slept beside him in the night, this woman whose name he did not yet know, interpreted. "Stephanie has brushed and pressed your suit and washed your shirt and underpants, and they are in your

114

room," she said. She looked up at Stephanie and then back to him. "She has not cleaned your pistol, she says."

Quite so, the pistol; he had forgotten the pistol. He would have to account for that somehow, but he begged that question for the moment and thanked Stephanie with some warmth. His own housekeeper at home would not have been kinder to him, he said, and he always cleaned his own firearms.

Stephanie nodded and went back into the house. She gave him a bit of a look before she departed, and though the gaunt face was as grim as ever, he sensed some kind of approval from her.

"Do you know why she likes you?" his hostess asked.

"I know it's not just because I thanked her," he said. "I know it's something else."

That seriousness of expression, full of histories of its own, was on her face and was strong in her eyes. "It's because you're a soldier," she said, and the eyes watched his, and then turned to the business of pouring coffee.

He thought about this; it seemed to be a kind of conundrum. As he held out his cup for the coffee, the tartan sleeve suggested an answer. "This is a soldier's," he said.

"Yes," she said. "Michel was a soldier." The cat was suddenly restless, but she held it and stroked it firmly before she would let it go. It jumped from her lap and off the terrace and ran till it came to the big pool in the middle of the lawn where it sat and flicked its paws angrily and began to wash itself.

"What was that about?" he asked.

"The cat? She doesn't like my grief. Michel died a year ago," she said, "a year and two months." She lifted her head and threw the hair off it, so that he could see everything in her face. "I'm not a coward," she said. "I don't hang on to him, but sometimes he comes up inside me."

He said: "The best days leave the longest shadows," and thought at once he had been trite. Then he thought, perhaps not, since it seemed to serve, for "Oh, yes," she said, and dropped her head and went inside her hair.

She emerged almost at once with her eyes wet but her face radiant, and gave him a curious kind of nod in which her neck dipped and came up again, but her face stayed level at him. She was a woman so given to the frank exchange that he felt himself either perceived or unworthy.

"I knew you were a soldier too," she said. "When we found the pistol on you. We looked at your papers to see who you were, to make sure, but I knew already. Eat, you poor man."

He took a brioche and spooned jam onto his plate. "Do you realize," he said, "I don't know your name. You know mine, except that they call me Harry, not Henry."

She said: "My name is Olivia," and then, "Harry," for the sound.

There was a great swirl of water in the pond before them and the back of a fish broke out of the water. The cat fell into a pose of utter astonishment.

"Dear God," Harry said, "carp, and what a size."

He understood all at once that the place was idyllic, that he was in an idyll, and therefore remembered that he would have to leave.

"You have to go," she said. He stared at her and she smiled. "Well, I know you, don't I?" she said. "Where do you have to go?"

"London," he said.

"I'll drive you," she said. "Your car is wrecked."

"Drive me where? To Orly?"

"No, to London. Are you in a great hurry, do you have to fly?"

"Listen," he said, "flying is fast when you're in the air, but they can do awful things to you on the ground."

"Would you like me to drive you?"

"It's a lot to ask of you," he said. "I would like it more than anything."

"Yes," she said. "So would I. We'll drive then?"

"We'll drive," he said.

"Dieppe to Newhaven," she said. "You'll be in London this afternoon."

As they ran through the forests of Compiègne, she said: "Why do you carry a pistol? Are you in Intelligence?"

"Yes," he said. "I am."

On the boat she said: "You were very unhappy last night. Did something terrible happen?"

"Yes," he said, and told her about rescuing Arkley from the carnage at the chateau.

While they were driving up through Sussex he told her everything that was on his mind, about Arkley, about the general and Lord Findo, and about Mrs Heron's friend who had died in Scotland.

When she had parked the car, their journey over, in Phillimore Gardens, he said to her: "I shouldn't have told you any of this stuff."

"I know," she said.

"It was impossible not to tell," he said. "You're a terrible woman."

"I do hope so," she said. "I would like to be a terrible woman."

They sat down four to tea. Harry and Olivia in chairs, the dog Bayard on the hearthrug, and the black cat Sacha on the piano. Sacha kept her eyes shut most of the time, but whenever Olivia looked at her the cat opened them and stared rudely.

Mrs Lyon came in with her coat on, ready to depart. "And there's this," she said, giving Harry an envelope, "from Miss Blake. I had it leaning on the tea caddy in case I forgot, and I near did, because I put the caddy on top of it efter I'd made your tea. I'll be here in the morn."

Bayard saw her to the door and watched gloomily as she went down the hall and away, and then came back to the fire.

"Thought it best," Harry read, "to leave this with Mrs

117

Lyon as it's unofficial. You told me to think about the island problem that came up when you were at the opera and I did, and decided that the best thing to do was to go there. So I have.

Sorrel

PS Don't *worry*. I'm a big girl now."

"Don't worry," said Harry. "Don't worry, she says."

"What's wrong?" Olivia asked him.

"It's Sorrel – I told you about her in the car. She's gone to that bloody island, what's it called? Islay, she's gone to Islay, the bloody girl."

He gave Olivia the note.

"What are you upset about?" Olivia asked.

"What am I upset about? It could be very unsafe, that's what I'm upset about."

"Bouf!" Olivia said, and shrugged. "Don't be so stupid, so chauvinist. She says she's a big girl now. I'd have done the same, I think."

Harry stared at her. Bayard twitched in his sleep, but the black cat Sacha opened her eyes and stared too, for a long while.

14

On the Isle of Islay off the west coast of Scotland, Sorrel was having a high old time.

She had flown to Glasgow, hired a car, bounced exuberantly up the Sound of Islay on the car ferry in a half gale, and got herself into a small hotel saying she had come to catch some trout and put in some walking.

In the bar, where the hotel's owner served her a gin and tonic, she added to these projects her intention of looking up her old history teacher from the university.

"Who would that be?" the man MacGillivray asked her.

"Marion Oliphant," Sorrel said blithely. "She retired up here."

MacGillivray was startled. "But surely," he said, and then broke off and began again. "Is she," he asked carefully, "a close friend of yours?"

"Hardly a friend at all, really," Sorrel said, "but she was a good teacher and I liked her. It's just that when I said I was coming here someone told me it was where she lived."

MacGillivray was a big man with red hair splashed with grey and a craggy face. She thought the concern he had shown suited it well, that she liked big soft-hearted men. "I'm afraid," he said, "I have to tell you that Professor Oliphant is dead. She died some weeks ago."

"How awful," Sorrel said. "But she was quite old, after all."

"Maybe," he said. "I don't know how old she was. The fact is that her house burnt down, and she was killed in the fire."

Sorrel put a hand to her mouth. "Oh, but that's dreadful," she said. "Poor Marion."

MacGillivray, in his turn, thought that the young woman made a picture, with her golden curls and those blue eyes, round and large, now in distress.

"I'm glad she wasn't a close friend," he said.

"Did she . . . do you think . . . ?"

"Well, they say it is the smoke that takes them," he said, "but it's a bad way to die. Here, let me fill that for you." He put the glass away and gave her another. "That's from me," he said, "for giving you the bad news."

"Thanks," Sorrel said. "She wasn't a friend, you know, but it's so terrible, isn't it?"

"Aye," he said. "It is terrible. There was a lot of us liked her. She'd had the house for years, you know, long before she retired. She was one of us."

"One of us be damned!" said the man at the other end of the bar. "Don't flatter yourself; don't flatter the rest of us. Marion was a highly individual woman. Strong character. Never ran with the flock. Give me another, will you, John?"

He was a man about fifty, dark and smoothly haired with a face that was all edges, pink and fresh as if it had just swum up a waterfall. He was wearing moleskin trousers that looked – could this be so? – tailored for him, and an Aran sweater, from which his long neck and small head emerged like a bird looking out of a nest. Sorrel thought the look of his eyes was pretty hard, but his smile was good enough.

"Hallo," he said to her. "You knew Marion, then. I'll miss her a lot. She had great moral fibre, that woman. Some people thought she was a bit nutty; not a bit of it. My name's Welland, James Welland."

MacGillivray put a glass in front of him and said: "He's an incomer, *and* a lawyer. Don't trust him."

"*Slainte* to you," Welland said ironically. "Half the island's incomers. If they weren't, you'd be out of business tomorrow."

"True enough," MacGillivray said. "Mind the bar for a few

minutes, will you? There'll not be many in now this time of the afternoon." He went out and left them.

"I'm Sorrel Blake," Sorrel said. "Are you the libel lawyer? *That* James Welland? You live up here?"

"As much as I can. Half London lives in the Highlands and Islands nowadays." He drank his whisky at a gulp. "And half of that half always seems to be living in my house."

"You must invite them," she said. "They wouldn't come unasked."

"God!" Welland said. "Women are tough nowadays. You can't get away with anything."

He went behind the bar with his glass. "Buy you another of those?"

"No thanks," Sorrel said. "I'm going to go upstairs and have a nap. I came up from London in one fell swoop, and I want to enjoy my evening."

"Here?" he said. "Among the tourists? You won't get much local colour in here, if that's what you're after. You'd better come up to the house for dinner and join the throng. John'll tell you where it is."

"That's warm-hearted, all right," Sorrel said. "Thanks, but I can't. These are the only kind of clothes I've got with me."

"Don't be an ass," he said. "You'll put their eye out, poncing around in their Paco Rabanes and Givenchys. Come as you are, jeans and sweater."

"You'll do the same?"

"If you want me to. Spoil the effect for you."

"All right then, don't. And I shall come. But," she said, "you tell me where it is. It would be a kind of promise of good manners to come, you know?"

He put the glass he had filled untasted on the bar, and gave her a terrific smile. "Yes," he said. "I know. It's a house called Killanet, and it's a grey crow-stepped gabled pile two point three miles south of here on the road to Bowmore, off to the left, and you'll see a sign clearly painted. Seven-thirty for eight."

"I'll look forward to it," Sorrel said.

"So will I," he said. "See you later."

At nine o'clock Sorrel was sitting in an enormously long and lofty dining room with her host on her left, a right-wing Home Counties MP called Turvey on her right, a woman of fifty opposite her who was apparently something in industry, called Annette, but whose surname Sorrel had failed to collect, and beside Annette, a German called Rupert Windisch.

Welland had told them how he and Sorrel met, over their shared acquaintance with the late Marion Oliphant. "You met her once here," he said to Annette, "you and Freddie."

"I remember her," Annette said. "She was quite an eccentric."

"She was nothing of the sort," Welland said with vigour. "She knew how a human being ought to live."

"James, I mean nothing critical of her," Annette said. "I liked her. But she lived up there in the most desolate part of the island, she said so herself, which is inhabited only by deer and feral sheep. What else – yes, she said she consulted Tarot cards, and threw the I Ching to see where her life was moving. Cultivated her garden and did flower paintings . . ."

"And had five cats and a goat and kept bees," Welland came in with no sign of the hoped-for good manners. "And played chess by herself against a computer, and did yoga and was wildly reclusive except for her forays down here. I don't call that eccentric. It's a tremendously good way to live. I'd like to live like that one day."

"You?" Turvey said. "This," and he coiled a manicured hand through the air, "is how you like to live."

"Is it really? Is it really?" Welland said, and his voice was very nearly angry. "It's how you like to live, Michael. I shall be sick of it before I'm fifty, I assure you. As it is I'm not quite well, it makes me not quite well."

Observing that his host had crossed the frontier into bad taste by being too personal about himself, Turvey changed the subject. "You were taught by Marion Oliphant?" he said to Sorrel.

"Yes, I was," she said, going overboard to be pleasant because she rather disliked Turvey, who had a red, tough, meaningless, manicured face. Seddall did not employ people who liked the company of politicians. "I read history at Oxford but Marion was my supervisor when I did my doctorate at Edinburgh."

"What was your thesis?" Turvey asked.

"Causes of the Great Northern War," Sorrel said, having spent the previous evening with an encyclopedia looking for a subject no one would be likely to challenge her on.

"What on earth was the Great Northern War?" said Turvey. "Were we in it?"

"No, we were not," Sorrel said. "Sweden, Russia, the Baltic states and some German ones."

"It was before the Keil Canal was built," Rupert Windisch said strangely, and Sorrel saw a sense of humour hiding on his expressionless face.

"I had worked that out, thank you," Turvey said.

The girl next to Windisch, a black-haired Scot called Catriona, said: "Samuel Greig."

With barely a second's pause Sorrel said: "Absolutely," and hoped for the best.

It came, from Annette, who leaned forward to say past Windisch: "Who is Samuel Greig, Catriona?"

"Peter the Great's admiral at Tallin. A Scotsman. Fought off the Swedes. Terrific gunnery." Catriona herself spoke like a rattle of musketry, and that and her expertise about Admiral Greig made Sorrel nervous.

The politician, however, was by this time impatient with aspects of history of which he knew nothing. "Gunnery," he said. "Annette's our gunnery expert at this table."

This led to most of the table looking at Annette. Sorrel speculated wildly. Had this woman with the good, quiet, forceful countenance held a commission in the Royal Horse Artillery?

"We don't know that yet, Michael," Annette said. "It's open to competition."

"Is it hell," Michael said. "Like the US forces sidearm was open to competition, and everyone knew long before they announced their decision that it was Biretta who were bound to get it. Why? Because it was the best weapon by the longest piece of chalk you ever saw. It's the same with Kalman's gunsight, and you know it, and the Defence Select Committee knows it, and if we voted on it it would be unanimous, I can tell you. I've spoken to every other member of the Committee, and not pushing either, just finding out."

"We're talking shop, Michael," Annette said, "at least, it's shop for me."

"Ah!" Windisch said. "My dear Annette, if you were an artist or a novelist we could talk about your work. You are an artist in electronics, we can talk about that."

"Well, Rupert," Annette said, pleasantly enough, "you can talk about electronics with Michael. It's your first day in Islay?" she said to Sorrel. "You'll like it. This is not really Islay, this kind of dinner, James would agree with me." Welland nodded and smiled benevolently. "In a way I can see what he means about Marion Oliphant living alone up there, that is Islay. Moor and hill, long white beaches, woods full of bluebells at this time of year. That's why I come here."

"It is why I come too," Windisch said. "It is one of the reasons I so much like to visit you and Freddie. It is idyllic," he said to Sorrel. "So far even from Europe, it seems to me, never mind from the world."

"This *is* Europe," Turvey said, dropping the dead hand of realpolitik into these pretty contemplations. "This is NATO territory, and now that you West Germans have got your way over standing down short-range nuclear missiles from German soil, NATO is going to need the best tank gunsight it can get, and Annette Kalman has produced it."

Annette Kalman, Sorrel was saying to herself. Of course, Annette *Kalman*.

"Whatever gunsight NATO tanks use," Windisch said, "the tank battles will be in Germany, Mr Turvey, and not in Islay, or Sussex. If there are to be battles, that is where they will be."

Kalman Electronics, Sorrel said to herself. This is a very high-powered quiet-looking lady indeed.

Turvey refreshed himself from his wineglass. "This is most frightfully good claret, James," he said, and returned to Windisch. "If the tank battles are to be fought in Germany, then you will want your tanks to have the best gunsight going. Kalman's got it, and if Annette won't speak up for herself, ask Freddie. Right, Freddie?" he said to the other end of the table.

"That's enough, Michael," Annette said. "Freddie's not in the firm."

"What's up?" Freddie demanded.

"Nothing for you to trouble about, Freddie," Welland said. "That *is* enough, you know, Michael. You stick to woofing about the claret for a bit, and let Annette mind her own business."

"Well, damn me!" Turvey said, recovering well. "Damn me, Mr Speaker, my apologies to the House. I feel strongly about it, and here you were, Annette. I've been embarrassing, I'm sorry."

Freddie looked a good deal older than his wife, but a very fit older man, with a long hatchet face, balding on the head, his shoulders still square. He leaned forward and gave his wife an indulgent eye, indulging what? Her distinction in her field, in the tough world of electronic business, one of the most competitive in the world? Her being in the limelight? It seemed odd for anyone to regard such a woman indulgently, but who was she, Sorrel Blake, to interpret glances between men and women she hardly knew?

They went into the walled garden for coffee, it being warm for May, a mini-heatwave. Welland walked her round the garden, away from what he had called the throng, along with his wife or girlfriend, whatever, who was a miniature Venus with red hair and a demure and enigmatic cast to her face, called Kate.

"He's a wild man, Michael Turvey," Welland said. "A pain in the ass, really."

"Why ask him then?" said Kate.

"I don't know. Because he's there. Anyway he's leaving tomorrow."

The sky was paled almost out of colour now and blackbird and thrush were singing out the day. Sorrel thought there could be no place more peaceful than this.

"You don't know shit about the Great Northern War, do you?" Welland said to Sorrel. Kate smiled at her and gave a kind of shrug of sympathy.

"Is this direct examination, or cross?" Sorrel said, stopping to look him in the eye.

"I don't know," he said. "I think I'm for you. It's not that easy to fool a lawyer of my kind. But where does that leave you with Marion? Am I to suppose you knew her or not? I mean, if you invented the thesis subject you said she guided you with, did you invent knowing her as well, that's what I have to wonder."

"How about this?" Sorrel said. "I care for her."

He looked round the garden. "That would do," he said. "I don't know what it means, but that would do."

"Are you going to give me away?" Sorrel asked.

"No, why should I? I incline to trust you," he said.

"Thanks," Sorrel said.

As the party, in the drawing room of the house now, broke up, Annette Kalman said to her: "Come and see us, won't you? Come and lunch with us. When can you? Tomorrow, the next day?"

"That's very kind," Sorrel said. "Can I come the day after tomorrow? Tomorrow I want to go up to Marion Oliphant's place, what's left of it. A kind of pilgrimage."

The indulgent Freddie, who was adroitly helping his wife on

with her coat, lost touch with what he was doing.

"Help!" Annette said. "Where's the sleeve? You're usually so good at doing this for women, Freddie. You manage to put the sleeves where they need to be. That's better."

As she got into her hired Sierra, Sorrel watched them drive off in their Saab 9000. Freddie spurted gravel as he went.

"My goodness, Sorrel Blake," she said. "Is something up?"

The next day she mailed her report of the dinner to Seddall, and drove along the top of Loch Indaal, sharing the road with bullocks, cows and calves, sheep and lambs, and struck north from farmland to moor, and finally onto a track into the hills.

It was another sunny day, but when she got out of the car the wind off the sea was cold, and she dived into the back for an extra sweater. Then she set off for Marion's cottage. When she found it her heart went into her mouth, because the place was beautiful. The house sat, or had sat, above a bay, a small bay that was a curve of sand, and the house itself was in a bay formed by the hills. The house was ruined walls and black ash, and about it was the garden, full and unharmed and still showing the tending of Marion Oliphant. Already the peonies were out, and lupins, and Icelandic poppies, and violets unknown to her. If ever a place had been loved by the one who dwelt there, it was this. Fruit trees were espaliered along a high wall protecting them from the northerly winds, a wall which she knew by instinct Marion Oliphant had built herself, of the same slatey blue stone that surrounded the fields she had driven through on the way here. Last night she had thought that there could be nowhere more full of peace than the walled garden where she walked with James Welland and Kate, and today she knew she had been wrong.

Sorrel decided not to weep, as an appropriate, though not fully understood, tribute to the maker of this place, and got to her feet and went down to the ruins of the house. The garden shed was standing, and she took a rake from it.

There had been rain since the fire and inside the shell of the house was filth to move along. She worked earnestly with the rake, expecting to find nothing, and finding nothing. She worked on though, with the minute movements of the archaeologist, until the sun was high.

She went up to the car for the packed lunch the hotel had put up for her, and saw a movement under it. There was a cat in there. Five cats, she remembered. She wondered if any of them had been in the house or if they were all let out at night.

She squatted down well away from the car and waited for the cat to come to her, which at length it did, but nervous in its approach until it let her stroke it, and tell it what a good cat it was, what a nice cat, what a pretty cat. In truth it was pretty, a black and white cat with a black face and a white streak up the centre of it running up from a white chin.

"Let's eat," she said to it. It ate some of the ham out of her sandwiches but was not ravenous, so she supposed it had been hunting for itself and done well at it.

On a hill, on the crest of a hill, in front of her about a mile away the sun glinted at her, and glinted again like a heliograph. There was someone up there with a glass.

"Cat, my dear," she said, "it is time to go. Let us be cool, calm, and collected, and remember to take off the safety catch, if that's what it comes to."

She wadded the remains of the lunch together, and stood up and stretched and looked back over the garden and the bay, and then lifted the cat and put it in the back of the car, and climbed in herself and turned it round.

Then she took the revolver out of the glove compartment and put it in the pocket in the door, and set off down the track. The cat began to wail.

"Me too," Sorrel said to it. "Me too! Keep your claws crossed. You do know, don't you, that Harry's going to be furious with us if anything happens."

The track went on winding round the hill, and there in front of her, not fifty yards away, was a big white BMW coming slowly towards her. By the time she had stopped it was thirty feet away and then ten feet, where it stopped.

The two front doors opened and two men got out, both tall men, one in a leather jacket and jeans, the other in a light Burberry coat, all belting and epaulettes.

Sorrel was out too, standing a little back from the open door of her car. She could see the hands of the man in the leather jacket, but Burberry's hands were in his pockets.

"Hallo?" she said.

They said nothing, but came towards her.

"Far enough," Sorrel said, and showed the revolver.

Burberry at once took out a pistol and fired three times into the Sierra and leather jacket vanished in a dive that took him to the other side of the car.

It was a face-off between Sorrel and Burberry, each looking into the barrel of a gun.

"Lower the weapon," leather jacket said from behind her.

Sorrel let her arm fall. A hand went over the revolver and took it from her.

"That was a moment, all right," Burberry said. "That was a moment."

"Yes, I suppose it was," leather jacket said. He held a card in front of Sorrel's face. "Police," he said. "Special Branch. What's this business with the weapon?"

"It's licensed," Sorrel said, "and with a permit to carry."

"But not to fire it at the filth," Burberry said.

"I didn't fire it," she said.

Leather jacket lifted his arm and fired a shot from Sorrel's revolver into the ground.

"Try telling that to the Judge," he said.

"Well, thank God you're police, anyway," Sorrel said. "We'll get it all sorted out."

"Ho, ho," Burberry said. "I like it. Get in the back of the BMW."

"What about the cat?" she said. "Can I bring the cat?"

"Cat?" Leather jacket looked into the Sierra and saw the

black and white cat cowering in the corner of the back seat, all its hair standing up and a snarl on it.

He put his hand in and the cat spat and latched onto it. He shook it off and it tore away round the hill, back towards the burnt-out house.

"Bugger the cat!" leather jacket said. "It's more dangerous than you are."

As she sat in the back of the BMW with Burberry beside her and the other man driving with one hand and licking blood off the other, it came to her that both of them spoke with south of England voices. Special Branch up here would surely be Scottish?

"Are you Strathclyde Police?" she asked. "Taking me to Glasgow, or where?"

"Yes, and yes," Burberry said, from somewhere in mid-Sussex. "Now shut up."

The car was still bucking down the track out of the hills. To the left of the track the land fell away, and to the right it rose.

"I need to pee," Sorrel said. "I really do."

The driver laughed and Burberry said: "Fat chance of that."

She squirmed sideways onto the seat with her back to the side of the car as if that eased her discomfort. She pulled up her knee and put a booted foot on the car seat and made a face, like a child out shopping with her mother caught in the predicament she had complained of.

"I do," she said. "I really do."

"Stow it," Burberry said, "or I'll clock you one."

The car went into a right-hand bend against the tilt of the road, fighting against the steering.

"Well, watch *out*!" Sorrel said, her eyes staring out of the window, and as Burberry lost that fraction of a second of attention she kicked him in the face with all her might, and even as she saw blood burst from his nose kicked him again, took muzzle flash on her thigh as she felt the bones break round his eye under her boot heel, and then ignored the inside of the car, opened the door and threw herself out, got up after an ineffec-

130

tual roll and ran on a shallow slant up the hillside, aiming for distance not for height.

She thought of nothing but running fast and not putting a foot wrong. She heard two pistol shots and then a group of them close together and ran on without looking back. She leapt a stream like a deer, cleared a drystone dike with one hand on a solid looking coping stone, and ran on till the hill began to turn.

She threw herself on the ground and crawled back, and saw leather jacket pounding after her a good seventy yards back, but not looking good.

Sorrel made a cast with her eyes and decided on her course, and set off again, still running but making for height now, putting herself to the test now, because the only hope she had left was to run leather jacket off his feet.

15

It was a long time since Carmichael had been in England. He drove up through Oxfordshire and Northamptonshire on the quiet roads. The may blossom was full on the hedges. There was green everywhere, pasture with cattle or sheep on it, crops of silage or young wheat, the parks of large houses and the lawns of lesser ones. The trees were already turning to the heavy green of summer, as if it had been a hot spring over here.

Carmichael drove slowly, the roof of the car open, the sky blue above him. He saw a church with a Norman tower ahead and slowed and pulled off the road at the gateway of the church. He got out and hoisted himself onto the graveyard wall and sat there smoking a cigarette. There was little traffic along this byroad, but he noticed everything that went past.

Carmichael thought that perhaps he missed England more than Mendham did. He could not be sure whether he actually felt a strong sentiment about it, but he liked being here. He liked this kind of day, and he liked this kind of day in the country. As to Mendham, it was hard to say. Whether it was because Mendham had been forced to leave England, or because his marriage had cracked up, one way or the other something weird had overtaken Mendham. He had never dealt with anyone so visibly untrustworthy as Mendham was now. Carmichael trusted nobody – not even Jane Winder, who seemed to hide nothing, who had been wonderful with him in bed, affectionate and kindly and obscene – but he trusted Mendham less than he trusted anyone.

He wondered why Mendham had brought him in for this job,

whether Mendham was setting him up in some way. He flicked the remains of the cigarette into the long grass at the foot of the wall, and smiled a secretive smile. If Mendham thought he was setting him up, he had another think coming.

Carmichael got back in the car.

About five miles along the road he drove round a village green and went back the way he had come, until he had reached the church again. He turned the car there and resumed his journey, drove through the village and went on. He had seen nothing to make him uneasy. No one was following him. He was clean, as he had promised he would be.

He checked in at the hotel at Crick, just off the motorway, and ate his solitary dinner with *The Times* propped up in front of him. He walked outside in the evening sun for ten minutes and made his way through the long corridors to his room at the back.

When he unlocked the door, the man he had come to see was lying on one of the beds with his hands behind his head, looking at the ceiling.

"You took your sweet time," he said.

"Negative," Carmichael said, deflecting this bit of power play with a drop shot, light over the net with a lot of spin on it. He opened a window and looked at the rabbits running about in the field beyond the fence.

"I suppose they're immune to myxamotosis now," he said.

The man on the bed turned his head till he could see the rabbits. "I don't know that they are," he said. "Not all of them certainly. You still come across it. Much smaller since the myx, though, don't you think?"

"Yes, they are," Carmichael said. "Disgusting way to set about killing them, introducing myxamotosis."

"I rather agree," the man on the bed said. "Not nearly so honest as this."

Carmichael had sensed it coming a mile off, and as the man on the bed brought a pistol from under the pillow Carmichael landed with one knee on his face and the other on his stomach, grasped the hand with the pistol in it in a ferocious grip and

133

pulled the arm to its length and chopped it at the ulnar nerve. The pistol fell to the floor and he went on over the bed and grabbed it.

He paid no attention to the man on the bed but made sure the room door was locked, checked out the bathroom, looked into the wardrobe, and then scouted from the window to make sure there was no outside backup. He closed the window and locked it, then drew the curtain.

He switched on the bed lamps and plugged in the electric kettle. "Tea or coffee?" he said. "Do you prefer decaffeinated?"

The victim of this dynamic assault rolled over on the bed and sat crouched on the edge of it, gasping to breathe. He clutched the bad arm in his good hand and watched the blood from his nose dripping onto an expensive navy blue pinstripe trouser leg.

"Damnation," he said. "You bastard, Carmichael."

"Right," Carmichael said. "That's exactly what I am, and that's exactly what you wanted to find out."

He tore open a sachet of Nescafé and emptied it into a cup. He put hot water into it and gave himself a cigarette and sat down.

The man on the bed came to his feet, preoccupied with the pain in his arm, his eye, his nose and his gut, and went into the bathroom and shut the door.

Carmichael smoked the cigarette and lit another one. He finished the cup of coffee.

The man came out of the bathroom, standing straight now, the nose no longer bleeding, the eye blinking and more closed than open, and the right arm hanging at his side.

"I don't know if I can work with you," he said. "I really don't." He sat on the bed again. "I want a drink."

"Call room service," Carmichael said.

"You are a *bastard*," the man said again, and called room service, having some difficulty because of the useless arm. He ordered two large Scotches and soda water on the side. "Don't pour it into the whisky, I'll do that myself."

134

He sat and stared at Carmichael, and Carmichael scrutinized him in return, seeing a lean, even underfleshed face, what you'd call a lantern-jawed face, long, hollowed at the temples, with dark hair lying flat now after being combed with tap water, a face half military half pirate, a rather old-fashioned British face. Three-piece suit to match, and a club tie of some sort, and a blue handkerchief with white spots in the breast pocket.

"All right," this land pirate said grudgingly. "You're everything I'd heard, but you knew I was going to do that, I know you did. You didn't have to make such a bloody meal of it."

There was a knock on the door and Carmichael went over and opened it. He took the tray from the boy and locked the door again. He made space for the tray on the locker between the beds, convenient for the other man, and went back to his chair.

"Listen," he said, "I don't play games, I don't rehearse, I don't practise. I just do."

The man on the bed took the first glass of whisky neat, in three swallows with a three-bar rest between each. He put the glass down and opened a bottle of soda and poured some into the second glass and watched the bubbles rise and explode into nothing.

"You're right," he said. "I asked for it. Damn you to hell, all the same."

Carmichael waited.

The man from MI5 said: "Your fee is £100,000. We have agreed that."

"Yes," Carmichael said.

"The man I want you to kill, when the time is ripe and not before; when I give you the signal, and not before, is a man in Army Intelligence called Harry Seddall."

Carmichael put everything he knew into controlling his face and his body and his breathing. He made no movement, did not reach for a cigarette or scratch his head or smooth the hair at the back of his neck.

For the second time in a week he felt the birthday of his life had come. If this kept up he'd be old before his time. He had an overpowering wish to go to bed again with Jane Winder.

"How high up in Army Intelligence is this Seddall?" he said.

"He's not the top, he's a colonel in rank, but he's their best," the man from MI5 said.

Carmichael pretended to look at these facts. "I guess £100,000 is about right for that," he said. "Why don't I just go and do it? Why do I wait for your signal?"

The other man drank some whisky and soda. "Because first of all," he said, "I'm going to dirty him up, get him sacked if I'm lucky, but take his reputation away at least. In that way, Carmichael, and this is important to me, there will be less anxiety when he is killed, less likelihood – none at all, I believe – of people in my business trying to find out why he's got himself killed. They will think they know why, and it will have nothing to do with you or me."

"How long will I have to wait?" Carmichael asked.

"Not long. Within a fortnight. The dirtying process has begun," the man from MI5 said.

Carmichael nodded, and allowed himself now to take a cigarette. The other man took the whisky and soda down to where there was one more mouthful to come.

Carmichael said: "The first third will be in the bank tomorrow?"

"It will be in your bank tomorrow," the MI5 man said. "Thirty-three and a third per cent. Phone the bank at noon. It has been arranged."

"It's a go, then," Carmichael said.

"So I should bloody hope," the other man said, and moved his right arm experimentally, "after all this." He took the last swallow of his Scotch and soda, and stood up. "You don't go back more than two years," he said. "Where do you come from, Carmichael?"

"You don't want to know," Carmichael said. "You don't want to find out, either. If you find out, I'll kill you."

They watched each other for a long moment, each seeing as much as he could of the other.

"What a violent fellow you are," the man from MI5 said.

"It's second nature to me now," Carmichael said.

The MI5 man went away.

16

Considine was in ruins. A helmet of bandage covered his scalp, a surgical collar held his neck, one arm was strapped to his body, and he was travelling in a wheelchair.

As he was trundled into the new Ministry of Defence building he raised his left arm up to present the wrist in front of his face and looked at his watch. He was late, but he was there.

"Get a move on," he said to the man pushing the chair, and then almost at once, "Christ! Be careful!"

To a repetition of similar exhortations they made their way to, and up in, the lift. They emerged from it to find themselves between two large Military Policemen.

"Considine," Considine said.

Along at the door to the Minister's conference room were three more. A captain, a sergeant and a corporal. The captain came towards him.

"Mr Considine," he said. "How are you, sir?"

"Never fitter," Considine said. "Get me in there, will you?"

The chair-pusher was sent down again in the lift and the captain wheeled the chair to the conference room and got Considine in there.

The Minister rose from his place. "Considine," he said. "This is above the call of duty. You really ought not to have come."

"I run the Security Service," Considine said. "If we're going to talk about this supposed mole, I have to be here."

"*Supposed* mole?" a voice said.

"Not now, Findo," the Minister said, and to the captain: "Fetch the doctor, will you?"

The doctor was a short compact man of thirty or so. He looked at the people ranged round the table, and at his patient, and took the handle of the wheelchair. "Let's go over to the windows, away from all these people," he said disrespectfully.

He shone a torch in Considine's eye, checked his pulse rate, listened to his heart, and examined the bandages.

"You're in lousy shape," he said. "Icarus after touchdown, I'd say."

"You're damn right I'm in lousy shape," Considine said. "Can you do anything about it?"

"They faxed your chart over to me," the doctor said, "you're pretty medicated already. Still, hold this, will you?"

He put a tube of pills into Considine's visible hand and went to the conference table, leaned over between Sir Edward Pinkney, Bart., of the Foreign Office and Miss Palmer, the Cabinet Office Deputy Secretary, and poured water from a carafe into a glass. He took the glass back to Considine and shook a pill out and gave it to him. Considine swallowed.

"Half an hour," the doctor said to the room at large, "and then I want him back in the ambulance and running for the Clinic. Is that understood? Meanwhile I shall wait in the anteroom and at the least sign," he sighed, "the least sign perceptible to the layman or laywoman that the patient has deteriorated I must be called in at once."

"Understood," Pinkney said.

"Where do you want him?" the doctor said.

"Here, if you will," the Minister said. "Beside me."

"Damn it, man," Considine said to the doctor as he was wheeled to the table. "I'm not a carcase in the meat market."

The doctor made none of the obvious replies. "Half an hour," he said, having parked Considine at the table, and went out, followed by the captain.

The Minister ran the edge of a hand across his smooth black hair. "You must take it as read, Considine, that I am extremely

139

happy you survived this atrocity, that all of us are extremely happy, and that we wish you a speedy recovery."

"Thanks," Considine said. "And if I may congratulate you on your escape also. Seddall did a good job there, Minister."

For the merest second the Minister looked vague, then he said: "Indeed he did."

He then inclined his head to Miss Palmer.

"Thank you, Minister," she said. "We have no more than adverted to the shelling of the chateau, Mr Considine, and are about to pass on from that, since all we know so far is that the Panhard armoured car was a version no longer in use by the French Army although sold by France to several Mediterranean and African countries, and that the explosion which destroyed it was not the result of fire by the patrol vehicles at the chateau but originated in the Panhard. The experts tell us the Panhard was programmed to self-destruct."

Miss Palmer, a frail figure of composed energy, who had beaten most of Whitehall's frontrunners to the post she held, sat back and looked at the Minister.

"General," Christopher Walpole said, "this so-called mole, if you please."

This to General Kenyon. If Seddall had been there it would have been obvious to him that Aubrey Kenyon was holding himself easy in the saddle and guiding with a light rein, as if riding across difficult and unknown country in the dark, with his senses alert for the least whisper of the enemy.

Kenyon sat back with one hand on his thigh and the other loose on the table at the end of a curved arm. There was no flash of the white teeth and no gnawing of the black moustache, and no showing of the vigour that carried him at a rate of knots up and down the swimming pool every morning. He looked like a bored lawyer at a board meeting, with his mind on dinner.

"Yes," Kenyon said. "This mole. I take it I'm going first because I'm at the bottom of the bill, since I have it only at secondhand from Colonel Seddall. According to Seddall's account he was told in a late telephone call last night by a Mr

Doffene of the Pentagon Intelligence Division that the BND in Bonn, the CIA in London, and the SCEDE in Paris, had each within the previous twenty-four hours had reports that a Soviet mole who had been here, in Britain, since and during the war, was going to make a break for Moscow, was going to be got out of the country and emerge in Moscow."

Julia Heron said: "That is the essence of it?"

Kenyon, who liked Mrs Heron, gave her a small smile across the table. "That's all of it," he said.

"It's not much, is it?" she said.

"It's not," Kenyon said.

The Minister said: "What credence does Seddall lay on it?"

"None," Kenyon said. "That is to say, none, one way or the other. Quite right too; not enough to evaluate."

"That may be so," Walpole said, "but in the present volatile state of relations with the Soviet Union it is important to put a value on it. And from the Government's standpoint and the standpoint of the Intelligence and Security Services it is vital to put a value on it. The worst-case scenario lurking there is this confounded Fifth Man the Press are always going on about. The Prime Minister, I myself, all of us, surely, are exercised at the prospect that a Fifth Man, call him X, is to be added to the Philby–MacLean–Burgess–Blunt quartet."

"It depends what he's been doing," Considine said. "If he exists, it depends on whether he's been active at all, or just lying low."

From beside Julia Heron, Lord Findo spoke. He was so slightly built as to be almost a miniature man. His face was of such a delicate structure it might have been built on a cage of chicken bones, but their formation had been kinder to him, for it was a sharply handsome face and with a good tough set to it. For all that, there was something about him. When he began to speak Julia's eyes were passing Miss Palmer, and though she saw not the least change of expression there, she detected with her woman's instinct the distaste for Findo in the woman opposite.

Lord Findo said: "Are you telling us, Considine, that as head of the Security Service you will be content that a mole who has been in Britain, for how long we cannot say but for some years, might make his way to Moscow and proclaim himself as such once arrived there – that you will be content with that, simply because he has been inactive?"

"No," was all Considine said.

"Then what are you telling us?" Lord Findo demanded. He had a light baritone voice, pleasant on the ear. None of it worked, Julia thought. She was not that taken with charming men, but less taken with charmless men, and Findo was charmless.

"I think," said Sir Edward Pinkney, "that Considine was saying that an inactive mole would have little to boast about. Also it will, it would, I should say, count for less if he had no connection with Intelligence and no connection with the Government service, whether political or professional." He flashed a smile at the head of the table. "I do beg your pardon," he said to the Minister, "I do not suggest that politicians are not professional."

"I'm not that sensitive," the Minister said. "Your point is well made. Considine, will you speak to this suggestion of a mole."

Considine had been sparing of energy, resting his depleted strength, and appeared no worse than when he came into the room. "I heard it from my opposite number in France, yes," he said. "He said they'd got it from a low-grade GRU defector who'd taken his wife from Lithuania on a shopping trip to Frankfurt. A lot of the mobile Soviets, the better off, in the Baltic states buy their clothes in Germany. However," he said, "I spoke to him on the phone this morning. He said they've lost track of their GRU man. They didn't put that much value on him as a defector per se, and he dodged his minder at the hospital they'd put him in and skipped."

Considine moved his free arm, as if in a shrug, and made a face at the pain that resulted. "I can't put a value on it either, any more than General Kenyon, but I have to put a figure for scepticism into the equation."

He looked round the faces at the table. "Arkley was with me," he said, "but Arkley's laid up. The only other first-hand account would be Seddall's. Why isn't he here?"

He looked at Kenyon, and Kenyon looked back. "I was told Seddall need not come," the general said.

In the silence that followed the Minister lifted his head and looked, as it were, at an ascending flight path receding from him along the line of the conference table.

"I am in a difficulty about Colonel Seddall," he said. "Findo?"

"Very well," Findo said. "Before the conference at the chateau," he said, "I had already spoken to General Kenyon about Seddall, being in duty bound to warn him that I had received information about Seddall that, to say the least, raised a question about him."

General Kenyon, metaphorically, readied his horse and drew his sabre. "That was the most you said, Findo. There was none of this 'to say the least' about it."

"There is a question about Seddall," Findo said. "I am developing an inquiry into Seddall, and can say no more than that. Indeed, it would be unfair to him to say more, but I cannot ignore what has been put before me."

Julia Heron, astounded and incredulous, broke all the rules of protocol. "This is totally absurd," she said. "Harry Seddall is one of the best men I ever met."

She caught Kenyon's eye and he shifted his head a trifle, telling her to stop now before she got in over her head.

It was Considine, known to be no admirer of Seddall, who saved her from rushing on regardless. "How the hell can there be a question about Seddall?" he said. "If there was a question about Seddall do you think MI5 wouldn't know about it? Personally I have no time for Seddall, but professionally I have to say he's done some extraordinary things. He's an Army man from way back, and his record there's unimpeachable. And if there's a question about Seddall, as you put it, where did you hear that question from? You're not running a service, Findo.

What are your resources? Who are you using to develop this inquiry you talk about?"

Miss Palmer, whether or no she felt distaste for Lord Findo, spoke up for Downing Street. "I do not speak within the framework of the law," she said, "but it is accepted in the Cabinet Office that there is the appearance of a prima facie case that may reach a point where it has to be answered."

Sir Edward Pinkney said: "I mean no offence to youself, Miss Palmer, but I find the language in which Seddall's reputation is being called in question too refined to inspire confidence. Minister," he said, turning his head up the table, "we can't stop at this. Either we must be told more or I, for one, cannot give credit to what Lord Findo has said."

"You have formed the Foreign Office view?" the Minister said in a voice like a whip. "You take a lot on yourself, Sir Edward." Having succeeded in stirring up his temper, the Minister found it possible to encourage Findo. "Besides," he said, "there is more to come."

A faint flush was running in Lord Findo's face, not the flush of embarrassment but of a man who found himself in his element. He sat forward in his chair and ran his quick grey eyes round everyone at the table, turning even to his neighbours to be sure of including everyone, to show that he felt complete control of the moment.

"I have resources, Considine," he said, "and what they are I may not tell you. This is the first thing."

"They're not MI5," Considine said, "and they're not Special Branch, or I'd have been told. What are you using, British Nuclear Fuels Police? Constabulary of the Royal Parks?"

To those who knew Considine as the dugong, it began to appear that being blown to hell and gone by a French 75 had effected a sea-change.

The Minister glared at the wounded Considine, and perceived the impossibility of chastising so gallant a figure. In any case, all this kind of stuff ran off Findo like water off a duck's back.

"Neither of those," he said. "So," he said, "having already, before the shelling of the chateau, a doubt about Seddall that is shared by the Cabinet Office," – Miss Palmer frowned but saw that this paraphrase of the Downing Street position could hardly be disclaimed – "I could not but notice that in removing the Secretary of State from the target area and holding him at gunpoint in another part of the chateau, Seddall," and here he paused and repeated that circuit of all the eyes in the room, "established himself also away from the target area, and that his assistant, Captain Churchyard, was uncommonly astute to suppose that the car, which was doing no more than run towards the house when he saw it, was likely to open fire and so threw himself to the floor and called for Seddall to do likewise."

The effect on those at the table was as if another shell from a French 75 had landed among them. They sat speechless as if in the first moments of trauma.

When the silence broke, it was broken in words and attitudes that remembered ancient principles of English life, as if they had been suddenly awoken in the spirits of those enured to decades of politic language and thought. They were principles that went back to Earl Bigod throwing his sword on the table, to Admiral Craddock throwing his inferior force to its doom against the German armoured cruisers at Coronel, to Oates going out into the blizzard, to Edith Cavell deploring that she had but one life to give for her country, and to Major Wolfe – who was later to cause the dying Montcalm to exclaim: "Oh God! Oh, Montreal!" – refusing to pistol a wounded Highlander after Culloden at the order of the Duke of Cumberland with the words: "My commission is at Your Royal Highness's disposal."

General Kenyon launched a look of contempt that went from Findo to the Minister, like a cannon at billiards, and said in a voice of fury: "This is infamous. Goddamit, sir, Harry Seddall saved your life! How the devil can you sit there and let this, this creature traduce an honourable and gallant soldier?"

The Minister had expected trouble, but he had not expected

this. He looked again along that imaginary flight path, and his face had paled. "Collect yourself, General Kenyon."

"Collect myself? Collect myself, sir!" Kenyon said, and came to his feet. "I'll be damned if I'll collect myself."

Sir Edward Pinkney, as pale as the Minister, also came to his feet, and as if they were at opposite ends of a seesaw, Kenyon sat down again. Sir Edward Pinkney, whose baronetcy, be it noted, had brought him nothing but itself – no rolling acres round an ancient house, no fortune in stocks and shares, not even a stamp collection – put his career on the line as Wolfe had done before the Butcher Cumberland.

"I find," he said with immeasurable scorn, "that I can no longer remain in this room."

He bowed to Julia Heron, gave the merest inflection of the same gesture to Miss Palmer, and made his way down the long table to the door. Having opened the door he turned, stared down the Secretary of State for Defence, darted a glance like a poignard at Findo, and went out.

He had left the door open behind him, and the startled faces of the Military Police showed for a moment before their captain swiftly pulled the door to again.

Julia Heron sat appalled, and all that would come into her mind in the way of articulate thought was the idea that she should move away from her seat next to Lord Findo, and that she should do so in order to make a statement, though she had no idea what that statement would be.

Accordingly, she rose and moved to the chair vacated by the departed Sir Edward, and immediately began to speak.

"Secretary of State," she said, and he gave her the floor with a movement of his head.

"At meetings such as this," Julia Heron said, "I represent the Home Office, and insofar as I attend as an individual it is only as one whose personal experience is germane to matter under discussion. It is not for me to advise the Secretary of State for Defence on a matter between himself and an Army officer; that would be for his own senior advisers, from within this Ministry."

Walpole bit his lip. Whether this was because he would have wished, with hindsight, to have had a senior adviser to support him; or because he felt that the absence of such an adviser in some way reduced the validity of the meeting; or merely that Julia was reminding him of her own standing; it was impossible to tell, but his discomfort encouraged her to go on.

"To speak first as an individual with experience of the matter under discussion, I find it my duty to advise you that in some years of experience of committees concerned with Intelligence and Security, and therefore with questions of such personnel as come before such committees, the knowledge I have acquired of Colonel Seddall leads me to confront the charges made against him by Lord Findo as contrary to all previous experience of him."

Findo came back at her at once. "You are a friend of Seddall?"

She thought of Seddall becoming hopelessly mixed up with his coat on the stairs of the Opera House, of their talk on the way to the restaurant after the opera. Yes, she was a friend of Harry Seddall.

"You mistake the character of this meeting, Lord Findo," she said. "It is not a court of law. Further, I am addressing the Secretary of State, and it would not be customary to interrupt me in my representing to him the position of the Home Office."

She waited, to see if he had anything more to say, but he did no more than continue to regard her out of grey basilisk eyes.

"As to the charges or suppositions laid against Colonel Seddall," she said, "at this moment they do not compare favourably with the case brought against Captain Dreyfus. I speak jurisprudentially," she said, as Walpole lifted his chin at her against this comparison. "In the first instance it is said that 'there is a question about Colonel Seddall', which is not much to say, and in any case the 'question' is not enlarged upon; and the second instance, the suggestion that Colonel Seddall removed you from the scene of danger in order to protect himself, we are asked to regard as being mutually sustained by and corroborative of the first.

"No court, Secretary of State, would allow a hypothesis to be built in this way on an unsupported allegation, or allow the idea that either of these strengthened, or even gave any colour of evidential merit, to the other. If Colonel Seddall, for example, asked to be court-martialled tomorrow on what is led against him, you could not do it. The Judge-Advocate would not let you do it."

The Minister raised his chin again, and again she came in fast. "I render formal advice, in the absence of formal advice being available to you at this meeting from your own Department.

"I have one more thing to say, as becomes my role here as Home Office representative, and it is this. Our understanding at the Home Office, so far as I am aware, is that Lord Findo chairs the committee considering the advisability of altering the structure of the Intelligence and Security Services. We had not understood that he in any way exercised the functions in intelligence or security matters of an executive officer responsible to a Minister of the Crown, and ultimately, therefore, to Parliament.

"I am not certain of my ground here, but I shall advise the Home Secretary to take legal opinion as to whether it is or is not constitutional for Lord Findo to exercise such functions, not being an officer of a duly constituted service entrusted with the safety of the realm. I believe that on my doing so the Home Secretary will consider himself obliged to consult the Attorney-General."

Mrs Heron thought she had finished, but she held the basilisk stare of Findo, and then looked along the table to Walpole.

"I'll say this, too," she said in a quite different voice. "You get an instinct in this line of country when you've been hunting over it as long as some of us here, and my instinct tells me there is chicane at the back of this, though at what distance behind the advice Lord Findo is receiving it is not for me to speculate."

She sat back and found herself being watched intently by

148

Miss Palmer, the voice of Downing Street. Of all those at the table, Palmer was the one who would most recognize the threat hidden in Julia's line of argument. The threat that somehow a member of Parliament might find himself adequately briefed to table a question to the Home Secretary or the Attorney-General, and so open Lord Findo's position to the more alert sections of the press.

There had been leaks enough, in all conscience, from the Civil Service before now. Julia looked as demure as she might, and met Palmer's frown with no trouble at all.

The gaze that spelled danger to her she did not meet, but felt it on her cheek as tangibly as if its owner had reached out and touched her.

It came from Lord Findo.

17

Harry met two of the chaps walking along Whitehall, a major called Hakluyt and another major called Fairn.

"Nice morning," Hakluyt said, "not sure that we're talking to you, though. One hears you did quite a number on Mr Secretary Walpole."

"Saved the blighter's life for him, that's what one hears," Fairn said.

"Anyone would have done the same," Harry said modestly.

"On the contrary," Hakluyt said, "nobody in his right mind would have done anything to prolong the existence of the unspeakable Walpole. Out to destroy the Army, Walpole is."

"Rotten thing to do, Seddall, just to get promotion," Fairn said.

"That's what it is," Hakluyt said. "Afraid he'll be stuck at colonel the rest of his life."

"Sucking up to the boss," Fairn said.

"Sucking up to the politicos," Hakluyt said earnestly, "that's what's so bad about it."

"Always thought you didn't like politicos, Seddall," Fairn said.

"I *don't* like 'em," Harry said. The three men stopped, having come to the parting of their ways. "I *want* to be stuck at colonel the rest of my life. I don't like generals either. I don't want to *be* a general."

"Goin' the wrong way about it, then," Hakluyt said. "What about your man, Kenyon? He's all right."

"Exception that proves the rule," Harry said.

"I can't hang around here listening to clichés," Fairn said. "We should ask him to dine in the mess, Johnnie. Do us no end of good to be in with a man like Seddall."

"I suppose we have to," Hakluyt said. "Must keep in with the right people. I'll send you a line, Harry, just try not to do anything like that again."

"Look forward to it," Harry said. "So long."

It was like being at school again, he thought, as he watched the two guardees walk off in their identical suits, identical bowlers, wielding identical umbrellas: like getting the piss taken for making the first eleven, all very jolly.

As he turned into the Office, though, the smile that had come to him faded. He was remembering what Kenyon had told him about Findo before he went to France.

Still, Findo would have to watch his step a bit, now that Harry Seddall was, presumably, in like silk with the Defence Secretary. It was a vulgar way to look at it, but there it was.

He reached his room, hung up the hat and coat, loaded up the coffee machine, and sat on the window ledge with a cigarette. There was fresh mail on his desk. It would wait.

The phone rang. As he left the window to go to it he noticed that the daffodils were fading suddenly. What to replace them with?

"Harry Seddall," he said.

It was the general. "Seddall," he said, "will you come up to my room, please." Kenyon sounded pretty rough; none of the usual good mornings, just straight in. "I have with me," he said, "Lord Findo."

Harry folded the letter in his hand and put it in a pocket. Lord Findo, eh? The way Kenyon spoke had been a warning, a preparation for a bad thing coming up. Harry went back to the window and put the palm of his hand behind one of the more flourishing daffodils, and jounced it lightly.

"I'll be talking to you," he said to it, and went upstairs.

*

151

Maggie Donovan stood up when he went into her office. Her hair was still chestnut. "I've to lock the outer door," she said, and did so.

"No one's to come in here while you're with the general and Lord Findo," she said. "Something's up. Do be careful. Count ten before you say anything."

"You're a nice person," he said. "Don't worry about it. I can't count up to ten, that's double figures."

"Count up to nine, then," she said.

"Nine I can do," he said. "Meanwhile, think about my daffodils. They're fading, and I'll want some quick blooms in that window box. Think about what they should be."

She smiled, but God, she looked anxious. This was all very worrying. He hardly knew the girl and she was looking anxious, as if he were a casualty already.

"The knot of your tie is under your left ear," she said, "and there's ash on your suit."

"Sure, sure," he said. "Think about the flowers for the window, will you?" and knocked on the general's door and went in.

Later, when he came out of General Kenyon's room, pulling the heavy oak door shut behind him without the least sound, as if there were a deadly ill patient behind it, she watched him come towards her.

He stopped beside her desk and she saw a tinge of red on that sallow brown tan of his. He looked, not at her, but at the door, as if he could see through it and along the corridor on the other side.

"I haven't thought about the flowers yet," she said. "I don't know enough about flowers."

"Never mind," he said, in a voice so slight she hardly heard him, "never mind about the flowers," and looked at her now, but it was as if she were a creature of no consequence.

"How did it go?" she asked.

He said nothing, only rapped his knuckles lightly on her desk by way of acknowledgement or farewell, turned the key, opened the door and went out.

When he was gone she went on seeing into those yellow eyes of his. They had been the eyes of an animal who smells the hunters on his trail, and she had read what they were saying to her: no matter what your rating in the jungle, you knew what fear was.

18

How did it go? He had heard her question and heard it still, but would not let it pass his inner ear. Before he answered it, he must first find refuge.

Tracking carefully to his room, making all the corners, taking easy steps up the flight of stairs, lifting his coat from the hanger and his hat from the hook with movements of meticulous simplicity, he cherished the suspended state that had come upon him, and would maybe last him a hundred years if he kept on moving, kept on being, not letting his mind light on anything at all.

Once in his room with his coat on his arm and his hat on his head, he sat down but knew at once that this was a mistake, so set off again as before, found his keys and locked the door, and went along and down, round the corners, along and down, down and out into the sunshine which was now not as it had been before; still as bright, to be sure, but perceived within a frame of vision that held the light in an edge of blackness: whether this was an optical thing purely, or some event in the brain, made an interesting question – it would in the future make an interesting question, but answering questions was forbidden and he let it go just in time, a risk narrowly avoided.

A taxi stopped to let down some Americans at the Banqueting House. He opened the door to them, doffing his hat courteously to the women and waiting patiently until they departed, and was surprised to find actions such as these, even to bending what felt like a pleasant expression upon them, so easy to perform.

He gave the name of a club at which the driver raised an eyebrow, since he could have walked it in no time, but the journey took place and he climbed the steps and went in to find the chief steward.

"Mr Piper," he said. "Good morning. I need a room to myself, perhaps for the rest of the day; also, a bottle of Scotch and a siphon, and a great pile of ham sandwiches. If anyone calls, I am not here."

"You are not here as often as we would wish, sir," Piper said. "If you will give me five minutes. Do you want to wait in my room? No one would intrude on you there."

"You're a great man, Mr Piper," Seddall said, and felt the miraculous control that had brought him here slipping away. "I dare say I'll be all right in the bar for a few minutes, this time of day."

In the bar, tenanted this early in the day by only three men, none of them known to Seddall, he took a stiff whisky to the window and occupied himself by staring into the street.

The question came again, too soon: how did it go? How *did* it bloody go? Like nothing you ever imagined, that's how it went, laddie. No, not yet, hang in there Seddall, Piper will be along in a minute, in a twinkling, in a trice. As he was about to call for another drink, Piper came, and led him upstairs and introduced him to a room at the back of the club.

"The key is on the inside of the door, sir," Piper said, "and I have assured myself that the bell is in working order. If you ring, no one but myself shall answer it."

Then Piper was gone, and Seddall had turned the key, and the crisis was on.

Much later he woke, lying in an armchair, and was astonished first to find that he had slept, and then by how long he had slept, for he could tell by the light in the room that it was evening.

He stretched his length, and as he came to life again from under the heavy pall of sleep the terrorizing meeting with the general and the man Findo moved forward from his memory. His eyes, without volition of his own, shifted warily over the room and kept returning to the door, until at last he stood up and crossed the room and made sure the door was locked.

That done he went to the window and looked out on the park, where a shower that came down as he slept had left its residue on leaves, grass, and flowers to glisten in the last of the sun. The trees laid long shadows on the ground where the birds fossicked at the wet earth, and dogs let loose for the last run of the day threw themselves in mad geometries across each other's tracks and put up the feeding birds, which loitered in the air until the canine riot went by, and came down again to their suppers. People strolled with their heads a little high, breathing the refreshed air under the paling blue of the sky.

"There is life," Harry Seddall said aloud to himself, "even after the Lord Findo," and went back into the room where the first of the dusk had begun to gather, and went about switching on lights.

One of them, an Edwardian contraption suspended from the ceiling by cords that ran on wheels, hung low above a round pedestal table of honey-coloured walnut, and the glow that fell from its red silk shade lit on the decanter full of whisky, the siphon in its silver basket, and Seddall's personal picnic of ham sandwiches kept fresh in an entrée dish, with pickles, mustard and what-have-you set out as skirmishers and a bowl of fruit in reserve.

With a sandwich in one hand, and a whisky and soda in the other, Seddall began to walk about the room looking at the strangely reliquarious collection of photographs on the walls: Petra, 1906, appeared in faded sepia that looked a good bit more than half as old as time. Each picture was named and dated in ink, in cobbled but legible handwriting. The Embassy garden, Constantinople, 1913, showed a woman of fifty or so with a half-manned chessboard in front of her; Constantinople, indeed, not yet Istanbul, those were the days. He liked the look of her, and hoped she was winning. He thought she probably was. A man and woman in riding breeches and boots, but standing beside an early 1930s touring car, was inscribed "In Goldie's Footsteps!" Goldie, Goldie? He knew who Goldie was, surely?

Nigeria, that was it, Sir George Goldie, founder of the Royal Niger Company. Petra, Constantinople, Nigeria – there was no logic to this collection. Seddall moved on, wandering from Africa to the Levant and across Arabia.

He completed his circuit of these dull but pleasant, anonymous but evocative, snapshots from unknown people's lives, by confronting a troop of the Sudan Camel Corps, 1933. This was a clearer photograph than the others, and the camel ridden by a subaltern on the left of the picture seemed ready to spit in his eye. He remembered the stinking slime an expectorating camel would come up with, and grinned at the creature, the malicious intent with which he endowed it lodged safe in history.

He felt the smile drier on his mouth and knew it was time to answer the question Maggie Donovan had thrown at him as he left the general's office, one long sleep and one short taxi ride ago.

"How did it go?" she had asked him.

This was how it had gone.

"Good morning, Harry," said Major-General Aubrey Kenyon.

"Morning, Aubrey."

"I don't think you know Lord Findo," the general said.

"How d'you do?" Harry said to the man sitting in the chair in the sunlight that made its direct entrance to the general's room, at this time of year, a good hour before it reached Harry's.

Lord Findo made none of the usual responses to this greeting, such as standing up to shake hands, or making a polite reply, or smiling or looking in Harry's direction. Harry found this strange. One met all sorts in Whitehall, but however contentious a meeting was to become, it was the custom to open with the superficial courtesies.

He was about to sit down in the chair waiting for him opposite the general's desk, when he saw that if he sat in it he would perceive that already sufficiently enigmatic peer as no more than an indecipherable shape against the sunlight. "Shan't be able to see," he said therefore to the general. "You won't mind if I lower the blind."

He had a glimpse of Findo making the involuntary and quickly aborted movements of protest, a hand lifting and falling again and the mouth opening and saying nothing, as he passed him those few inches too close to be quite careful of that private space a man holds round him. Fuck, Harry thought, enunciating well but silently to himself, the good Lord Findo, and pulled out a bandana handkerchief and blew his nose while he contemplated the nice day outside, and then drew the blind down slowly, and went back and sat down.

At the start of the working day General Kenyon could be relied on to look like a man who had a good battle plan ready and was all set to launch his troops against the enemy. But not this morning. This morning he looked as if the opposing general had arrived on the ground first, and had got Kenyon heavily outnumbered and with his back to the river. He looked as well founded as ever, but there was a hazed look in his eye and his body was stiff with tension.

"Lord Findo has something to say to you," Kenyon said.

Lord Findo repeated the movements he had made when Harry near-missed into his airspace, but this time he spoke. "I believe it would come better from you, General Kenyon," he said.

The voice was hi-falutin' to excess, as if it had progressed from the drawl they use at Cambridge into some Church of England bishopric. Findo was curiously small, too small, not just in height, which was not much less than Harry's: but small all over, as if he had stopped growing before he left school. The head was not much bigger than a boy's, the shoulders were narrow, the hands clasped on his stomach hardly made one fist between them.

Findo might have been short-changed in the way of size, but there was a being of some force inside that puny frame. Under a close crop of grey hair too wirelike, apparently, to lie down before the brush, was a face cast in a mould so stern and gloomy that it seemed out of place in the ordinary world, or today's world. It was a face out of another age, a portrait to find reproduced in some history of one of the darker lives of the sixteenth century.

The general, nevertheless, replied curtly to the forbidding countenance. "What you have to say to Colonel Seddall would not come better from me, Lord Findo. In fact it would not come well from me at all. It impugns the character of one of my officers, and yet you have still not made clear to me the basis on which it rests."

At this hint of what he was about to hear Seddall found that his head had dropped forward as if he had been stabbed in the vitals, which he noticed as a sudden premonitory action even as it happened. He stayed like that, his eyes on the carpet between his feet, and felt his forces gather and his whole self come alert.

Findo's reply was mocking. " 'One of my officers', General Kenyon? We are in the world of intelligence here, which is the world of spies," laying an emphasis on the word that deprecated wonderfully what it represented. You might have thought he had run a finger along a mantelpiece and found dirt. "When I hear you of the Army talk in that way, I know that the great idea behind it all, and which you are too shy to mention, is honour. There is no honour among spies, general. I understand that this morning, with myself and Seddall here face to face in your office, you feel yourself to be a passionate Dreyfusard. That cuts no ice with me."

A considerable silence followed this, and Seddall lifted his head to find that Lord Findo remained as still and sombre as if he were the Grand Inquisitor in Madrid. The general, on the other hand, was gazing at the peer, while his soldier's back grew even straighter, and gained in height until it became a vertical cliff.

Seddall, although he was able to understand that the general's display of outrage was appropriate and magnificent, could have done without it. The mention of Captain Dreyfus had built like the pealing of the tocsin on the alarm that had already sprung up in him. What was Dreyfus to him, or he to Dreyfus? He felt the adrenalin course through him at an alarming rate, and to see if he could perform a controlled physical action he took the Gauloises and the lighter from his pocket and lit one. His hands were only just steady.

Like a fox accepting the inevitable as the yelping of the pack draws near, he emerged, as it were, from the bracken. "I gather I'm concerned in this," he said. "So someone," and he found that drawing on the cigarette had taken his first deep breath for some time, and paused to let the blue smoke issue from his throat, "so someone will have to tell me what's up."

The general's head, and it might have been the movement of the commendatore's statue coming to life at the close of Don Giovanni, turned stiffly towards Seddall. Kenyon was still on his high horse, but the hand had fallen from the sword. "As you know," he said, "as I told you last week, it is Lord Findo's view, Seddall, that there is what he calls 'a question' about you," he said.

"No," Findo said, and spoke at last to Seddall, spoke neither politely nor rudely, but with a dispassionate and bloodless voice. "I have not formed, or rather my committee has not formed, a view. We have been advised that there is a question about you, and that is what I have said to General Kenyon."

It had been plain from the start that Findo was hostile, but it was only in this moment of Findo's speaking to him directly that Harry picked out of the air, where the smoke of his cigarette coiled into the quiet and filtered light in the space between them, the force of the enmity the man was directing towards him.

Yet Findo was a man he had never met, and of whose existence he had until now been no more than vaguely aware.

"I seem to hear you all right," Harry said. He let the words come out in a casual drawl, while the alarm grew inside him. When did it become panic? "It's just that I don't understand what you're saying. What does it mean – 'There is a question about me?'"

He studied Findo now with real, indeed with zealous and

profound, curiosity, and quite without thought of what he was doing, leaned forward to see into his eyes. They were grey, and they alone in that small collected being showed the intensity of the life in him. If there was emotion there, however, Harry could not make out what it was. He peered shamelessly at Findo, and Findo looked back at him. Findo's eyes showed no hatred, for example, not even dislike or repugnance, nothing to corroborate Seddall's sure and deepening knowledge that behind them was a will determined on his destruction.

The voice of his enemy, that dry and hi-falutin' and objective voice, spoke with unnatural speed, like a Minister in the House of Commons reading a reply prepared for him by his staff.

"That there is a question," it said, "about a member of our Intelligence or Security staff means that he or she cannot be counted as reliable. It does not mean that he or she is not reliable, only that it is not possible to be certain either way."

So much of Seddall's attention was given to trying to make out what lay behind the impassive exterior. The result was that the sense of Findo's words did not reach him until some time after they were spoken.

Because of this he did not leap up and punch him on the nose, or tell him he was a lying blackguard, or a shit and a liar, depending on the vocabulary of the moment. He just said: "Yes. Go on."

"Is that all you have to say?" Findo demanded. "You do not seem alarmed, or surprised. Do you have nothing to say in your defence?"

"Pshaw," Seddall heard himself say, as if he had been reading too much Dickens. "I'm not surprised because General Kenyon's told me this much already. Of course I'm alarmed, goes without saying. As to my defence, that's what I want to know, what I've to defend myself against. So tell me."

The Grand Inquisitorial face found itself a smile, a bit of a smile at any rate, as if an unused centimetre of thread had been found on the screw of the thumbikins. "I cannot tell you," it said, "until my investigators have completed their inquiry."

Harry sat back and looked at Kenyon. "Who are his investigators?"

The general looked back. His eyes were not crafty, but they were not honest either. "One, I don't know," he said. "Two, I couldn't tell you if I did, probably. All I can tell you is that you were discussed at a meeting chaired by the Secretary of State yesterday, and it was agreed Lord Findo and I should tell you of the situation." He turned his head to Findo. "Tell him the rest."

"Some play was made," Findo said, "at yesterday's meeting, with the part you played during the attack on the chateau, holding the Secretary of State in your room, at gunpoint I believe, in order to give the appearance of saving his life."

"The appearance," Harry said in a dead voice.

"Quite so," Findo said, "the appearance. I have pointed out two elements in this charade of yours – "

"Charade?" Harry interrupted him. "I see."

" – the first is the assiduous way you went round the conference questioning the French security arrangements, and making great play with the use of identical, numbered, computer-connected attaché cases," Findo said, "and the second, is that, having in this way laid the groundwork, as you fancied it to be, for you to make the inspired guess that a bomb was to be taken into the conference room, you then removed yourself from the target area of the armoured car attack by claiming to protect the Minister from a threat to his security."

Seddall had been carrying the start of his extensive sentence in his head since it began. He was amazed with how well his brain was working. "Pointed out to whom?" he said.

"To the Cabinet Office, to which as you should know, I report directly," replied Findo, as who would say, I have the Emperor's ear, "and to the Secretary of State himself, to Christopher Walpole."

"To Walpole," Seddall said. "And what did Walpole say to that?"

"He conceded," Findo said, "the unassailable logic of my argument." Findo turned his fine and miniature head to

Kenyon. "As a result of these questions about you, Colonel Seddall, it was agreed at the meeting that General Kenyon should say to you what he will now tell you."

"Hold on a moment," Seddall said. "Are you telling me I am now thought by the Cabinet Office and the Defence Secretary to have been behind the attack on the chateau? If so, what am I doing sitting here listening to you? Why am I not in the Tower of London or somewhere?"

Seddall was deeply interested in his own behaviour, which he felt to be unbalanced. He was aware that the panic he kept expecting to feel had very likely set in already, and that it was perhaps this which had put him in the rather odd state where he was suspended from receiving the full reality of what was happening to him.

He knew that he was in the very act of being dealt a major wound by this man; that the trauma protected him from the pain; and that fear prevented him from opening his eyes to the severity of the wound.

"Why am I at liberty?" he said. "Why have Special Branch or the Military Police not charged me?"

The general, who had been quiet too long for his own comfort, came on very formal. "Lord Findo goes too far – "

"I do nothing of the sort," Findo said at once.

"Yes, sir," the general said. "By God you do. All that is held against you, Harry, is suspicion of Heaven knows what brought against you by these mysterious investigators of Lord Findo's. And on top of that, this, this twisted argument of his about the chateau."

Harry smiled at Findo, and was shocked to see the change in the other man's face. It must have been a bad smile. "So tell me, Aubrey," he said, still watching Findo, "where do I stand on this business at the chateau? Did I have a good hunch, albeit for the wrong reasons, and save his life, or did I train these people in the armoured car that shot the place to hell?"

"Lord Findo is to be given time to develop his inquiries," Kenyon said. "As far as this office is concerned, I am to send you on indefinite leave until these matters are cleared up one way or the other."

"Are you, by God?" Seddall said, and moved his eyes to Kenyon. "And to think that out there," he nodded out of the window, "not an hour ago, I was saying that you were the exception among generals."

"That's enough," Kenyon said. "Remember who you're talking to."

Still with his eyes on Kenyon's, Seddall said: "Yes, sir. I do."

He stood up, feeling his muscles as fatigued as if he'd just done a fifteen-mile hill walk. He had a thought, and sat down again. He leaned towards Findo and prodded him on the knee-cap.

"I just don't accept what you're doing to me. Oh, yes, for the time being I'll go wherever it is I go while you and your henchmen get up to your little tricks, but," he said, "I'm not going to take all this shit lying down. You've set out to wreck me without a shred of evidence. For some reason you simply haven't got the guts to utter. Well, all right, fine. Just don't think, don't for one moment think, that you're going to get away with it. You play dirty, Findo, I'll play dirty, and before I'm finished with you you'll find there are rules being broken that you've never even heard of."

"You are threatening me," Findo said. "Hear him, General, he is threatening me!"

"I have not heard him threaten you," Kenyon said.

"There you are, then," Harry said to Lord Findo. "Where the offence is, let the great axe fall."

Findo's head flicked to the side as if he had been struck, but he came back in a way that, in some other situation than this, might have earned Harry's respect. "Th'offence," Findo said. "Where th'offence is, let the great axe fall."

Harry got up again, felt a trembling in his body but disciplined it as hard as he might. He went out, and closed the door behind him very softly, very gently.

That was how it had gone.

*

"I'm a little drunk," he said.

She leaned on the doorpost. The dog Bayard stood at her knee. "Not on my account, I hope," she said.

"You stole that from a movie," he said. "Cary Grant said it to, to this woman. No, not on your account. I've got trouble, Olivia. I'm in deep trouble."

She took his hand and walked him inside like that, hand in hand. "You've been drinking whisky," she said. "Do you want whisky, or will you have coffee? It is just made."

"Coffee. Thank God you're here," he said, and then as one making a discovery, so that she was more puzzled than hurt, "but you'll have to leave here," he said to her. "It's not safe for you, not now."

"Be calm," she said. "Let me have your coat. That's right."

In the drawing room Bayard put his chin on the arm of Seddall's chair and regarded him with his tail waving a slow and steady emotional pulse.

"He knows I'm in trouble," Harry said.

The black cat Sacha, a more selfish and neurotic creature, stayed up on the piano and lashed her tail against the atmosphere of this trouble.

"Yes," Olivia said, "I think I do too, but I'm not going away. I'm not going home so soon, now that we've met."

"You have to leave this house, Olivia," he said. "I was followed home; quite openly. These people will do anything. At the very least, and I mean the very least, they might go through the house. So I want you out of it."

"I'm not going back to France," she said. "If it is necessary, then I'll go to a hotel. So, why don't you tell me about all this trouble you are in." Olivia settled on the floor with her coffee and tucked his dressing gown round her knees.

He told her about his day. She faced him and watched him through all of it. Under the stroke of Seddall's hand on his head, Bayard settled beside him and drooled onto the carpet.

"Harry, my very dear man, what will you do?"

He had spoken to her as one recounting a history, a personal history; so that at moments of recollected emotion he broke off, and ceased stroking the dog to wipe at the tension on the back of his neck.

Now, when she asked him what he would do, a wild look came into his face. "Well," he said. "'I shall do such things, I know not what they are, but they shall be the terror of the earth.' That's what Good King Lear said, and you've got to be clear of here while I do them."

"Then I will be," she said, "but I will not go back to France."

"Olivia," he said, "I can't have you go to a hotel. I'd feel truly bad to think I'd asked you to leave my house and go to a hotel. Will you go down to the country with Mrs Lyon?"

"To the country? To where in the country?"

"I have a house near Wells in Somerset."

"That makes me very happy, Harry," she said. "Yes, I'll go there."

"Tomorrow," he said. "First thing."

19

Charles Doffene stepped onto the rue des Saussaies and made his way towards the Champs Elysées. His limber and vigorous stride took him rapidly along the avenue de Marigny with no appearance of haste, and he went past the armed soldiery outside the Elysée Palace without a sideways glance. He was a man occupied with his thoughts, as indifferent to the fact that he was passing the Presidency of the Republic as to the unseasonal rigour of the day: one of those where the clouds persist as no more than a veil to obscure the warmth of the sun and the blueness of the sky, and tantalise you with the knowledge that above them, up there, it is fine weather.

No more aristocratic figure had walked Paris in the time of the Bourbons. The slim height, the carriage of the head, the active but inscrutable eye, and the harsh composure of the dark face, combined into a distinction that separated him from those among whom he moved. When he stopped opposite the Marigny Theatre a taxi wavered at the sight of him, and at the slightest movement of his head came to the kerb.

The car was a Mercedes, tolerably new, and whisked him with an exhilarating apportionment of risk and skill across the river and down the boulevard St Germain until he called it to a halt.

There were plenty of people sitting outside the café, confident that the sun would emerge triumphant at the imminent hour of noon, but Doffene went through the doorway in the wall of glass and polished wood, and found Jennifer already entabled.

"Hi," she said, as he sat down. "Not good, huh?"

"No," Doffene said. "Not good." He looked around him. "Pretty busy."

"Don't excite yourself," Jennifer said. "It's coming, a large espresso and a cognac. I saw you out there paying off the cab."

"Excite myself," he said, "that was excitement?"

"For you, that was excitement," she said.

The drinks arrived.

"What's the scoop?" Jennifer said, when they had regaled themselves a little.

"The scoop," said Doffene, "is that forensic has come up with the news that there is nothing for forensic to come up with in the remains of that scout car."

"Armoured car, for God's sake," Jennifer said. "It was carrying a damn great cannon, Charlie."

"I stand corrected," Doffene said, and produced a piece of paper from his pocket. "It was a Panhard AML-90 armoured car and almost as out of date as Noah's Ark, but in the seventies they were being sold to half the states in Africa and a couple in South America." He put the paper away again. "This was a specially adapted model, though. This baby was provided with an incendiary device probably time-triggered by the first firing of the gun, a very warm incendiary device. The crew went down to zilch at so many thousand degrees centigrade the heat of it would have melted the Arctic icecap. There is nothing in there, Jennifer, but a smear of burnt meringue."

"I guess it's what we expected," Jennifer said. "It's certainly what I expected when I saw the wreck up there."

"I know, but I also expect those forensic geniuses to come up with miracles, because they sometimes do."

"Not this time. So that's that trail closed off."

"Yeah. That leaves us looking at the arms dealers, and that's all it leaves us looking at."

He finished the coffee and gave himself what would have been a jolt of cognac, except that the cognac was so smooth.

"Ah," he said, and his face, at last, looked pleased with itself. "When's Nick joining us?"

"I was just going to tell you," Jennifer said. "Nick's gone to Brussels."

"What for? Is he going home?"

"No, you dope. Why would he go home by Brussels? Do you know where Brussels is? It's in Belgium."

"Take it easy. I can't think wisely and well all the time. So why's he gone to Brussels?"

"He went to see Sir John Arkley this morning, who is coming along not bad, considering he's just had a leg blown off. Pretty sick and weak, but able to talk a little. And what Arkley wants," Jennifer said with a kind of grim and approving satisfaction, "is to get even. Nick told him the line he was on was the merchants of death, that he was trying to source the car, this Panhard? Arkley told him to go and see a man in Brussels."

When he had made a contract with the waiter for more refreshment, Doffene said: "This man in Brussels: who's he?"

"Who knows?" Jennifer said, and gently napkined an inebriated wasp off her white cashmere lapel. "Arkley told Nick the man owes him. He's calling in the debt. Arkley said to Nick: '*Fiat justitia, ruat coelum*'. It means: 'let justice be done, though the heavens fall'."

Doffene looked at her. "Thank you," he said.

"The idea being, that if the guy doesn't come through, the heavens will fall on him."

"I don't know what that's got to do with justice."

"I guess Arkley's being a bit subjective. If I were in Arkley's shoes, I would be too."

"Shoe," Doffene said. "Shoe."

"You didn't have to say that. In any case, Arkley wasn't just being rhetorical. He told Nick that would be the password."

"*Fiat justitia*," Nick Churchyard said into the telephone at the airport.

169

"*Ruat coelum,*" the voice said.

The voice gave him an address, and directions. The address was not in Brussels. "Hire a car. No taxis."

Churchyard drove towards Leuven and turned off south on the road to the place called Everberg. The house was easy to find. It stood by itself behind half an acre or more of neat, colourfully bedded, but characterless garden. It was one of those modern houses now commonplace in France and Belgium that stood on a mound which concealed the cellar; a graceless building on a dull tract of land.

It occurred to Churchyard, however, that it afforded a clear field of view for miles around, and when he drove in and round the house he saw that it boasted a rear drive (of a length that would have cost, in his terms, a fortune) which ran westward for a good half mile, a ribbon of fresh tarmac as straight as an arrow that joined another road from that by which he had come.

On the apron where he parked his hired Peugeot was a Lancia-Maserati, the car that looked at first sight like an ordinary Lancia until you noticed the badge; a car that would rip down that back drive in seconds.

The man who opened the heavy oak door was short, with great breadth of shoulder. A man in his forties with hair cut *en brosse*, and one of those French businessman's faces that show energy and experience, but have retained a trace of the cheerful vitality of the schoolboy.

He said nothing but gestured vigorously with his arm, and Churchyard found himself in a living room whose furnishings might have been bought in one lot out of a large store.

He went over to one of the windows. He struck the glass with his knuckles. The sound was solid and the vibration nil. "You're a careful man," he said.

"Yes," his host said.

He was not, however, playing the part of a host. He did not ask Churchyard to sit and he offered him nothing to drink, neither tea nor coffee nor alcohol.

"You deal in arms yourself, Monsieur . . .?" Churchyard said.

"Don't be a fool," the man said. "You can find out who I am, what I do, from our mutual contact, but we are not here for that. We are here for one thing only."

"All right," Churchyard said. "Who sold that old Panhard to whom?"

"To whom, I have no idea of any kind. Who sold it I don't know, but I have made an educated guess as to three men the most likely, and another educated guess as to who is the most likely of these three; this last is a very educated guess, and I think it was he. You may write down the three names and where they live, because if I insisted on your memorising them you would write them down anyway as soon as you were out of here.

"But first: you have never been here. Your life hangs on that, I give you my assurance and that of our mutual contact to this effect. If you divulge anything of me or this place of meeting to anyone, even the team you are working with, even to your boss, whoever he is, you will be a dead man."

"That's coming it a bit," Churchyard said. "Our mutual contact would never go for that."

"You are quite ignorant. Our mutual contact certainly would. Do not doubt it. Ask him when you see him. This is a world you know nothing about, and – you want some advice? – you want to live long enough to know *anything* about it, you grow up very fast and learn to be very, very frightened."

He took time out to study Churchyard receiving this, and digesting it. Then he said: "I am sorry it is you. I would not like to work with you. You think you can dip your toe in this world and be part of it. This is not so. You dive in and swim, little man, or you remain a dilletante and a danger to everyone. No one will want to know you. Excuse me for one moment," he said, and went out of the room.

Churchyard caught glimpses of him through the open door as he passed in and out of the hall. He went in and out of the rooms of the house, that was all, and when he came back in again he went to each of the windows and looked out.

He turned back into the room. "All right," he said to

Churchyard. "Here are the names, the best name first. Get out your pen and paper."

When he was done he said without irony, as to a child: "Now tuck them away safely in your pocket. That's right."

He escorted Churchyard to the door of the house, and when Churchyard was outside, the man said: "Wait. Listen to me. I have meant everything I said. Remember also what you said, that I am a careful man."

He shut the door.

Churchyard, driving away, was for a while stunned by the way he had been dealt with. Then he began to feel humiliated.

20

Seddall sat in the Ristorante Calabrese and waited moodily for Lethington.

He was moody because he was a long way from home, and because somehow he seemed to have got into a state of war with the management. He was not so far from home as these Italians were from their Calabria, but in this particular ristorante on the outer edge of west London he felt himself an exile in a far land. Tables and chairs were varnished to a yellow that outshone the going down of the sun on Annapurna's snow; businessmen like gangsters in sharp suits entertained each other and their women on a scale that spoke either of high generosity or low dealings with the Inland Revenue; and in a loud voice from many speakers burning Pavarotti loved and sang.

The war had started when the waiter presented the menu, which was bound in full calf and impressive enough to have been a Heads of Government signature copy of the Treaty of Versailles.

"You will have something to drink while you wait for your friend?"

"My friend?"

If the tall, handsome, stupid-looking young man from the shore of the Tyrrhenian Sea had known Lethington, he might have understood that the idea of his being a friend would be a hard thing for Seddall to accept. Instead he was baffled, a condition which southern Italians detest.

"You have reserved for two? We do not take bookings for only one on Saturday nights."

He had withdrawn the offered menu three inches, and Seddall reached out and took it from him, both acting instinctively like two children tussling for possession of a prized object, so that when Seddall pulled it from the man's resisting fingers it was a declaration of war.

"It is a reservation for two," Seddall said. "I shall eat now, my colleague will arrive at nine."

Together they looked at their watches.

"But it is just eight o'clock!" the waiter exclaimed.

"Yes. Five past, I make it," Seddall said. "I don't want an aperitif. I'll have a large espresso. You have espresso?"

"Espresso!" The waiter was astounded. "You reserve a table to have an espresso? You don't want dinner? You don't need the menu?"

He grabbed the treasured volume, but Harry, whose verbal agility had been left behind by the speed with which the other raced to wrong conclusions, abandoned explanation and kept a firm hold on it.

"Stop that," he said.

The waiter went away.

People at the tables round about cast hostile glances at Seddall as if he was a problem and therefore had no right to be there, and one man in particular peered at him, through eyes half closed by cigar smoke, for longer than the rest. It was a hard stare, steady as a rifle barrel aimed across the nice bare shoulder of the woman opposite him. The woman turned to see the target of this unwavering regard and Harry smiled at her, a bit lopsided since he had just finished lighting a Gaulloise and the cigarette was still in his mouth, but then his smile was often like that.

She laughed at him over the nice shoulder. Her companion moved his stare to her and said something short and violent, and she turned back to him, still laughing and fanning a hand in the air above their table to disperse the smoke of his cigar; but before her eyes left Harry they had given him a look of such candid friendliness and sudden, intimate inquiry, that he found himself elevated into a better frame of mind. The black hair and that message from the dark blue eyes roused him to a state of pleasant speculation.

Even when the foreground of his vision became the red white and green sash that separated the white shirt of the waiter from the black trousers, he refused to descend from the better mood he now occupied. He was helped in this by the fact that the waiter brought with him the double espresso, and spilled none into the saucer as he set it down. Seddall and the waiter examined one another. Neither showed remorse, but hostilities had plainly been suspended.

Seddall ordered Parma ham and chicken cacciatora.

The waiter wrote this down. "You *do* want to eat," he said, and nodded to himself. "Then perhaps you want some wine now too."

"Perhaps I do," Seddall said. "Suggest something."

The waiter thought about this: was it an aggressive command, or a continuance of the peace? "Brunello di Montalcino," he said.

"Good."

The waiter thought again, recalling the word Seddall had used to describe Lethington. "You are not waiting for your colleague? You will eat alone?"

Clearly this peculiarity, which had been the cause of their little war, was inexplicable. Seddall sought to console him. "I have my book," he said, and illustrated this by stroking its pages where it lay open before him on the table.

He moved his hands aside as the waiter reached for it. "Catherine de Medici," he said, reading the title page, "by Pasolini. A tough woman," he said approvingly, and as if apologizing for knowing already what Seddall might not have read far enough to discover, he added: "My sister lives in Florence. She is a tough woman too."

"Catherine de Medici was a strong woman," Seddall said, "but tender as well."

The waiter frowned. Was this stress on the nuance between two words a breach of the truce? He gave Seddall the benefit of

175

the doubt. "Strong, tough." He departed, and came back with the ham and its attendant melon. So with his book open at the chapter telling how the gallant Catherine prepared Forli to meet the onslaught of Cesare Borgia, Seddall fell to.

As the meal and the siege of Forli progressed, the relationship between Seddall and the waiter continued to improve; the laments, rages, and exhilarations of Pavarotti in his various roles were muted at the request of a party of newcomers; the vivacities and laughter of the woman with the beautiful bare shoulders seemed increasingly to Seddall to be directed at himself rather than at the ill-favoured man opposite her, and since she had her back to Seddall he found this feeling within him to be of particular portent; and altogether he came to a favourable view of the Ristorante Calabrese, which earlier he had so much disliked.

As the Gorgonzola followed the chicken, however, and although the wine of Montalcino grew less in the bottle and more inside Seddall, the approach of nine o'clock diminished his sense of well-being as if a shadow had fallen across the sun.

Tonight the shadow took palpable form. The table to Seddall's left, which had been empty since half-past eight, was occupied by a youth and two girls who talked vigorously, busied themselves with menus, with disposing of purses, lighting cigarettes, and laughing hard at the slightest opportunity, all this with closed faces and the physical restraints of nervous actors at an audition. None, though he looked openly at them, looked at Seddall. The table at his left was then occupied by two men of about thirty, a pair of heavies in sober suits who came gracelessly close to the table while their predecessors were still collecting themselves to leave. One of the two allowed himself a long sight of Seddall as if his eyes were making a mental photograph of singularly slow aperture.

After these outriders, sharp on nine o'clock, Lethington came.

Six feet tall but with the appearance of being taller by reason of his thinness, lanky but with a muscular stride and active bearing, dark brown hair with a red tinge to it and clipped moustache of the same, he came in at the door and walked straight to Seddall to sit down across from him in what could have been no more than a one-second clip of film. He had a long death's head with hollow cheeks, hollows to hold his eyes, and a hollow under the jawbone. The eyes shifted all the time, casting about for errors, exits, surprises; the eyes of a witness testifying under oath in a bad cause. They were brown, and moved out of step with the head, for if it turned on its overlong neck to the left they lingered on the right, and by the time they moved left to conform the head was off somewhere else again. The physical movement was a symptom of the man's restless, probing, ambitious interior character. There was no peace to be had near him.

"Lethington," Harry said warmly, "Good to see you."

Lethington made a sound in his throat like a dog's bark, and showed long clean teeth in a smile. "Don't give me that, Seddall. You'd as soon see a spider in your soup as me across the table. So how are you? Are you going to make trouble? Or are you going to go quietly? Resign your commission or whatever you people do and just fade away."

"Oh, fade away, I think," Harry said. "The forces arrayed against me are too strong. Fade away, that's the thing."

"I'll just bet you will, you busy little bastard. You're a better liar than I am, Seddall, and that's saying something."

He picked up the wine bottle and read the label. "Not bad for a dump like this," he said. He filled a glass in front of him with the last of the Montalcino and drank half of it at a gulp. "Not bad," he said again, and drank the rest of it.

"You like the dregs?" Harry said.

"What dregs? That stuff's only four years old. Anyway, I'm not one of your Fancy Dan Whitehall wine warriors, as you perfectly damn well know." He looked off to one side and yelled: "Waiter!" At the same time his right arm rose vertically into the air and stayed there. He waited like that, silent and unmoving, for a full minute, until the waiter came up on his left side.

"You want the menu, sir?"

Lethington brought his right arm down and looked at his left wrist. "No, I don't want the menu, we've used up our time for that. I want food. You've eaten already," he said to Harry, "for some mysterious reason of your own, and you're still alive. What did you have?"

Harry told him.

"I'll have the chicken." He took the empty bottle by the base and held it back over his shoulder. "Another bottle of that." He had not looked at the waiter.

The waiter looked at Harry as if he was beginning to understand what war was really like. "You don't want the Parma ham?" He took the bottle by the neck.

Lethington studied the tips of the fingers that had been holding the bottle, as if there might be some news about Parma there. "I don't want your ham. I want your chicken cacciatora, and I want a lot of boiled potatoes, and I want a bottle of wine."

There was something heartbroken in the waiter's face, so Harry kept all sympathy out of his own, not to make it worse for him. Lethington had taken the whip hand and if there was nothing the waiter could do about it, there was nothing for anyone else to do either.

When the waiter had gone, Harry said: "Where'd you get your manners from?"

"From my dear old grandmother, I expect," Lethington answered, and came out with a hugely pleasant smile, remarkable in such an awful man. "I'm having a nice time," he said. "Don't spoil it."

He picked up Harry's pack of Gaulloise from the tablecloth and took two from it, passing one over. "You must have got here an hour early," he said. "Looking the place over?"

"Why would I do that?" Harry lit the cigarettes. "Are we going to discuss matters of State security? I could have come to Curzon Street to do that. Then you wouldn't have had to stack the table with deaf ears."

Lethington straightened himself and took in the two heavies talking in widely spaced monosyllables to his left, and the vivacious trio acting out their over-scripted three-hander on his right. "They're mine all right. You were smart to pick them out, Seddall, but not that smart, and you know it." He crouched over the table again. "Because *they're* not that smart, and you know that too. What they are, all of them, is straight, safe, secure – and they're mine. So here I can talk to you, in this neck of the woods where no one ever comes."

"Once more," Seddall said. "I could have come to Curzon Street, or you could have come to Defence."

Impatiently Lethington put out his cigarette in the ashtray. "It is for privacy that we have come here," he said. "It is for privacy that we have my people sitting on either side of us. I want to talk to you privately and I don't want any gossip about us meeting."

Harry watched a short stout man in a dinner suit approach carrying a plate of what might well be chicken cacciatora, and in his wake the familiar waiter with a bottle of wine. "You expect me not to gossip?" he said.

"That's what I expect."

As Lethington spoke the dish was put in front of him together with another holding potatoes and green beans. Without removing his attention from Seddall he said at once: "I asked for lots of potatoes, and I did not ask for beans."

No one answered him. The waiter looked at the stout man who nodded, and the waiter then displayed the wine to Lethington, who said simply: "More potatoes, no beans."

In response to another nod, the waiter set the bottle on the table and withdrew. The stout man remained behind Lethington's elbow. He was big in the shoulders and the dinner jacket sat well on them. He had a round head, almost bald, a smooth brown-skinned face, and black eyes, calm and controlled, but with some other quality in them that moved Seddall to look at the table where the two heavies sat. Sure enough, they were poised and ready, watching the stout man as if he might pull a knife or a gun at any moment. All this over potatoes, Seddall thought.

He turned back to the tableau across his own table and saw

that the stout man was aware of the two heavies, for he let a corner of his mouth twist dismissively as his eyes met Seddall's. When Seddall moved his eyes down to Lethington's he was surprised to see nothing in them but merriment.

"This is not the man who was here before, is it, Harry?" he asked.

"No, this is a different man."

"Do you think if I eat my potatoes like a good little boy, I'll get some more?"

The stout man pulled out the empty chair beside Lethington and sat down. "This is my restaurant," he said, with a lot of Calabria in his voice. "If you ask *me* these questions about potatoes, you won't get to eat any potatoes, any cacciatora."

"No wine either, I suppose," and Lethington moved his torso to face the man directly.

"No wine."

"Out?"

"Out."

Lethington flicked a glance half way to the heavies and back to the stout man and raised his eyebrows.

The stout man looked at his knees and up at Lethington and shook his head. "Out," he said again.

Lethington rasped the palm of his hand down the side of his face. "Do I have to eat the beans too?"

The stout man reached over and took one of the beans and ate it, then picked up the napkin beside him and touched his mouth and wiped the tips of his fingers with it. "If it were me," he said, "I should eat the beans. Nothing wrong with them."

"I'll eat the beans." He brought out that refulgent smile. "Enjoyed meeting you," he said.

The stout man went on looking at him for a little and then said, "Yes, you have. I can see that."

Lethington, suddenly, wore a very grave expression. "You don't reciprocate?"

The stout man leaned forward towards him. "You will not eat here again. They," and he jerked a thumb over his shoulder, "will not eat here again." He pointed at the now rather subdued trio at the other table. "They will not eat here again."

Lethington's right elbow rested on the table, and he swung the hand round to point the forefinger at Seddall. "What about him?"

"He will be welcome," the stout man said, and immediately noticing the breach of politeness in having referred to Seddall in the third person, he said to him directly: "You will be welcome."

"Why he, and not these three, at any rate?"

The stout man shifted his gaze to the two girls and their escort. "Because you belong to an organization and you are being unserious with the power that gives you. I don't know what your organization is and don't want to know. I just don't want it around."

Lethington, in his turn, leaned close to the other man. "How do you know he doesn't belong to it?"

The stout man shook his head once, to say the question was merely trivial.

"You know my organization could put you out of business?" Lethington said, still leaning close.

The man's face changed for no longer than it takes a bat to flit across the moon, and then was the same as before, but in the glimpse it had shown a menace so violent, and so sure of its power, that Seddall knew it spoke of something more than a hidden character in the individual.

Lethington, it seemed, thought the same, for he asked: "Where do you come from?"

The stout man, who had said nothing to Lethington's previous question, said nothing to this one either. It was as if he listened to Lethington simply in order to learn. Now he put his hands on his knees and sighed. "There is still steam from the cacciatora," he said, "but if you want I shall send over fresh vegetables."

Lethington held up a hand, conceding defeat. "No, I shall eat these."

The stout man nodded once more, then he said: "The waiter is a better man than you. It is just that he is still young. *He* is not scum."

Lethington's body convulsed where he sat, but he met the man's eye while his chin jerked up and the colour rushed to his face.

The stout man stood up, but still he watched Lethington. "*Buon appetito*," he said at last, and went away.

Lethington continued, lost in a trance, to confront the space where he had been, then turned stiffly to the table.

"Game, set and match to the home team," he said, and peeled a great gobbet of the stewed chicken off the bone with his fork and stuffed it into his mouth. While he was chewing this he tipped the potatoes and some of the beans from their dish onto his plate and began crushing the potatoes into the gravy like a schoolboy free of supervision.

"You can eat his food?" Harry said. "We're not leaving?"

"I can eat his food, and you can bet your favourite escritoire we're not leaving," Lethington said, and gathered a hummock of mashed potato lovingly onto his fork.

"I'm surprised you can stomach it. I'm surprised it doesn't stick in your throat."

"Nothing sticks in my throat." Lethington shoved the potato into his mouth and swallowed it at a gulp, as if to demonstrate the flexibility of his gullet.

"Eat your nice beans," Harry said.

"Fuck you," Lethington said cheerfully, but he took in a forkful of the green beans.

Such resilience after humiliation, in a man of Lethington's pride and temper, was alarming. Seddall thought he knew quite a lot about Lethington, but this volatility pointed to a degree of confidence in himself that was so exalted it was overweening, and if Harry had been sure what psychopathic meant he might have applied that description too.

He knew that Lethington, who was now chomping chicken, potatoes and beans with vigorous enjoyment, had been angry enough a few minutes ago to kick the stout man in the balls and out of his chair if he had wanted to; and he knew that he had wanted to and would have done it, even had he been here entirely on his own, if the impulse took him.

Lethington, therefore, had restrained himself because he had an agenda for this meeting, and set some store by it. Lethington was on a scent and would let nothing lift his nose from it in case he lost the line.

The object of these reflections belched softly and wiped his mouth thoroughly with his napkin. "Well, Harry," he said. From the triumphant, rotten expression on him Seddall knew a bad moment had come.

"Well Harry what?" he asked.

Lethington angled his face towards the greasy plate in front of him and looked up at Seddall. "Your place or mine, Harry? This place has served its purpose."

"I've got a headache," Seddall said. "Why don't I just drop you off?"

Lethington lifted his head and smiled with those good white teeth, but he said nothing.

Seddall said nothing too, and lifted his hand to ask for the check, but Lethington laid a gentle finger into Seddall's cuff and coaxed his arm down.

"There's something you need to hear, Seddall. You're in a trap, and I laid it for you. So, your place or mine?"

"I don't want you in my house," Harry said, "but we'll go there."

Lethington took a piece of bread from the basket and wiped it around and about on the cold refuse of his plate, and put it in his mouth.

He poured himself a glass of wine and washed it down.

21

The dog was sitting on the hall floor when Harry came home, but Sacha the black cat waited on top of the piano in the drawing room to exchange those caresses of mutual respect which must be conducted at a level.

These courtesies accomplished, Harry went through to the kitchen to put decaffeinated grounds in the coffee filter, and then returned to the drawing room where he sat in an armchair with the dog at his knee and the cat ensconced on the back of the chair opposite.

"We three," Harry said, fumbling the cigarettes out of his pocket, "make a lot of wisdom in one room, the intellects, imaginations and experience, of one cat," – he employed Sacha's order of precedence – "one human, and one dog, hey Bayard?" He scratched the dog's ear with his lighter and lit the Gaulloise, taking in a large draught of smoke and letting it trickle slowly out of his mouth.

Bayard licked Harry's hand, but Sacha simply watched.

"You've got the right instincts, old son," Harry said to Bayard. "This thing is getting to be very messy, and I'm in the middle of it. And this bastard thinks I'm down on the ground already, and he's got himself set to put the boot in."

He was pleased to see Sacha show concern. At least she stopped licking the paw with which she had just started to wash her already glossy pelt, and looked at him.

"The thing is," he told the cat earnestly, but then he found he didn't know what the thing was. Sacha blinked at him, the paw still suspended, wanting more.

Harry waved his cigarette about expressively, and Sacha stopped being wise and became foolish, weaving her head about like a mongoose facing an unusually vivacious snake. "Simmer down," Harry said. "It's quite simple, really. Either we fight the good fight and win, or the three of us can retire now and go and live in the country. Sure, we'll retire under a cloud, but who cares about a blot on the escutcheon?"

Bayard shifted his position, and Sacha thought of moles, voles, mice, and the innocence of rabbits. "On the other hand," he said, "it's not much of an escutcheon as it is. Why make it worse?"

The three of them communed in silence after that until the doorbell rang, and Harry let in his unwanted guest.

"We meet again," Lethington said, but to the dog, not to his host. Bayard backed and turned and went off to his basket in the kitchen. "You should get yourself a guard dog, Seddall."

Seddall went slowly into the drawing room while he worked out this business about Bayard and guard dogs. He sat down and when Lethington came in said to him: "You've been into this house?"

"I most certainly have. Went through it with the lads six weeks ago."

"Since you're here to talk to me privately, as you put it, does that mean the lads were in again this evening to check it out for you?"

"Of course they were. If I'm going to bare my soul I don't want it recorded on some crafty in-house system, do I?"

At the notion of Lethington baring his appalling soul a particularly insulting smile came onto Seddall's face, and he let it stay there for as long as it wanted, because he was finding it hard to come to grips with the emotions that had burst open inside him at the news that Lethington had put a team through his house.

Anger was uppermost, but a deep feeling of violation, the astounded sense that the natural order of things had been subverted, was the cause of it. The strength of these feelings bewildered him, and he was shocked that he was bewildered, and began to wonder if he was now afraid of Lethington.

Seddall had a detestable vision of how it must have been, the team devoted to their business of rummaging, reading and copying, taking colour pictures of every room like estate agents with a sideline in blackmail; while Lethington himself prowled slowly through the house, turning door handles that Seddall habitually turned, sitting in chairs he sat in; opening drawers to scrutinize their contents, stroking furniture, studying paintings, rugs, and views from windows; turning the leaves of books, weighing silver in his hand, peering at china, making a piece of crystal ring with the negligent flick of a fingernail while he stood there sniffing out the nature of the man whose home this was.

He was at it now, his head cocked towards the painting of the Seine at Pontoise while he played with the stopper of a decanter on the table beside him, and his attention roved from there, from the picture of the riverside town and the crystal in his hand, to the black cat Sacha – back on top of the piano but at the edge farthest from the intruder – and to Seddall, of whose life these objects and that creature were all part.

Suddenly, watching him, Seddall had had enough. "Sit down, Lethington," he said, "and get it over. I don't keep those pictures for people like you to look at, and the men who painted them wouldn't like it either."

Lethington let the stopper drop gently into the neck of the decanter. "What do you think this is?" he said, "the fourth form at St Dominic's?" He came down the room. "Do you know what this is?" He stood in front of Seddall, his tall lean figure with its death's-head face impassioned by some internal energy, and flourished an arm round his head like a fanatical tank commander signalling the start of a desperate attack. "This is the eye of the hurricane, Harry, that's what this is. This room, this house, this whole damn city, you."

Past Lethington's elbow Harry saw the crimson and yellow of Olivia's tulips, fine sculpted heads strong with colour, unconscious of the hurricane in whose eye, it seemed, they sat. Seddall scratched his own less beautiful, more thinly decorated, head, which was doing its best to make sense of Lethington's outburst.

He sought to win time for it to do this. "I'll fetch coffee," he said.

Lethington, however, came with him to the kitchen. "I think we should use this," he said, opening a cupboard and laying his hand unerringly on a Queen Anne coffee pot. He put some hot water from the tap into it and swung it in small circles – an old-fashioned housewife warming the teapot – while Seddall put cups and saucers on a tray.

"This is precisely the sort of thing I mean," Lethington said, emptying the water out and handing the elegant artefact to his reluctant host, but tapping the lid with his forefinger before he let it go.

Seddall switched off the coffee machine and poured the coffee into the nominated receptacle. "I know," he said, "To you it's a storm-cone waiting to be hoisted."

Lethington took up the tray and handed it to Seddall. "Take this," he said, "before I throw it" – not joking, the true hard edge in his voice – "through your kitchen window," but then he stood in the doorway, a roadblock on the route back to the drawing room, oblivious to everything except the need to have his passionate argument heard.

Seddall put the tray down and sat himself on a high stool and idly poured coffee into two cups, using the casual understatement of movement with which one humours a madman.

"The hurricane will come, and we are living as if all storms are in the past. Security and Intelligence will be downgraded into one Service, because the East and the West are to be friends now, now and forever, do you see?" Lethington spoke the words earnestly but with calm. "A committee of Privy Counsellors recommends it and the Government will do it. Privy Counsellors! As if Henry VIII were still on the throne. Privy Counsellors! Every political flavour there, all of them past it, all at that too great age when compromise and consensus seem to them wise and divinely illuminated judgment; so the Government puts it to the Americans, the Americans say do it, neat, good notion. They say it because it will make sure the CIA and the FBI and the rest of them will stay top dogs, not that they need any help there right now because whatever shit they get into they lie low and come up squeaky clean, as they call it, when the stink dies down.''

"Here," Harry said, and pulled the other stool round him towards Lethington. "Have some coffee."

"Are you listening?" He had not moved from the doorway.

"I'm listening. I'm listening all right."

Lethington had his right hand up in front of him and was watching the thumb rub nervously on the forefinger. He put the hand down and took the stool and sat on it, swallowed some coffee, and went on.

"Look at Whitehall these days," he said.

His tone was relaxed now, that of a man feeling himself reasonable and cogent and knowing himself in command of a good brief.

"Look at Downing Street. The seat of power, correct? Well, it was once, Seddall, but it's not now. Oh, they get themselves a good press, and they're *in* power, they can do what they like *inside* the country, but outside it . . .''

Words failed him, and he made a large, wild motion of the arms above his head to signify despair. Real despair, Seddall recognized; despair as in the Tragedies. Bayard in his basket woke up, at some convulsion in the forest where his dreams had been, and went hurriedly out. Seddall heard him padding upstairs.

Lethington rubbed his hands over his face and gave his shoulders a shake, and seemed to become once again the reasoning advocate for his thesis. "They don't have power now, they don't even have authority. If they had authority, they would have silenced all these squealers who came along after Mr Spycatcher Wright, leaking their wretched secrets to the media, and to so-called Intelligence experts cashing in with their own books on the market Wright opened up for them. If they had *authority*,

188

they would have used the power they had to silence Wright and the rest of them, the whole pestilential gang of them, instead of pissing about with legislation and litigation. *I* could have fixed their wagons, no trouble at all, no problem, no hardship either, believe you me: Wright and all the rest of them."

He held out his cup for more coffee and his face showed Seddall an amiable, euphoric, grinning, lustful, retrospective satisfaction at the exhilarating memory of what might have been, of how well it would have been done.

"Oh, I would have fixed their wagons, all right," he said, with much good humour. "There would have been a long silence behind me after I'd done with them."

Seddall thought that Lethington went up and down from one mood to another like a yo-yo, and wondered that his constitution could stand it; for how long it would survive before – before what? He wished he could have taped this, not just to have a record for the more obvious reasons, but to let someone hear it who knew about people like Lethington. If there were people like Lethington.

"Exactly how would you have fixed their wagons?" he asked.

"Don't play the innocent, Seddall. You know exactly how. There's only one thing to do if you want to silence a man the long way."

Harry, in his role as the unwilling confidant of the mood-swinging Lethington, looked at this in regard to himself and felt unhappy.

"That's a bit extreme, surely?" he said.

"That's it, you see, Seddall! What do you think being in secret work means? Do you think it's a job like any other? Like carving out a career in Marks & Spencer? Yes, you do. You all do. They all do. They think it's a job for gentlemen, like merchant banking or publishing or what have you. They go to the right schools and wear the right ties and know each other's fathers from way back, and belong to the clubs, and the only time they're not born that way they come in as grotty little grammar school scholarship boys from God knows where and they become like that as hard and as fast as they can, and of course both lots produce traitors, don't they, you know that."

Harry eased himself off the stool. "Let's go through to the front."

Lethington nodded. As they walked to the drawing room, Harry said: "There's nothing much wrong with your school, Lethington, that I've heard."

"That's no answer, that's no answer at all. I didn't let it turn me into a post-Victorian backward-looking snob flying a desk and playing schoolboy games all my life. That," he said, throwing himself onto the couch, "is what I mean by your Queen Anne coffee pot and this whole house and the way you live. I've nothing against that as such except by God I have, which is that if you'd all gone to Borstal and spent five years in the Foreign Legion, which is *not* as romantic as Beau Geste seemed to find it, you'd all be better fitted for what you're supposed to be doing."

He took a glass of brandy from Seddall and sent some of it down, and said: "That's better. I'm a rough son of a bitch, and I'm dishonourable, you can't turn your back on me. I'm good at my job, and that's what makes me good at it."

This was a new mood again, and Harry did not expect to like this one very much, neither the mood nor the willing and deliberate exposure the man was making of himself. Lethington confirmed this apprehension for him.

"That's why you had your dinner before I came, I know that, so that you wouldn't have to eat with me. *You* wouldn't eat with me! You'd eat with a *capo da Mafia* who'd made his bones when he was sixteen and had men murdered by the hundred, and you'd eat with an oil sheikh who had his wives flogged before breakfast because they're ignorant foreigners who don't know any better, but you wouldn't eat with me because I'm one of us but I'm a cad and a low hound, whatever you like, I knew that's why you'd eaten the moment I came in. Now," and he worked his way clumsily out of the couch to lean forward, so urgent was it to him to make his point, "now you'll be eating with me willy-nilly, my lad, and you will need, you will certainly need, one very long spoon indeed."

Seddall did not take Lethington up on his threat that in future they would be messing together. "Tell me about this hurricane," he said instead, and admired the light in his cognac. Then he turned to Lethington sitting on the edge of the couch with the empty glass in his hand, and watched the malign zest fall in his face as he accepted that Seddall had refused to pick up his cue.

"You want to hear about the hurricane? I'll tell you about the hurricane. But after that I'll tell you why you're going to be in my pocket, Seddall, and why you'll have to swallow it too." He held out his glass. "What about a refill?"

Harry was really irritated by this. "You can mix your own metaphors, Lethington, so surely to God you can mix your own drinks." He knew this was childish, but he enjoyed it all the same. Besides, he had learned something that might be useful in this behaviour of Lethington's, telling Harry he was going to do him dirt and then asking him for a drink the moment after. It displayed an odd blindness to how people reacted. It was as if he did not expect his own policy of massive ill will to be taken personally by its individual victims; as if, say, he might tell a man he was about to kill him, and then ask him if he would kindly cash a cheque before the fatal act.

Lethington – no hard feelings, apparently – brought the decanter and replenished both their glasses. Then he settled himself on the floor with his back against the facing armchair – Sacha's chair; where was Sacha? Still on the piano, watching and listening – and set the decanter beside him. How he makes himself at home, Seddall thought, irritated afresh. He wondered just how big a cheque Lethington might ask a man to cash for him, before slipping the knife in.

"Here we are in the eye of the hurricane," Lethington said, back in one of his better moods, "with our club ties, our clubs, our club fenders, our careers that might take us to better clubs, although never to the best unless that's where we start. Here we are with our networks, our technique, our computers, our

191

controllers, our conferences, our centuries of policy, empire and war with the whole apparatus of modern techno-thought grafted onto them, and what have we decided to do with all these assets?"

"I dunno. Tell me."

"We have decided to become the little friend of all the world, but I should have said that in capitals," and he enunciated with stress on the initial letters like an eccentric schoolmaster drumming home pronunciation, the same phrase: "The Little Friend Of All The World." Seddall was startled. The mimicry was indescribably camp and effective, and although Lethington was recumbent he put his whole body as well as his facial expression into it, not only becoming an actor but also becoming yet another aspect of himself. How often did Lethington do this, come out from the shelter of the unshowing face and the neutral manner, the visibly well-together personality and urbane mode of conduct, that were the hallmark of men in his profession, or trade, or vocation?

He saw that Lethington was watching him like a hawk; still learning, the intrusive, persistent, bastard.

Harry signalled to him to continue.

"The little friend," Lethington said at once, "of Europe, of Russia, of China. It's happened before, and each time it happens we seem to believe it. It happened with Europe after Bonaparte; with Russia after Dulles and Eisenhower, and I use their names because we go with the American line always, did it then and we're doing it again now; with China after Mao. Next thing you know we'll double-cross the oil states in the Gulf and be friends with the Shi'ite Moslems. Which is a good case in point, because all they would have to do is stop calling for Jihad against the Infidel West – and stop sending their ineffectual terrorists to blow up airliners full of irrelevant people, and work away at looking like what we think are good guys. All any of these nations have to do is say they're our brothers and we fall for it."

He became suddenly depressed and at the same time began to

show signs of fatigue, even of exhaustion, an exhaustion buried far inside him that surfaced only when he let it. He lay there with his chin on his chest for so long that Seddall feared he was declining into a stupor of sleep from which it might be difficult to rouse him. Then he came to himself with a great shuddering yawn. He fixed Seddall with a long, mordant look, and smiled quickly to himself, at himself, and reached his arm and poured brandy into his glass. The stopper he had been playing with earlier went back into the decanter with so loud a sound that Seddall flinched for it.

"One for the road," Lethington said. "What it comes down to is this, you see. If Military Intelligence Five and Military Intelligence Six are to become one, then I have to head it. That's what it comes down to."

This was too much for Seddall. "You're not even head of Five, man. There's Considine and Banks, and after them you're only third equal with about seven others, and that would only be on the warmest estimate of you, and no one, Lethington, is going to get that warm."

"Considine is wrecked," Lethington said.

"I know that. But he'll be back."

"No he won't. They may let him soldier on for a bit, but they'll have to ease him out, and they'll do it."

"Banks then. He's not wrecked."

"Oh no," Lethington said, perking up a good deal under the influence of cognac or malice, and very likely both. "Banks has been gambling, my dear Seddall, and is not only broke, but far too far in debt to last much longer as number two, never mind becoming number one."

"I don't believe it," Seddall said, and he didn't.

"Not in the clubs, you dolt. Stock Exchange. Could happen to anyone, but who it happened to is Banks."

"Whom," Harry said, wanting to get rid of this man and do some thinking.

"Right. Whom. Do you want me to go through the seven?"

"No, I don't want you to go through the seven," Harry said.

"Set aside your lot for the moment. What about Six? What about Arkley?"

Lethington dropped his head to one side and laughed silently. "Ah," he said, "that is a sad thing. Sir John Arkley is minus a leg." He did some more silent laughter. "Your friend Arkley will not be back."

"Arkley is hardly my friend," Harry said shortly.

"More so than I am," Lethington said, and embarked on a slow series of movements that brought him, climbing backwards as it were up the armchair behind him with the glass still in his hand, to his feet.

He reached for an inside pocket and drew out a manilla envelope thickly filled, for when he slung it onto the floor at Seddall's feet it landed with a thump.

"Read that," he said, "before you get on the blower to anyone about tonight's little talk. It is a Security Service report on one Harry Seddall, and it is, I can tell you, very worrying.

"In fact," he said, and tilted back his head to drain the last of the brandy from his glass, which he tossed into the chair behind him, "if I were to do my duty, on the basis of that report I would put the collar on you right now, old son. I should know, me and my little gang have been putting it together for a long time now. The people you've been meeting on the Embankment in parked cars at night with the lights off, you wouldn't believe."

"Name one, just one," but the bad feeling that had come up in him at the Ristorante Calabrese was back.

"F.W. Schaller, then. How about Freidrich Wilhelm Schaller, a German, sorry, an East German, naturalized Soviet citizen, currently on the staff of the Soviet Embassy?"

"Never heard of him."

"Oh, Seddall, that's what they all say. You can do better than that."

Lethington touched the envelope with his foot and said something Harry had never found sinister before this night.

"Don't call us, Seddall, because we shall certainly call you. You just bone up on that little piece of fiction there. And be

194

very careful to keep it safe. It would do me no harm if other people saw it, but it would do you no good at all."

He made for the door and lurched as he passed the piano, grabbing at it for support. In a split second Sacha leapt at his head, hung onto his scalp with her forepaws and clawed, shrieking horribly, at his face with her hind claws. She was off up the stairs before her wounded opponent could lift a hand in his defence. Sacha, whether or not she had taken his move towards her as an attack, had not just been scared, she had been in a fury of rage. Lethington's face was streaked with bloody scratches, some of them deeper than scratches, because the blood was running down.

Lethington did not touch his damaged face, but only stared at the doorway through which the cat had vanished.

"Come on," Harry said. "We'll have blood on the carpet in another minute."

Standing with Lethington at the top of the stairs under the bright moon, he found himself laughing.

"What is it?" Lethington demanded.

"You don't want to know."

"I want to know, Seddall."

"It's nothing very much. It's just that the lesser mammals don't piss around like us, wasting a lot of words, do they, Lethington? When they decide to do a thing, they just do it. Like that cat of mine."

Lethington steadied himself onto his left foot and clenched his right fist, and the man now standing at the passenger door of his car began to make the move towards the house. Lethington eased out his fingers and waved the man back, and went down the steps.

He still hadn't touched his face.

Harry watched the car drive away, and went back inside to do his homework.

22

When he had locked and bolted the door Seddall went back up the hall a little way and then hunched into himself and put his hands in his pockets, and leaned a shoulder against the wall and stood looking at nothing.

He was looking inside himself for a reaction, and could not find one, not enough of one. He had reacted to Findo all right, the day before. Findo had put him into a state of panic which, when it was past, had been succeeded by one of intelligent fear. Seddall had thought this to be healthy, considering that Findo had scared the living shit out of him.

Now it seemed to Seddall that Lethington had done that to him and more. Lethington had spent the evening displaying himself as a recklessly dangerous man, a man not only cunning with ambition but also with a demon of chaos in him who would destroy others – destroy perhaps anything – to satisfy that demon, and who would himself walk callously into risk for the sake of it. He had done this as part of a considered purpose, and he had done it too out of a primitive instinct, to build on the fear with which Findo had assaulted Seddall the day before.

Now, in the immediate aftermath of Lethington, Seddall felt not panic, not even fear, but lassitude. He could suppose that he had been manipulated into this, that the full weight of this unsuspected, objective and cold-blooded enmity being laid on him over the twenty-four hours, and tonight's revelation of the extent to which a plot had already been prepared against him, had been designed to paralyze him; but the fact that he could see how this had been done to him did not make the effect any less real.

He picked himself off the wall. He had no god-damned energy in him, but he could make a start.

As if on cue, the small black cat appeared in the doorway of the drawing room and arched her back. Her hair had not yet settled from her hatred of Lethington, and still stood up a little here and there, so that she had a rare dishevelled look to her. She sat herself in the doorway and fixed her green eyes on him.

"All right, Sacha," he said. "All right. Let's at least check out this phoney document Lethington's concocted on me. Let us just see if we can find a hole in it."

He went into the drawing room, and like a fielder with no runs at risk who drops a lazy arm to collect a slowly rolling ball, he scooped up the spurious dossier Lethington had tossed onto the carpet and dumped it on an armchair. He took off his jacket, lifted his diary out of its pocket, and let the jacket fall. He lifted the top of a Victorian writing desk and rummaged in at the back of it and found his diary for last year; had a second thought about letting his jacket lie on the floor and folded it over the back of the couch, took his pen from it, and shrugged out of the shoulder rig with the thirty-eight in its holster and put that with the jacket.

He laid the pen and the diaries on top of the dossier, took through to the kitchen the detritus of glasses and coffee things left from Lethington's visit, and made a small fresh pot of filtered coffee.

Ensconced at last in the armchair with the dossier on his knee, he began to match the dates of the nefarious meetings it alleged against him with the record of his social career laid out in the first diary.

This had an unexpected effect on him. It had been a lonely year, with plenty of empty evenings for Lethington to build up into his imaginary double life of Harry Seddall, and as Harry worked through these parallel calendars of his existence, the real and the invented, contradictory feelings began to play on him.

For one thing now there was Olivia. He did not quite

197

understand what this meant, except that everything that was wrong with his life, that had been wrong last year, or was wrong now – even to this threat of disaster that Findo and Lethington had brought on him – was outmatched by the fact of Olivia.

He laid the papers aside, and went for a walk around the room. He stopped to talk with Sacha at her perch on top of the Bechstein, but something, perhaps this sickness that was passing through him, made him uncongenial to her, and she jerked herself away from his attempt to caress her.

"Wash yourself, then," he said to her. "Your hair's all at sixes and sevens still."

Indeed it was, bristling as if Lethington had left behind him, to lie on the air in the house, the scent of danger that had issued from him all evening.

Harry poured the last of the coffee into his cup, and settled again to looking for actual events that might provide alibis, here and there, against Lethington's dossier.

"August 16," he read. "Subject left MoD (old building) 5 p.m. Taxi to SNCF office on Piccadilly. Paid off taxi. Taxi turned down Duke Street and subject almost at once emerged from Fortnum's side door and re-entered taxi. Followed taxi to Battersea where subject dismounted" – dismounted? – "and entered pub-restaurant The Cocked Hat. Subject still drinking heavily: drank three large neat whiskies in rapid succession and took another to table where he was joined by two members of Soviet Trade Mission, Vassily Krnov and Liena Smirnova, both known members of KGB, at 7.23 p.m." – 7.23 p.m.? Exactitudes so pretentious were surely unpersuasive?

Harry knew better than that. The whole document was so much a spiritual copy of genuine surveillance reports that its very style would inspire belief. But who, in God's name, would believe that he, Harry Seddall, would sell out his country to the Russians? If he had set out to put the skids under Harry Seddall he'd have concocted something far more cunning. Disloyal dealings, say the unsanctioned share of secret information, with an ally, West Germany or the United States. The Russian card was such an old and well-thumbed card to play, surely any intelligence group or committee sitting in judgment would see it coming a mile off?

He supposed he knew better than that too. The worn stereotype was instantly recognizable, roused easily understood reflexes, raised a spectre so familiar that alarm would be spontaneous and sincere, and guilt would be assumed in the quarters where it mattered more from precedent than any question of likelihood.

He thought that the quick clean line of Lethington's cunning was an exceedingly frightening thing to have coming at one.

Lethington's cunning, he thought, the quick clean line of Lethington's cunning, and felt a chill on the back of his neck. He put up a hand to rub it and knew a flicker of irritation, almost as though it was a twinge of some familiar ailment that had touched him.

He threw the papers aside again, suddenly restless with himself, and said to Sacha on the piano: "What the hell, Sacha. What the hell."

But Sacha was no longer there.

Seddall stood up, thinking of a drink, or more coffee. Then he thought his stomach had taken enough of these, and decided on bed preceded by a glass of milk.

In the hall he felt the night air cool on his face and had even begun to smile at the realization that it was a draught from the back door which had laid its chill on the back of his neck (not the aftertaste of Lethington), but in the same instant the smile stopped.

The back door was bloody open, and it had been locked. Both doors had been locked, he knew it. He had made sure of the back door when he came in, and of the front door when Lethington went out.

Without further thought he let the reflexes take over.

"That's funny," he said, as if he were shrugging it off, went down the three steps to the back door, shut and locked it, came back up the three steps to the cupboard that held the alarm and activated it. He did all this as fast as he could without putting vibes of haste or alarm into the air.

He went to the drawing room door and switched off the lights, decided to leave the lights on in the hall. He did not go into the drawing room to collect his revolver. He went to the door and touched the switch and moved to the stairs and ran up into the darkness at the top of the house, ran with what felt like winged feet into the dark, ran as fleet and sure as a startled deer, ran the gauntlet, ran with it in his mind that he was running the gauntlet even as he climbed past the first floor, passing through the internal dusk of the house; took the landing at a leap on the circumference of a wheel axled by a hand to the banister with his eye flinching at the whirl of doors more and less open, of the corridor black in its depth like a cave where any terror might lurk; on and up into the night where the staircase ended and into his bedroom, flighting his sight round it in the glim from the windows, from the street lights below, finding it empty, feeling it empty; not shutting the door but going to the tallboy and taking the Browning (working the slide) and the spare clip from the drawer and laying himself on the carpet, his body angled back from the door in the protection of the wall; his eyes watching the staircase, adapting it to the pale glow of light that lifted into the stairwell.

Thanked his lucky stars, and waited, knowing now there was someone in the house, sensing the other human presence in the house.

As pants the hart for cooling streams. The line – where was it from? – fell absurdly into his head as he lay there with the pistol held loose and ready in his hand, lay there trying not to puff like a grampus while his respiration got itself back to normal from that miraculous ascent in which, it seemed to him, he had soared up the stairs on a single breath.

These glimpses of panting harts and puffing grampuses came and went as images thrown up by flashes of lightning, random electric discharges flying from the high state of activity to which his brain had moved: they deflected nothing of the intensity with which he was putting himself to the spaces of the house outside that doorway.

Minutiae of sound reached him from the silences of the rooms below. He felt his hearing to be as sensitive as if he had the audio system of a bat, felt all his senses pitched to their highest by the old magic that always came back to him when he was alert to danger. He felt more alive than he could remember.

Life in the old dog yet. Yes, well, let's keep it that way.

He listened and sensed his way throughout the house, into the bathroom and two other rooms on this floor, the bathroom to the left outside the doorway, the other two rooms to the right of it; down one flight to the study, the bedroom, the other bathroom; down to the ground floor, to kitchen, dining room and drawing room; to everywhere at once.

He felt presence close and presence farther off. He was keyed up for anything except what happened next.

A growling sound rose from the depths of the house. His eyes went wide in amazement before he recognized what it was. It was the Berlin Philharmonic performing Beethoven's Triple Concerto on the CD player in the drawing room, and that low rumbling of the strings would rise in a few bars to a crescendo.

If the idea was to suggest to him that the enemy's strength was massed belowstairs, and about to make an escalade under cover of the sound when it burst forth from von Karajan's tremendous band, it was an idea that Seddall rejected on the instant.

There was a man up here. The music was a signal to him. He might not know the concerto but he'd know the music grew loud sooner or later.

The fool came at the first crescendo and Seddall was right with him, riding music that he knew like the back of his hand. The man leapt past the doorway, fired twice from a silenced pistol and said, "Oh, ach," as the Browning nailed him in flight.

Seddall wriggled himself forward.

Up into his vision came galloping the impromptu disc jockey, shaped by the pale light rising from the stairwell but doubtless unaware that it betrayed him. Doubtless, to his innocent and unadjusted eyes, it was all dark up there.

For him, it was about to be all dark forever.

The nine millimetre bullet tossed the man out of his stride against the stairs, where – for von Karajan had reached the diminuendo – out of the brief but dreadful thrashing sounds of his astonished body either he or his ruined lungs vented a shriek that was the worst thing Seddall had heard since . . . Well, it was bad, a hard thing to hear. The man and his scream died, bubbling in his blood, and the music came up again and went on its exhilarating way.

Seddall threw the light switch on the landing and made sure of what his instinct already knew. Both men were dead, both shot in about the same place except that the man on the landing had taken his in front, and made less mess as well as less noise.

With the adrenalin running in him like a promise of immortality Seddall went tearing recklessly through the rooms on the top floor like a terrier searching out a badger's sett – putting lights on as he went, filling the house with light – through the floor below, through the ground floor (returning the Berlin Philharmonic to silence as he passed) and found them empty.

He shuttered and curtained the dining room and the kitchen and made sure of the already closed shutters in the drawing room, made sure again of the doors and the alarm. Somewhere in all this he met Sacha descending into the hall.

"You were up there?" he said. "I rather think you tipped me off," he said, "so thanks. Sorry about all the noise."

Her fur was still staring, but not that much. She looked cool, he thought, a cool cat. If she'd been upstairs all she'd think was that there were two dead strangers, or intruders, if she thought of them as intruders, lying up there in their own blood.

Blood and bodies were nothing to Sacha, except that the best ones made good eating. She came with him to the drawing room and jumped up on the piano, and blinked at Harry pleasantly, as if he was rather a cool cat himself, a good clean killer, and set to washing herself.

Harry sat down and gave himself a cigarette and thought about the furniture in his bedroom. He wondered if the two shots that laddie had fired – what had he been doing, shooting blind? Hoping to draw fire and learn the position of the target? – had spoiled anything. He'd have to replace whole quantities of stair-carpet. He was watching Sacha at her ablutions, and was startled to find his mind on the same track.

There were things to be done. Go through their pockets, in case they'd been careless and left a trace? He was not ready for that yet. He was not ready for anything very much.

He did not want to have killed two men in his own house, his home. As soon as he had said that to himself he wondered how true it was, how much it truly disturbed him, and at once began to feel it was not true. It was an artificial response, the expected response of urban civilized man, but he was not urban civilized man, sitting here with a Browning automatic in his hand, resting on his thigh.

Sacha had the right of it: after the tumult and the shouting die, clean up and look forward to the next meal. He got up and laid the pistol on the mantelpiece and went over to the cat and stroked her, hard over her head and back and the forefinger along the tail. She started to purr, and with a stroke of her paw that was both pretty and witty together hit him on the nose with just enough claw extended to draw blood. She looked at him and then dropped to the floor and went out. He heard the flap in the kitchen window fall back. Sacha was not eating out of tins tonight.

Time for his own cleaning up. He thought it was one for Special Branch. The General had lifted his Ministry of Defence pass, but apart from that he was simply on leave. There was nothing to stop him using channels he would normally use.

"Mind you," he said to himself. "Normally you'd report this kind of dust-up to the boss."

But to hell with that. He was going to stay away from the higher levels of command. He was going to deal with guys he knew, guys he'd worked with before, until this business was sorted out.

"Well that's an improvement, Seddall." He spoke to himself again. "You're going to sort it out, are you, just like that?"

Sure. So Gerald Kenna at Special Branch was the thing, failing whom young Gatenby, Gatenby was back in London. He picked up his diary from beside the chair where it lay with the other one on top of Lethington's dossier, and found Kenna's home number. He went to the phone and reached out his hand, and as if by osmosis it began to ring.

He hesitated. This could be the genius who had sent these now deceased assassins after him, Lethington or whoever. He picked up the receiver and said nothing.

"Harry," the phone said. "Harry, are you there?"

It was Sorrel's voice.

"Am I glad to hear you," he said.

"You're bloody lucky to hear me," Sorrel said. "I've been lurking in the hills up here like a partisan or something. Two heavies tried to kidnap me or take me prisoner or whatever you'd call it."

"Are you all right? I mean you sound all right," he said. "In fact, you sound curiously all right."

"I feel terrific," Sorrel said. "These were not very classy thugs and they know bugger all about the country."

"I should tell you," Harry said. "This phone's most likely got a bug on it."

There was a silence. "I don't think it matters," Sorrel said. "They'll have reported back by now. I've sent a letter to that drop address of yours. I've holed up with a man who doesn't know enough to be worried. I won't tell you where. He'll get me off the island in case the heavies are still about."

. He wanted to ask her if she had learned something, but could not, not with another ear on the line.

He thought he would give a message to the other ear, if it was there. "We're not doing badly," he said to her. "You've slipped your heavies and I've got two aspiring assassins weltering in their gore upstairs."

"My dear," Sorrel said. "What times we do live in. Well done you."

"Yeah," Harry said. "Listen, my name is mud at the Ministry, so we're working out of here. Get in touch here or any of the other ways you know about. Get here soon, if you can. I may be hauled off to the Tower at any moment."

"Well, don't worry if you are," Sorrel said. "We'll get you out of there."

"It's refreshing to talk to you, Sorrel," he said. "You may be a damn fool about some things but you see matters in a good perspective."

"Well, thanks," she said. "Take care."

"Also you," he said.

Sacha came in with a dead blackbird, and laid it at his feet as an offering.

How good it was to be surrounded by supportive colleagues. He dialled Kenna's number.

In a rented flat in North Kensington's Sumner Place, Carmichael opened the door to Lethington, let him in and shut it fast.

"What the hell do you want?" he said. "I don't want to be seen near you."

"It's the middle of the night," Lethington said. "Nobody's seeing anybody."

He sniffed. There was a nice smell of bacon and eggs coming from the kitchenette. He followed Carmichael to the frying pan. Carmichael was good at this. The four rashers of bacon looked perfect. The eggs were well formed, just in the pan. Carmichael scooped fat over them with a spoon and placed the spoon carefully on a saucer.

Lethington said: "What was the idea of sending those two idiots in after Seddall? That was you, I take it?"

"That was me," Carmichael said. He put a plate in the sink and let it sit there with the hot tap running on it. He put two slices of bread in the electric toaster. "You've got two minutes," he said.

Lethington ignored this crack. "All you've done is alert Seddall," he said.

Carmichael said: "You've spent your evening alerting him, haven't you?"

"I've spent the evening putting the frighteners on him. I've scared him," Lethington said. "Violence doesn't scare him. He's good at violence."

"I want him to know I'm coming," Carmichael said. "At the end I'll want him to know it's me. That's why I sent these two punks in. I would have been seriously upset if they'd killed him."

The toaster clicked up. The bread was inadequately toasted, so Carmichael pressed it down again. He turned the bacon.

"You do see how I'm fixed," he said. "I can only give you one more minute. I like my bacon and eggs just exactly right."

"I'm not paying you to work out a vendetta against Seddall. I'm paying you to kill him," Lethington said.

"I'll kill him," Carmichael said, "and I'll kill him how I want to kill him. If you don't like that you can take a running fuck at a rolling doughnut." He took the bacon from the pan and laid it on a sheet of paper towel. "That is, if you find you're fit enough."

The toast popped up again.

Lethington turned on his heel and went out.

23

When the car came off the boat at Harwich a four-striper opened the door beside von Harma and said: "Everybody out, please."

He went on standing there, holding the door, as if von Harma might make a dash for it. After all, von Harma was on the List.

"You will have to stand back," von Harma said. "I have difficulty in leaving the car."

The four-striper, who had a small group of acolytes at his back, found this to be a hiccup in the smooth flow of his authority, and his vexation showed.

He stepped back, however, and waited.

"I must wait for my wheelchair," von Harma said.

"Passport," the Customs man said.

"My driver has the passports," von Harma said.

Peter the driver was at the back of the car with Calder. He unlocked the boot, hoisted out the wheelchair, and unfolded it. Calder took over, and pushed it round to where von Harma sat waiting. It took Calder and Peter to extract von Harma from the back of the Daimler and establish him in the wheelchair. Calder got behind the chair and began to push it away from the car.

"Get me a rug," von Harma said. "Do you want me to freeze to death?"

Calder fetched the rug and swathed von Harma's lower half in it.

The rug was sable. The four-striper made it an occasion to connect von Harma with the idea of brutality. "A lot of little animals have been killed for that one," he said.

"Russian little animals," von Harma said, and made a repellent deprecating movement of the head, as if in his terms that Russian made the difference, and stroked heartlessly, with a gesture so light that his fingers seemed to just touch the beautiful pelt. It came to Calder, as an invasion of intolerable reality, that there had been a time when von Harma would have said: "Russian little animals" and meant it of human beings. There had been an eloquence in the slightness of the gesture, an eloquence both wonderfully and appallingly deliberate, to convey that in an earlier day the precise original of this heartless, graceful, fleeting touch might have been made upon the head of some child destined by von Harma for a forest grave.

Von Harma looked up for a moment at the Customs officer and then, finding nothing to interest him there (nothing to interest him in the officer's face, wrenched from the secure lines of its belligerence into naked chaos by this glimpse of the abyss), demanded from Calder a cigarette. "Good," he said when he had inhaled. "Now put me at a little distance from this *galère*, and be careful, damn you."

The chances of von Harma freezing to death, even if he had been as frail as he pretended, would have been slight. It was one of these fine seacoast days that Boudin loved to paint, with white clouds passaging across blue sky and the breeze from off the sea – from the south-west, with enough cool in it to refresh but not chilly enough to take the warmth from the sunshine – perceptibly invigorating all but the most morose constitutions among those coming and going on their travels.

When Calder had pushed the wheelchair between fifteen and twenty feet from the car, von Harma said: "This should be far enough, do you think? I think perhaps I might have been more offensive to you, in this role of petulant and arrogant invalid to my nurse-companion. What is your feeling?"

"Oh, my feeling is so far, so good," Calder said. "I assure you I do not feel insufficiently humiliated. You do it with the most natural ease."

"Take care," von Harma said. "Resent me later, all you wish. Now we must play our parts with belief. I believe we have a Thermos of coffee in the car. They are pretending to take their search seriously, and since we may be here for a while, it would look well if you were to serve me coffee, if I were to demand it of you. You might also turn the chair, so that I can look at the sea, and not watch them turning out my car."

"Do it yourself," Calder said, preparing to depart.

"Now, now," von Harma chided him. "You must be subservient to the last. Remember, we are concerned to save your life."

Calder found himself caught, in the exact sense, on the hop, and knew that his movements as he complied with the autocrat's wish were charged with all the impotent chagrin his part called for.

The seats were out of the car, the bonnet was open, the boot was being emptied. Peter, having presented the passports, stood at the back of the car watching events there. His face was impassive but rancour emanated from every line of his stance.

"His excellency requires coffee," Calder said to him. Overdoing it, perhaps: at Calder's use of the honorific, the driver's eyebrows had flickered.

Nevertheless he repeated the message instantly. "The *freiherr* requires coffee," he said to the Customs men. "It is in that case." He pointed to it, where it sat on the ground – on a waterproof sheet doubtless set there by Peter – beside seven or eight solid suitcases.

The officer in charge had drifted up from the front of the car. "Oh, the *freiherr* does, does he? The *freiherr* can . . ."

"The *freiherr* can what?" Calder demanded, assuming with sudden recklessness the dominating character of the head of a university department. Play-acting or no, he had no time for all this aggro, for these childish games being acted out by men old enough to know better.

He knew he was being illogical and foolish, that the officer with four stripes on his arm, who had certainly taken courses in

209

command management, was merely showing his team how to keep such unwelcome visitors as war criminals on MI5's Special List – the B List, had von Harma called it? some initial or other – waiting about on the dockside so that an MI5 man could take a good look at them.

That was reason talking, though, and Calder had run out of reason. The Customs officer's provocation of von Harma, and the contemptuous indifference with which von Harma, in return, had revealed the character expected of him, were to Calder equally dehumanized acts of behaviour: facetious performances whose script was based on a reality in which millions of people had been slaughtered.

So: "The *freiherr* can what?" he demanded, irritated even as he spoke to find that he seemed to be defending von Harma, when what he was doing was defending himself against these hostilities which opened so deep a disturbance inside him.

And he bent down and opened the case, which held in its leather interior, safely and variously stored in pockets or secured by clips, a Thermos jug and eighteenth century Schwarzlot porcelain.

"Do you want to search this cup?" he said. "Or this saucer? Do you want to try the coffee, to find if on the tongue the sugar may not have the taste of some narcotic illegitimate?"

Why he had run on into this inverted, mock-poetic, pseudo-archaic speech he had no idea, except that the use of it came to him unbidden as the perfect weapon, as the bow from which to fire the tone of elaborate sarcasm to which he resorted when he felt himself attacked.

He had the top off the Thermos, coffee in a cup, the cup on a saucer, and these he extended to the astonished officer with such certitude of will that an arm with four gold rings on it came up and took the saucer from him.

The officer sipped from the cup and put it back on the saucer. "Not bad," he said. He lifted the cup again and drank the coffee down, and while he drank it stared at Calder over the rim of the cup.

When the cup was empty he returned it to Calder. "The sugar," he said.

Calder unscrewed the lid and handed him the silver sugar bowl and a silver coffee spoon. He experienced the sensation of being on stage in a Viennese political comedy.

The officer kept his beefy face, his cold grey eyes, hard at Calder. He sniffed the Demerara sugar. He probed into it with the spoon spilling it freely on the ground. He returned the spoon to Calder, and took a pinch of sugar in his fingers and tasted it. He gave Calder the bowl.

He addressed himself to the four men who had been rummaging in the car but had suspended the operation to watch this little scene.

"Put it all back," he said. "The party's over."

He turned again to Calder. "And you," he said, "you put the old bastard back in the car." He took off his cap and moved his head about as if to cool it in the breeze. He looked across the roof of the car at von Harma in his wheelchair, and then he gazed up into the sky, and his eyes tightened as if at some emotion that had to be kept private. "Get him off my harbour," he said.

He went on looking at the sky. He replaced the cap on his head. "For my money," he said, "you two deserve each other."

He walked away, leaving his men to get the pieces back together.

24

"Shoes off, sir. Socks too, if I were you."

From the middle distance came those resonations of the slightest sound which swimming pools, theatres and concert halls share with great churches, and which give impartially to all of them the sense of harbouring a religious rite.

Harry, therefore, found nothing incongruous in leaving his shoes and socks on a bench and, dressed otherwise as for the street but with his hat in one hand and a paper bag in the other, making his way to the scene of the general's morning worship of whatever god inspired him to those endlessly spun lengths of the pool.

When he had entered the precincts of the pool he squatted on his toes, quite far back from the edge, and watched Kenyon swim. Kenyon swam something like a butterfly stroke, and with his black hair, the way he rose and sank gave him the appearance of a seal on the waves of the sea.

He completed a length, made the turn, and set off down the pool, rapt in his own world of movement through the water. Seddall had heard swimmers speak of a suspended, trance-like state that came when they swam many lengths, in which the swimming became automatic, and the state of being akin to that of meditation in the sense of the Eastern religions.

He stood up and walked to the head of the pool, and sat on a bench against the wall. The seal made its turn at the far end and came towards him, travelling slowly in its half-brisk, half-clumsy bounding movements, alone in its adopted element.

Seddall wondered if Kenyon was entranced, he wondered what the trance of a general was like, and he wondered if Kenyon, as he came in his series of small surges up the pool, saw him sitting here on the bench.

The general approached, his burly shoulders heaving him on his way, the water sleeking his hair to that seal's pelt look. Seddall was aware of the exact moment when the swimmer recognized him. He did not know how he knew this. There had been no change in the general's stroke, no interruption to the rhythm of his progress, but from the figure splashing along in solitary splendour through the chlorinated water above the cerulean tiles a signal had passed as much as to say: "So, it's you, Seddall. What are you doing here?"

The general reached the top of the pool and came to a mooring with a hand on the rail. He shook his head and brushed the water off his face and out of his hair, and looked at the watch on his wrist.

"Not bad," he said.

"Never occurred to me," Seddall said.

"What never occurred to you?" Kenyon asked.

"That you timed yourself. I thought you just swam," Seddall said.

"I'm a competitive man," Kenyon said.

"You compete against yourself?" Seddall said.

"I don't see anyone else, do you?" Kenyon said. "What the hell are you doing here, anyway?"

He lifted himself out of the pool, and stood there with water dripping off him. From a rather clumsy-looking swimmer he became a hefty, tanned, and muscular body, in such remarkable physical condition for his age that Seddall had a nasty feeling he might be thrown into the water if he said anything too provocative.

"Thought we might have a little drink," he said, "clear a few things up."

"I'm not going to talk here," Kenyon said. "I'm starting to shiver already."

"Albert's making some coffee for us," Seddall said, "and I've brought these." He let Kenyon see into the paper bag.

"Croissants!" Kenyon said. "How do you know Albert? Is this a club of yours?"

"I seem to belong to a lot of odd clubs," Seddall said. "I just don't use 'em much. Do you want yours warmed up? Albert says he'll put them in the microwave if we give him one."

"You get on better with Albert than I do," Kenyon said with some chagrin. "He's never offered me a cup of coffee after my swim."

"Well, he's not a chef or a barman," Seddall said. "It's not his job, he's just the early man. I expect you never offered him a croissant, did you? See you upstairs."

Kenyon went off with the quaint energetic waddle that besets the athletic stride on a slippery tile surface. Watching him go, Seddall knew a small feeling of contentment. He thought this business about Albert had got Kenyon on the run rather. In psychological warfare, every little helped.

After a while he followed on, stepping carelessly in Kenyon's wake, and wondered if one handkerchief would do to dry his feet, or if it would take both of them.

"All right, then." Kenyon, who still had all his handkerchiefs, used one of them to brush bits of croissant off the blue suiting. "What do you want to know? You realize I shouldn't be talking to you."

"I don't see why you shouldn't be talking to me," Harry said. "A man's innocent until he's proved guilty. I'm not in the Tower yet, I'm not even charged with anything. What you mean is that I'm not safe to be seen with in case you get tarred with the same brush. Which is why I've come here at what is practically dawn where nobody will see us except young Albert."

"Albert's sixty if he's a day," Kenyon said. "What do you want to know?"

Harry found he had worked himself into such a state that he

214

was about to mop up the crumbs with a wet handkerchief. He threw the soggy object away and lit a cigarette. Let the crumbs fall where they may.

"Well," Harry said. "It may be I owe you an apology. I've no way of knowing, have I? You've taken my MoD pass, barred me from the office, held me at arm's length, refused my calls. I don't know if you're for me or against me, or sitting on the sidelines, or ready to throw me to the wolves, or what. I want to know about six things," he said. "Are you quitting, I mean, are you going to retire while the going's good, or are you sticking? Whose side are you on? What's Findo to you? What about Lethington? What do you know about him? I mean, have you ever actually noticed his existence? Are he and Findo like that," he held up a hand with two fingers crossed, "or are they likely to stab each other in the back . . . ?"

Kenyon sat upright in the small chair, with his elbows on the arms and his hands clasped lightly. Harry noticed what big knuckles he had, and remembered that Kenyon had been a boxer, Army welter-weight champion, was that it? Still, he was a general now, generals kept everything under control, they didn't lose their heads and start throwing punches at people when they grew irritated. The general looked very much under control now.

He was. "I had a report this morning from Superintendent Kenna at Special Branch, about the goings-on at your house last night. You'll have expected Kenna to let me know about it," he said. He rocked once, forward and back in his chair. "Two of them, with the old Browning, eh? Always a good weapon that. In the right hands," he added courteously. "What do you think I've been doing, you bloody fool? I've been waiting to see some cards on the table. You never showed me any cards, not until now. Nor has Findo. All I know about Findo is that he's one of the Prime Minister's pets, and a power-hungry little weasel as well. Thank you, Albert," he said.

Albert had brought another pot of coffee. Albert looked well past sixty, Harry thought. Seventy, more like. He would stay in the job here until he dropped, and he would always be called young Albert for reasons only he could remember, and when he did, at last, drop, the club would not be able to find anyone to do the odd assortment of tasks performed by Albert.

"I say," the general said, sniffing in the aroma of Albert's coffee, "that does smell good. Cup of coffee after my swim, I must say it goes down well."

Albert was short, bent in the middle, but he had seen this coming a mile off. "I don't know," he said. His face was lean and ruddy, innocent and wily, and it was the face of a man who lived in his own world and was the only one who understood it. "I don't know," Albert said, and moved nimbly off.

"What does that mean?" Kenyon said. "That he won't make a habit of it?"

"Where were you brought up?" Harry said. "He wants a quid pro quo."

"Can't give a club servant money for special favours," Kenyon said. "It isn't done."

"Well, not unless you give him rather a lot of money, if he's in a fix of some kind," Harry said. Kenyon looked at him strongly, but Harry kept his face empty. "You grow asparagus, don't you?"

"Albert's not going to want asparagus!"

"How do you know? Maybe he dotes on it. Anyway," Harry said. "He'll want it if you tell him it's from your garden. Favours exchanged between equals, that sort of thing."

"Well," Kenyon said, and clapped his hands together silently, "the asparagus will be ready soon. Yes, yes. I see." He studied Seddall, learning him. "What else d'you want to know."

"You're a tanks man," Seddall said. "What do you know about the Kalman gunsight? Come to think of it, what can you tell me about Annette Kalman?"

The atmosphere between them exploded.

"God damn you!" the general said. "God damn you for a sneaky little bastard, Harry Seddall!" He was almost incoherent with rage. "Asparagus, you shit! God, they warned me about you. I've a good mind to . . . Asparagus, and then 'Come to that, what can you tell me about, about Annette?' "

Harry was listening so hard to the fact that Kenyon had not added the surname 'Kalman' to his 'Annette', and to the way he had actually said her name; listening back to discover whether Kenyon had been going to add the surname and had simply stopped short in the incoherence of his anger, or whether he had said Annette *pur sang* because it would not occur to him to add her surname – as if he knew her well; listening, with some distaste for himself, because he sensed he had heard something in the way Kenyon had said Annette, as if he had more than known her well: listening so intently that he hardly reacted to the state the general was in, perceiving Kenyon's fury objectively as supportive evidence, and seeing no threat in the clenching of those massive fists and the suffusion of blood in the choleric face.

"Take it easy, Aubrey," he said. "If there's been anything between you and Annette Kalman I knew nothing about it. Till now," he said. "Till now, all I was hoping was that you might be able to tell me about the Kalman gunsight: in the running for the new battle tank, is that right?"

Behind Seddall, the cheerful early morning voices of swimmers on their way to the pool came into the bar. Their passage through the room imposed enough sense of social requirement to take the heat out of Kenyon.

The general – Seddall had read about this as a way of easing plethoric pressure but had never seen it done – ran a finger round the inside of his collar.

With his head screwed round to one side and the forefinger still in place he stared obliquely at Seddall. The look in his eyes was a mixture to see: they were angry, hard, suspicious and hangdog all at once.

"Is that true, Harry?" he said.

"Of course it's true, for God's sake. What sort of interest could that sort of thing possibly have for me," Seddall said, "with the problems I've got on my plate?"

217

He felt the answer was at once truthful and disingenuous. He meant it, all right, but at the same time something was forming in the back of his mind. He could not see it yet, but he would; he knew he would.

Kenyon, however, appeared to take the assurance on its face value. "I don't believe anyone knows, you understand, no one else, that is." The hangdog look was now in the ascendant, but he had better manners than to ask outright for Seddall's discretion.

"No one will learn it from me," Harry said. "Tell me about her tank sight. Is it the best on offer? The Army's going to take it?"

"She's very beautiful, Annette, but it's not only that . . ."

Harry interrupted him. He had been afraid of this. Being the sole confidant of a man in, or as it might be recently out of, an affair, could be a pain in the neck.

"The gunsight, Aubrey," he said, "the gunsight's what I'm interested in."

"Well, that's it, dammit," Kenyon said. "The gunsight's a brilliant piece of work. She's an electronics wizard, and as well as that she's a really strong woman, terrific strength of character and tough as old boots in that business world of hers. She built that company of hers up from scratch, and her husband, well he's not much, you know. A kind of consort, you could say."

Harry leaned forward. "Aubrey," he said, "if you're going to tell me he's not man enough for her, and you are, I'll puke on the spot. Tell me about the fucking gunsight, will you?"

"I think it very likely to be the best," Kenyon said. "They're test-firing against the competition next week, but that won't decide it. It's already been decided. Kalman Electronics won't get it. Too pricey, that's the argument, but there's more to it than that. It's a NATO question too, and the political complications with the Allies – well, you know what that's like, in Europe alone; and of course the Americans have a bloody great axe to grind too, when it comes to defence contracts."

Kenyon sighed, and an expression of wry and bitter recollection came onto his face. "It's bloody disgusting, the way they wheel and deal with this kind of thing. It's not just the contract for the gunsight that goes on the table: it's anything else anyone's got to sell or buy. X may have a civil aircraft engine on the stocks, Y may want oil investment, A wants to cut down on troops on the ground in West Germany, B needs to sell a naval weapons system, C may want to oblige someone in the Middle East, for God's sake, and is willing to buy silence by sliding the contract towards D. The ramifications go on forever. It's tough luck on Annette."

"Dear God," Harry said. "That's why you made yourself so unpopular at Procurement. You were fighting for the Kalman gunsight."

"Damn right I was," Kenyon said, "but there was nothing improper about that, let me tell you."

"I'm sure of it," Harry said.

He was sure, at any rate, that Kenyon was sure of it. And he wondered, with an awful sense that his scepticism might be miscoloured by prurience, who had made the first move in the affair between Aubrey Kenyon and Annette Kalman? How far would a nice girl go in the way of business?

He cheered up a bit. He knew it was a dirty line of thought, but the question eased him out from under the oppression that Kenyon's rather heavy devotion had been laying on him.

Also, it seemed to him that whatever had come into the back of his mind, when Kenyon let the cat out of the bag about his affair with Annette Kalman, had moved a little forward.

"Why don't you," the general said, "go down and see the thing in action for yourself?"

"What thing?" Seddall asked, deeply irritated: Kenyon's question had delayed the diffident revelation that had been making its way to the front of his mind.

"The Kalman gunsight," Kenyon said.

"I might," Seddall said. "I might, at that." He felt confused. "Are you going? I mean . . ."

"You mean because of Annette?" The general was almost

boisterous. "Like a first-night, that what you mean? Yes, I think I shall be expected."

"Well, hell," Harry said, "if we meet, are we speaking to each other, or what?"

"Oh, I think we are," Kenyon said.

"That's a change. When we started this talk you didn't want to be seen in the same room with me," Harry said. "What's different now?"

The general looked clever. "Work it out, Harry. Work it out for yourself."

"Ah, Albert," he said, as young Albert came to remove the debris of their breakfast. "I wonder if you like asparagus? It's going to be overflowing my garden any day now."

"I'll have to sweep the floor," Albert said gloomily, "all them crumbs. Asparagus would go down a treat," he said.

He smiled like a child, and said the word again. "A treat," he said.

25

"I think Kalman knows," Sorrel said. "I'm afraid this omelette hasn't really worked."

"It looks perfectly workmanlike to me," Harry said. "It's a mess, certainly, but perfectly cooked, which is all that counts with omelettes."

"I'll do mine. You start in or it'll be a waste. It was that moment when he was helping her on with her coat," Sorrel said. She put butter in the iron pan, and there was a hiatus while she watched it heat, and poured the eggs and stirred them about.

"Help yourself to things," she said as she joined him at the table. "How is it?" she asked.

"Delicious. Tell me about this coat business. It wasn't in your letter."

"It meant nothing to me then," she said. "He was helping her into her coat when they were leaving after dinner."

Sorrel ate some omelette and did some remembering.

"Yes, that's it," she said. "Annette's arms didn't find the sleeves, you know? And Annette made a remark, a crack at him really, very camouflaged and therefore snide, to the effect that he was usually so good at holding a coat for a woman. And he gave such a look, I didn't know what it meant at the time."

"What do you think it means now?"

"This is all hindsight and madly intuitive," Sorrel said. "I think what was going on was this, that he knows she's been having an affair, and that she has a feeling he knows, but they haven't spoken about it to each other, so it's not acknowledged."

"I wonder if it's going to mean something," Harry said. "What's he like?"

"He doesn't really present himself," Sorrel said. "I could give characters to all the other men at that dinner table, but not to him. Either he's a hider, or there's not much to him. He's a lot older than she is, I can tell you that."

"What's a lot?" Harry asked, and it came out more sharply than he would have expected.

Sorrel gave him a look. "Twenty years or so, I'd say. Why did you ask it like that?"

"Ah, twenty years, that is a lot," Harry said. He took cheese: molten Brie. "We're risking listeria and salmonella left, right and centre," he said. "I asked it like that," he said, "because I seem to have met a woman."

"You have, haven't you," Sorrel said. "I can tell, looking at you. It's a real thing, is that right?"

"Who knows these days? Feels like it. May be," Harry said. "She's French, called Olivia. She's down at Carolside. I think perhaps you should go and join her, and I'll follow. We do well in the country. You did well up on that island. These heavies you escaped from, who do you think they were?"

"I think they were typical MI5 urban yokels, ex-police route, probably. As a matter of fact," Sorrel said, "I think the reason I got away was that they weren't as ready to shoot as I was. I don't think they were the kind to have knocked off poor Marion."

"More hindsight and intuition?" Harry said.

"Not entirely," Sorrel said. "Professional experience and judgment are in there too."

"It's true," he said. "They are."

She got up and went round the table. Her arms circled his neck from behind and she kissed his cheek. "I'm glad about your Olivia person," she said. "You deserve an Olivia person."

"Do I? That's a nice thing to say."

He watched her making the coffee, a lithe and cheerful, tough girl-woman, with a strong lush body and auburn-shot gold hair.

222

"You're looking pretty brisk," he said.

"Yes, yes," Sorrel said, as one who had experienced before the transferred sexual benevolence of the recently infatuated, "I know. Here's your coffee. Now, what's next on the agenda?"

"I'm going to Edinburgh to see this lawyer Julia Heron's landed me with. I was trying," Harry said, "to find out something, anything he could tell me, about this letter the late Marion Oliphant left for him to send to America, to a professor in New York State, and all he can remember, he says, is that the man was a professor. But there's something else, I know there is." He lit himself a cigarette. "When I said, was that absolutely all he could tell me, there was one of those stops in the talk, and then he said, 'Nothing else I can say to you on the telephone,' very stuffy and sanctimonious all of a sudden."

"Maybe that was professional integrity," Sorrel said.

"Uh-huh, you mean *that's* what happens north of Watford?" Harry said. "Maybe that's what it was, but I think he was scared. So I think it might be worth the trip. I mean, any least glimmer of illumination on what the hell's going on will be just terribly welcome."

Sorrel got up to open a window and let some of the smoke out. She stood looking down into the street.

"What have we got?" she said. "What we've got is separate strands. There's the chateau being shot up, and the weird stuff you picked up from that American, Doffene, about MI5 being out to get you; we've got Marion Oliphant dead, and thinking MI5 was out to get her, according to Julia Heron; we've got Lethington as the megalomaniac conspirator who's faked evidence to put you on the spot, and says this is to blackmail you with, but five minutes later his boys, presumably his boys, are rushing up the stairs to kill you, so God knows what he means."

She came back to the table and poured more coffee, and sat down. "And before that we've got Lord Findo coming on at Kenyon about you and then we've got you being rubbished by that committee; and we've got Annette's affair with General Kenyon, and Marion Oliphant being one of the community the

Kalmans move in when they're up there. It's time, Holmes, for the injection of heroin and the inspiring violin music."

"That's exactly what it's time for," Harry said, "because if we don't see daylight soon they'll be playing the wrong sort of violin music, and we won't be around to hear it."

He put out his cigarette. "Right now, though, what about running me out to the airport? I've got a flight about three."

In the car he said: "Fill me in on Nick Churchyard."

He took off his shoes and inclined the seat back and put a foot up on the dashboard, and wished he could drive the way Sorrel drove. She nourished second and third gears to the limits of their torque in a way to which he could never hope to aspire, and accepted offerings that became available on the road, which he would have regarded as no more than chances and some of them mighty thin chances at that, with a certainty that let her shift the car through the traffic with mind, hands and instinct as sure as those of a lapidary at work on a rough diamond.

"Use the ashtray, for God's sake," Sorrel said, and pulled it out for him.

"Damn it, it fell off," he said. "I wasn't looking at the ash, I was waiting for that truck to come through the door at me."

"He and I knew exactly what we were doing," Sorrel said. "Nick and these Americans, Doffene and a woman called Jennifer . . ."

"Nick was much taken with the woman called Jennifer," Harry said.

"I thought he might be," Sorrel said. "I heard him blush over the phone, the poor fish. I thought our Nick was a hard case."

"He's a hard case, all right. Even Achilles had his heel, remember, but look what he did to Hector."

They did not speak for a bit. Whether Sorrel was visualizing Churchyard tearing round Troy with Hector's corpse dragging behind his chariot, Harry did not know, and he rather hoped not. He hoped she was concentrating on what she was doing with this chariot made by Alfa-Romeo.

"Has this car got turbo, or something?" he said as the traffic grew lighter and some road opened before them.

"This car has a normally aspirated engine," Sorrel said. "I'm just driving it, that's all. Nick said he had been given a list of people through a contact of Arkley's, to whom he, this contact, would have gone, if he'd wanted a Panhard armoured car and crew to take out that conference for him. Nick went to see Arkley and Arkley sent him to see this man. Three names on the list."

"Arkley's *that* much better?"

"Arkley's that much better," Sorrel said, "partly because he's in a tearing rage with whoever had his leg shot off for him. Yes, they're moving him to London this week. Anyway, MI6 in Paris – because however much some chaps in MI6 may be glad to see the back of Arkley, they can't let their boss have his leg blown off and not do something about it – apparently put the fear of God into this contact, and he seems to have put it into Nick. Nick was rather subdued, talking about him."

Seddall said: "See the back of Arkley? They'll be lucky."

"He's lost his leg, Harry, for God's sake."

"He's in Intelligence, he's not an Olympic hurdler. He does not," Seddall said, "need two legs to think his crafty thoughts. And I'll tell you this," he said, "when Arkley's up and hobbling about again he'll just love having a tin leg."

"Don't say that, I don't like it. Nobody can love having a tin leg."

The car flew down the dual carriageway, as if Sorrel had put her foot down to get away from the place where Seddall had shown the less pleasant side of himself.

"They're going to, well, call on the three," she said, "and see what they can find out."

"Uh-huh," Harry said. "Well, let's not think about that. Let's think about you going to Carolside. It's likely to be your last visit, come to think about it. The farmhouse is about ready to move into. I'll be glad to see the last of that dreadful pile."

"Are you going to sell it?"

"Sell it? It's a crumbling old jerry-built Victorian ruin. It's not sellable. I'm going to blow it up."

"You were brought up there. Won't you miss it?"

"Listen, if you had been brought up there, with a father like my father, you'd want to shell it to pieces."

"So-ho," she said.

"Yeah," he said. "So-ho is about right. Will you mind going down there? It's not only that if there are wars breaking out all round us we'll do better on our own ground; I'm exercised about Olivia. They'll know by now that they can get at me through her, whoever they are, they'll know that. That's why I thought better of asking her to go back to France. So in a way, I'm asking you to watch out for her."

He got another of those quick side glances. "I thought you said she can look after herself."

"So she can, damn it, but don't be a fool, Sorrel. I don't know that much about her, but she can't be a trained and dirty fighter like you."

Sorrel smiled at the road flying to meet her. "Thanks," she said. "You're paying me quite a compliment, asking me to watch out for Olivia. No, I'll like to do it, of course I shall."

Harry unwound himself from the intricate convolutions he had imposed upon his limbs, and made himself and the seat upright. He took out a keyring and with some cursing and a broken nail managed to take a key off it.

"When you have a free hand," he said, "take this. It's the key of the gun cupboard. You might want to get in some shooting. So might Olivia, and I forgot to give it to her. Take Bayard too, will you?"

Sorrel put out her hand, palm up, and he laid the key on it. "Thanks," she said, dropping it into the door pocket, "I'm a better shot than I am an angler. I felt a real phoney up on Islay."

"You did all right on Islay," he said. "Yes, you did all right on Islay. There's that to think about too, isn't there?"

*

The plane put him down at Edinburgh Airport, and the taxi put him down in Charlotte Square. Refulgent in the late afternoon sunlight, the confident nobility of proportion of the square's north and south sides, the domed weight of the church on the west side facing eastward across the fresh green of the central garden down the elegant boulevard of George Street, stopped him on the pavement.

It was all so clean, its face as youthful and unused as when the stone was cut and laid. He stood on the steps of the Roxburghe Hotel and turned to look again across the square. He knew why he preferred London. London had a used face; he liked a used face.

He entered the hotel, took note of the time, and checked in.

"I have to rush," he told the desk. "I'll leave my bag with you."

Out again in the square he strolled to his appointment with the lawyer of Marion Oliphant, deceased.

He climbed a flight of stairs and entered a surpassingly handsome Georgian room on the drawing-room floor of a house where men, such as he who rose from behind the desk, had once lived instead of merely working.

Seddall did not hang about, waiting to gather his impressions of this one. He put all his antennae at him to suss out who he was.

"Colonel Seddall," he said, and came round the desk to shake hands, "I'm Alec Crawfurd. Do sit down. Good flight, I hope?"

Seddall said the things, and went on taking in Alec Crawfurd. He stood to six feet, was about fifty years old, had a tall face with a short military moustache, but it was a face that had seen no wars. It was weathered enough to have been on the golf course, but not for a yachtsman, and was hardly tanned. With that black hair, had Crawfurd been in the habit of travelling where the sun shone hot and long, there would have been more to show for it on his skin. A man who stayed in his own country, then: where he knew who he was, where it was safe?

He behaved with confidence, he wore authority of a kind. But what kind? The kind, perhaps, that came from being always certain of what he knew, of what he was doing, of where he placed himself among his peers. There was nothing wrong with the suit: a man of tolerable wealth.

Up and at 'em, Harry thought, no time like the present.

"There was something you couldn't tell me on the phone," he said. "What was that?"

Crawfurd moved his head down a slope that left his eyes looking upwards and sideways at this sudden questioner. No rough-and-tumble of the courts behind this one, Harry thought.

And then got a surprise. "I see," Crawfurd said. "I think we should perhaps leave here. We could go to my club, it's only five minutes walk. Discuss this over a drink, and if we're still talking to each other, we might have dinner."

Time played for by Crawfurd, and Seddall bamboozled by courtesy. They went outside again, walked a bit of George Street, turned down to Princes Street, and entered a building that appeared to have been done up as an oil company headquarters. When Harry stepped out of the lift, however, he found an acceptable, almost acceptable, mix of pre-twenty-first century and olde clubbe styles.

"Not bad," he said.

"It's not, is it?" Crawfurd said. "Took me time to get used to it, when it was poshed up like this, but I rather like it."

They sat themselves with gin and tonic, in a room yet lightly occupied but beginning to fill with those who left their desks on the stroke of six.

Crawfurd took a first sip, put the glass down, and went straight at it. "Dr Oliphant," he said, "was a perfectly normal client until she died, excepting only that she left an envelope marked 'To be opened in the event of my death'. When I opened it, it had in it a letter addressed to a man in the United States, a professor at a university in New York State, and a note to me, asking me to post the letter."

He took a second sip, this one more of a swallow. "So I

posted it," he said, and thought nothing of it. It's a very straight-forward request, isn't it? And I was so appalled by the manner of her death that I took no particular interest in the letter."

"What did the inquest say?" Harry asked. "There was an inquest?"

"Yes, there was. We call them fatal accident inquiries," Crawfurd said. "They're held before a sheriff, roughly equivalent to your county court judge in England. We don't have coroners in Scotland. The decision was, an accident. That she suffocated in the smoke when the house went up. I have to tell you," he said, "that in such a case the inclination is to say that the victim of a fire suffocated in the smoke rather than burned to death. It is probably the case, in most fire deaths, and it saves any relatives some portion of their grief."

"You're telling me it was a painful death, as like as not," Harry said.

"As like as not," Crawfurd said. He had eyes of grey, as cold now as the winter sea. "An excruciating death." He took a sip, and then a swallow, which emptied his glass.

He put a handkerchief to his mouth and tucked it away again. "Unless, of course, she was murdered," he said, cool as anything. "Killed first and left to burn, or knocked unconscious first, either of those; perhaps strangled, poisoned, probably not stabbed, certainly not shot if it was to seem that she died in a fire that she accidentally started herself."

He regarded Harry, as if he might reasonably expect to be given some answer.

It was clear to Harry by now that this was a man to reckon with. He tried something. "When I spoke to you on the phone from London," he said, "it seemed to me that the reason you would not divulge more over the phone was that you were frightened of something."

Crawfurd had ordered more gin, and it came. He let it sit there.

"I was," he said. "I am now, rather. Can you show me some sort of, what do they call it, ID?"

He examined it and gave it back. "Ministry of Defence; it looks awfully respectable, I suppose," he said.

He looked at Harry for a long number of seconds, and Harry did not try to look bland, he just looked back.

Crawfurd nodded, and vented a considerable sigh. "Two men from MI5 came to see me. What are you smiling at?"

"Five," Harry said. "Hunting in couples, like hounds."

"I thought they hunted in packs," Crawfurd said. "I'm an Edinburgh bourgeois, I don't hunt." He waved it away. "They asked me about Marion Oliphant. They wanted to know if there was a deed box they could look through, that kind of thing. Anything I could tell them, they wanted to know."

He went back, now, to the gin. "I told them to come back later in the day, and I spoke to some people, senior colleagues in the firm, the Law Society, that sort of thing; for guidance, you understand. A client's private affairs vis-à-vis the Crown's need to know, you could put it like that.

"I don't know," he said. "I may have made a bad decision. I showed them the will in which you and Mrs Heron were named executors. I told them about the letter, that it had gone to a professor at a university in up-state New York."

Harry took in some gin, then some more, a lot of gin. "I see," he said. "Yes, I see," and drained his glass.

"As soon as I'd done," Crawfurd said, "or almost as soon, it occurred to me that I should have consulted the executors."

"I dunno," Harry said. "I don't see a breach of ethics there. The Crown is the Crown. We owe a duty to the Crown."

"I owe a duty to my client," Crawfurd said. "I'm glad you take it like that, that nothing's gone wrong out of it?"

"Nothing," Harry lied, seeing Lethington's motive laid out before him like a backdrop, as clear as Edinburgh Castle outside the window up there on its rock, picked out by the levelling sun.

"What made you feel," Harry said, "that you didn't want to talk about this on the phone?"

"I read newspapers," Crawfurd said. "There have been some

strange things written about the secret services lately, and I began to have doubts, and the doubts began to work on me. Was I mistaken? Have I dragged you up here for nothing?"

"It is always wise," Harry said carefully, "to be discreet in matters of this kind."

Crawfurd gave a smile – it had great charm – that mocked them both. "You talk like a lawyer," he said. "Will you have dinner?"

"I should have liked that beyond anything," Harry said, "but I think I must get back to London."

On the pavement, outside the club, they looked across Princes Street at the castle. "A stout hold of war," Harry said archaically.

Crawfurd was amused. "It's fired on the city in its time."

"Has it indeed?" By a convoluted osmotic process Harry thought of Lethington. He pictured him up there on that half-moon battery, laying a gun on himself and Crawfurd, regardless of the innocent crowds making their way home in Edinburgh's rush hour. Innocent crowds wouldn't worry Lethington worth a damn.

Seddall thought that Crawfurd would prove to be not only the vital link but also the vital voice, and that he needed the great and the good in Whitehall to hear that voice: as things stood right now, Seddall's word on its own was worth nothing in Whitehall.

He thought that Crawfurd could be an easy target for even the most commonplace assassin, if a decision was made to silence that voice.

He wondered if he had been followed from London.

"I'd like dinner," he said, not quite politely, "after all."

Crawfurd was startled; ready to feel put out. "By all means," he said, "but why this sudden change?"

The answer was not quite direct. "Because I think I should invite myself to your home overnight. Do you have family?"

Crawfurd was making close scrutiny now, interested in this abruptly alien mind at work. "My wife, who's with her bridge

231

four this evening. Twin daughters, in America, doing post-graduate at different universities. Two cairn terriers and a cat."

"I hope they're noisy dogs," Seddall said, and turned back into the club.

Going up again in the lift, Crawfurd said: "I'm beginning to get a glimmer, but why do you want to stay tonight?"

"I carry a pistol," Seddall said. "That's why."

With lamb cutlets and claret on the table, Seddall felt he was thinking well at last. Lethington's men, whether they were regular MI5 or Lethington's private thugs provided with all the credentials, had carried to their master the surprising news that Seddall was an executor of Marion Oliphant's estate.

Lethington had at once embarked on his plan to discredit Seddall, knowing that Dr Oliphant had prepared an in-the-event-of-my-death letter to a man in America; but it didn't matter where the man was, Lethington had probably got him by now; he was probably ashes in an urn by now in some cemetery in New York State.

What mattered was that Lethington knew Seddall would learn about the letter, and that Seddall would at least start wondering, and might very well start wondering too much for Lethington's peace of mind: not that Lethington went in for peace of mind, but you know what I mean, Seddall said to himself.

Lethington would also know, however, that Julia Heron was the other executor, and Heron and Seddall together were names that would give him to think deeply, since she was high in the counsels of secret intelligence. Seddall, had he not been chewing lamb, would have chewed his lip: he knew now why he had felt watched during that supper with Julia after the opera.

He had a nasty feeling that if Lethington knew what was happening here in Edinburgh right now he would start to cut off the loose ends of the threads tying him into all this: he would start killing. Seddall would have to talk to Julia. The sooner the better.

Crawfurd, sharing this silent dinner, was enough engaged in his companion's unusual professional style to say readily: "Let me show you," when Seddall said he must find a telephone.

"Julia Heron," her voice said.

"Julia," he said. "It's Harry Seddall. I want you to leave your house, this very minute – well, this very half-hour, anyway – and go where it's absolutely safe, abroad, anywhere, so long as its safe. I think the crisis is going down, and there could be bodies piled up like the stage in a Restoration tragedy. I don't want yours to be one. And Julia, this line will not be safe, there'll be a bug on your phone."

"I'll digest all that," she said. " Wait."

He waited, longer than he thought it would have taken for Julia Heron, that considerable woman, to digest even such news as he had given.

"You're still there?" her voice said at last, and he said he was. "I have a captain RN dining here," she said. "He'll think what to do."

"Good," he said, "but go, go now."

"My dear," she said, "he's standing here waving his car keys at me. I shall be in good hands. Look to yourself."

The phone clicked in his ear.

He dialled again. "Sorrel," he said, "that friend of yours, the lad with the ginger hair who's in the Regiment," he italicized the words. "Are you still on good terms with him?"

There was a silence of more than a moment, then she said: "Yes, you could say that. When he's in London we exchange the last favours, now and then, you know."

"Great Scott," he said. "Don't talk dirty, woman, I'm in a respectable club."

"I'm not talking dirty," she said. "It's friendship between woman and man, that's all. You have some need of him?"

"I want four of his buddies, including him if possible, to look after a man and his wife for maybe three days, here in

233

Edinburgh, and I want them here tomorrow noon. Fix it and I'll call you later."

"It's done," Sorrel said.

"And be ready to go down to Carolside after we speak again, which will be in about two hours," he said. "I want you off to Carolside tonight, don't wait till tomorrow. Don't trust your phone. Watch your back. The hounds of hell are in winter's traces, all that sort of thing."

"Showdown time," she said. "The enemy might strike anywhere, do anything. I've got it."

"That's right," he said. "That's right. Talk to you later."

He went back to the dining room and found Crawfurd reading a newspaper with every appearance of patience. "I thought you'd as soon go on to the cheese," Crawfurd said. "You'd eaten most of the lamb, not worth having it kept warm."

"You're being extremely kind," Harry said.

"It may be," Crawfurd said, "that the boot's on the other foot."

"There's a high proportion of enlightened self-interest, I assure you. Stilton, thank you, perfect choice. We have a lot to do," Harry said. "I'm going to ask you to swear an affidavit, or something like that, which I can show to Ten Downing Street along with my report. Are any of the colleagues you consulted establishment enough for their word to carry an absolute guarantee of authenticity to that address? I'm not talking about *doubting* anybody's word, you understand, but these are politicians and bureaucrats I have to get the message through to, and I need them to sit up and take notice at once.

"You can take it that your client was certainly murdered," Seddall went on, "and that there have been subsequent and there are continuing skullduggeries."

The sun had gone, and the castle was dark and lowering against a clouded sky. He remembered Sorrel's description of Marion Oliphant's house, a carpet of ash in a setting of flowers. He thought that he hated men like Lethington.

"How would this do?" Crawfurd said. "I consulted the

Deputy Keeper of the Signet, who is in effect the chairman of the society of solicitors to which I belong. Armed with a statement from him of what passed between him and myself, the Lord Advocate . . ."

Harry made a question of his face, since it was full of Stilton.

"The Lord Advocate is the Scottish equivalent of the Attorney-General," Crawfurd said, "and a Minister of the Crown. I know he was in London yesterday. The Lord Advocate could get attention at Downing Street."

"Well, would he do it?" Seddall asked.

"Of course he'd do it," Crawfurd said, surprised. "We all know each other here, we lawyers. I'll convince the Deputy Keeper, he'll convince the Lord Advocate, and the Lord Advocate will convince Downing Street."

Seddall smiled what felt like the best smile he'd come up with for weeks. "You Scotch lawyers don't beat about the bush, do you?" he said.

Crawfurd said: "Don't deceive yourself. When there are bushes to be beaten about, we beat them as periphrastically as anybody. Come and meet my wife."

Crawfurd stood up. Seddall, about to do the same, turned part sideways in his chair and went on sitting there, looking into what was now a roomful of men in business suits but hardly seeing them, seeing only a haze of blue and black and grey, with heads turning to each other, heads bending to their food.

He remembered himself, and came to his feet.

"What was that about?" Crawfurd asked him. "More action-planning?"

"No," Harry said. "I was thinking about that posthumous letter your Dr Oliphant left for you to post. However well-intentioned she may have been, it was like a death warrant, that letter to Professor Whoever."

"You think it's all up with him?" Crawfurd said.

"That's what I have to think," Harry said. "Even if the letter was a warning, it will have been nip and tuck with him. Nip and tuck," he said again.

26

Nip and tuck was what it was. If Calder had been in a state to consider objectively descriptions of his situation, he would have agreed that nip and tuck were the words to use.

But Calder was not in that state.

Calder was alone again, on the run again, and the shock of the event that had put him there had left him capable of nothing but moving as well as his legs would move; which was not very well. They did not entirely refuse their office, his legs, but they would not stride, there was a restriction in their operation as if his central nervous system had sent out the wrong message to his sinews.

For the message in his head was move on, move *away*, on down the street and round the corner, on down the next street to the next corner. Calder felt, indignantly, that fear should be more useful to him than this.

They spent several nights on the road after they left Harwich, travelling westward, keeping clear of London, and then turning south past Oxford towards Bath, covering hardly any distance each day.

At each hotel they had stopped at, von Harma conducted himself like the commander of an isolated army unit on campaign who had patrols out searching for any sign of other military activity, friend or foe.

For the most part this consisted of Peter using the phone while von Harma sat waiting for his reports.

236

"Intelligence," von Harma explained to Calder, "is like any other industry. If you can afford it, you can buy into it."

"You buy it from Government intelligence services?" Calder asked. "You mean you can bribe their agents?"

If there had been any capacity for amusement in von Harma, it would have shown then, but the pale eyes that glanced at Calder remained as always, as if they were made of glass.

"You are so unused to the ways of the world, my Calder," von Harma said. "You are a wonder to me. Sometimes, you can bribe, but it is seldom necessary, but it is time consuming and not that fruitful: bribable intelligence officers invariably feel that they have a personal stake on the table, and tend to make demands on you to satisfy their need for reassurances of various kinds. You are to tell them that they are good fellows, that you value what they have done for you, that you insure their future against risk; you have to tell them all sorts of rubbish, which you do not mean, simply to satisfy their need for neurotic dialogue."

Von Harma looked across at the man busy on the phone. "Peter is good at it. He has been a non-commissioned officer, and with such men he is stern and humane, or so they think, and if they believe it is called for, he is stern and humane and respectful. But it is a great waste of his time, and his time is valuable to me, so I seldom resort to bribery.

"No, my dear Calder, when I say intelligence is an industry and you can buy into it, I mean just that. I have bought into a first-rank security company in Munich, that is all."

There was a knock on the door. "Ah," von Harma said. "If you would be so kind, but wait first for Peter."

Peter laid the receiver on the table and stood so that he would be behind the door when it opened. At each of the hotels, Peter had gone upstairs to approve the rooms. He would not take a room where the door was hinged to open close against a side wall. When Calder asked him what he looked for in a room, Peter told him about the doors. "Security consists of fractions in your favour, and fractions against you," he said. "If you can move a fraction from one balance to the other, you should do so."

Calder had given it as his view that this business with the doors was tantamount to pedantry, and it was because of this that Peter answered him in terms of fractions. He had quite taken to Calder since the business with the Customs at Harwich. "The *freiherr* killed a lot of Jews," he said. "He killed Russians and Poles as well, but the Mossad have long memories. The Mossad do not make threats, when they have decided to make a target of a man, they strike without warning. Of course they do, it is the sensible way. So I am careful about doors as I am about a hundred or so other things. It becomes second nature, and it is my work."

Now, when Calder opened the door, not Mossad but a maid with a teatray came into the room. When she had gone, Peter returned to the phone, spoke briefly, and hung up.

While Calder nourished himself with smoked salmon sandwiches, Peter and von Harma spoke together in German. Calder was used to this, and it did not seem rude to him. It seemed only natural that the German High Command should communicate in German.

"So far, so good," von Harma said at last. "It appears that your Colonel Seddall is indeed going to his house in Somerset. He has sent Miss Sorrel Blake there to join Madame Tesson."

He began to cough drily, and swallowed some tea. "Peter," he said, "you will continue."

"It is a large house," Peter said. "Not a schloss, you understand, but a large house standing very much by itself, on its own land, grass and trees," he looked at his notes, "and all surrounded by bocage country, hedges, ditches, fields. It is called Carolside and the nearest town of any size is called Wellington. Now," he said, "this is of interest tactically, because Colonel Seddall has said to Miss Blake," and he looked again at his notes, "that they do well in the country, and in the way he said it . . ."

"The context," von Harma said. "In the context in which he said it, he means they do well in the country, better than in the town, when engaging their enemies. It appears that his difficulties with the man Lethington of their MI5 are approaching the crisis, and that Seddall is in a state of some confidence, but expecting perhaps armed attack."

He stopped there in response to a gesture from von Harma. "Peter has said that in this event we may want to bring in some men to help ensure that your Colonel Seddall," he inclined his head slightly at Calder, "who is your lifeline, shall we say, remains alive if there is an attack on him. It seems that in a day or two he may be in a position to clear his name, but until then he chooses to look after himself. It seems in any case that the affair he is dealing with has complications that would concern his government and that is one that he will wish to keep secret: our knowledge here is more sketchy, but it sounds to me as if, should Seddall succeed, there will afterwards be a hush-hush."

It was the first solecism Calder had heard in von Harma's English, and without a thought Calder said: "That it will be hushed up, you mean."

Peter looked out of the window. Von Harma looked at Calder and the corners of his eyes squeezed themselves a little together. There was no change of expression in his face, but Calder understood that it was one thing for von Harma to compliment Peter's excellent command of English, and another thing for Calder to seek to improve von Harma's, particularly in front of Peter.

"Peter," von Harma said, "has summoned a reinforcement and ordered it to accommodate itself in twos and threes in hotels in Taunton, where weapons and vehicles will be supplied to it."

His eyes relaxed. If he had been a man who smiled, Calder thought, he would have smiled then. "So we shall go to Bath, and quite soon, it is possible, you will reach your Colonel Seddall."

Calder was about to issue the appropriate expression of gratitude to von Harma for bringing him safely to what had seemed, at one time, an impossible destination, and found that he could not. The obstacle was simply that von Harma, who should, according to natural justice, be suffering the tortures of the damned, was still here in this world, able to own a private intelligence network and a private security company that supplied armed men to his need.

The fact that all of this was being done on Calder's behalf did not serve to ease his knowledge that he was being a moral hypocrite purely out of fear. If he survived all this, if his life went on for a few years into an afterwards, he would carry the burden von Harma's protection was laying on him as a moral guilt, a guilt that shared von Harma's own appalling guilt.

He said nothing. He looked at von Harma, and saw that the German knew.

Von Harma lifted his forefinger. "Now I shall rest," he said, "and will hope to see you at dinner."

As Calder rose to leave, von Harma said: "I told you this would happen to you."

"It is true, you did," Calder said, "but it is worse than I had thought it would be."

"You feel you have been altered," von Harma said. "With you it is not irremediable."

Calder knew that he was being reminded of something about von Harma of which he had been aware from the first: von Harma was already a dead presence, already one of the damned.

It was a day of rain and high wind. They drove through the buffeting downpour and in heavy traffic down the Oxford by-pass to Swindon then west along the M4 motorway, and they drove much of the way in silence.

Calder was glad he was not driving. Peter constantly had the windscreen wipers going at their highest speed to clear away the muck as well as the torrential rain. He sat back in his corner and von Harma in his, with a late symphony by Mozart, and then another, to soothe their passage. It vexed Calder that he could not be sure which symphonies they were, except that neither was the Jupiter.

His mind was doing its best to work itself up into a ferment, to hit him with a kaleidoscope of mental photographs, as of the man Seddall, whom he had never seen and who appeared therefore only as a figure, variously welcoming him and assuring him that now he was safe, on the one hand, and being shot – Seddall being shot – by von Harma's over-enthusiastic reinforcement from Germany on the other; photographs of the man he had left with the corpse in the trunk of his car in America being devoured by maggots that had bred on the corpse; photographs of von Harma going down to hell in a scene no more imaginative than to be a steal from the last act of *Don Giovanni*, which did not seem to Calder to be sufficiently hellish, since he had always had the unsettled feeling that the Don would carry on much as before once he'd had the chance to charm the Devil with an aria or two.

Certainly von Harma, with the one exception that he was doing Calder a good turn, seemed still to conduct himself, given the changes that had taken place in the world, very much as he would have done as an officer of the occupying power in an invaded country: the difference was, that von Harma operated now across frontiers, rode under no swastika banner, concealed the fact that he had an army at his heels, or at least ready to answer to his call.

Calder recognized too, now, that he had a dislike of the von Harma he actually knew, as opposed to the von Harma the war criminal, whom he had not known. This arose from his idea that von Harma perceived himself as a kind of modern Flying Dutchman, upon whom the dire hand of fate had been laid. Von Harma did not open himself to such intimacy as would have been required for Calder to feel justified in this idea, but that was, to him, immaterial. It was an idea that had grown in him during the time they had travelled together; he was stuck with it, and whether he was employing it as a rationalization or not he did not care to examine. He simply knew that he had come to find being held in close quarters with von Harma next to intolerable.

For the twentieth time he reached for a cigarette before he recalled that von Harma detested cigarette smoke in his car. Calder felt sweat break out on him, and if von Harma had not, at last, begun to talk, he did not know what effect the increasing strain might have had on him.

"When I was in Estonia during the war," von Harma said, not so much out of the blue as out of the cloud of rain in which they moved, "one of our batteries, which had not been long at the front, had a Latvian liaison officer attached to it.

"We were expecting a counterattack by the Russians across a marsh. We had seen them massing in the woods beyond the marsh at daybreak. It was February, and though there had been some thaw that had done away with recent snow, more snow was forecast. The cold was raw. When the wind comes across that Livonian plain off the Baltic it pierces you to the marrow."

The car ran blind down the fast lane, passing a succession of lorries which threw out a turbulence of air and a steady deluge of their own to meet the torrent falling from the sky. When they emerged from this dark, aquatic world, the sky before them was changing. White clouds outnumbered the grey, and behind them the imminent sun shone bright, and was already gleaming on the landscape.

"Ah, that's better," von Harma said. "Where was I? Yes, it was dawn. We began firing on the Russians on the other side of the marsh, and kept it up for hours. Their casualties, as we afterwards found, were extremely heavy. A pine forest is a doubtful haven from artillery; the splinters from the trees wreak havoc, severe wounds, most severe, you will realize. Not that the Russians were using it, or being permitted by their officers, to use it as a haven. They did not lie down, for example, but stood fire until they were blown up, and more then took their place."

They were bowling along in a clear sunlight now, and Calder hoped this narrative might take an upward and less bloody turn. Peter, on the other hand, had an ear cocked towards the narrator: his kind of story, doubtless.

"This went on for hours, you understand. At noon, the

Latvian liaison officer said to the battery commander he had at last understood what was going on.

" 'We are shelling them to bits,' the battery commander said. 'We are breaking up their attack before it starts.'

" 'No,' the Latvian said. 'What is going on, is that the Russians are waiting in the marsh to launch their attack.'

"Well," von Harma said, "the notion was absurd. How could men spend hours up to their heads in water in weather like that and be in any condition to attack? We continued to shell the wood. At dusk, after a whole day of it, they came out of the marsh and took the battery and threw us back nearly ten kilometres."

Calder saw Peter smile with satisfaction in the mirror. "Good for them," Calder said, with some spite in his tone.

Von Harma heard it. "Certainly," he said, "good for them. Is that, however, all it tells you?"

"What else?" Calder said. "I am not a military man."

"It told me," von Harma said, "that the phrase 'Know your enemy' is meaningless. You must believe your enemy capable of anything, even if to you it is unthinkable."

"That is why you have lasted so long?" Calder said crudely.

In the mirror, Peter frowned, but von Harma said only: "It is one of the reasons."

Silence fell, and Peter returned them to Mozart. Calder at once recognized the minuet as being from No. 39 in E Flat. It was a small triumph, but his first today. He felt rather more alert.

They ran into the outskirts of Bath with the road steaming itself dry in the heat of the sun. As they approached a filling station Peter said: "We need fuel."

"Very well," von Harma said.

The trio to the minuet sang cheerfully and was repeated while Peter poured petrol into the tank. When he had paid for it, and came back to the car, von Harma said: "They have a car-wash. Let us use it."

"I can wash the car when we reach the hotel," Peter said.

"You will polish it," von Harma said, "when we reach the hotel. It is a hotel of some elegance, I do not wish to arrive with the car in this state. It is covered with filth from our journey."

"I must then buy a . . . I do not know what it is called, but the driver before me was buying one. A plastic that feeds into a slot in the car-wash."

"A token," von Harma said. "Then buy one, by all means."

To enter the car-wash Peter drove off the apron of the filling station and round behind the office building. There were two cars in front of them, and one just leaving the car-wash to emerge again on the apron, having completed the circuit.

Calder saw his opportunity, and felt for his cigarettes. "I shall jump out and have a smoke," he said, "while you go through the car-wash."

"Do not smoke too close to the petrol pumps," von Harma said. It sounded almost like a joke, but von Harma never joked.

Calder shrugged, and left the Daimler. He perched on a wall, already dry, from where he would be able to glimpse, past the corner of the office, the car come out after its bath.

It was now a beautiful day, a thrush sang near him with extra vigour after the rain, as if to make up for lost time. "You should be down on the ground catching worms," Calder said, "not up in that tree. Place will be hotching with worms after that rain."

He basked in the sun, in the song of the thrush, and in the absence of von Harma; he began to relax, in this release from a claustrophobia that was doing no good to his psyche. He wondered what Seddall was like, if he really could do something to help him. It had begun to occur to him that Seddall was quite likely living a perfectly normal life, and that all the excitements with which von Harma had embroidered it were a fiction of his and Peter's. Sitting here on this wall, deciding not to light a second cigarette, he felt real, and escaped from the unreality that he experienced in the company of von Harma. He did not think von Harma and his man lived real lives. Their lives were imaginary.

Calder's mind, in short, was babbling because he was, for the moment, pleasantly situated.

The Daimler entered the car-wash and was covered with a layer of foam, to the strains, presumably, of the last movement of Mozart's 39th.

A big black car at the farthest petrol pump reversed from the pump, turning hard to its left, and ran back to the mouth of the car-wash, where the Daimler was smothered in its cocoon of white foam.

Peering past the corner of the building, through the fore-shortening diagonally aligned mass of pumps, forecourt pillars, vehicles and people, Calder did not at once believe what some hidden instinct had begun to say to him; but the instinct moved him from his perch.

He walked to the corner of the building, to the first pump, and past the bonnet of the car there. He had reached the pillar in the middle rank of pumps when flame and noise erupted from the rear window of the black car, erupted and went on, stopped for what seemed no more than a second and erupted again.

He could not work that out. Why stop in the middle of it?

The roller of the car-wash had travelled the length of the Daimler by now. Water flooded down to clear off the foam and through it you could see blood and bloody bits of stuff being splashed onto the insides of the windows. Von Harma and Peter were being shot to pieces. One of the side windows blew out and some of the bloody bits of stuff flew out of the car and smeared themselves quite high up on the wire-reinforced glass wall of the car-wash, and slid slowly down as if they had some special adhesive life in them – life in them still – that resisted the pressure of the water of the car-wash.

The noise and flame stopped, but those bits of one or other, or both, of the slaughtered Germans, went on sliding down inside that glazed wall.

With part of his sight Calder saw the black car leave, and he heard the squeal of tyres and the blare of car horns, but his whole being was fixed on the car-wash carrying on with its programme, its mechanical mind unconscious that it had become a tomb: he watched with meticulous care as the gantry carried its hot-air blower along above the soaped, scrubbed, and showered Daimler and then, at the same slow and steady pace, back again to the front of the car. Until the machine stopped.

At the rear of the car he saw a red something, and in the front only a shape, for the wire-strengthened glass of the car wash was not clear. He heard screams and shouts and one voice whimpering, and realized he had been hearing them for some time. People, a few of the people in the forecourt, were moving slowly towards the Daimler and suddenly one of them ran, and when he saw what was in there stopped and stared and then came away again, flapping his arms slowly like tired wings as if to say, Don't go there, you don't want to see what's in there.

Calder did not want to see what was in there. Calder wanted to go away from where he was. He let go of the pillar and found that he could stand. He blinked once or twice and felt his head move from side to side at odd angles, and turned and bumped into the car behind him.

"Sorry," he said, "I'm so sorry," to the owner, who was standing on the other side of the bonnet with his mouth agape. Their eyes met.

"I don't know," the man said. "I never . . . I never . . ."

Calder walked past him and out of the forecourt onto the pavement. His body was hardly under his control but he had a clear message from his mind: they would have a man there, someone in that crowd of innocents will be there to see that everyone died. He'll be doubting already if he's close enough; in a moment he'll be at the car and he'll know.

There was a street to the left and Calder took it, and at the next corner turned and went on, and turned again, making a maze of his passage among these suburban houses.

After a while words began to repeat in his head that he had not the nervous energy to silence, though he could not say what they meant.

"They came out of the marsh," the words said, over and over in his head. He felt that he was perhaps going mad, because he did not know what they meant. He had forgotten von Harma's story.

27

It was a house between Abbeville and Dieppe, in a small park on the edge of its village. Having found it, they drove through the village without stopping, scouted the country round about, and dined early at a restaurant in Saint Valery-sur-Somme.

"Cheap but classy," Doffene said afterwards, as they left Saint Valery in the dusk. "You never know in France. Boy, that duck!"

" 'You never know in France!' " Jennifer repeated. "Don't be so racist."

"I not being racist, babe," said Doffene, imitating a stereotype of black speech that probably never was on land or sea, "I being aristocratic. My folks was *guelowar* in Senegal. The kingly race, babe, and a matrilineage. You can be proud to know me on two counts."

"I'll certainly try harder," Jennifer said, "but I don't know that I'll make it. Nick might." She let her hand rest on Nick Churchyard's thigh. "The English are suckers for the aristocracy."

Churchyard, who was driving, kept his eyes on the road and smiled. He was humming, not very musically, a tune that seemed to snatch from time to time at being *Parlez moi d'amour*. He seemed to Doffene to be not quite with them, as if he was looking forward to an evening of some private but immensurable satisfaction. Which was odd, considering what they were going to do.

Perhaps the Englishman was just celebrating to himself his rhapsody with Jennifer. Well, Doffene had no trouble with that. Our Jennifer was what Pauline Kael in the *New Yorker* would have called a hot chick.

"Take your hand off that boy," he said. "We got work to do tonight."

Churchyard came out of his privacy. "Isn't 'boy' an opprobrious usage?" he asked.

"From you to me," Doffene said, "opprobrious is what it would be. From me to you, it's jealousy."

"Why, Charlie," Jennifer said. "How nice of you."

"All right now, let's concentrate," Doffene said. "We're getting there."

Wafts of mist had begun to drift up over the fields, bringing that visual increment that contributes to the sense of peace in a quiet pastoral country at the approach of nightfall. Doffene lowered the window to let the cool air refresh him.

He tightened his spirit to handle what lay ahead. What a man has to do, he thought, a man just goes and does.

"It's close," he said.

"I remember it," Churchyard said, and slowed the car. "We turn here and the other turn's not far down."

The car came to a stand at the field gate they had chosen. They walked the edges of the field, which was in wheat, and went over the fence into another, which took them to the wall of the little park round the house.

From over the wall, the sound subdued a little by the small wood of beech trees, came the sound of a rotary mower. "At this time of night," Jennifer said, "how can he see to cut the grass?"

"We can see our feet," Churchyard said reasonably. "I've done it, there's something about mowing grass late into the evening. I wonder if it's our target, or one of his bodyguards."

They climbed the wall and dropped into the wood, which they penetrated till they could see the man working on the lawn. "That's not the main man," Doffene said. "That guy's short and broad, and our guy's tall and skinny, right?"

"That's right," Churchyard said. "One of the bodyguards. I'll take him if you like, you two go to the house."

"That's good," Doffene said. "There should be two in the house, we can handle that; so can you keep the mower going till we tell you it's done?"

"Understood," Churchyard said.

"We'll go that way, along the back, in the back door by the kitchen," Doffene said. "These lighted windows, that's where he'll likely be."

The house had the feel of a summer pavilion. It was on two floors, long in proportion to its depth. From where they stood they saw most clearly the end wall, with the front of the house receding in a narrow perspective. The front had six tall windows with its door centred up a short but elegant flight of stairs. They could see no lights along the front, but in the two windows of the end wall, the windows Doffene had marked, cracks of light showed round the shutters.

"Take your time," Doffene said. "Pick your moment. It may take me ten minutes to deal with the alarm; it's not a wonderful system. But we don't need to synchronize. When you're set, just do it. We'll do the same."

He punched Churchyard lightly behind the shoulder and he and Jennifer went off through the wood, and round the corner of the house, and out of sight.

The grass-cutter was working in straight swathes at a diagonal to and from the wood. It was all too simple, really, Churchyard thought. He moved forward as the man began to cut away from the wood, and lay low, hunkered down in the bushes, humming that French song, until his target had returned and started back again.

Churchyard bounded out and hit him on the back of the neck, at which he fell to the ground. Churchyard hit him again to make sure, and then dragged him into the wood while the mower stood there making its noise. He thought he had possibly not killed the man, so he tied him up and stuffed a handkerchief in his mouth.

He went out onto the lawn, and continued the grass-mowing in the style of his predecessor, following the same line, and almost at once finding pleasure in making a neat job of it. He had caught the fellow an awful crack the second time. He supposed he might in fact die. It was a sweet mower this. You could hardly see the grass now, and the mist they had seen on the fields was forming in the lightest way and in one or two places on the lawn.

He hoped someone would come and rake the grass cuttings away tomorrow. It was essential with a rotary mower, otherwise the cuttings fouled the growing grass, did it no good at all really.

"Want to sit in?" Doffene had said.

"Not the best thing, do you think?" Churchyard had said in return. "Not if you and Jennifer make a team, as you do. Not if I'm not working on him myself."

It was past two in the morning now, and the three of them sat in the man's study, at the other end of the house from where the man himself sat bound to his chair, in the cellar under the kitchen, waiting for the next interrogation.

They were getting nowhere.

"He knows it all," Doffene said. "Hell, he was in Algeria before he became an arms dealer. He thinks we're softies. He *knows* we're softies."

The team had failed, and when the team had failed, Churchyard had tried and failed, and then the team had tried again, and Churchyard again. They could not wait all night. Help came up from the village in the morning, but they had to be away long before that. They had to because of the car. A strange car by the road at night, a sideroad like that, could be anything to the rare passer-by. In daytime, among a farmer's fields, it became an object of curiosity to that farmer; and farmers notice everything that goes on within their sphere of influence. Farm people get up early, and if the farmer got interested he would be a back trail to their car, and the car a back trail to them.

They could not wait much longer.

Churchyard said: "I learned a trick. I was in . . . I learned a trick. I'll try it. OK?"

"Try it," Doffene said.

When Churchyard was gone, Doffene said: "I guess we could take the guy away with us."

"I guess," Jennifer said. "I think Nick might get the name out of him. He's good, don't you think?"

"Good at what?" Doffene said. "I don't judge him yet; I haven't seen him do that much."

"He seemed suddenly confident," Jennifer said, "that he could get the name out of him."

"We'll see," Doffene said. "I sure to God hope so, but we'll see."

After a while Churchyard came back into the room. There was a high colour on his face and his face glistened, and his eyes were brilliant and he held his head high and his chin forward. He was full of pride.

"I have the name," he said. "Let's go."

He told them the name.

"So it's the London end," Doffene said. "Yeah, let's go. Our friend in the cellar will have to start running when he gets loose. His life will be hard to hold onto for a while."

"His life?" Churchyard said. "He hasn't got it any more."

Churchyard still had that proud look shining on him, and as he spoke the words his lips, moving, held in every shape their fine and chiselled beauty. He looked heroic and vibrant with life, with the grandeur of one who knew also about death. It would all have fitted him better if he had just taken part in the charge of the Light Brigade, than if he had tortured a man to death.

Jennifer turned to Doffene and buried her face in his shoulder. "Oh hell, Charlie," she said. "Oh hell."

Doffene stroked her hair once. "I know," he said. "I know."

Churchyard led the way out of the house, and with the others coming after, went down into the mist.

*

In a fine olde inne in the south-west of England which, although it had inglenooks and blackened beams low enough to take your scalp off, was rated as having *grand confort* in Michelin as well as a *restaurant agréable*, Carmichael said to Mrs Jane Winder: "What the fuck are you doing here?"

She was looking very terrific in black stretch pants, black boots and a white shirt. The first sight of her breasts pushing at the crisp Swiss cotton of that shirt sang straight into his gut. He loved the woman.

He changed his tune. "You look wonderful," he said. "You match the ceiling," he said idiotically. "Black and white."

"Here's looking at it," Jane Winder said, and began to undress.

In fact it was a four-poster bed with a canopy, and with Jane Winder nobody had a monopoly of looking at the ceiling, but then nobody cared.

After about an hour she stretched her body from head to toe and found herself grasping the bedposts.

"She shall have bondage wherever she goes," she said, "but that can wait till after dinner. We have some talking to do."

In the dining room she told him to order. He asked for mousseline of salmon, the roast beef of old England, and from the wine list threw in Pouilly-fumé and a Chambertin.

"No wine," Jane Winder said. "I want to fuck you sober."

"Perrier," Carmichael said. "No ice for Jane," he remembered.

"How sweet," she said, "that you should say 'No ice for Jane'."

"I can never bring myself to say 'for madame' or 'for the lady'," he said.

"You're exactly right, Alexander," she said. "Other people are human too."

The mousseline was perfect. She said so. "You had bad luck with Calder again," she said.

"Listen," Carmichael said. "Calder may be a hundred and three years old, but the little shit's a pro, whatever Mendham

253

says. I mean, he was in the car with the others when it went round to the car-wash, and when the shooting stopped, where was he?''

"John," she said, "is getting nervous. In fact, John is getting very nervous. By the way," she said, "the von Harma security *gemein* or *geselschaft* or whatever it is that von Harma owned a lot of is a big client of ours. Not that they'll mind, they'll screw von Harma's share out of the widow, but John is very paranoid, you know. He's afraid that in Munich they'll view your having zotzed von Harma as a hostile act."

"The old kraut got in the way, that's all," Carmichael said. "I love the way you say zotzed. Say 'Zotz the little fuckers', for me."

"Zotz the little fuckers," she said.

"Thank you," he said. "When you came out with that in Washington," he said, "I really went for you."

"I think that's sweet," she said.

They fell upon the blood-pink perfect beef, guaranteed free of hormone injections in the literature in their bedrooms which they had, admittedly, not yet had time to read, with willing teeth and ready stomachs.

"Oh, Jesus," he said, and looked at her.

"Yes, but we need to eat, and look how we're saving time for us, getting all this nasty business talk done."

"Everything you say is right," he said, and fell to again.

"John is afraid," she said, "that the reason you've failed with Calder is that your mind's set on this guy Seddall."

Death came into his eyes and looked at her.

"Oh, Jesus," she said, in her turn. "I love it when you do that."

"You're not scared of me, what I do, one bit, are you?" he said.

"Not one bit. I'm scared only because of how much I love you."

He put his hand on the white linen cloth, and she did things to it with her fingernails. "So," she said, "what about that?"

"So what about it?" he said. "You guys have cleared it up that Calder's running for Seddall, and I've followed Calder this far and this far he's certainly making a line for Seddall. So I'll go to this place of Seddall's and get the two of them. Ends problem, end of story."

"How clear-eyed you are when it comes to business, Alexander."

"You know, from you, that's a real compliment."

"It's a sincere compliment," she said. "It's important in a relationship, to acknowledge the other person's right to, and need for, self-esteem. And I think you and I are going to have a very good relationship indeed, because we have everything going for us. I want you to know," she said, "although you may have detected it in me already, that I have killed two people, which I thought I ought to do since I'm in the business, and it is my belief that the good businesswoman ought to know what it is she's sending people out to do."

"Oh, Jesus," he said. "Do you need coffee?"

"Yes," she said firmly, "keep your powder dry a little longer. We have one thing to settle. When you go after Calder and Seddall, I'm coming with you."

"No," he shouted.

The waiter appeared.

"Alexander took too much mustard with his last mouthful," Jane Winder explained. "Just coffee, please."

"No," Alexander said, at a lower decibel count.

"Yes," she said. "I can shoot the eye out of a cow four times out of five at thirty feet, with my Beretta 92SB, a special version of the pistol now ordered in volume for the US Army, and I have shot a lot of cows in developing this expertise, and emotionally speaking it is not easy to shoot away those big, brown, ruminant eyes, so you will understand that if I saw an infant with golden curls like the child Shirley Temple about to throw a grenade at you, I would slaughter her without compunction.

"And," she said, "now that I have found you I am going to do everything I can to make it that you stay alive, even if I have to shoot you in the fucking kneecap to stop you going out there without exceptional back-up."

"The kneecap?" he said.

"Well, she said. "In the foot. One or two toes, maybe. Am I coming with you?"

"Maybe it would be best," he said. "It would certainly be good."

"Nothing with us will ever be good," she said. "It will always be the best." She sipped coffee. "I've burnt my tongue," she said. "Who needs this kind of pain. Are you into bondage, Alexander?"

"I'm into anything," he said, "so long as it's with you."

"Then let's go upstairs."

When she was naked she went to her suitcase, which she had brought into Carmichael's room and had not yet made time to unpack, and took from it four broad long strong silk ribbons.

She put a foot up on a chair and tied one of the ribbons round one ankle, and then the same with the other ankle. She was for these minutes like a dancer portrayed by Degas, grave, beautiful, devoted to the art for which she was arranging herself, and because she possessed this devotion, wise.

She made Carmichael, who was sitting on the edge of the bed, stand up, and kissed him all over, and then lay down on the bed.

"You will tie me up first," she said, "because when you are tied up, after I have finished with you," she said with love, "finished is what you will be."

Lethington was on the warpath, which is to say he was in his element. Driving down to Somerset he felt like Xenophon leading his ten thousand to the sea, Sherman starting his march through Georgia, and Abd el-Krim hounding the Spaniards to defeat at Melilla, all rolled into one.

Adrenalin coursed through him like an elixir of the gods. If he had made out the words of the ancient song that sang in his blood he would have felt himself the last of a warrior race in a world coming down to chaos, that in chaos only he was at home, to chaos only he was the worthy opponent: if chaos was to come a good man would ride against it into the dark and go down, laughing, laughing, into the gulf.

The words that were in his head, however, came not from the ancestry of his wild being but from his phone tappers, who told him he had lost control of the game he had started; that the top-rated and overpaid assassin Carmichael had farted about too long, savouring the impending outcome of his *own* personal vendetta against Seddall (whatever, in the name of all creation, *that* might be about); and Harry bloody Seddall had in the mean-time found out more than it was good for him to know, and worse for Lethington that Seddall did know: unless in this mad dash to avert disaster he could put paid to Seddall, and his sidekick Sorrel Blake, before Seddall got himself a hearing in Whitehall.

After which, Lethington promised himself, he would deal with Carmichael, and after that, who can say, he thought. Need Findo live? A man was as well to wipe out his allies as his enemies, once they had served their purpose. Lethington laughed aloud. He who sups with me, he told himself merrily, had best use a toasting fork.

So, Lethington raced down to Somerset at the wheel of his 6 Series BMW, with a Range Rover full of his best boys and girls running a mile in front of him, and another, full of his second best, a mile behind; Lethington, on his ride to victory or ven-geance; Lethington with blood in his eye, and with his mind cracking and his spirit soaring; Lethington with he knew not what still to play for.

From Edinburgh, in his chartered aircraft, Seddall had got as far as the Scottish–English Border when the starboard engine went and the pilot put them down at Carlisle.

Now he sat in the express to Birmingham (change for Bristol) and thought he had made a bad decision. He should have hired a fast car, a Porsche or something like that, and gone for Somerset like a bat out of hell. He thought of Olivia, of Sorrel – and even of the thrawn Mrs Lyon – staked out there, it now seemed to him, like so many goats to fetch the tigers out of their jungle.

What could three women do against the forces that might, at any moment, be unleashed upon them? Well, quite a lot, actually, those three, but by the living God, he wished he was there with them right now.

He had a bad feeling under his heart, and a flicker of nausea in his throat, and against these symptoms he glared steadily out of the window at the flying countryside, and prayed as to a forgotten god.

28

The Alfa wound its way down the steep and coiling road, a road sunk between high banks from which sprang hedges of oak and beech and hawthorn gone wild, to leap to twenty feet and more in height. The light was in the sky, a sky of palest blue flowered with faint crimson by the unrisen sun. Sometimes overhead the hedges met and intertwined, so that Sorrel went in and out of tunnels and foliage, a passage dappled with light and dark, and even in the tunnels dappled again by the white flash of May blossom waking to the day.

She went round a corner and turned off between two stone pillars with pineapples on top, opening to a track that swung to the right, dipped into a coppice and then climbed to a ridge where the woodland ended and rough pasture spread out on either side.

When the Alfa mounted the ridge the sun struck at her eyes from across the valley, bright and blinding but welcome for all that. Sorrel stopped the car and got out. Bayard followed, wagged his tail for politeness, inspected a few molehills, and set off at a canter for the house. Sorrel stretched herself, her arms reaching to the empyrean, and grunted and stamped and strode about. It was too damp with dew to sit on the grass, so she sat on the side of the car seat with the door open and her legs outside and revelled in the morning air, fresh but soft.

There was the house, on the other side of the valley, about two miles away, a long building set on the far slope with a tower over the door. She began to drowse in the first suggestion of warmth from the sun, and set off again down the track thinking of breakfast. The car rattled across a cattle-grid and was in among sheep and well grown lambs, crossed another grid, and went down over the bridge and up to the house.

Carolside was a house of less grace than its name. It had been built by Seddall's great-grandfather, a successful career soldier and a great looter in India and Africa, who did not become a gentleman until he had retired and could afford to offer the appearance of being nice in his behaviour. General Seddall had enjoyed a good eye for intrinsic worth in small and portable objects, but in larger matters his aesthetic sense had been all to seek (as his contemporaries might have, and probably had, said), and between them he and his architect had come up with a monster.

It was built of grey stone and shaped as a shooting lodge that had grown beyond its station. The windows were ogival-arched Gothic, and the decoration about them had given much bad work to good stonemasons. It was on two floors except for the tower, which reached to four, on top of which the general had flown his flag to show that he was still holding out. The top of the tower, and the roofline of the rest of the building, were topped with fanciful crenellations indefensible both militarily and artistically.

The door itself, oversized and studded with iron, proclaimed the baronial, medieval-romantic fixation, and led, as Sorrel knew, to an entrance hall that would have taken a tennis court and soared strangely in wooden vaulting to the top of the house, carrying with it part of the way a staircase that divided and led to the first-floor galleries which gave onto the bedrooms.

The door, however, was locked, and Sorrel sat herself on one of the two cannon that flanked it (all that the general had won from the British campaign that toppled the Emperor Theodore of Abyssinia; a step up in rank, but no profit), to wait for the house to come to life.

Her eye scanned the country about, remembering the ground, recalling it to her mind from outings when she had walked or shot in this isolated valley. Strategically the house was hopeless. It could be fired at, from cover, all around. She went, reflexively to the car, and took out her bag where she had packed her pistol along with everything else, and turned to find Bayard coming round from the back of the house.

"Made the rounds, have you?" Sorrel said to him, taking the weight of his paws on her hip and ruffling the liver and white head. "What a big old fellow you are, Bayard."

There was the sound of a key turning and bolts going back, and Mrs Lyon opened the front door.

"It's yourself, then," Mrs Lyon said. "You'll be needing your coffee and your breakfast forbye, driving all night, a slip of a thing like you."

Sorrel accepted this slander gracefully, and went with Mrs Lyon through the cavernous hall and along the corridor to the kitchen.

Sorrel Blake had porridge and cream and bacon and eggs inside her by the time Olivia Tesson came downstairs.

To Mrs Lyon's offer of the same Olivia said, "No, no, thank you, just bread and coffee for me, please," with precisely that distracted air of being *affairée* in which Sorrel recognized a Frenchwoman wary of competition.

Simultaneously with their greetings, they measured each other. Sorrel was pleased for Harry, and knew that Olivia's reserve meant that she was supposing it likely that Sorrel and Harry had, somewhere along the line, been lovers.

This irritated Sorrel rather a lot, not just because it meant that in her thirties she looked good enough to be a bimbo, and Olivia had therefore allowed herself to suppose that she might well be one; Sorrel knew she looked good, but lots of women looked good, and whether from man or woman it pissed her off to have it implied that she was anybody's for a poke of chips.

Still, she could let that pass, since it was an outthrow of Olivia Tesson's newness in her relationship with Harry. What irritated her most was having to go to the trouble of dealing with the over-acute susceptibilities of that newness; she found the Tesson woman's – the Tesson woman, for God's sake! Calm

261

down, she told herself – she found *Olivia's* indulgence in these susceptibilities too pretty for words, when there was serious business to take care of.

"We'll be back in a moment," she said firmly to Mrs Lyon, who was that moment pouring boiling water onto the coffee she had ground for Olivia. "Come," she said with the same firmness to Olivia, "I want to show you something."

She took her outside, where she found the sun was already higher than she expected, and looked automatically at the watch on her wrist.

"Olivia," she said, "I expect us to be friends, but who knows about these things? Meanwhile, we have a day before us in which we have to be colleagues, allies if you like, and perhaps take some risks together, and I don't want any least *arrière pensée* between us in your estimate of me. So I need to say to you that Harry and I have never been lovers. We are extremely good friends, and the connection between us has only, ever, been either that of friendship or that of professional colleagues."

Olivia made no charming gesture of deprecation, no winsome movement of facial expression, which was a point in her favour. "You detected it?" she said. "I apologize. It is simply that I disliked the idea that I might be meeting, so soon after I have met him, a former girlfriend of his, so at home in his house."

"That would not be agreeable for you," Sorrel said, "but it is not the case, and," she said straightly, "it irritates the hell out of me to have had to say this to you. All right?"

Sorrel could see that this was not as Mlle Nice-Girl as Olivia had expected, not what Olivia would think quite polite when a misunderstanding had been dealt with: but, tough titty, she thought. She wanted this thing ironed out smooth, and she'd rather have Olivia know what to expect from her, and dislike her for it, than start the day with concessions to whatever style of social palliative Olivia might be accustomed.

Olivia looked at her, looked across the valley for a moment

and met her eyes again. "*D'accord*," she said. "Let us go on in and share that coffee."

"Harry telephoned me," Olivia said at the kitchen table, which was ten feet long and four wide, and took up no room at all in the big flagstoned kitchen. "He said we may expect to be attacked."

While she spoke Olivia was tying her hair back with a coloured square of silk that she had rolled up. Her breasts were just the right size. Lucky woman, Sorrel thought. Her own were too big for comfort, and would be a damn nuisance today if she had to do some of the running about she thought likely. She eased her shoulders, which had a habit of developing an ache these days after a hard fast drive in the car. She wondered if the weight of her breasts might be a cause: two kilos was a lot of weight to ask her shoulders to carry.

She noticed that she was being not quite objective about Olivia. Well, then, stow it, she told herself. There was no trace of alarm in Olivia's large and luminous eyes, or on that beautiful mouth.

"That's the picture," Sorrel said, "if they're about already, and if it was me I'd be about already, a car could be a trap for us. I think we should take to the bushes. Up behind the house is the way to go. The woods come right down."

"We should go soon," Olivia said. "There is no reason not to."

Mrs Lyon, who had been listening as if they were discussing the day's housekeeping, said: "I'll get some food tegither. Ham and bread and cheese and the like, and a puckle aiples and toma-toes for the drought. Five meenits and I'll be wi' ye. Ye'll can cairry it in yin o' his majesty's gamebags apiece. I'll no cairry onything. I'll be pit tae't tae keep up wi' ye as it is. And I'm no shootin' a gun, I cannae abide a gun."

She went out to the larder and came back at once. "And I'm no haudin' on tae the dug, either. I'll come wi' ye, but I intend tae be a liability. I'm ower old for these capers. Sae lang as it's understood."

She went off again.

"So much for the commisariat," Sorrel said. "Let's take a look at the gun cupboard."

An hour later they had taken up a temporary position high above the house, and Sorrel went off to scout for a better one on the height of land, and for signs of enemy activity.

"If you hear what you think is me coming back," she said, "don't believe it unless Bayard wags his tail. He'll growl if it's someone else. You won't mind my saying," she added, "that that's a hell of a weapon you've got there, for its size." She stopped there delicately.

That weapon was a .243 Ruger deer rifle. Sorrel had used it herself, and had fired it at a petrol can full of water to see what it could do. The can had peeled apart at the impact of the high velocity bullet. She did want actually to ask Olivia not to shoot her. She hoped the hint might be enough.

"Don't worry," Olivia said. "I won't shoot you. My husband was in the Army." Sorrel admired the smile that remembered him, not quite a smile, but an eloquence that passed over the face.

"Oh," Sorrel said. "*Ca explique tout*," and moved out.

Mrs Lyon, meanwhile, sat back with a knee up, wearing Black Watch tartan breeks she had donned for the occasion, and Seddall's spyglass resting on the knee, scanning the terrain below and across from her.

"My man wis a keeper on Ardverickie," she had explained, "there's naethin' ye'll can teach me about usin' the glass."

After a while Bayard stood and began wagging his tail, and Sorrel was back. "I've found it," she said. "Let's move."

Found it she had, a hollow in the top of the hill left by the roots of a fallen oak, where the trees on the forward slope were sparse so that they had a clear survey of the house and the valley, and where the forest, on this eminence, was too exposed for undergrowth to flourish, so that they had clear lanes of sight through the trees about them.

Here they disposed themselves with what combinations of

vigilance and comfort they could find. Bayard, uncertain whom to adopt, moved from one to another until, being a French dog, he decided on the Francophone. He settled himself beside Olivia, and waited for the day to grow.

29

It was under a night of storm and flying sky that Harry Seddall came home to Carolside. He came not into the westward end of the valley as Sorrel had done, but from the east, forcing the hired Sierra up a hopeless trail into a fir plantation until it grounded.

He tucked his trouser ends into his socks, put a dark polo-necked sweater over his shirt, and resumed the jacket of the suit so that he could store ammunition in its pockets: clips of 9 mm. in the right and a box of thirty-eights in the left. He holstered the automatic under his arm and the revolver at his waist.

It was his country, he knew it like the back of his hand. He went through the gate in the deer fence and set off loping through the plantation at an easy pace, knowing he had two miles or more to go and knowing he was not as fit as he should be for this; too many cigarettes, too little exercise.

The trail became a path and the path, after a while, lost confidence in its identity, so he put up an arm to guard against the boughs of the firs and thrust on through them, heedless of what scratches he took so long as his eyes were safe.

He heard a pair of deer, startled by his passage, thrashing away from him, and wondered what they did about their eyes. Then he cursed to himself, because there would be the deer fence on the other side of the plantation, and no time to cast this way and that along the fence on the chance of finding another gate. The fence was there, all right, and he hoisted himself up and over it into upland grass.

He slowed to a walk for a while to steady himself. He did not like the pounding of his heart, and swore to live a better life in future. He was keyed up and letting it make him tense, which was no way to be. He was keyed up because there was so much at stake, but the way to save his stake, and win the hand, was to channel the nervous energy that ran through him.

He made himself walk with his head up beneath the fitful moon, beneath the scudding clouds, to bring himself back to being one with the land. He put up a hare that had lain crouched in its form and felt the muscles of his mouth relax: there was good lore, old lore in a hare, it came as a good omen.

Off to his right a fox barked. The night was his, he was one with the night. He came to the hanging wood at the end of the valley with the wind soughing in the branches above him.

Lethington came into the valley like a troop of the Long Range Desert Group emerging from the Grand Erg Oriental to have a biff at Rommel.

After the first cattle-grid Lethington halted his combat group and the vehicles pulled off the track onto the pasture among the sheep.

To his driver he said: "You're not going to leave your vehicle like this, are you?"

"What do you mean?" the woman said.

"Turn the damn thing round, is what I mean," Lethington said. "Leave it facing out. Does it not occur to you we might want to leave in a hurry?"

She started the engine and swung the car round, killing a lamb in the process. She switched off again and doused the lights, and sat there saying, "Oh dear, the poor little thing."

The sheep's mother and her surviving lamb stood a little off, visible in the light of the moon, and bleated sadly.

The woman started to weep.

Lethington stared at her. "What the hell are you crying for?" he said. "That lamb would have been meat inside a month anyway. And we're going to kill people tonight."

"That's different," the woman said.

"That's different," Lethington said mockingly. Then he thought that it was different. He had no time to work out what this was about, but it was different. "Come on," he said. "It never knew what hit it. Pull your socks up."

Lethington Force dismounted from its vehicles and went down into the night, leaning into the wind that drove through the valley, to confront its leader's destiny. All in dark clothes and wearing ski-masks, each of them carrying a Heckler and Koch sub-machine gun, they could have been any bunch of terrorists on the job.

This, however, was not how it seemed to the exalted Lethington. Lethington felt himself to be the commander of a flying column making the night raid par excellence. At the appropriate signposts he had waved away his patrols to cover the heights along the north and south sides of his valley, and his main assault was about to be launched. These were copybook tactics, and as to the cause they served, Lethington went down to battle under no flag save that of knowing the mission he went on was his own, and for him this was patriotism enough.

At the bridge he sent three of his people across, one of them to scout up to the house, another to go with him as connecting file, and the third to stand picket on the far side. The remainder he held with him, and spaced them along the top of the river bank.

Himself he went down beside the bridge. Standing there, sheltered from the wind, he looked up at the house. The dark tower rose, its character emancipated, either by the dark or by the watcher's spirit, into a pinnacle of menace. It threw down to the man so far below it the challenge that the medieval donjon threw, the challenge not of defiance but of threat, to be appalled by it and yet to make the attempt.

The moon escaped from the clouds running across the sky. Lethington looked into the bubbling stream, greeting its reflection with a handsome smile, for he had on the moment found he had no personal hatred for Seddall, only the pure desire to see him dead, to destroy what was his.

It was the perfect night. The moon, when he lifted his face to the sky, stared back pale, implacable, favouring none beneath, neither Lethington nor Seddall, nor any other on the earth. So should it be.

"What's Hecate to him," he said to it, "or he to Hecate?" and climbed the river bank to wait for what news his men might bring him.

Carmichael and Jane Winder had left their car in a road-man's lay-by, and since noon had lain on the south side of the valley and watched the front of the house. They made a simple picnic lunch of truffled paté from Perigord and airborne strawberries, provided by the hotel, and all the time they watched. They did not make love. It was their first operation together and they were being good, to show each other that they could do this.

In the middle of the afternoon Jane Winder laughed.

"What is it?" Carmichael asked her.

"I was thinking of a line of T.S. Eliot. I don't know where it comes from."

"What line?" he said.

"A hard coming they had of it," she said.

"Thanks a lot," Carmichael said.

"I'm sorry," she said. "If it's any help, I don't think that's what he meant."

"Not much help," he said. "I wonder what's going on over there."

They had seen not a sign of life all afternoon.

"Seddall should be there by now," he said. "He's supposed to be there by now to protect his women, according to Lethington."

"No women to protect, for all that we know," she said. "Perhaps they've flown the coop."

"Perhaps," Carmichael said. "I should have thought Calder would be here by now too," he said.

"We must be patient," she said.

269

"I have used patience before," he said. "There is a large experience of patience in the profession of killing people."

"I do urge you, Alexander," she said, "to be sparing of your irony. I have little practice at being supportive, and that is what I am trying to be."

"That's fair," he said.

They watched the house.

Late in the afternoon they saw a shepherd with his dogs cross a footbridge upstream from the house. He walked up the pasture, the sheep coming to meet him, and on out of sight. After a while he and his dogs went back over the stream and away.

"That bridge will be invisible from the house," Carmichael said.

The shepherd was all the human life they saw in the valley during their watch, and when evening fell, and no lights came on in the house, they made ready to move. The day drew in, and still there were no lights, no sign of life. They descended into the valley, keeping to cover, and went over the footbridge.

They passed through a small wilderness of tall old trees, on a mulch of many years of oak and elm and chestnut leaves, negotiating underbrush and deadfall. A parliament of jackdaws drifted overhead and cawed into the rising wind, into the thickening dusk.

A stone's throw from the rear quarters of the house they stopped in the last concealment of this rough wood. There was a back door, there were windows on two floors, overlooking the space they would have to cross.

"Right," Carmichael said. "Here goes nothing. If anything moves, kill it."

Jane Winder had the Beretta in her fist. "Off safety," she said.

He made his start within the wood and broke from it running full pelt onto the open space and made the door. He paused there barely a moment, and then she saw it yield under his hand. He vanished inside.

Behind her, jackdaws descended into silence. The tree-tops

270

tossed in the wind. It was half-dark now. When he appeared again at the door she hardly saw his beckoning hand.

"No one in this bit of the house," Carmichael said when she reached him, panting. "No one upstairs or down. But this is only the kitchen-and-servant stuff. Now we go through it all." The key was in the door, and he locked it.

They went through what he called the kitchen and servant stuff again, for Carmichael was a careful man. Then they went through the whole house on this pattern, that he went into the rooms while she kept sentinel outside. There were three other outside doors, and his first care was to lock these.

Within an hour they knew the house was empty, and that three women were, though absent, in residence. They knew, too, who they were: in Olivia Tesson's room was her passport, and in Sorrel's bag, lying in the hall, was hers.

"Why the passport?" Jane Winder said of Sorrel. "She lives here."

"Sorrel always carries her passport," Carmichael said.

"I'd forgotten you knew her," she said.

"You work with Seddall, you work with Sorrel," he said. "All right," he said. "No sign of Seddall, he's not here yet. Tesson and the housekeeper already here. Bed made up for Sorrel but her bag here in the hall, she hasn't moved in yet, all she did was arrive. These are the first facts.

"The second facts are," and he spoke fast, his mind working fast, "remains of breakfast still on the kitchen table, and a space among the rifles in the gun cupboard, and a space among the shotguns, and the door of the cupboard still open, and both cars sitting outside there. So what have they done?"

"It strongly suggests," Jane Winder said, "that they have armed up and taken to the tall timber."

"First thing this morning," Carmichael said. "I think up there behind the house, that's where I'd be."

"How romantic," Jane said. "Your friend Sorrel holed up there on the hill like Gene Tierney in *Belle Starr*. I like her."

"Don't like her," Carmichael said. "She's a tough cookie. Think of her like that."

He said: "Who are Gene Tierney and Belle Starr?"

In the darkness of the great hall of Carolside, Jane Winder bit her lip.

The report that came to Lethington was that there were two cars on the gravel beside the house, but there was no sign of life in it: so either the occupants were in a defensive posture, or everyone in the house had gone to bed early – it was just after eleven – or the house was, for whatever reason, empty. There were four doors into the house, and all locked.

"We'll go in," Lethington said. "I haven't come here to pussyfoot about."

He left the woman who had run over the lamb to guard the line of retreat, and took the rest up to the house. Impatience was climbing in him. "You come with me," he said. "The rest of you along the front."

At a back window he said to the man with him: "Break the glass. Open it. The wind'll drown the noise."

They found themselves in the kitchen. "Leave one outside and fetch the others, tell them to bring the petrol."

He waited by the door that led from the kitchen into the house, and listened to the wind. "A gale," he said aloud to himself. "It will be an inferno."

When his people came he took them into the hall. The moon shone through the windows. "Wood," he said. "It's made of wood."

Two of the men went through the ground-floor rooms while the rest splashed the petrol about in the hall and on the wooden staircase. The ground-floor was reported empty. Lethington's inferno was ready to spring into its life.

"Out," he said. "Everybody out. Get back to the transport."

He himself withdrew into the kitchen passage, drew the phosphorous grenade from the pocket of his safari jacket and held it in his hand. Terror, awe, and exhilaration burst up in him. He wanted to wait, to fear and cherish this magical object.

Into his ears, over the sound of the gale, the crackle of gunfire came. "Oh-ho!" he said, and threw the grenade well into the hall and sprinted to the kitchen. He heard the fire smack into life, its light flew past him, its heat touched him.

He slammed the kitchen door and in the kitchen risked to wait, to wait for one more moment. First he heard the breathing of the fire like the slow surge of a maelstrom, and then at once it soared until he might have been in Africa again; standing again by the Zambesi falls.

He forced himself out of the window and ran for the trees at the side of the house, letting off the safety of the Heckler and Koch as he ran. As he crossed the space the clouds were over the moon, and as he ran in among the trees the moon came out at the same moment that he felt a tug at his jacket, saw a gun flash and the figure of the shooter behind it.

He let rip with automatic fire and heard the shout from his target. He went to the ground and shoved a new magazine into the pistol grip of the Steyer. The rest of the gunfire was behind him. He flung a look behind him and caught a glimpse of light tearing open the night and figures running in it like demons in hell about their work.

In the wood his victim gave a smaller shout, and Lethington moved forward warily, heaving himself on his elbows. He came near the man and saw the sheen of his pistol lying where it had fallen. He threw it into the undergrowth and went up to the man, and saw that he had no time at all left to live.

The man spoke, not a groan but a sad and painful whisper. "*Gott*," the man said. "*Gott*."

"*Gott* indeed," Lethington said, not with any kind of irony, but utterly perplexed. There were not supposed to be any Germans in this scenario.

He decided on a tactical withdrawal in the face of this unquantified threat, and passed among the trees to emerge well clear of the action, away from the great illumination of the blaze, at a point where he could descend slantwise to reach the bridge.

And he paused once to look over at the house, and saw a figure framed in a window above the kitchen, a woman's figure outlined against the flames behind her. The woman dropped, held first at the length of a man's arm. Hell's teeth: Seddall for a certainty. Lethington ran like a panther to the strike.

As the woman came to her feet a burst of 9mm. from his Steyer threw her against the wall and then the weapon went lifeless in his hand. The man dropping from the window screamed and bent over the torn woman, and screamed again, and came up and screamed at Lethington while gunfire flashed in his hand. Lethington ran for the bridge and reached it, and crossed it.

The girl was there. She was still there, the girl who had run over the lamb. "Hold the bridge," he yelled at her, and ran on.

The girl, seeing herself deserted and the enemy in hot pursuit of her departing leader, rolled intelligently down the bank and crouched under the bridge. "Hold it yourself, Horatius," she said to the running stream.

As Lethington raced towards the vehicles, thinking even while he ran that they were facing *out*, ready to go, a firefight erupted in front of him. One of his troop's Land Rovers had no sooner lurched into movement than a fusillade of shots rang out and it stopped. His people piled out and went to the ground and returned fire. The Land Rover blew up.

Lethington swerved and began to run towards the other end of the valley. A bullet took him high in the back and he fell. Where he lay he saw his inferno burst through the roof of the house and leap upwards, a flood of fire soaring to the heavens, its great spirit hurled about by the gale as if it were in agony.

He felt no pain in his own body, so great was the agony he saw in those tormented flames. "Ah, ah," he said, and again, "ah!"

Then he understood that there was no pain to speak of, it must have been a ricochet from the gunfight, perhaps no more than a bruise. He scouted a look back to the bridge and there was the man Carmichael coming on, not running like a hare, not like a greyhound; a kind of stumble in his running, as if he was not in whole charge of his movements; but running nevertheless, coming on. There was an unnerving implacability in this difficult but determined pursuit.

Lethington got hold of the Heckler and Koch and reloaded it. He turned his eyes to the darkness, waited until they had begun to get used to the night, and came up crouching and loped off towards the empty end of the valley, away from Carmichael; away from the burning house; away from the gunfight between his boys and girls and... who were they, for God's sake, who had come onto the scene and opened fire like that out of the blue? Well, out of the black.

That was pretty tough shooting, the way they had gone about it. Just opened up and started shooting like there was no tomorrow. Well, Lethington thought, against hardcases like these, there would be a good few tomorrows missing among his boys and girls.

He stopped thinking about what was going on behind him, stopped trying to read implications, and ran forward into the dark, into the nowhere that lay ahead of him.

After a while he looked behind him and thought he saw, against what distance had now rendered the illumination rather than the furious glare of the burning house, glimpses of the kind of movement Carmichael would be making if he was still stumbling along in that dogged, unhappy pursuit.

Lead him on, Lethington thought. Lead him away into that unknown country up ahead, and then lay for him. He steadied again into his long, careful, self-preserving gait.

From time to time, during the course of the long day, Bayard had taken Sorrel or Olivia off with him to prove the wood, and

275

each time they had come back it was again beside Olivia he had settled.

Now as she sat awake while the others slept, he came to his feet beside her, pointing into the darkness and making the lowest rumble of a growl.

"*Tais-toi!*" Olivia said.

Listening, she thought that now and then, on a whim of the wind, she heard voices. She stood up, took the rifle, touched Sorrel lightly on the shoulder and when she saw her waken went with Bayard towards the sound that had alerted him.

The ground was soft underfoot from the recent rain. The moon was out and Olivia drifted from tree to tree. Their tops were heaving in the gale but down here in the forest the noise was like a roof overhead and she could hear, separated from the storm above, the sounds about her.

The voices became more clear and she came on their owners so suddenly she was taken by surprise, and stepped back quickly but with care, feeling behind her with her feet, until she had a beech tree between her and the scene before her.

"Stay quiet," she said to Bayard.

There were three men with their backs to her, who formed a ring round a man sitting in a sleeping bag. The three men had sub-machine guns in their hands and the man on the ground was expecting to be killed. She saw it in the set of his shoulders and his head.

One of the men said: "I can't do it, not like this."

"It's him," one of the others said. "What more do you want?"

Olivia lifted the Ruger to her shoulder and took her stance.

"It's too cold-blooded," the first man said. "There can't be any need for it."

"Then I'll do it," the second man said, and made some movement with the sub-machine gun.

Olivia fired and slid the bolt of the deer rifle back and forward again. The shot took him high in the right shoulder and threw him down, where he lay silent and probably dying, Olivia knew, from the violence of the bullet.

His companions too were silent and shocked, then one of them began to turn. "Stand!" Olivia said, preparing to fire in the same second, but even as he threw himself to the ground a shotgun blazed off to her right and he began to die more dreadfully than his colleague.

The third man stretched his arms wide and let the submachine gun hang from its sling. Sorrel stepped out of the trees, stepped wide round the man groaning and tossing in her path, and took the gun from the survivor. She took a pistol from his belt, a knife from his boot.

Olivia went forward, since Sorrel, although she had thrown away the knife, was now holding three firearms, none of them, so far as Olivia knew, on safety.

"I'll look after him," she said to Sorrel, and to the man: "Walk forward, hug that tree. Now slide down, wrap your legs round it, more, and more. Good."

"That's a good trick," Sorrel said. She unloaded the pistol and sub-machine gun and set them on the ground, and took the weapons of the two casualties and did the same with them.

The man in the sleeping bag sat without moving, his eyes on the man who had been writhing from the shotgun wounds, but was now almost still.

"Are you all right?" Sorrel said to him.

"Just about," he said.

"What are you . . .?" she had been going to ask him what he was doing here, but it had become, even as she asked him, an oddly impolite question to a man who had just come close to being murdered.

"I'm looking for a house called Carolside," he said. "I've come across country, by the map. I'm quite exhausted, so I stopped to rest and then thought I might as well sleep here. I'm used to sleeping in the woods. It's not much of a camp," he said, as if this were an apology, "but I had to disguise myself as a hiker in a hurry. There are people after me."

"Why Carolside?" Sorrel said.

"I've been advised to see a man called Harry Seddall," the man said.

"There's some American in your voice," she said. "Who are you?"

"James Calder, Professor James Calder," he said, "of Wade University, New York."

"Yes," Sorrel said. "Well, you've come to the right place."

Seddall came out of the hanging wood into the full light of the moon and saw, a mile away down and across the valley, the great fire destroying his house.

At the same moment he heard the rifle, and soon afterwards the shotgun, up on the hill. Not poachers, not with the rifle too. He set off again, not for the house but for the hill, since it was a better than even chance that these weapons meant Olivia and Sorrel. The people he had been tangling with lately would have trendier weapons than those.

He had walked ten paces into the meadow when the words came.

"Stop right there," they said. "Lift the hands."

Seddall did these things, and Lethington came round into his view.

"Ah!" Lethington said. "The lord and master himself. Where's the pistol?"

"Shoulder holster," Harry said.

Lethington stepped close, but not too close. "I can see you," he said, "better than you can see me." Harry was facing the moon. "Three fingers on the butt; pick it out of there and let it fall."

Harry lifted out the automatic and dropped it.

"Now you move back away from it," Lethington said, and picked it up and hurled it behind him. "I don't have much time, there's a man called Carmichael after me. This job didn't really go too well, but there'll be another day."

"After this?" Harry said, and nodded at his burning house.

278

"That firing on the hill, what do you suppose that was?"

"I think some of my lads got into trouble," Lethington said. "Do you have gamekeepers out, looking for intruders?"

"I only have half a gamekeeper," Harry said. "Share him with a neighbour. No, I have no gamekeepers lurking up there."

"My boys and girls are carrying these," Lethington said, and rapped the Heckler and Koch. "Terrific rate of fire."

"Only if you fire it," Harry said.

"Quite. I'm afraid these lads of mine are as children in the woods. Still, I am not as a child, in the woods or anywhere else. So now we must say goodbye to each other."

Harry had a desperate wish to see Olivia before he died, and knew he wasn't going to. The black cloud coming towards the moon would be too late for him; it was too late for him anyway. Whatever change the clouds made to the visibility would not be enough, and Lethington could simply draw that nasty weapon on a line from right to left and that would be that.

"There is just one thing," Harry said, and his voice was a little rough.

"What's that, then?" Lethington asked, and looked down the meadow the way he had come for the merest fraction of a second, and then his eyes were back on Harry again.

Four shots, spaced, came out of the meadow where Lethington's glance had flicked just a moment ago. Long shooting, judging by the muzzle flash, but one caught Harry in the arm and spun him round so he went on falling, fell on his stomach and put his hand in to get the revolver from his belt.

The raving of the Heckler and Koch filled his ears and when the first shock of that was over, and no annihilating blast of bullets tore into him, he looked up and saw Lethington kneeling, one knee on the grass and the other up to steady him, shooting at a figure that came on out of the night, running and stumbling like a marathon runner with nothing left.

The racket of the sub-machine gun stopped and Lethington took out a pistol and aimed it carefully at the figure staggering up the meadow towards them. Lethington fired once and the figure was stopped, then bent over and came on.

Harry, from behind and to the left of his target, shot Lethington three times, starting with the head and moving the Smith & Wesson down for the heart. Lethington went over and lay still.

The man called Carmichael reached Lethington. He stood over him in that crouch he had taken when Lethington last fired at him. Of Harry, eight feet away, he took no notice.

"You killed her," he said to the body lying there, and Harry saw tears on his face and heard them in his voice. An extraordinary feeling began to grow in him that he had known this man before.

"Oh, you killed her," the man said, and fired his pistol three times into Lethington and then the weapon was empty.

He collapsed, in his crouch, until he was sitting, and sat there looking at the grass, holding the gun in his hand, cherishing it.

And Harry recognized him: remembered him as a man he had come up against once – how long ago was it now? – a man he had humiliated so deeply he had wiped him from his memory.

A mixture of pain and superstitious awe rose in him at this strange meeting, as if fate had brought them together in this valley that was his home; as if the gods of some other age had brought them to it, and were watching them now from that moon, from that wild sky, from out of the flying wind.

Harry went down on his toes in front of this man he had known. The sub-machine gun had taken chunks out of the man's left arm and his side but one bullet, probably that carefully aimed shot from Lethington's pistol, had taken him in the chest.

"Gyseman," Harry said to the man called Carmichael. "Gyseman, it's me, Harry Seddall."

The face came up weeping. "I would have killed you too," Gyseman said earnestly, as if somehow he had let Harry down, "but he killed her, he *killed* her."

"I know," Harry said. "I know."

He wondered who Gyseman was talking about.

"I loved her," Gyseman said. "Do you think I'll see her again?"

"Listen," Harry said. "You'll see her, Gyseman. It's certain." Then: "Gyseman," he said.

"Yes."

"She's a great woman," Harry said. "When you see her, give her my love."

Gyseman smiled. "I'll do that," he said. "Thanks."

Tears flooded from his eyes and blood from his mouth, and he turned onto his side and died.

As he went on down the meadow towards the hillside he heard the joyous bark, and here came Bayard, and then he saw people and heard the call: "Harry? Harry!"

It was Olivia? It was Olivia, but two men came with her.

She held him with both hands on the forearm, the good arm, thank God, as if to anchor him there; and that was all, but it was enough.

"You're all right?" he said.

"Yes," she said. "You too?"

"Me too," he said.

In the moonlight he could see her eyes, large and wise.

"These are friends, I take it," he said.

"Not enemies at least."

A voice with a German accent said: "Good evening. I think you are Colonel Seddall?"

"Harry Seddall, yes."

"Perhaps there is no need for you to know who I am, who we are," the German said. "We have had a firefight with the people who attacked your house, and they are either dead or wounded or held prisoner. It would be convenient if you would let us dispose of the bodies, care for the wounded, and set the prisoners free somewhere in London. I think they are illegal, and will have no story to tell."

"You know these people better than I do," Harry said to

281

Olivia, "whoever the hell they are. What do you think?"

"A Professor Calder has come," Olivia said, "from America."

"The devil he has!"

"Yes. And these men were sent to protect him, and you too they say. If they will do what they say, Sorrel and I have thought it would be convenient. They are Germans. They will certainly be very efficient."

"Thank you, Madame," the German said, with a whisper of irony in his tone.

"Do it," Harry said, "but by God do it fast."

"We are ready to leave," the German said.

"Then thank you," Harry said. "Thank you a great deal, and goodnight."

The Germans disappeared into the night.

"Hallo, Olivia," Harry said, "and thank God."

"Hallo, Harry."

"Not this arm," Harry said, "it's a little distempered."

Bayard turned his back and sat, and waited.

30

Seddall, wearing a pair of borrowed gumboots, came paddling through the ashes of his house and stood at the top of the steps looking down at Bayard. There had been much to see to, and he had not yet slept.

"Nice new day," he said to the dog. "Quite a nice new day, don't you think?"

Bayard was sitting in the sun, and had been sitting long enough not to be confident of an early departure from this strange scene on this strange morning, where a house that had been here yesterday was not, in the real sense of house, here any more; where a lot of uncertainly preoccupied strangers cluttered up the landscape; and where the smell of wet ash confused some far better smells. So he waved his tail in a polite but half-hearted way, and waited.

"Dog's got more sense than his boss," the warrant officer in charge of the standby fire tender said.

"Fucking right," his corporal said. "That lot's just fucking gasping to come down."

"I wish you'd come out of there, sir," the warrant officer bawled. "That tower won't stand like that forever."

Seddall looked up the shell of the tower to the blue sky. It was like looking up the black inside of an oversized chimney.

He came down the steps and joined the men at the fire tender.

The warrant officer said: "Wish I'd seen the fire. It was all over bar the smouldering when we got here." The corporal caught his eye. "Hell," the warrant officer said. "I don't mean to be unfeeling, sir."

283

"Not a bit of it," Seddall said cheerily. "Don't you worry about that. I'm glad to see the back of the place. It was a whale of a blaze, all right."

A Ministry of Defence police sergeant came round the end of the tender and stamped to attention. "Sir," he said vigorously. "Devon and Cornwall Constabulary are holding a man at the road end. He says he's come to see you."

The local police were at the extremities of the valley, and the military were within.

"He'll have a name," Seddall said.

"A Professor Calder, sir," the man said. "They say he sounds a bit American."

"A Professor Calder. You're talking to the Devon cops from your vehicle? I'll come with you."

He went the few yards along the terrace, walking briskly for the first time that morning.

"Handset to Colonel Seddall," the sergeant said to the driver.

"Putting Colonel Seddall onto you now," the driver said to the handset.

Harry began to feel they were all about to fire an artillery piece.

"Give me that thing," he said. "Seddall," he said to it. "You have a Professor Calder there?"

"So he claims, sir," the police voice said. "His passport shows different."

"What is this, dammit, the Third Reich?" Harry said. "He slept at my house last night. Let him through."

"Now then, sir," the police voice said, "now then. That can't be right. Your house burnt down last night."

"Not *that* house, you blithering idiot," Harry said. "The farmhouse."

There was a silence while the voice tried to make sense of this. "I'll drive him up to you right away," it said at last.

*

The car stopped on the far side of the bridge and an oldish man got out. A large policeman got out too and handed the man a light rucksack and a tall shepherd's crook of a stick, waved to Seddall across the stream, and drove off again.

They met at the middle of the bridge. "Professor Calder?" Harry said. "I'm Harry Seddall."

Calder looked up at the fire tender and the shell of the house. "Another fire?" he said. "Never thought I'd live to see you, Seddall." His eyes were still on the house.

"A fire, all right; but why do you say 'another'?" Seddall asked.

"Well, aren't you Marion Oliphant's executor?" Calder said. "Don't you know how she died?"

Seddall's conscience smote him a surprising blow. He had forgotten Marion Oliphant; forgotten that she had been found in the ashes of her house, and that her death lay at the beginning of all that had reached its climax in the burning of his own; forgotten that it was because of some link with her that Calder was here.

"You had a letter from her?" he said.

"I still have it," Calder said, and made to reach for it, but found he had a rucksack in one hand and a tall walking staff in the other. He looked at these articles in some surprise and simply let them fall.

Seddall bent to pick them up. "Oh," Calder said impatiently, "leave them. They're just props. I got them after von Harma and Peter were shot up, to disguise myself as a hiker."

"Von Harma and Peter?" Seddall said. "Shot up?"

"Yes, yes," Calder said. "They had taken the Daimler through the car-wash, but I'd got out to have a cigarette. Can I ask you, do you have a cigarette?"

"Only these," Seddall said, and produced the Gauloises. As he lit Calder's cigarette, he said: "It sounds as if you have a story to tell."

"Von Harma? The assassins? All that?" Calder said.

"The assassins," Seddall repeated the word, doing his best

not to smile at these unperturbed locutions from a man who, he was beginning to understand, had been put to it to survive. "Indeed, yes. I'd like to hear about the assassins. Normally I'd ask you up to the house, but as you see."

Calder sat on the stone parapet of the bridge, and told him about the warning letter from Marion Oliphant, about the assassins who had come for him in upper New York State, about Mexico and von Harma.

When he was done he threw the remains of his second cigarette into the stream. For some reason the two men sitting side by side looked everywhere but at each other.

"You had quite a run," Seddall said.

Calder, in recalling that time of forty years ago at Bletchley Park with Marion Oliphant, had not yet given him a name. Seddall longed for a name, but did not dare ask for it. Calder looked so washed-out, sustained by some inspiration of will but worn from the weeks of risk he had been through; and had recalled the past with so much inner difficulty, that Seddall feared the direct question — who was that man, Marion's other lover, who had been offered the Russian temptation beside the lily pond? — would drive the name down into the inaccessible depths of Calder's memory.

"Yes," Calder said, "I had quite a run, but now I'm here, and I hope you'll be able to explain some things to me."

"And I rather hope you'll be able to explain some things to me," Seddall said. "We need more comfort than this. Let's go and find ourselves some lunch in a decent pub."

"That would suit me very well," Calder said. "I feel too hyped up to rest right now. I have not yet said, I am extremely sorry about your house."

"I never liked it," Harry said. "I mean that seriously. I was going to get rid of it anyway."

It occurred to him that he might become rather bored with having to say this to people in the next few days.

*

"Some of us stayed at Woburn Abbey, you know," Calder said, "and were bussed in to Bletchley Park. She would never have admitted it, but there was a part of Marion that hunted for a mystical line into nature. She despised Wordsworth for it, but it was there in herself."

Seddall was eating good Cheddar, but Calder had finished eating, and caressed Bayard's ear, and watched the comfort of the log fire.

"She liked the night," Calder said. "She liked to be outside at night. She would get off the bus, sometimes, by herself, and walk from the gate to Woburn through the park. It had an extraordinary effect on her, to pass among the azaleas and rhododendrons, and see the antlers of the deer rise above the mist while the animals themselves were hidden by it."

Seddall, who had taken all the Cheddar he could stomach, took more and masticated as slowly as he might, earnest to bring no alteration to this state of things in which Calder played with the dog's ear, and remembered himself while the logs hissed and flickered in the grate, and communed easily with his memories of Marion Oliphant.

"That was why she liked to be on the lily pond at night," Calder said, and Seddall closed his eyes against the impulse to break the restraint that held him. "She liked to let the punt drift, to make love and let the motion of that take the punt where it would. She liked to be out making love under a gale of wind, or on a night of mist that gauzed the bright moon into a ghost."

Calder stopped as if the recollection held him fixed there, his eyes on the fire, but then made a sardonic smile, his critical ear, perhaps, hearing the imitative echo in that poetical lapse.

"It was on one of those nights, with the moon making a halo in the mist," Calder said, "that we heard them making their proposal to Smith to work for the Russians. We had made love and were just holding each other, and the punt had drifted in under an overhanging tree, and come to rest against the bank." He sighed. "It spoiled that night for us. It spoiled everything for us. Marion went off it, after that, she was so worked up about what Smith might do. It was from that I learned Smith was her lover too; had been her lover too. Not that I'd have cared about that. She just went off it."

Seddall thrust away the cheese plate. He began to breathe again, and in so doing discovered that his respiration had shallowed almost to asphyxiation.

"Smith," he said to himself, much chagrined. There was no one called Smith in the scheme of things. "Smith?" he said aloud, and heard the indignation in his voice.

"John Smith," Calder said, and rested silent.

John Smith! John Bloody Smith, of all names. Had the irrelevant – as it had proved to be – name been Roderick Arbuthnott, it would have been bad enough, but that it should be the commonest name in the English nomenclature hit Seddall like an insult.

He lit himself a cigarette and threw the pack on the table in front of Calder. It was, for him, a graceless act. Calder did not seem to notice, however, but took a cigarette from it and reached out a hand for Seddall's lighter.

Seddall stood up to go to the bar for beer.

Over the flame, round the cigarette, Calder said: "Yes, Smith was his name. Except that it was Smythe, I remember now. Smythe with a y, and an e on the end, but it was pronounced Smith. I doubt if he was persuaded, you know. He was not formed enough. He was impressionable enough to flirt with Communism, since he was in that set with Burgess and Maclean, but he was not tough enough to break the mould he was born from. It was Marion who grew so anxious about it all."

Seddall had stopped listening. As a lightly stroked piano key rouses a harmonic, an echo had sung softly in Seddall's memory.

He stood, suspended, and then went to the bar with the slow and automatic walk of the somnambulist, asked for, paid for, and picked up the beer, and came back to his seat, where he sat down slowly as if afraid to wake himself up.

"Smythe," he said in a companionable voice as if conversing with himself, "with a y and an e. Smythe. There's a Smythe in this." Then he exclaimed loudly and let the glass beer mug fall, more or less, on the table, so that it clattered and spilled. "There is a Smythe in this! Dear God, there is a Smythe in this!"

He took up the mug again and gulped down a lot of beer. "It's our bloody Lloyd George creation, Calder, it's the bloody" – and even in this hilarity caution came to him and his tone fell – "the bloody Lord Findo. The bloody Lord Findo was plain John Smythe before he inherited."

The man from the Cabinet Office, whose name was Walton, had a pallor that might have been achieved by going straight from a double first at Oxford through a chain of think-tanks and into Downing Street. He had an angular face and light eyes and colourless hair that knew its place.

When he looked at you he recognized at once what he saw, since he knew no occasion to perceive more than the first sketch his eyes printed for him. For this reason the encouraging appearance of inquiry was an illusion. The inquiry was constant and internal: it meant only that he had read his brief, knew his agenda, was aware of his planned programme for the rest of the day, and was continuously, though without effort, consulting the activity of the moment in its relation to these elements, which composed his existence.

He neither inspired, nor sought to inspire, respect, since he carried the authority of his office and knew its effect to be inevitable.

On the way to Welbeck Street he had said to Kenyon and Seddall: "I don't think we need to prearrange any of this. We know what we're going to do. We don't need a script. Do you agree?"

Findo had been expecting Walton, but not the other two. The dilapidation that had set in as soon as he saw them was now far gone, and he had reached that stage of tranquillity that follows the first shock of exposure, and results from the easing of guilt by confession.

"It was you," he said to General Kenyon, "who started it all."

"I?" the general was startled.

"Yes, you," Findo said. "You went shooting on that Scottish island, of all God-forsaken places to go shooting, took a cottage or something, roughing it rather, I thought. You told me you'd met Marion Oliphant."

Seddall stood at a window, out of it now, after narrating what he had heard from Calder in the pub. He had been gazing down into the street, but at this he looked over at Kenyon and saw him turn red, and then redder. He might have smiled, knowing what must have occasioned the visit to Islay and the rented holiday cottage, but Walton had his eyes on the general too. One had one's loyalties, after all.

"At a dinner party," Findo said. "Met her at a dinner party and somehow it came up about my chairing this committee on the intelligence and security services. Then I met you at some damned function in London and you had nothing better to do than tell me how *interested* she was to hear it."

"Good God!" the general said. "So I did. I'd forgotten all about it." Seddall could feel the general not looking his way, aware that Seddall knew perfectly well why he would forget whatever subject he had chosen to focus on, in order to avoid letting Annette Kalman's name drift into their conversation. No one who was having an affair, and who flushed as easily as Kenyon, could risk letting social chat stray onto the forbidden territory.

"Deeply interested, you said she was. Almost agitated," Findo said.

His mouth had gone dry and he licked his lips. "I need a drink," he said.

"I'll get it," Walton said at once, and Seddall knew he was afraid of suicide, taking place here and now, with the Cabinet Office present. "What would you like?"

"A very weak whisky, please," Findo said. "A great deal of soda, if you will."

Seddall, in spite of himself, was unhappy. Findo sat low in an armchair and appeared very small and defenceless, surrounded in his own home by these hostile judges. It was a pleasant home too. This drawing room was large and light. The oak floor was well rugged, the bookshelves were as well stocked with new books as with old, and the furniture was either covered with flax-coloured linen or waxed to a deep and satisfying polish.

Well, so the room was likeable. What had that to say to anything? He turned back to Welbeck Street, and wondered how Olivia was getting on. He wished this business was over. It was as good as over for him. He could have left now, but it would seem to be a kind of cowardice; one of the kinds of cowardice he would not allow himself.

"So I did what I could do," Findo said. The words ought to have sounded good, but there was not enough conviction in the way they were spoken. "I went to MI5, to Lethington."

"Why Lethington?" Harry heard himself ask.

Findo met his eyes across the room, over the rim of the glass. "I knew him," was all he said.

Well, there was no law against knowing Lethington, whatever else might be hidden in that reply.

"I told Lethington of my early association with these Communists at Bletchley," Findo said. "I was never a Communist myself, you understand, but the association with Maclean and that lot would have been impossible for me, if it became known."

They could make what they liked of that.

He took some of the weak whisky and soda. "It was not long after that," he said, "that Lethington sent me a cutting from a newspaper, which reported the death of Marion Oliphant in the burning of her house."

He shut his eyes for what seemed a long time, and emitted breath in a long sigh, and opened them. "He had me then. I did not have the energy of will to act decisively, and if I had ever resolved what I might best do after that, it would have been too

291

late. I had hesitated in the dilemma too long, and so I simply stayed in it. Until now," he said. "Until you came."

On the pavement below the Downing Street driver had taken Bayard out of the car, and was walking him on the leash. Bayard, driven up incontinently from too short a sojourn in the country, showed no interest in the smells and sights of a Welbeck Street at evening. He wore an air of dutiful gratitude, like a great-uncle being walked by a child.

"What more do you want?" Findo said. "You know about Lethington now. He was a monster, a Sparafucile come off the stage and run amok in the audience."

"I don't want," Harry said, in an awful, mordant, drawl, "to hear that kind of stuff. You knew there'd been murder done, and that more mayhem was going on around you – I mean, Findo, for Christ's sake, *think* about that chateau full of dead and dying, and Arkley with his leg blown off! Think about it, damn you! And don't spin us smart lines about villains from grand opera."

Findo's face began to shake and the glass fell to the floor and shattered.

"Doctor time," Walton said, and went to the phone.

"What happens now?" Kenyon said. "Do you get him to write a letter of resignation? When he comes out of that?"

Findo's body was shaken all over from within, the man was taking in air in desperate gulps as if he might choke, and had begun to slobber.

"No need," Walton said. "His committee has completed its work and the report will not, of course, be published, since its remit concerned the security and intelligence services."

"Privy counsellors?" Harry said. "They won't wear that. The committee know they've not completed their work."

"Do not concern yourself," Walton said. "If they are not content, an accommodation that contents them will be reached."

The doorbell rang, and Walton went out. A doctor and two ambulance attendants came back with him.

"Be careful," Walton said to them. "There is broken glass on the floor there." To Kenyon and Seddall he said: "Shall we go?"

At the car, Walton said to Seddall: "The Defence Secretary wants to see you. Can I drop you off at the Ministry?"

"No, you can't, thanks all the same."

"What do you mean?" the general said.

"I mean I don't want to see the Defence Secretary," Harry said. "I want to have something to eat, and a good sleep, and first thing in the morning I want to get back to Carolside. Well," and his mouth smiled up at one side and down at the other, "back to the farm, actually." The dog nudged the back of his knee. "Hallo, Bayard. Won't be a moment."

Walton said: "He feels he owes you an apology, I understand."

"Does he?" Harry said. "I really don't believe we know each other well enough for that kind of thing."

"Dear God, Harry!" the general said. "Sometimes you're the worst behaved man I've ever met, and sometimes you're the most insufferable prig."

"That could be me, all right," Harry said. "It does sound like me."

"An officer can't *refuse* to see the Secretary of Defence," Kenyon said.

Walton flicked over his wrist to see if he was slipping out of schedule.

"Well, now," Harry said. "I rather think he can, not that it matters to me either way. He threw me to the wolves without asking me what I had to say about it, and I have an earnest wish not to meet him again."

Walton, not as if he cared much about the outcome, said: "I daresay he wants to make some amends."

"Quite so," the general said. "I know you saved his life for him, Harry, but you must admit that afterwards appearances became misleading."

"I don't give a shit about saving his fucking life for him," Harry said. "I don't want to see the bloody man, that's all."

"You're being unreasonable," the general said.

"I'm not famous for being reasonable."

Bayard, as if this line signified the end of discussion, yawned, walked into the car, and heaved himself onto the back seat. The three debaters, and the driver who was holding the door, all looked at him. They understood that it was time to depart.

"Where do you want to go?" Walton said. "Let me drop you off anyway."

"I want to have dinner," Harry said, "somewhere quaint and old-fashioned, where they'll let Bayard come too."

"Very well," Walton said. "Get in. After you, General."

"You can do this?" Harry asked, much surprised. "You know of such a place?"

"Certainly," Walton said.

He gave the driver the name.

Arkley had just been shaved. His eyes gleamed with an evil lustre into those of the nurse who was wiping his face with the flannel.

She was in that moment of nubile age and body where sexuality emanates with each breath. Arkley, ancient by comparison, could hardly contain himself. "When I go home," he said, "I shall need someone to look after me."

"It won't be me," she said. "I know what you mean by look after. There are girls who like older men. Find one of them."

"I want you," Arkley said. "You can marry me, damn you, if that's what it takes."

"It would take that," the girl said, "but that won't do it. You only want me for bed."

"Christ," Arkley said. "Don't tell me you're a person in your own right, don't tell me you're one of those."

"You're a lot better," she said. "You can shave yourself tomorrow. And I damn well am one of those."

"Tell her what she's missing, Seddall," Arkley said.

"Not a lot," Harry said. "I wouldn't wonder if you had wives from here to Jakarta, either. You're an untrustworthy bastard in everything else."

"Try to behave," the nurse said to Arkley, and left them.

"You look better than you did when I last saw you," Harry said.

"You got me out of there," Arkley said.

"I'll live to regret it."

"I hope so." Arkley said. "So will someone else, when I get out of here."

"I have bad news for you on that score," Harry said. "Can I smoke in this place?"

"No," Arkley said, "but do it. That filth you smoke will remind me of the real world. This place is too sanitized for a man of my depravity. What's this bad news you've got for me?"

"The chateau," Harry said. "Lethington was behind that, behind everything: Lethington at Five?"

"I know Lethington, for pity's sake. D'you think this," and he waved at the cage over his legs, "has put me in my dotage?"

"What'll I use for an ashtray?"

"Use the handbasin. So what about Lethington?"

"He's dead." Harry said. He ran the cold tap to wash away the ash.

"Damn that," Arkley said. "Damn it. If ever a man loved vengeance, I am that man. Tell me the tale."

"Can't stay long," Harry said. "I've got the dog outside in the car."

"Tell it," Arkley said.

Harry told it.

"You had a lot of luck," Arkley said. "When you get down to it, you just muddled through."

"Arkley," Harry said. "Do you think that doesn't frighten me?"

"I could have helped you, if I'd been up and about," Arkley said, "and if I'd thought it suited my book. So Lethington wanted to be top of the heap, hey? By God, he went at it, didn't he? Trying to knock off the competition at the chateau, doing in that unfortunate woman just to get a hold on Findo, hiring Mendham's little mob to do some of his dirty work. What a man! I don't know who else could have done all that, except for myself."

"That thought occurred to me also."

"I believe you," Arkley said, deeply pleased. "Just wait till I'm back at my desk."

"You're going back to your desk?"

"What the devil did you think? Did you think I wouldn't want to be the first director-general of the Secret Intelligence Service with a wooden leg? I could have told you about Findo's wife, you know. I knew that family."

"Wouldn't have helped much," Harry said. "I only heard about that yesterday morning when Calder gave me Marion Oliphant's letter. After that all we had to do was look in *Who's Who*. You knew the father?"

Arkley declined to be brushed aside in this offhand way. "It would have been odd if I didn't," he said. "CIA head of station in London? In the days when the CIA really meant something? No wonder the Oliphant woman got excited."

"We still don't know how the Oliphant woman knew he was CIA."

"Don't we?" Arkley said, purbright with satisfaction. "Try this. They were PhD students, or something like that anyway, at Yale together. And when I say together, Seddall, I mean together. There was more to Marion Oliphant than meets the eye."

"You're a bloody computer, Arkley!" Harry said. "Actually, I'm dumbfounded. The next thing you'll be telling me she worked for you."

"I shall, shall I?" Arkley said.

There was a spell of hard eye contact which ended in deadlock.

Arkley said: "I knew the daughter too. A likely lass. Not at all the thing for Findo. I was surprised it lasted, what, three years. Can't think what came over him."

Seddall looked at him.

"I'm not Findo," Arkley said. "You think that creature would be a mistake?" He nodded at the door.

"I think it would be a mistake for her, Arkley," Harry said. "Do you know what you ought to do while you're laid up."

Arkley became wary. "What?" he said.

"You ought to advertise in *The Times*," Harry said. "How would it go? 'Top spy, dominant older male, wooden leg, seeks submissive Mata Hari in flower of young womanhood to share top secrets'."

Arkley stared at him.

"You could audition them here," Harry said.

"Reach me the pen and paper out of that locker," Arkley said, "and then you can cut along, there's a good chap."

Only in the car did the black cat Sacha lose some of her character for independence. She did not yowl plaintively, nor defecate out of fear, like some of the lesser cats, and she still kept her distance from Seddall; but it was in the car, and nowhere else, that she accepted the moral protection of Bayard.

She lay across the French spaniel's forelegs with her head into the back of the seat, and sheltered under his jowl, and surrendered herself to whatever dreams might come. When you got down to it, a car journey meant the country, and the country meant, to Sacha, an unsurpassed killing ground.

Harry, bounding down the M4 towards Olivia, glanced over his shoulder at them and took their comradeship for a good sign. If Sacha could make an entente with the French, how could Seddall fail?

He remembered what General Pershing had said when he arrived with the American Expeditionary Force in the First World War to pay back America's Revolutionary debt to

France. He remembered that Pershing's wife and daughters had been burned to death in their home in San Francisco when the general had been down on the Mexican border, and hoped he was not acquiring a neurosis about burning houses.

But mostly he remembered what Pershing said when he stepped onto French soil.

Harry said it aloud, for Olivia: "*Lafayette, nous voici,*" he said, and the needle on the rev counter ran towards the red.